By Vicki Pettersson

THE SCENT OF SHADOWS
The First Sign of the Zodiac

THE TASTE OF NIGHT
The Second Sign of the Zodiac

THE TOUCH OF TWILIGHT
The Third Sign of the Zodiac

CITY OF SOULS
The Fourth Sign of the Zodiac

City of Souls

THE FOURTH SIGN OF THE ZODIAC

VICKI PETTERSSON

An Imprint of HarperCollins*Publishers*

EOS
An Imprint of HarperCollins*Publishers*
10 East 53rd Street
New York, New York 10022-5299

Copyright © 2009 by Vicki Pettersson
Author photo © 2007 by Derik Klein
Cover art by Tony Mauro
ISBN 978-0-06-145678-7
www.eosbooks.com

First Eos paperback printing: July 2009

HarperCollins® and Eos® are registered trademarks of HarperCollins Publishers.

Printed in the U.S.A.

10 9 8 7 6 5 4 3 2 1

To Susan Agassi-Hughes – because true friends are family, too.

Acknowledgments

Thanks go to my editor, Diana Gill—simultaneously my creative nemesis and savior. My ever-deepening respect and gratitude is yours. Also to Emily Krump, for hard work behind the scenes . . . and cupcakes. You do know how to keep an author going. To my agent, Miriam Kriss, for providing valuable and timely insight—even if it means staying up half the night to do so. To Suzanne Frank, Susan Adrian, and Joy Maiorana for honest, demanding, and critical feedback. (I will, naturally, blame any textual errors on you.) Finally, to Raven and the marvelous regulars on my message board. Thank you for the daily laughter, the chats, and your continual support. It's an honor to write for each of you.

City of Souls

1

Hanging out in the perfumed, puke-inducing dressing room of an overpriced boutique was hardly my idea of a good time, but right now it was the only place I could get a moment to myself. Olivia Archer—debutante, casino heiress, and lingerie expert—had been my much beloved sister, and while I still mourned her passing everyday, *being* her was more involved than I'd ever expected. There were benefits to attend, bachelors to date . . . silk negligees to be purchased. And tonight there was a bachelorette party for one of her BFFs. More than two hundred women flitted around at what had mushroomed into one of the social events of the year. That was why I had to escape behind a pink velvet-covered stall door just to send a text message. Though this wasn't just any text message.

Where the hell are you?

There. Cryptic enough that if intercepted no one would know it was a text sent from one superhero to another. Imploring enough that Vanessa would find me as soon as possible. She knew these über-feminine social events made me twitchy.

As if on cue, the door to the dressing room was flung

open wide, banging against the opposite side to rattle the wall mirrors. " . . . I mean, she can't just get married like everyone else, can she?"

"Please. That woman lives for attention."

I came to attention too, because I knew those voices. Lena Carradine and Madeleine Cross, two of society's finest.

And they were talking about one of *my* mortals, I thought, narrowing my eyes to peek through a crack in my dressing stall.

"No, first she has to celebrate for an entire week here," Lena said, flipping back a lock of her auburn hair. Extensions, I sneered, getting a good glimpse of the false locks and mentally patting my own back. Six months ago I never would've spotted the bonding glue. "Spend more money than has ever been spent on a Las Vegas wedding—"

"Well, it's not *her* money, is it?"

My phone vibrated in my hand. I looked down.

where R U

I frowned. Vanessa Valen knew exactly where I was. She was supposed to be with me. And what was with the truncated text? Her work as a reporter might just be a cover, but it'd been chosen precisely because she had the grammar bug. She hated sloppy texts.

Just hurry. I wrote back. *I can't do this by myself.*

I tucked the phone back in my Dior and smiled wryly. As an agent of Light, I could have just as easily been talking about our enemy Shadow agents, paranormal beings who fed off negative energy, manipulating the mortal population in order to stir up dissension and chaos. Or I could have been referencing a recent training session with the rest of our troop, a matriarchal corps based on the signs of the Zodiac. But no, I meant enduring a whole evening surrounded by society women whose verbal sniping made supernatural battles look like sandbox swipes. As if on cue, Madeleine joined in.

"And then fly off for another weeklong Indian celebration. I mean, where is Hindu, anyway?"

"It's where the guy in your iPhone lives."

I'd only taken over my deceased sister's identity, life, and lifestyle a year ago, but I'd already met Lena and Madeleine. Saying they were self-absorbed and vain was like saying Madonna craved attention. It was a hunger without end.

And now they were devouring one of their own. "And talk about tacky. I mean, are we in her native Texas with all these gourmet barbecue sauce party favors?"

Okay, so she had a point there. The hot sauce didn't exactly fit with the boudoir theme.

"Or some third world country with their barbaric beauty customs?"

Lena was referring to the henna that had been painstakingly applied to our hands the day before, intricate whorls, dots, and swoops that had turned our bodies into eastern art. Mine had been a beautiful mandala, often depicted in sand paintings by Buddhist monks. I'd chosen it because it symbolized the cosmos that—as a member of Zodiac troop 175, paranormal division, Las Vegas—had recently become a very important part of my life. Yet the drawing had washed off in the shower without leaving the faintest trace of red dye. The woman of the hour, Suzanne, had been devastated.

"Or just Vegas, with that gawdy neon runway and over-sized disco ball?"

Wait, wait. Texas and India were one matter. But pick on my hometown? Now I'd had enough. Besides, what normal person didn't like disco balls?

Kicking open the door of the dressing room stall, I had the satisfaction of seeing them both gasp and whirl, hands to chests and mouths. Sure, it was an entrance more befitting Joanna Archer than her perfect socialite sister, Olivia, but I was trying to make a point . . . and, again, I was both.

"You're forgetting something ladies," I said, slipping in front of the beveled three-way mirror. I patted the back of my long blond hair. "She's marrying an Indian prince."

Madeleine could only respond by lifting her chin. Her face had been long frozen into a permanent expression of surprise. Botulism was so unpredictable. "So what's next? A friggin' tepee and a sweat lodge?"

"Indian, sweetie," I emphasized, pointing to the middle of my forehead. "Dot, not feather."

"Yes, and one of the most esteemed businessmen of our generation." The words flowed more smoothly than the silk pooling at Suzanne's feet as she glided in from the festivities. The notes of Chopin were muted by the shutting of the door as she shot a conspiratorial wink my way. "How I snagged him, I'll never know."

I smiled at the well-timed entrance.

I knew how. I'd sent Suzanne and Cher on a trip to Fiji the month before to remove them from the direct line of fire of supernatural enemies who'd see them dead just to get to me. True to form, Suzanne had returned engaged to a high-profile textiles magnate so wealthy he made every casino tycoon in town look like a pauper. Including Olivia's father—and the man I'd once thought was mine, too— Xavier Archer.

Of course, the big news on the gossip circuit was the question Suzanne had just voiced. How had a forty-something-year-old widow enticed a younger, infamous bachelor with homes in Bombay and London, a chalet in the south of France, and romantic liaisons on every continent, into suddenly becoming the marrying kind? The announcement of their million-dollar wedding hadn't only made headlines in Vegas, it'd been blazed across the international press, complete with full accounts of past trysts on each side, and close-up shots of the size of the diamond on her left hand.

The one, I noted, that she lifted now to brush back a tendril of honeyed hair. It was obviously the first time Lena had seen the rock up close since she gaped like an air-deprived guppy, though Madeleine pretended not to notice. Still, the scent of envy wafted from her like fresh-cut grass gone sour.

If there was one thing I had, it was a strong sense of smell.

Suzanne glided to my side and we both turned to the mirror, physically aligned across, and in front of, the other women. I was in the Vegas Girl uniform—designer jeans, expensive heels, and tiny top—appropriate for my socialite cover, though not too ostentatious. I could still move comfortably and hide my blades. Suzanne, on the other hand, wore a traditional Indian wedding lengha, the full-length blue and gold skirt marrying well with the intricate bindi sparking off her forehead. However, hidden beneath it all was a pair of crystal and sequined-encrusted cowboy boots, because she insisted on being comfortable. *Bless her heart.* I didn't have the heart to tell her she looked like a culturally confused Barbie doll.

"I do so admire your confidence, Suzanne," Lena finally said, eyes arrowing cruelly on the toes of those sparkling shit-kickers. "I'd be afraid a younger, perkier model would come by and snag him right back."

"Of course you would," Suzanne clucked sympathetically. Lena didn't seem to know how to take that.

"How long does the prenup last?" Madeleine asked, in an overly high voice. "Mine was good for ten years."

"But those first nine were good ones, weren't they?" Suzanne shot back, unperturbed. "And you guys did throw the best parties."

"I still do," Madeleine huffed.

"Well I wouldn't know. I haven't been invited since Harry left." She tilted her head so that her bindi winked. "That's very interesting, now that I think about it."

Realizing the pickle she'd gotten herself into, Madeleine stiffened. I knew that her former husband, like all the former husbands in this social circle, had courted Suzanne for a bit after his divorce, but I didn't know what Madeleine found more insulting, that or the way Suzanne had quickly, gently, shot him down.

"Well, there's my fabulous Christmas fete next month. I'll make sure my assistant has your current address."

"Great. Tell her it hasn't changed."

I put my hand on Suz's arm, like I'd just realized something. "And next year her assistant can just forward it to the palace."

Suzanne tilted her face up to mine. "Oh, that does simplify things, doesn't it?"

I nodded sweetly.

Madeleine swallowed tightly. "Come, Lena. The Martino girls just got back from Europe. I want to hear all about the Milan shows."

They left in a cloud of burnt sugar—their pique—and marinated violets—their perfume—and Suzanne said nothing for a moment, studying her nails like they were of great interest. I knew she was mentally rebuilding the wall of morale Madeleine's and Lena's words had chipped at. I'd done the same enough times as Olivia that I recognized the need, so I fumbled in my bag and began lacquering my lips in the mirror.

"Suz, can I ask you a question?" I finally said, pulling the gloss wand away.

"Sure, honey."

I rubbed my lips together. "Well, Madeleine and Lena have a point. Women around the world have been trying to attract Arun for years. So why—"

"Why me?" she asked with a raised brow.

"Why *not* you?" I said hurriedly, patting her arm. "But . . . why do *you* think he chose you?"

She thought for a moment, and then smiled. "Well, I'm attractive enough I suppose. And my pedigree is acceptable to his family, even though I'm widowed, and I'm a westerner."

"There are other attractive, available, acceptable women out there," I pointed out.

She inclined her head. "But most of them are afflicted. They're ill. Like Lena and Maddy. Pretty enough, but . . . "

She let her words trail off and shrugged like I should know what she meant. I didn't. "Afflicted with what?"

Suzanne took me by the shoulders. "Here. Look in the mirror."

I did so reluctantly. I confess, my exterior sometimes overwhelmed me, and it wasn't just because I looked like the sister I'd lost and loved. She was just so . . . much. Blond locks, sky blue eyes, breasts that were perkier than a game show host, and a waist that had been so perfectly nipped and tucked I looked like a bendable straw.

I was so much.

"There's this mental illness, right? It's called 'anhedonia.' It means 'without pleasure.' You can look it up, though all you really have to do is look around." She motioned to the door the other women had disappeared through, and to the world at large. "A good deal of people, mostly women, spend their entire lives in this state. It's a sort of half-death. But if you recognize this, you can fix it."

"How?" I asked, immediately wishing I hadn't. I ducked my head, unable to meet either her reflection in the mirror, or mine.

Suzanne smiled, not noticing my discomfort, or pretending not to. "You focus on bliss. Small pleasures. Fill your day with as many as you can fit into twenty-four hours. You devote every possible moment not to fulfilling another person—a man—but yourself."

I wrinkled my nose. "Sounds hedonistic."

"But once you can do this, you start attracting everyone to you. You don't need to compare yourself to some other girl, no matter how young or firm or perky she is." She smiled at me through the mirror, a better match for Olivia's sister than I had ever been. The thought didn't bother me as much as it once had. I was beginning to realize that friends were actually the family you chose.

"Trust me. A woman like this, one at her best? We're the

color of the world. We're the light and the beauty. So." Suzanne straightened. "Focus on your pleasure, and the man you want can't help but realize . . . "

I waited, but she only sighed, suddenly teary-eyed.

"That he's incidental?" I finished for her.

"That he may be a prince . . . but you're a goddess."

I smiled at that. "Yes," I said softly. "You certainly are."

She grinned, then frowned. "This just isn't right."

"What? Oh, those women? Don't worry about them. They're just jealous."

"No, I mean that I'm so happy." She spread her hands out in front of her, and I noted that her henna designs hadn't faded. "I'm happier than I've ever been, and you're going through such a rough time."

I wracked my brain to figure out what she was referring to, finally settling on the only subject she'd know about. The one the entire city was talking about: Xavier Archer's health.

Suzanne looked at me with concern. I lowered my eyes to keep from rolling them. Though I'd once believed Xavier was my father too, we'd never gotten along. I think he'd known from the beginning that he hadn't fathered me, but he'd fallen so hard for my mother he didn't let that stop him from raising me as his own. Still, he'd never liked me. Kids can tell that kind of thing from the start. So the image of the last time I'd seen him, frail and huddled under a pile of blankets, didn't exactly make me want to shed a tear. However, Olivia would. "The doctors are still hopeful," I said vaguely.

Suzanne put her arm around my shoulder and gave me a quick hug. After nearly a year of hanging out with her—via Olivia's best friend, Cher—I knew her scent well. Spiced gardenias and warm vanilla, a sensory telling of her spirit and good health. It *was* somewhat addictive, and no wonder Arun had fallen so hard. Pheromones tied into a goddess complex? What man had a chance?

"Come on," she said, pulling my hair to the side and taking me by both shoulders. "Let's try to take your mind off it for a bit. Ready for a lingerie trunk show? You can help me pick out my wedding trousseau."

She couldn't help herself, she was already beaming. It made me feel like the older woman in this relationship, but I smiled, and linked my arm in hers. "That sounds great, my goddess."

Half turning to me, she pushed open the door. "You're a goddess too, you know."

I shrugged and returned her smile, but said nothing as I followed her back into the chaos of her prewedding festivities. I'd go ahead and leave the pleasure and bliss and indulgences to Suzanne. After all, I thought, smiling to myself. I didn't need to be a goddess . . . I was a superhero.

A male attendant wearing nothing but a white loincloth and a beautiful smile met us just outside the dressing room. "Champagne?"

"Absolutely," Suzanne murmured, scooping a flute off the silver tray before cutting her way to the center of the ballroom. I lifted my own glass, smiling as I watched her go. The ballroom Arun had rented for the night was decked out like an elaborate Roman temple, with white pillars, busts of forgotten emperors and gods, and mosaics of Apollo and Alexander the Great. Landscape portraits hung along walls draped in silks, and white candles of all sizes pooled off waist-high pedestals, threatening to set the guests afire.

There was a make-it-yourself sachet bar at the back of the room, while more menservants wandered about with expensive lotions and perfumes, others carrying silver trays bearing exotic fruits, fresh vegetables, mini-quiches, and sandwiches. It was, I thought, a brothel and buffet mixed into one.

Snagging a sampling of strawberries dipped in chocolate, I followed Suzanne to the front of the stage, looking to the press row for Vanessa. Eyes stared back at me, a few bright bulbs flashed, but none of them were my ally's. I checked my phone for a message once seated, but there was still nothing. Maybe she'd had a breaking story to follow. She usually covered the crime beat, investigating anything that hinted of Shadow activity. Our aliases were carefully chosen so we could search out our enemies and thwart their plans. Or, if really lucky, take them out if it did nothing to impact the mortal population. It had been mere curiosity—the same curiosity Lena and Madeleine exhibited in the bathroom, minus the envy—that'd had Vanessa begging for a ticket to this event.

"These mortals are capricious, aren't they?" she'd said, glancing over the perfumed and embossed invitation when I handed it to her. She was asking me because while she'd been reared as a member of the troop, I'd been raised as one of the mortals they protected. My metamorphosis last year from normal human being into twenty-first-century superheroine had taken both allies and enemies in the paranormal world by surprise. As for me, up until that point I'd thought superheroes were pop culture myths. That the emerging glyph on my chest, which now lit under attack, was just a severe case of heartburn.

That the attack that nearly killed me as a teen had been random.

I thought of Suzanne, and her stepdaughter Cher, who had been Olivia's first and only best friend. "Well, these particular ones are capricious."

"Oh, not them. I think your friends are great."

I didn't correct her about the women being "my" friends, as I might have in the past. Like everything else that had been Olivia Archer's—her luxury condo, her car, her cat, and her wardrobe—what was hers was now mine. This had been difficult at first, and I was a bit thrown by how quickly people had forgotten me—Joanna Archer—and the tragic circumstances of my "death." But I had a new life now, and all these women were a part of it.

But I was interested in what Vanessa thought of my mortal playmates. They were flighty, weak, shallow when the tide was out—everything she was not. So what could she possibly find likable? "How so?"

"Well, first of all, they didn't have the advantage of growing up in a matriarchal society. I'd hate to be seen as the weaker sex." She shuddered, and I half smiled, knowing what she meant. Zodiac women enjoyed an elevated status the rest of the world's women couldn't fathom. "They also have to deal with lessened physical abilities, so they rely more on their minds and feminine skills to get what they want."

Which reminded me of Cher's unwritten motto: Flirting—it's a tool, not a weapon.

I shook my head. "They just don't know any better. It's the ignorance of being mortal."

And before enduring an attack that had broken my body and spirit, I'd been gleefully ignorant. But all of that—mortality, injury, getting by in a man's world—was well behind me. I had powers that enabled me to heal from man-made weapons, run faster, leap higher, and be stronger than any human could ever conceive. I could materialize walls from thin air and conjure plant life amid the most arid of terrain. My lungs had expanded like wings in my chest, and my every sense soared with each inhalation. It was like giving sight to someone who'd been blind since birth.

Mortality, I knew now, sucked.

Vanessa shook her head, like I'd said it aloud. "Not for your mother. She knew what she'd be giving up, and she chose mortality."

"She did it for me." And that was why and how I had all my powers. Zoe Archer had given hers over to me to save me from that long ago attack. But then she'd disappeared.

"But it's her very humanity that keeps her safe. That fragile flesh is as strong an armament as an Amazon's shield. She has the power to totally disappear. Becoming one of these capricious humans is her supernatural legacy. Now *that's* power."

But power and legacy weren't the words that came to mind as I sipped my champagne and looked around now. I wished Vanessa were there so I could see what she'd make of the male attendants in oversized diapers, and the sparkling white runway soon to be filled with bridal lingerie. At least I didn't have to be *in* the show this time, I thought, staring up at the runway. Maybe I was actually getting better at navigating the world as Olivia Archer.

"I'm sorry again about the henna," Suzanne said, settling next to me in a puff of scent and silk and crystal embroidery. Lightbulbs flashed like mad from the photographer's row as Cher joined us. "I know how long you waited as it was applied."

"It wasn't exactly a hardship." I'd been massaged and served finger food and drink the whole time. I patted her hand, careful to keep the printless pads of my fingertips—the one true giveaway of my Zodiac status—from touching her soft hand.

"Well I, for one, am extremely disappointed," Cher said, sending a little finger wave to Madeleine and Lena just behind us. She was dressed similarly to her stepmother, having gotten fully on board with the whole "ethnic thing," as she called it. Her lengha had gold threads and colored gems handcrafted throughout, and revealed her navel, where another bright gem winked merrily. "I was test-driving a real tattoo. I wanted to put a butterfly right behind my right earlobe."

Suzanne settled the fishtail of her gown around her legs. The shimmering jacquard winked elegantly in the pooling candlelight. "You mean for when you and your old man move into the double-wide?"

"Mama, your southern Baptist roots are showing! Tattoos are not trashy. They're mainstream now. Just ask Angelina Jolie."

"I will, next time Arun and I vacation with their clan

in St. Moritz." She made sure to say that loudly enough for Madeleine to hear. I smiled and sipped my wine. "And these weren't just random designs or tattoos. Arun helped me assemble the collection, explaining each one's significance in his culture."

"They were beautiful," I said, thinking again of the assorted mandalas. The delicate whorls and dots of the one I'd chosen had been almost mesmerizing . . . all the way up until they washed down my drain.

"Arun says they're magic," Suzanne replied, edging close, her tone dreamy at the magic of the man. Short courtship or not, she truly appeared to be in love. "They establish a sacred place on the body."

"Oh, well that's probably why they washed off," Cher said, waving the whole issue away. "There are no sacred spaces left on our bodies."

I snorted before I could help myself. At some point in the last year my acute grief over Olivia's death had lessened to the point that my mind skipped more to the memories of her happy life, much of which included these two women. I'd even begun thinking of my impersonation of her as a sort of tribute, a way to keep her memory alive. Cher and Suzanne had been her greatest friends, and for that alone I'd be ever grateful, but their friendship helped cloak my real identity now, and that added weight to my gratitude.

So as the lights dimmed to low, I smiled as one of the biggest weapons in my undercover arsenal began clapping her hands excitedly. "Oh, goodie!" Cher giggled. "Here we go."

The elegant notes of a violin filled the hall, the notes of Pachelbel's Canon swelling as the chiffon curtains at the runway's entrance slowly parted. Every smiling face turned Suzanne's way. There was a smattering of applause and a delicious surge of anticipation, an emotion I could now pick out by scent. It was sugary and light, like softened vanilla and whipped cream. I inhaled deeply of the collective emotion . . .

And a big cake rolled into the room.

I tilted my head, sniffing. Shit, I couldn't tell the difference between the anticipation and the cake?

"Is it someone's fucking birthday too?" Madeleine muttered under her breath, as the giant cake slowly made its way down the runway. It was frosted entirely in white with red roses, giant chunks of glitter sparking from each bloom's center. Madeleine's remark was too low for Suzanne and Cher to hear, but I had no such problem. I turned and she sunk back in her seat at my glare. One word from me and she'd be sitting out the wedding of the decade. She smiled weakly, and I turned back around.

The music altered, the Canon disappearing beneath a low, techno throb, like a heartbeat picking up pace, and the genteel society women were suddenly sitting straight in their seats, straining to keep their eyes on the cake as it glided down the forty foot catwalk. Maybe it was the lowered lighting, maybe the free-flowing champagne, maybe the cake itself amidst a group who allowed themselves to lunch only on lettuce and white wine, but the emotion I now scented was a growing hunger, the biting hook of cinnamon and allspice and a small dusting of pepper. The cake began a slow rotation too, and the music swelled.

"That's not a birthday cake," Lena cried next to Madeleine, standing to clap her hands with everyone else. "It's—"

"Beefcake!" Cher jumped to her feet as the top of the cake burst open, sparkly icing flying, music pounding, women screaming, and a shirtless man suddenly gyrating like his hips could power a vehicle.

"That's some filling!" Suzanne, the forty-something-year-old blushing bride, squealed in my ear.

Cher clapped madly on my other side.

I took one good look at the man's face and spewed champagne all down the front of my enhanced bust line.

Coughing, I wiped the tears from my eyes, and made brief eye contact with the dancer, still humping air, his pelvis doing things that were illegal in Suzanne's home state.

He paused in his dance of love long enough to locate me. Thank God superheroes didn't have the power to kill with looks alone. Because my ally and onetime lover—Hunter Lorenzo—shot me a look so wilting I would have keeled over in that moment. Instead, I swallowed hard, and set down my champagne glass, excusing myself to little notice. Hunter kept dancing, Cher pulled out some bills, and Suzanne headed to the stage to cop a feel.

I didn't laugh.

Vanessa hadn't shown. Hunter had just burst from a cake. I didn't know exactly what that meant, but like another superhero spotting the bat signal against the night sky, I knew that whatever it was, it couldn't be good.

2

"That was horrifying."

"No, it wasn't that bad," I assured Hunter as I handed him a towel. We were backstage, shuttled to a corner of the dressing room while models wearing—or not wearing—lingerie trotted out pieces for Suzanne's trousseau. I mentally marked a particularly cute peignoir for later. "You've actually got rhythm."

Unamused, Hunter snatched the towel from my hands and wiped icing from his chest. I found myself staring a moment too long, and looked away before he could catch me. It was the first time we'd been alone since the end of our affair a month ago, and by "affair" I meant something that'd ended almost as soon as it began.

As he turned his back—his beautiful back—to me, I pulled on a black trench coat and reminded myself that starting a relationship on the rebound was asking for heartache. Though the tension between Hunter and me had gradually eased, that didn't mean we were back to normal. Our interactions were stilted, the pauses filled almost to bursting with everything we were trying not to say, or even think. There was absolutely zero innuendo or sexual tautness, and there'd always been at least that. Even my teasing had no effect, as if what once stood between us had never even existed.

It's resolve, I thought as I switched into sturdy soled boots. I knew how it felt to have an indecision finally put to rest. I'd done the same with my last boyfriend, Ben, so I recognized the hardened glaze shellacking Hunter's once soft feelings for me. When resting on me, his expression was faraway yet focused, like he was seeing past skin and blood and bone and laying his mind's eye at the base of my spine.

It wouldn't have been so bad, I thought, tucking my heels into my bag, if I didn't have the memory of how he'd once let that knowing gaze linger on places only lovers found of interest. He'd once captured and followed the length and shape of my fingers, clearly reimagining them on himself. He'd memorized the curve of my wrists, which he once held and bit and raised above me in bed in willing surrender. He'd run his jawline along the muscles in my calves, taking pains to caress them before sliding them around his sides, covering himself in a second skin.

All of that was suddenly barricaded behind a wall of something he wanted more, but as there was no end to the things on this earth a man could want, I had no idea what it was.

But I did know that despite our physical attraction, and a mental connection once forged through magic, Hunter had his own dark secrets. The ones I was aware of—an undercover callboy identity, a cameo appearance with someone in the Shadow manuals, a daughter no one else knew about— were only the beginning. Experience had taught me that beneath such jagged tips lay emotional icebergs, and Hunter, I thought, stealing a glance as he pulled a long-sleeved collared shirt over his head, looked like an unsinkable ship going it alone. For some reason, it made me fear for him.

"What's your problem, anyway?" I said, careful to keep my voice light. "I mean, this is well within your line of work, right?"

I was referring to that secret work as a male escort, even though I knew it was only a cover in his search for someone, or something, else. Hey, I had to deal with the Jessica Rabbit references in my cover, so why should I let the facts stop me?

"I don't do that anymore."

"I know." He'd sold his Mustang, cancelled his private number, and disappeared from the escort brochures, leaving behind only wistful memories of lonely women. What I didn't know was why. I couldn't tell from his demeanor whether he'd found what he was looking for or if he'd given up altogether. And the dead calm of his gaze told me he wasn't saying.

"So where's the real stripper?"

He jerked his head. "Still in the cake."

I snorted, and crossed to the corner to peer inside. Sure enough, there was a hunky stripper inside, sleeping like a well-built baby. "You climbed into a cake with another man?"

"Shut up, Jo." He crossed the room, and for a moment it looked like he was going to keep on coming, and *that* was something you didn't want Hunter Lorenzo to do. I stepped back, but he only yanked his black pants from the center of the cake, checking them for frosting before pulling them on. "How else was I supposed to infiltrate the land of estrogen?"

"You wouldn't have had to if Vanessa had shown up."

"Exactly." He flipped a cap on to conceal his hair and facial features.

I frowned. "What?"

"She's missing." He jerked his head to the door, assuming I'd follow. "Let's roll."

Missing? I shook my head, but willed my feet into moving. "No. She'll be here. I was just texting . . . "

where R U

The text had no punctuation. Vanessa, as I'd known earlier, would never do that.

"Oh, my God." No, I pleased silently. Visions of Vanessa laughing and smiling and blowing kisses raced through my head. Not her. Not *anyone*, but . . . the Shadows couldn't have Vanessa. I picked up my pace.

Hunter led me from the ballroom, careful to keep a discreet distance between us. I put an extra sway in my hips but kept up the pace. We had to get clear of Valhalla, and the Eye-in-the-Sky security system, before we could look like we actually knew each other. Here, in the Archer dynasty's hallowed gaming halls, we were Olivia Archer and Employee.

"We think they got her while she was on her way to you, so they shouldn't be far." Hunter nodded to another guard, who goggled at me when we passed. I shot him a smile that could melt iron and kept walking. "Same message sent to everyone on her contact list. Riddick, Jewell, and Warren were all together when they got it. It's how we figured it out so quickly."

And Hunter, who acted as a security guard at Valhalla when not saving the world, had been the closest to me. I should've known he wouldn't have taken off his uniform and climbed into a cake unless the situation was absolutely dire. "Whoever has her is trying to use her to get to me, aren't they?"

where R U

He lifted one shoulder noncommittally, which meant yes, and pushed through the door into the open air. Beyond Valhalla's ornate porte cochere and winding drive, Las Vegas stretched like a winking rainbow, light scoring the ground and sky.

Hunter halted as we reached the fountains, lifting his phone to his ear. I bit my lip, waiting as he listened silently, nodded once, and hung up. "Gregor traced the call."

"Find the phone?"

"Yes."

"And Vanessa with it?" My heart pounded as I waited for the answer.

"Sorta." He turned his back to the street and gazed back up at the casino.

Worry washed over me from head to toe. "What do you mean 'sort of'?"

"The phone was wrapped in a package. With a bow." His slumped shoulders gave away the bad news before he spoke again. "And her tongue."

We raced across Maryland south of the university, the busy street teeming with college students letting off weekend steam and enough traffic that we had to dodge headlights. The sound of laughter and music rang from the off-campus apartments, the gas stations were bright, and the restaurants dim but bustling.

It wasn't until I spotted the tiny variable star winking above the side entrance of a tavern that I realized where Hunter was leading me. I stifled a groan, knowing it would only earn me an arch look. This tiny star marked a portal, an entrance into the washed-out flip side of reality. If you knew how to look, they could be found almost anywhere.

But that didn't mean I liked entering them. Sure, it reduced the chances of being spotted by both mortals and Shadows, but reality's flip side reduced the landscape into a hazy black-and-white line drawing, and the molecules comprising air zinged in my mouth with every breath, snapping in my throat when I swallowed. Most disconcerting, though, was never knowing what lurked on the other side of these supernatural thoroughfares. The weather was capricious, the terrain more like something found on another planet than this one, and the basic universal rules—like time and space, and sometimes even gravity—were as bendable as straws.

I followed Hunter through the dented metal door, eyes

locked on the portal's star for as long as possible, though I knew it wouldn't wink out until the entry closed behind us. As soon as it had, the street sounds ceased, and we took a moment to acclimate ourselves to what looked like a street scene from some grainy gumshoe film set in the forties.

"I mean to solve this crime, ya see, and you're not going to like it, ya see."

I snorted, gratified that Hunter was thinking along the same lines, and we started off down Rainbow Boulevard, a good fifteen miles from where we'd entered. Entries and exits between the two sides never matched up.

We walked on, easier without the threat of Shadows to contend with. In the past we'd found snow or rain or rainbows shaped like lucky horseshoes marring the landscape, but this time there was a knotty ball of power gathered in the sky. The clouds were dense around the center bulge, the layers extended in frayed wisps, which disappeared at the valley's edges. It was as if the victim of a very large spider had been wrapped up tight. Every so often there was a flash, like sheet lightning was caught in that bulbous center. I gave thanks that the odd cloud bump was only on this side of the portals, and caught Hunter giving it a wary glance as well.

Yet even given that, what really stood out in the achromatic gloom was the one thing that shouldn't have been there at all.

Us.

In the smeared, dulled, monochromatic milieu, Hunter's aura pooled around him like a full-body halo, a snapping gold that played off his burnished skin like light cutting on glass. It trailed behind him as he walked, a colorful cloak dissipating with the absence of heat from his body. I lifted my hand to run it through the trailing light when he wasn't looking, sending sparks pinging from my skin in his wake.

Which was how I noted my aura, or lack of it. Aura represented life force, and what had once fairly pulsed in a vibrant red band was now nothing more than a wispy cloud, barely colored at all.

"Worse than the last time," I said, ducking my head when I realized Hunter had heard. But it was. Thankfully, he said nothing, and we continued on in silence until we reached the Spring Valley Park, and the others. Six agents of Light were gathered under a green steel awning, and they greeted us with subdued nods. The two newest agents, Riddick and Jewell, were flanking Felix, who was only a little older but already a senior troop member. Tekla, mysterious and tiny, was an island unto herself as usual. Gregor was behind Micah, our troop's physician, and was using his one good arm to unconsciously rub at the stump of the other as he watched Micah rifle in a trash bin. Hunter and I joined the first three agents and were quickly filled in.

They'd found two more body parts. Micah was pushing aside soda bottles, empty fast food wrappers, and bags of chips, in search of a third body part that we all could readily smell. He finally found it—an ear—and added it with a sigh to his growing collection. He wouldn't throw them away, I knew. No matter what happened to Vanessa, we would later burn them as relics, give our thanks for her sacrifice, and if needed send up prayers for her soul.

I turned at a sound, and found my troop leader jogging toward us, though it took me a moment to recognize him. Warren Clarke had a multitude of covers meant to keep the Shadows from tracking him, though his favorite was that of a weary, timeworn indigent. His matted hair, crusted fingernails, and bloodshot eyes regularly sent people scurrying the other way, but the Shadows had recently put a new agent on patrol in the city's homeless shelters, so Warren decided to take time off, appearing as a regular Joe instead.

He jerked his head in the direction he'd just come and we followed without a word. Colorful auras trailed behind the others, reminding me again of my faded red hue. I didn't have time to regret it much beyond that, though. Two hundred yards away we found a big toe with shiny silver polish. Micah's giant shoulders drooped. Tekla bent to pick it up.

They weren't trying to kill Vanessa. Not yet. No, these were just tokens. Teasers. Her tongue left in the middle of the street, her right ear in the trash. They'd severed a thumb, and left it hanging like an ornament on a tree. Very creative. We also found her hair, which didn't technically count as a body part, but it was the one thing that took the same amount of time to grow on us as it would on a mortal, so the shearing was symbolic. I looked at the mass of shining dark curls and couldn't help my tears.

As the body parts were too small to attract mortal attention, we found each one through Vanessa's blood and unique scent, all of us attuned to the macabre signage pointing us in her direction.

"I think I'm going to be sick," Jewell said when we came across Vanessa's perfect, petite, and now severed nose. It was as if they were chopping off every available appendage, severing all the bits that came together to identify her as a whole.

"Don't you dare!" Felix whirled, and his tears rolled from their tracks, disappeared into the night. He wiped a hand over his face, leaving a smear of dirt. "She has to endure this. It shouldn't be so hard for *you*."

Felix, normally engaging and easygoing, fisted his hand in his already tousled hair like he wanted to pull it out. It wasn't just that he'd grown up with Vanessa in the underground sanctuary that housed the agents of Light and their children, their world. The two junior agents had quietly become an item in the last year, and he was having a hard time keeping his emotions from burning like acid in the air.

Tekla, our troop's Seer, wise woman, and senior troop member, placed a hand on his shoulder. "She didn't mean that, Felix. She didn't mean anything by it."

"She is not just parts . . . " He shook off Tekla, but kept on shaking. "She's not . . . "

Hunter and I looked at each other, then he jerked his head and we silently followed.

We followed the body parts all the way into Chinatown.

"This can't be right," Riddick said as we turned onto Spring Mountain Road. "All of Chinatown is a safe zone."

Safe zones were places where neither side of the Zodiac could touch the other, and were built in around the entire city. Even an agent's paranormal weapon, their personal conduit, was useless in such a place.

Gregor squinted at the faux Imperial skyline. "You sure it's not residual? Has Vanessa been here before?"

"It's fresh blood," Micah said, voice strained. Felix winced.

"So why would they lead us somewhere they can't touch us?"

"I know why." It was the first time Warren had spoken since Hunter and I joined them, and the timing was telling. It was only recently that I'd begun to realize his quietude was much like his indigent cover, designed to make us overlook him . . . and that he had such a great stake in our lives. Meanwhile the wheels were turning behind that sturdy frame, his mind ever-working, and all to an end that he'd already pinpointed at his personal destination. "They want to make a trade."

I swallowed hard. There was only one person they'd be willing to trade the life of a full-fledged agent of Light for—only one thing we had that they wanted. Our world's chosen one. The Kairos. Me.

They were torturing Vanessa because of me.

I was careful not to let Felix see my face as my stomach roiled.

"No trade."

"Of course not."

Felix frowned and bit his lip, and he didn't look at me.

I took a breath. "Wait. There has—"

Tekla stayed a hand on my arm, but spoke loudly enough for Felix to hear. "No, Jo. We'll get her back without risking you. Now put on your mask. And start searching for a portal. We can't enter a safe zone on this side of reality."

We found one, and we entered it as a team, as one.

3

⟩⟩   At one time only three people knew I was masquerading as my sister, the socialite and casino heiress Olivia Archer. It had been a month since the other agents of Light found out I was Joanna Archer beneath all this Stepford perfection, but other than Regan DuPree—now an outcast and rogue agent—the entire Shadow Zodiac was still clueless about my cover identity. Everyone in the mortal world believed Joanna Archer had died a year ago in a fall from a high-rise building, and it was out of this destruction of my old identity that my true life was birthed. In order to keep that life, it was imperative the Shadows never discover my Olivia Archer identity.

So I made one last check of my mask before we collectively slipped under the turned-up eaves of a strip mall impersonating a Chinese temple. The red tile rooftops appeared black in the moonless night, and we stole past the crowded restaurants on the lower levels, where menus I couldn't read were pressed against the windows and the people inside were munching contentedly on dim sum and pot stickers. Ignoring the scent of steamed food, we instead followed that of fresh blood and rotting flesh, heading one by one up a wide concrete staircase to the empty furniture stores above.

Antiques shops comprised most of the retail space, Buddhas and dragons and Shaolin warriors all peering out from the window displays in wary dismay, but we kept going, the macabre scents intensifying as we neared a Chinese bakery. The Shadows weren't even trying to conceal their location.

Warren, sotto voce. "Make a net."

We put some distance between us, so the splitting of ranks would appear natural, though we were running short a couple of agents. Chandra, whom I'd displaced, was now serving the troop in an auxiliary role only, and Kimber was no longer strong enough to run with us. As she blamed me for that lack, I didn't exactly mourn her absence. Yet it was at the moment that everyone pulled out their conduits that I felt most vulnerable. That now-rogue agent, Regan, had stolen mine after being expelled from the Shadow troop. I had to settle for a mortal weapon until Hunter could make me a new one. The Micro Uzi was a poor substitute for a conduit, but you took what you could get.

The bakery was abnormally large, with giant plate-glass windows sporting tiered wedding cakes that overlooked the ornamental patio and the lights of passing traffic on Spring Mountain Road beyond. There was no way to sneak up unseen, but we didn't need to in a safe zone. So we walked single file through the sole glass door, propped open to let the scent of Shadows—and Vanessa—waft outside.

The table and chair clusters had been cleared from the room's center, and bakery cases lined the opposite wall, while red paper lanterns set on a low glow shot an eerie light through the cavernous shop's middle. There were coffee and tea stations, and a curtained doorway leading into a kitchen, but the Shadows were clustered at one side of the elongated room, tilting our attention that way. It was like they were baiting us. But for what?

And then, as they parted ranks, I decided they'd been luring us in for a close-up of the carnage they'd wreaked upon Vanessa's once pristine body. She was trussed to a chair like a victim in a gangster movie, except the ropes wrapped only around her core, leaving limbs and remaining appendages free for further attack. But they'd dispensed with the toying games now. In addition to her shorn hair and missing nose, and the ear and digits we'd already found, there was a foot lying beneath her chair.

They had done this because of me.

It was all I could do to hold back a wail.

Felix didn't. His cry rose out of him like a siren, but guttural and borne from his belly. He strained forward, but Gregor and Micah were already flanking him in anticipation. They held him until he stopped struggling, but his voice had awoken something in Vanessa. She lifted her head, which had been lolling, and though it took her a moment to focus, seeing us brought her to life. She shook her head from side to side, gurgling as she strained against her bonds, eyes bulging, the movement making the blood flow free in her mouth again. After all she'd been through, it was a testament to her will that she could still move at all.

Other than the man securing her, the Shadows fanned out, and we each gravitated almost unconsciously to our opposite on the Zodiac. Felix dutifully followed Sloane, the Shadow Capricorn, who fucked with him by arching the farthest away from Vanessa. Though I didn't will it, I found myself bisecting the room to stand directly in front of our captured Leo. My opposite, the Sagittarian Shadow and their troop leader, was missing.

"So what now?" Warren finally asked. I could tell by the tightness constricting his voice that it rubbed him to ask, but right now the Shadows were firmly in control.

"We wait," said the man securing Vanessa, the man—I could tell from scent—who'd defiled our Zodiac's Leo. This was the first time I'd met him, but I recognized him from the Shadow manuals. Harrison Lamb was Micah's opposite, the Shadow side's new Virgo. I'd killed his uncle Ajax nine months earlier, and because of Ajax's prowess and brutality, Harrison hadn't been expected to succeed Ajax until later in life.

Yet despite his sudden rise in rank, he was surprisingly self-possessed. He moved with grace, wore his paranoia with an ease that said he'd rather be wrong than dead, and hardly made any effort to withhold the smell—or in the Shadows' case, the *stench*—that rose with emotion, giving him away to his enemies. I took in a good whiff, committing the scent to memory: Gucci cologne laid over an ashy sack of skin laid over a marinating stew of organs laid over decaying bone.

In short? Shadow.

Harrison stretched and yawned, bloodied fingers splayed to the ceiling like he was completely unconcerned that a six-foot, seven-inch agent of Light was creeping up on him. In contrast to his current posturing, Micah was a gentle soul where his troop was concerned, using a sweet disposition and his surgeon's skill to attend to our health. Though his fury sat atop his emotions like oil upon water, I could already see him calculating how to put Vanessa back together, how to reattach and regrow and erase all the damage the Shadows had done.

Harrison saw it too. "Don't worry, Micah. We used mortal knives to cut away the fat. They all regenerate . . . eventually."

But it would be an excruciating process. We couldn't die from the strike of man-made weaponry, but we felt the pain just as acutely.

Micah's jaw clenched and he took an involuntary step forward. Harrison unsheathed a barbed poker from the holder behind his back, immediately stilling the advance. The unspoken message was clear. If Micah kept moving, Harrison would instead drag Vanessa outside the safe zone and use his personal weapon upon her . . . and then she'd never heal.

"So what are we waiting for?" I asked. For us to give in? For my allies to turn me over? To allow Vanessa to go to her tortuous death without a fight? I narrowed my eyes on Harrison's responding grin, thinking if that were the case, it was going to be a long wait.

Vanessa's renewed struggle drew every eye. She was wild, almost fierce now, gagging on the blood her movement caused to seep from her mouth and nose. Harrison leaned down like he was concerned, then looked in turn at each of us, dark humor giving life to his eyes. He continued this cruel pantomime, glancing back and forth in exaggerated concern, before letting all expression drop from his face as his gaze arrowed in on Felix. Lifting one side of his mouth, his skeleton momentarily flashed, as if revealed on an X ray. Then his smile was back, and he was slipping a hand over Vanessa's mouth and nose. She began suffocating immediately.

When I was younger I didn't fully understand why it was so distressing to see a woman specifically brutalized by a man. As a victim, I'd identified with anyone who'd ever been forcibly overcome by another. Violence was impervious to gender, and it didn't always come in physical form either.

It was only as I grew older, and especially once I'd gained strength no mortal woman *or* man could know, that I realized why this was such an abomination. Yes, using a physical force on someone smaller than you was immoral. But an attack on a woman was an additional insult—it was an attack on life itself. Every strong man—down to the worst rapist and murderer—had once been nurtured, if only for a small while, by the softness and solace of a woman's body. To turn upon that was a desecration, and in our world—a matriarchal society where power was passed through the woman's bloodline—it was absolute blasphemy.

And Felix—as good and strong a man as any—still took his solace in Vanessa. He reveled in her wit and smile, her laugh and, yes, her body. She was his soft spot. So, despite it being a safe zone, he lunged.

The Shadow conduits still didn't appear. Their power was useless in a safe zone, but what could be done—what I didn't know how to do the first time I was attacked in a safe zone—was to turn the attacking agent's power against them. It was a more dangerous sort of power because, as any soldier knew, it was easier to defeat an enemy if they were already at war with themselves. It would have been enough for Harrison to face down Felix alone, but the Shadow troop timed their defense so perfectly it was clear they'd anticipated this response. When Felix was no more than five feet from Harrison, they all held up a hand, ringing him in silent negation.

He didn't freeze, as I'd thought would happen to an agent trapped in a cloud of their own power. Instead he thrashed as he was lifted from the ground, fighting invisible bindings, like he was being pulled from every side at once. One hand clutched at his throat when he hit the ground, the other at his chest, and he flopped like a fish on a dry bank. This eventually dropped off into random twitches, pitching the Shadows' laughter even higher.

I didn't move, nor did any of the other agents of Light. I'd been warned against trying to help someone who'd breached a safe zone . . . warned too that no one would help me if I did the same. The bond between troop members was so strong that the negative energy would be transferred, and we'd both end up being strangled by our power.

No, not strangled, I thought, watching Felix heaving. *Drowned.*

"Anyone else want to try?" Harrison asked lightly as Felix continued to gasp. I swallowed hard. At least the gasping was an improvement. And his limbs had fallen still, so the power was abating, being reabsorbed. "How about you, little Kairos? I mean, you're the cause of all this. Want to take a long shot at redemption?"

"Why don't you give it a go, Harrison?" I said. "I mean, take out the Kairos, the woman of legend, and you'll go down as one of the most powerful, badass Shadows of all time."

His eyes flickered like he was briefly considering it, but a sneer quickly replaced the look. "In a safe zone? Do you think I'm stupid?"

"Yes. Ugly, foul-smelling, and inbred too."

His gaze flat-lined. "Well, I'm not the single-handed cause of my entire troop's collapse."

"Nor am I." I wasn't responsible for someone else's evil, even if I was the target.

"Oh, but you are. You broke your changeling, right? And breaking the changeling of Light, that one special little child, is what caused the manuals of Light not to be written. So now the children of the world can't read of your antics in comic book form. Their fertile little minds don't birth the dreams and power that give you the energy to fight us. Your entire troop is weakened."

"We're not getting weaker."

He held out his bloodied hands. "We're getting stronger, so it's the same thing."

Because their manuals were still being recorded, detailing the battle between good and evil, and sold in comic book shops all over the nation. The fact that manuals vital to our survival were masquerading as comic books wasn't as oxymoronic as it might seem. There was something to be said for hiding in plain sight, and though truth might be stranger than fiction, in this case they were one and the same.

So Harrison had an ugly, foul-smelling point. Despite our demigod status in this smoggy, bright valley, our micro-universe was as fragile as a rain forest's. Knock out one little organism, and suddenly the whole ecosystem was thrown off balance.

"So you're not the almighty savior of the Zodiac," Harrison pushed, with a lift of his chin. "You're a hindrance to your troop."

Though I'd gotten better in recent months at controlling my anger, I decided Harrison could use a reminder of just whose daughter I was. So I opened the darkness in my heart, locked in the middle of the light one, and lifted my lids to reveal a gaze as smoldering and bright as the sun's flashing core. I let my cheekbones rise to press at my skin, and felt it pull tight across my forehead. I imagined my skull gleaming, almost glowing white against my skin, while the rising pressure and the smoke from my pores brought to life a pounding headache. I ignored that until I knew my dark eyes—the only thing visible beneath my mask—had completed their transition into glowing red coals. When Harrison shuddered involuntarily, violently, I smiled sweetly and let the demonic mask fade.

Yet he recovered quickly . . . and came back for more. "That's just a parlor trick. We've no real use for you."

"Then why do you want her so badly?" Hunter piped up, arms folded over his chest. His expression was shuttered, like he was observing events that didn't involve him, but I knew better. Hunter was a tactician and warrior, and wasn't so much at rest right now as he was coiled and waiting.

Meanwhile, Felix was finally sitting up, head hanging forward and mouth open, like his power was pouring from his throat.

"*I* don't." Harrison began idly picking through the pastry case, lifting and considering a good half-dozen sweet buns before replacing them, leaving a trail of Vanessa's blood on each one. He turned his attention back to me. "But your daddy does, and he's been doing everything in his power to get to you."

I thought of what I knew about the Tulpa's power: the ability to touch people in their dreams, take over his agents' bodies and turn them inside out, and how he could stud the sky with black holes, insert someone inside them, and make it all disappear. And those were only the homicidal abilities I'd seen firsthand. He'd been at rest for much of the time I'd known him, trying to court me into joining his troop, and abandon the Light for the Shadow. He was beyond that now, and as lethal as his wrath had been in the past, it was nothing compared to the complete, unbridled hatred he felt for me since our last encounter. Great.

"Then what do *you* want?"

"Right now?" He stuffed a moon cake in his mouth and spoke around it. "A cappuccino."

Felix struggled to his feet but didn't move forward. "You prick—"

"Shhh . . . " Harrison put a bloody finger to his lips. "He's coming . . . "

And in a strange unspoken harmony, agents of both Shadow and Light turned toward the wall of windows to watch the Shadow leader, the Tulpa, drop as if from the heavens, landing onto the false pagoda patio like a descending UFO. Of course, a living being that had been created rather than birthed really *was* as otherworldly as all that. I swallowed hard and stepped forward to face him because he was also my opposite on the Zodiac. The Shadow Archer. Their troop leader.

My birth father.

A tulpa was a thought-form; a being so vividly imagined it became an actual person. Tibetan monks had honed this skill for centuries through visualization, meditation, and extreme discipline, though this tulpa had been birthed from the mind of a westerner . . . and a twisted one at that. Once actualized, the Tulpa had become unnaturally powerful. There was no known way to kill him. In fact, if we attempted to do so with one of our conduits, the energy put behind the attempt actually funneled more power into him. So we battled his agents, while searching hopefully for his invisible Achilles' heel, but steered clear of direct battle with him whenever possible.

Yet we'd recently discovered that the nature of his birth was also his weakness. His creator had been killed before he could gift the Tulpa with a name, so his title *was* his name. His ability to alter his appearance entirely was a power, but it was also a sign that he lacked permanence in the world, and *that* was a weakness.

His appearance today was a cross between a Wall Street executive and a construction worker, interesting, as he took the physical form of a person's expectations. I'd seen him as a casino mobster, a suave college instructor . . . and a hairless, spine-horned demon. To be honest, that was the visage I preferred. At least I knew exactly what I was up against when staring into the face of a demon.

My allies pulled in tighter as a result of his arrival, but we held our ground. As powerful as the Tulpa was, even he couldn't violate a safe zone.

"My gawd, Harrison. You've practically dismantled that agent. And yet her allies are just standing around talking." He sauntered into the entry, hemmed in the doorway like he was both posing for a picture and caught in its frame. He smiled slyly at me. "And you call yourself the Kairos."

That's what *they* called me. "I call myself the Archer."

"And Joanna," he said lightly, tilting his head. "What else?"

"Nothing I can repeat in such polite company."

His eyes traced the mask covering my eyes, temples, and hairline, and his fingers twitched reflexively, causing me to smile. He'd been angling for my Olivia Archer identity for months now.

Reining in the need for a little while longer, he folded his hands before him and settled into himself. "Well, you should check the temper, daughter. That's how I pinpointed you."

That brought my black humor to an abrupt halt. "My temper?"

"Anger is a gift. In this case, my gift to you. It lurks in your heart as surely as my blood resides in your veins. It's how I found you."

"Bullshit." I was not linked to the foul nonhuman being. Not in any way that mattered. "You orchestrated this."

He shrugged. "Of course. But I can't stand around waiting all day for my troop to capture an agent of Light, torture her—bonus points for inventiveness, Harrison—"

Harrison smiled, and both Felix and Micah strained forward like they were leashed.

"—and draw the rest of you in. I'm a busy man."

"Yes, your dates with Skamar must keep your calendar quite full," I said.

Finally, a barb that hit home. His overly pleasant expression fell and his nostrils widened. Skamar was the Tulpa's nemesis, enemy, and equal. Also a tulpa, and as such, she was the first being he'd never been able to completely overcome. And though new to the valley, she also had a power he did not: she was named.

Where was Skamar, anyway?

The Tulpa settled himself, pulled at his jacket sleeves, then sniffed once as he lifted his nose into the air. His placid gaze landed directly on me.

"Kill them," he said softly. The glyphs on every agent of Light's chest shot to life. Depicted in comic books as a superhero's lettering across the chest, they only did so when in danger, but we were in a safe zone, so for a moment no one moved.

Then the Tulpa tilted his head and the Shadows surged forward. I saw hands go up all around the room, the Light deflecting the advance and turning the Shadow agents' powers upon themselves. But they kept on coming. Vanessa managed to force a scream past her tongueless mouth, and it hit me then, as it did all the Light: she hadn't been struggling so vehemently to get free. She'd been struggling to warn us. *We were not safe here.*

I only had one second to return my attention to the Tulpa, catching the anger and hatred in the red flare of his eyes, before the order of the world turned upside down. He flicked a finger, and even though I was twenty feet away,

I was catapulted through the air to slam head first into an ornate concrete pillar. On one level I was aware of the activity around me—the Light fleeing, conduits useless, no offense available to them but a good defense; the Shadow chasing, battle cries in their throats; Vanessa struggling, screaming and forgotten on the far side of the bakery—but blanketing all that concern was one greater than the rest.

I lifted my head slowly and found the Tulpa staring at me, his eyes as glittering and hard as our city's night-soaked grid of lights. He bared teeth of chipped granite . . . and he charged.

I froze amidst the pile of crumbled plaster, knowing I'd never escape that wheeling vortex of limbs. He was a rocket, faster than anything I'd ever seen, and when a scream escaped that decaying mouth, the building shook, plaster and tiles fell from the ceiling, bulbs shattered in their sockets, and I ducked.

A wall of sheet silver appeared between us, too instantly for the Tulpa to avoid. The crash was like a car wreck, and I looked over to find Tekla with both arms outstretched. So we weren't *entirely* powerless.

"Get Vanessa!" she yelled, flinging up wall after wall as the Tulpa, screaming now, continued to punch through them. I bolted. We were lucky; Vanessa's opposite was Regan, now an outcast, and Tekla's had been Zell, whom I'd helped kill last month. But the Cancerian Shadow, Drake, had heard Tekla's cry, and was reaching for Vanessa along with me. Without thinking, I pulled out the Micro Uzi—the weapon I'd thought useless—and rolled off an ear-shattering round from arm's distance away. No, mortal weapons wouldn't kill him. But as evidenced by Vanessa—they were still effective. He jerked backward, spraying blood.

I didn't waste time on Vanessa's ropes. I just swung the Uzi to one side and picked up the entire chair with the other hand. It wasn't heavy, just awkward, and with Tekla covering my back, thrusting up walls to cover my retreat, I ran.

Outside, I vaulted over the ornamental wall, silently apologizing to Vanessa for the rough landing, but kept spraying bullets at anything that moved . . . or moved too fast. I was one of those things, of course—fleeing so fast that all the mortals would see was a blur—but fast and fast enough were two different things.

With our lives depending on it, I put on the speed. I needed to be the latter.

4

My phone rang in my pocket.

"Peppermill. Cab. Hurry."

Warren. Without preamble. Or good-bye.

Carrying Vanessa as gingerly as possible, I headed to the Peppermill Lounge, formerly another safe zone. Gregor masqueraded in the mortal world as a cab driver and regularly parked behind the classic Vegas lounge. So I knew both he and Warren had made it there safely.

Fifteen minutes later, Hunter and Felix gingerly took Vanessa from my arms. Micah patted the space next to him in the cab, which meant there wasn't a lot of it, and I clamored into the backseat, practically on his lap as I pulled the door shut behind me.

"We'll have to circle because of all the blood," Warren told Gregor, who took off in a screech of rubber and exhaust. Vanessa's blood was already scenting the air.

Gregor nodded. "I'll hit the beltway from the Strip. It circles the entire valley."

"One pass," Warren agreed. "Then we drop Micah, Hunter, and Vanessa at the warehouse."

Located in industrial Vegas, the troop's warehouse wasn't a safe zone, but right now it was as safe as we were

going to get. Hunter, our weapons master, crafted our conduits there, but more importantly, there was a panic room
where Vanessa could hide.

"I'm going too," Felix said in a tight voice. Warren drew
in a breath, but only hesitated momentarily before nodding.
Felix would be a wreck if he was trapped in the sanctuary,
not knowing how Vanessa was doing. He was a wreck now,
arms hanging helplessly, afraid to touch her anywhere. She
groaned as we hit a speed bump.

"Where's Tekla?" I asked as we flew up the on ramp.

No one answered.

"Where's Tekla?" If she'd gone down while saving
me . . . after Vanessa had endured *this* because of me . . .

"Calm the fuck down!" Warren yelled, half turning in
his seat. "He's following us!"

"I'm trying." But the thought of the Tulpa tracking us
had the opposite effect of calming me. Gregor glared at me
through the rearview mirror.

"Jo!"

"Shut up!" I closed my eyes and thought of grassy fields
and fuzzy bunnies and shit. But my anxiety had spiked
and the fields were burning up behind my lids, the bunnies
turning into blood-splattered carcasses.

I realized belatedly that Warren was yelling at me. " . . .
if you would listen!"

I opened my eyes. "What?"

"You have to go."

"Go?" My heart jumped again. Where the hell was I
supposed to go? There were no safe zones any longer.
No place to hide and heal and find refuge from our
enemies.

"Go away, for one. The Tulpa will be able to track us
because of you."

Keeping the troop safe, then. As always.

He sighed, and worked to calm himself as well. "Look,
I'm not just throwing you out on your own. Find Skamar.
Make her tell you about Midheaven."

"Midheaven?" Hunter turned to stare at Warren. The cab fell oddly silent.

Warren held Hunter's look for a long moment, then blew out a breath and tried to tuck a tuft of hair behind an ear, a habit left over from the days when it was dreadlocked. It was an uncharacteristically nervous gesture. "Just tell her about the safe zones. She'll tell you how to walk the line so you can get help, and do it without—"

He turned back at a sharp crack behind us, followed shortly by a sonic boom, as if the sky was made of ice floes, shifting and breaking apart. The Tulpa was having a fit. And he wasn't far off.

I shivered when he raised a brow at me. He wanted me to leave *now*? "Wait—"

"We can't."

"But—"

"You broke the changeling, Joanna! You caused the fall of our safe zones! You're the only one who can fix it, and the answer is in Midheaven!"

"But—"

"Look, we'll find you as soon as possible. Let me get the rest of the troop safe first. You alone can fix this. Go find Skamar. Go be someone else—"

"Find her where?" The female tulpa had a habit of disappearing for days at a time, reemerging only to battle with my homicidal father. She was as elusive now as she'd been in her previous incarnation as my doppelgänger. "Be who?"

Warren looked out the back windshield again. The Tulpa seemed to be dropping back.

"Anyone," he finally answered, voice ragged with fatigue. "Just . . . don't be Jo."

I drew back, stunned. He turned back around, and the others refused to meet my eye. I stroked the butt of my Uzi like it was a security blanket.

Warren, finally realizing I wasn't going to say anything, muttered one word. "Micah."

There was barely any room for Micah to turn his head, much less his body, but he managed to shoot me a look of sympathy as he shrugged. "Sorry, Jo."

"For wh—"

My ass hit the ground before my feet, as did my head and palms and right cheek as I flipped over myself. The cab was nothing but a wink of distant taillights by the time I looked up, and I cursed as I limped to the side of the road. Sure I was already healing from the fall. The *push,* I corrected, as I began walking in the opposite direction. But what the hell was I supposed to do alone, with an automatic weapon, and instructions to be anybody but me?

They threw me out at the north end of the Las Vegas Beltway, at the top of Charleston, near a chichi casino where savvy locals played and an upscale boutique mall housing independent eateries and one-off shops. It was late now, all the shops closed, and the indoor/outdoor restaurants were shut tight to the winter chill. I set my Micro Uzi on the wall of a marble white fountain, and figuring a head cold was better than a decapitation, climbed in to wash off the remainder of Vanessa's blood and scent.

"Don't be Joanna," I muttered, flipping my mask atop my head like an oversized headband. I loosened my low knot and tried not to be offended by Warren's parting remark—or the skid marks on my ass—and shook out my hair. It was fine, really. I impersonated Olivia the majority of time anyway. And subtracting my real name from the equation did nothing to diminish my status in the troop: the Archer of the Zodiac, the Kairos, and the chosen one of our entire world.

Right?

Sighing, I climbed from the fountain and kept walking. *Like I knew.* Spotting a hedge of struggling boxwoods lining the glossy, stamped sidewalk, I trailed my hand idly above them as I passed. A gentle pulse from my mind, then a moment where I could almost feel *green* in my fingertips, which throbbed as I forced energy downward. Bright leaves unfurled beneath my palm and the trunks wobbled then stilled, their roots strengthening. Birthing plant life from nothing—it was a skill, and mark, of Light.

"See?" I muttered, mollified by the show of power. I wasn't a hindrance to my troop. I could control my temper. I could thrive as a superhero. I could help . . . at least when I wasn't screwing up. I sighed again.

Besides, others could call me what they wanted—Joanna, Olivia, Kairos, Archer—what really mattered was how I saw myself. "Warrior."

That word was the only thing that'd enabled me to keep moving through a world after the attack on my life as a teen, and in a world where much of the population had been larger and stronger and faster than me. It let me maximize the strength I did have, and had me honing abilities other women—and even men—never considered necessary. It'd taken years of intense martial training, but after a time I'd turned my weaknesses into weapons.

And that was *before* I became a superhero.

As for the Kairos designation, well that's where things got a little more complicated. Being the underworld's "chosen one" sounded wonderfully auspicious . . . until you realized it was all a big mistake. My mother, an agent of Light, had been sleeping with the Tulpa—getting in close, looking for a way to kill him—when a quick trip to the drugstore confirmed she was the proud new owner of a pregnancy stick sporting two pink lines. She was lucky I hadn't popped out with fangs and claws.

For reasons known only to her, she then kept my existence from *both* sides of the Zodiac, so my metamorphosis into an agent a year ago had completely shaken up the landscape of Las Vegas's paranormal war. Sure, I was reportedly destined to bring ultimate victory to whatever side I fought for, but that was tied to bringing certain signs, or portents, to life. So far I'd managed the first three through trial, and mostly error. The fourth one, though? I'd fumbled that completely.

As Drake had taunted, I'd inadvertently injured a changeling, Jasmine Chan, who was absolutely essential to our continued existence. Changelings were mortals who lived and died as any other, except for their childhood years, when imagination and belief extended to things unseen. Each side, Shadow and Light, had changelings who kept the secrets of the Zodiac, and passed them on to the next generation, while making sure mortal kids knew and believed in us as well. Those little minds were like fuel cells providing our troops with extra energy to fight the opposing side. Obviously the ability to suspend disbelief—to believe in superheroes—generally passed along with youth, which was why even the changelings eventually had to forget us entirely.

It was now time for Jasmine to do this; in short, it was time for her to grow up, but she couldn't—or simply wouldn't—which had effectively put the brakes on any flexible new minds reading and believing in our stories. The fear was that if I didn't figure out how to fix Jasmine soon, our troop would gradually weaken. Our alternate realities would fade away, our portals would close, and we would cease to exist altogether.

But now, finding the elusive Skamar, and getting her to tell me how to "walk the line," would supposedly help with that. I wondered why Warren wouldn't instruct her to help me prior to this, or why it took the loss of our safe zones to light some sort of fire under his ass. Meanwhile I waved my hand over a cluster of star jasmine, which bloomed so fully, so immediately, that the air was honeysuckle sweet in seconds. I smiled.

See? I hadn't broken everything. And over the past year I'd gotten used to the "superhero" designation too. It was my job and calling, and despite its dangers, and my repeated screw-ups, and the sacrifices required of me, it was one I'd begun to love.

Any warrior would.

5

Setting out to find Skamar and actually doing so were two different things. She'd been at war with the Tulpa essentially from the moment she'd been "birthed" or fully realized in this world, so she didn't have a home, any contact information, or even the ubiquitous cell phone. Still, randomly wandering the city was the least effective way of finding someone in short order. So the next morning, under an unseasonably warm sky, I headed to the one place I knew I could leave word that I was looking for her.

The parking lot of the pink-stuccoed strip mall where Master Comics was housed was only half full when I drove by, but I parked a few blocks away at a day spa Cher had once dragged me to, and walked back.

Although none of the Shadows knew about my Olivia Archer cover identity, I still felt exposed just waltzing up to the building in the middle of the day. Perhaps I should have taken the added precaution of approaching via a portal. It wouldn't necessarily have kept me from being spotted by an observant Shadow, but the black and white camouflage might get me past the inattentive.

"Too late now," I muttered, reaching the storefront.

I visually tagged two portal entrances—one alongside a sewer grate, and another above the passenger side of an abandoned car—options if I had to flee, priceless in a world where I suddenly found myself with too few.

Oddly, I also found the entrance locked. I glanced around, but the OPEN sign was bright orange against the glass front, and the hours of operation hadn't changed. I gave the door another tug, and when it didn't budge, found a sliver of space between a Green Lantern poster and the ever-popular Spider-Man and peeked inside. The shop was teeming with children. I saw Kylee and Kade, two of the newest changelings, and Douglas, the little shit who used his body to shield the Shadows from harm when they were in the shop, but none of them looked my way. Even when I rapped on the glass, they just continued perusing comics and playing games too complicated for the mind of someone as simple as me.

"Excuse me."

I glanced over to find a skinny kid staring up at me, arms so straight at his sides I wanted to tell him to fall at ease. He was watching me open-mouthed, as if mesmerized by a movie screen. As if, I thought with a degree of annoyance, he was watching a horror flick. Unwilling to continue with the absurd stare-down, I stepped aside, and he pressed his back against the glass, inching toward the door. I got a whiff of adrenaline and fear, but before I could grab the handle he slipped inside, cowbells jangled . . . and the door rocketed shut behind him. I stepped back, looked around, and tried to follow. It might as well have been a handle attached to a cement wall for all the good it did.

What was going on?

Squinting between Spider-Man's legs, I saw the kid who'd slipped inside point to me, and a man's head popped into view. I waved . . . with my middle finger.

Zane Silver scowled in reply. He was the shop's owner . . . and though he looked like a nerd who got off on things like freeze-dried ice cream and collectible sock monkeys, he was really a seventy-three-year-old man trapped in time. It was that whole "great power requires great responsibility" maxim at work. He had the ability to mentally watch the events of our world and record them in comic book form—a gift, sure—but ever since he'd accepted the position of record keeper, he couldn't resign until someone else took over the duty. Nobody'd been willing to in a good half century, so a retirement including bridge games and gumming his food was a long way off.

Drawing back, Zane then reappeared outside of what I'd begun thinking of as his command center, circling the counter grumpily to head my way. I rolled my eyes, straightened, and waited for him to let me in.

"What the hell—" I began as soon as the door swung open.

"Go away!" he snarled, and began pulling the door shut again. I barely got my foot wedged between the door and frame.

"Let me in, Zane! It's dangerous out here."

"That's because *you're* out there. Now go away."

And with that, he stomped on my foot, kicked my leg out of the way, and pulled the door shut.

"Evil, psychotic, geriatric Martian . . . !" I hopped on one foot while cradling the other, and decided to stop complimenting him. He couldn't hear me anyway. Fine. If the old coot wasn't going to let me in this way, I'd break in via the rooftop skylight. That's what I'd done last time.

Bound to the building as surely as he was bound to his service, Zane worked on the lower floor and lived on the upper, with groceries, mail, take-out food, and dry-cleaning—for all his valuable T-shirts—delivered to his door. If he even attempted to leave—and he hadn't in the time I'd known him—then the voices in his head that helped transcribe our world's events would turn on him and drive him into madness.

I kinda felt sorry for the guy, even as I removed a skylight pane for my break-in. After all, I'd probably be cranky too if World of Warcraft action figures were the highlight of my existence. Then pain splintered my limbs like slivers of glass were being inserted via my nail beds. Sizzling sounded nearby, and I found myself on my back, staring up at a blank, blue sky. I blew a tendril of burnt hair from my eyes, wondering if my appendages were missing from my body. Because I couldn't feel any of them.

"Wow! That was great! It was like she was yanked backward on a fisherman's hook!"

"Awesome."

"Do it again!" The first voice said, and I felt a light thump on the rooftop as someone hopped up and down. "Zane! Zane! Make her do it again!"

I grunted in objection and pushed myself to a sitting position, having to squint to focus. Two blurred silhouettes sharpened, but blurred again when they shifted. A rat's nest of shit-brown hair appeared behind them at the half-open skylight, followed by chunky cheeks and a body that had to be wedged through carefully to access the roof. Zane joined the two nimble preteens already there, a remote control in his hand. I looked at it balefully.

"About time, Archer. I've been dying to try out my new toy." Zane put his hands on his hips, belly jutting from below his T-shirt as he inspected me for damage. He, and the changelings, knew exactly who I was, what I looked like, and what I was trying to do. They weren't allowed to say, just as they couldn't tip the balance the other way and reveal those selfsame details to us about the Shadows.

"Let me guess," I said, wiggling my toes. All still there. "You've got cameras up here?"

"Sensors, man!" The first kid, whom I now recognized as Dylan, was so excited he had to draw heavily on his inhaler. Shoving it back into his pocket, he pointed. "Under that wadded up newspaper . . . inside that Coke can over there too."

"Awesome, huh?" said the other kid again. Kade. He had a habit of turning every statement into a question.

The high-pitched excitement did nothing to help the buzzing in my head. "Please, please, piss off."

"My mother would be mad if she heard you talk to me like that."

"She can—"

Dylan knew what I was going to say. "Don't talk about my mother!"

"Yeah, because politics, religion, and mothers are off limits," I muttered, clamoring to my feet. The jolt had been a thankfully short, if powerful, shock.

Zane was looking at me with a down-turned mouth. "You really shouldn't talk to kids that way."

"They're not going to remember it anyway," I said. All memory of this time in their lives would be erased upon onset of puberty. Just as it *should* have been for Jasmine, I thought, reminding myself why I was there. "Besides, they shouldn't go around electrocuting people."

"Zap this bitch again, Zane!" Dylan was still pissed about his mother.

I held out my hands as Zane cocked his thumb above the red button. "Look, I just need some help."

"You're dangerous, Archer. You could get us all killed. Just look at Jasmine."

"I didn't touch her!"

"You did. You touched her inside. You displaced part of her *chi* with your own. You've split her soul in half."

Accidentally split it in half. I sighed. "Okay, but I'm trying to figure out how to fix her. The manual detailing how to do that would be a big help."

Because such a thing had been done before. An agent named Jaden Jacks had displaced a changeling's aura, and the details of how he'd ultimately fixed the kid were somewhere in the Shadow manuals. It was just a matter of finding it, impossible without spending months in the effort . . . and if Zane wouldn't let me in.

As expected, he shook his head. "As record keeper, I can't reveal anything that might unbalance the equilibrium of the Zodiac. I work for both sides."

Shadow agents couldn't read the manuals of Light, and

vice versa. It kept a sort of cosmic balance between the two sides. But I could read both sides, I thought irritably, because I *was* both. This had caused the Shadow manuals to be altered somewhere—there were fewer thought bubbles detailing what a featured Shadow agent was planning; more once they'd already acted—so I didn't see why Zane couldn't just throw me a bone.

"I'm trying to bring it back in to balance," I said.

He shrugged. "You fucked up and now karma is weighing down the scales in the Shadows' favor. You'll have to find it yourself."

"Why don't you just kill Jasmine?" Kade said snottily.

I took a threatening step toward him instead.

Wide-eyed, he backed straight into Dylan, who landed flat on his butt. I smirked. His voice cracked as he yelled. "What? Like you haven't thought of it. You're half Shadow! You live for that shit, right?"

"If your mother could hear you now," I muttered, because I *hadn't* thought of it. It would have never occurred to me . . . but now it was in my mind. I turned back to Zane, who was watching me closely. "Is he serious?"

"See! She's interested!"

"Shut up, Dylan." I glared over my shoulder. He fumbled his inhaler. "I'm . . . curious."

"It's simple, Archer. Jasmine's like a leech, sucking your power from you in long, slow pulses. If you want to reunite your split aura in your body, along with all the powers she's been siphoning off, then she's gotta die."

It wasn't the first time these kids had said that. They knew of Jaden Jacks and the changeling he'd injured, though the report of the child's death was more of an assumption. The kid and Jacks hadn't been seen since, not even in a manual, and that was odd. Full-fledged troop members couldn't leave the valley. It was one of the maxims that ruled our existence.

"Jas knows it, too," said Dylan. "That's why she doesn't come around here anymore. Well, that . . . and because she's spending time with Li."

Li. I swallowed hard. Li, who was eight years old, and clamoring to take over Jasmine's position. Li, who'd somehow been injured when the Tulpa had attacked me. Li, who was deteriorating by the day because of that injury, and would continue to do so until I figured out a way to fix her sister.

And that's when the manuals had stopped being written. That's what was keeping the fourth sign of the Zodiac from coming to pass.

"Look, I don't want to kill Jas." *Or her little sister.* "I want to find the manual that shows how Jacks healed his changeling, or find Jacks himself. Barring that, I need to find Skamar so she can tell me how to 'walk the line.'"

I muttered this last bit, rolling Warren's words over in my mind, still having no idea exactly what they meant.

"What did you say?" Zane asked sharply.

"I said I need to find Skamar. If I leave a message with you, can I be sure she'll get it?"

"Skamar's in hiding. She needs safe zones to recover from her battles with the Tulpa, and you've done away with those." I opened my mouth to object, but he was already waving that subject away. "But go back to the part after that. About walking the line. Who told you that?"

I tilted my head, caught by his sudden interest, and his seriousness. "My troop leader."

He lifted a brow. "Warren Clarke?"

"No. Jabba the Hutt. He also said to tell you he needs an octogenarian to help round out his criminal empire. You may have a future yet."

Zane scowled. I was about to write off his question, but then I remembered how anything that happened in Las Vegas's underworld ended up in a manual within two weeks. I continued staring at him until the silence elongated uncomfortably between us. From the expression blanketing his face, I knew what he'd say even before the question was out of my mouth. "You know about Midheaven too, don't you?"

"Of course. I know everything relevant to our world."

I'd asked him once before if he thought Midheaven was a myth. At the time, though, I hadn't had Warren's permission to do so.

"Let me guess. You can't tell me anything about that world, right? Some sort of cosmic checks-and-balances, right?" That would be right in keeping with the same powerful law that prevented the changelings from telling their favored troop members about the opposing side's actions. The same reason the little sickos who favored the Shadows knew, but couldn't tell, of my Olivia Archer cover identity.

"I can't tell you," he confirmed, with a shrug, "but not because it's forbidden. Midheaven's energy doesn't register over here. That's why it's not in any manual. It's another world entirely."

"But one Warren now wants me to enter." Because he knew, or at least thought, that Jaden Jacks was over there? Or that Jacks could tell me how to fix Jasmine? It would make sense. Zane clearly didn't know what had happened to the kid, and as he'd said, he knew everything that happened in *this* world. But how was I going to get to Midheaven if I couldn't find Skamar in order to learn how to walk this "line"?

"It has to be because of the safe zones," Zane was muttering, shaking his head like he was perplexed. "He'd never reveal its physical existence otherwise . . ."

Yeah, what about that? I fisted my hands on my hips. "Why?"

"Because it'd be better if it didn't even exist," he said in that eerily serious way that made me want to giggle and shiver at the same time. "Midheaven is a pocket of distended reality. It's distorted, and a place for people—usually rogue agents—to hide. It serves as a way to escape detection as they made their way into the valley."

"Ahh . . . " Now it was making sense. Rogues were agents, either Light or Shadow, who'd been cast out of their home troops either due to personal infractions or political unrest. In other words, if their troop was disbanded or destroyed.

If that happened, they were free to leave the city they'd formerly served and become independent agents. They officially became rogues when they entered another largely populated city, where another troop already resided. There could only be one star sign for each position on the Zodiac, so even entering a city with a full Zodiac was seen as a challenge. We had orders to slay them on sight. That's why Regan was no longer a threat. No one on either side of the Zodiac would stand up for her now. "So Warren didn't tell us about Midheaven because of the rogue agents."

"He didn't tell you about it," Zane said direly, "because it's a twisted place, and it twists you in return. You go in one person, you come out another."

"Experience shapes people," I countered.

"Midheaven strips them."

Shaking my head, I decided this was already turning into an infinite circle. Find Skamar to find Jacks to fix Jas and restore our safe zones. Yet I needed a safe zone in order to find Skamar and Jacks, to fix Jasmine and restore those safe spaces. "What a clusterfuck."

I hopped to the ledge, already considering my next step—beyond the one that would have me leaping thirty feet to the alley floor—when Zane, still in zealot-geek mode, stopped me.

"Don't you want to hear the song?"

I looked up at the bright, wide sky, wondering when the minutia of this world was going to stop bitch-slapping me. I stepped off the ledge and turned.

"I love songs," said Kade. Dylan hit him. Anxious to get on with the business of saving the world, I'd like to have done the same, but Zane was already clearing his throat, straightening formally, and widening his stance. Then he began crooning like he was headlining at the Sands with a half-full martini in one hand.

Beneath the neon glowing bright here
Lies a land of starry skies

Look below dear, not in the middle
But kill the rushlight in two tries.

"Wow," I said, and he shot me a rare smile. "Put on a button-down shirt and a few gold chains and you'd have yourself a career."

His face fell. "Shut up."

"No, seriously. You're not half bad."

"It's not funny!" He began pacing, fat face clouded and red. "You'll memorize that if you know what's good for you. That shit can save your life!"

I thought of all the other shit that was supposed to be helping me too. "Let me see if I've got this right. I've got to find a tulpa, walk the 'line,' enter Midheaven, and find a Shadow agent . . . and the only clue is a badly written murder ballad?"

He pursed his lips, then shrugged. "Pretty much."

I hit the ledge again. "Good-bye, Zane."

"Don't come back here, Archer. Not unless you've fixed this."

Twisting, I cocked a fist on my hip, but my brows drew together when I saw what he was holding aloft. It was a beat-up photo of a freckle-faced boy, sandy-haired and lanky with youth. I'd never seen the kid before, but I knew who he was. Zane would only carry a worn photo of one kid with him at all times. "Jacks' changeling."

"His name was Ricky," he said, voice edged in granite. "And I don't want to lose any more."

He meant changelings. Jaw clenched, I swallowed hard. "You haven't lost this one yet."

And I was going to do everything in my power to make sure we didn't. Even if it meant entering a fabled world armed with nothing but a song.

6

Though finding a way to bring the fourth sign of the Zodiac to life was currently my greatest worry, it wasn't my only one. Despite my rebirth last November as Olivia, and as a twenty-first century super-heroine, what was really surprising were the things that hadn't changed. For example, the Tulpa still sported a hard-on for my mother's death, my mother continued to elude him, and I was still forced to interact with the enigmatic, powerful—and recently reclusive—Xavier Archer.

An anonymous note this time last year—one I now knew had been sent by the Shadows—had relieved us both of the notion that Xavier was my real father. Of course, the note failed to mention that my real father was the Tulpa, but that was because the Tulpa hadn't known of my existence either.

Was there anything, I thought wryly, that my mother couldn't make disappear?

So I wheeled down Las Vegas's most famous sun-baked street and returned to the site of Suzanne's opulent bridal shower the night before. Valhalla was Xavier's premiere hotel, and though ironic, I had to put in an appearance here just so I could safely disappear later. I needed the Olivia identity, and I couldn't risk drawing anyone's attention by switching up my routine without notice.

So despite my newfound power, status, and knowledge, I still had to kowtow to a mortal man I hated. There was a silver lining, though. Everything belonging to Xavier also belonged to the Tulpa. My real father was my fake father's benefactor. In return for money, Xavier fronted the Tulpa's many businesses. My ultimate goal? Bring them both down . . . but in order to do that, I had to stick close to a man I'd despised for years. Xavier.

So that's one of the reasons why Olivia Archer—casino heiress and social debutante—regularly worked an eight-hour shift where she'd earn less than she'd spend on a bottle of wine. It was another way to get inside Valhalla's hallowed walls, which we believed was the headquarters for the Tulpa's organization. Xavier had initially refused me, and then, when he realized I wouldn't be swayed, started me in the gift shop, hoping that would cure this inexplicable whim to actually work for a living. It hadn't—I wanted more than spending money; I wanted retribution—and so the news that he wanted to see me at his home office before my shift even began had me holding back a smile . . . and had Ginny, my small-minded boss, grinding her teeth.

"Maybe he wants to give me a raise," I told her with false excitement. More likely he was going to move me to a new, more socially appropriate department now that I'd proven I wasn't giving up. Ginny huffed and turned away while my coworker, Janet, gave me a hopeful thumbs-up. I hoofed it down to Uniforms, used the adjacent locker room to change into a more Oliviaesque outfit, and handed in my work clothes for a fresh set that I might or might not need the next day. I locked these away in my appointed locker— I couldn't be caught ferrying around a Valhalla uniform if a Shadow did happen to track me—then headed to my car in the employee lot, where I was both surprised, and not, to find Felix waiting.

"You my babysitter?" I asked, purposely keeping my tone light. Anything heavy looked like it would knock him over. He was dressed in his usual jeans, with a faded gray T-shirt, untucked, and hair streaked with caramel highlights, deliberately unbrushed. But the expression on his face wasn't one I'd ever seen on him before. He'd aged a decade since the night before.

"Yes, and you've been naughty," he tried, but his grin slipped from his new face. "Come here and let me give you a spanking."

"My daddy would kick your ass if you tried," I said softly.

"Your daddy wants to kick my ass anyway." He snorted. "And yours, for that matter."

I put a hand to his arm, steadying us both for my question. "Vanessa?"

"Micah's taking care of her." Tears welled so quickly, they'd clearly been lurking beneath the surface. "It's going to take time, though."

I nodded because there was nothing to say. Normally we healed in an instant from mortal wounds. But there was nothing normal about what the Shadows had done to Vanessa. "I'm so sorry, Felix."

"It's not your fault."

I shook my head. "They were angling for me, and I broke the safe zones, plus—"

"Jo!" His voice must have come out even more loudly than he intended, because even he jumped. "They're Shadows. They'd have done it anyway."

I hesitated, biting my lip. "I saw you, Felix. When Warren told us they wanted to make a trade, Vanessa for me . . . " I didn't look away when he flushed because I wanted him to know I'd seen . . . and I understood.

He looked me in the eye then, so serious it was like I didn't know him. I *didn't* know him, I realized in the next moment. Vanessa's torture had changed him. He looked more like Hunter now; something had touched him in a way that he would always bear a scar. I too had the same sort of scar. "No. Warren was right. No matter what they did to Vanessa, we wouldn't have made a trade. Not even a lateral one, agent for agent. And certainly not for . . . "

The Kairos. I cringed. The title didn't make me feel special . . . and it certainly didn't make me feel like the savior of the supernatural underworld. Instead it made me feel like a thing rather than a person. Again, all I could say was "I'm sorry."

He looked down, and the warrior-look disappeared in the slump of his shoulders.

"Warren doesn't know I'm here," he said, blurting the confession out like it was burning his tongue. "He told us about Midheaven after you left. That he'd always known it existed, that he'd kept it from us for our own good."

I wasn't surprised. "Did anyone ask about the Shadow side?"

"What do you mean?"

"I mean, did they know about Midheaven even while we didn't?"

Felix's brows drew down like he didn't understand why that was important, so I knew that no one had thought to bring it up. It was significant, though, because if the Shadows knew of it, and Jacks had disappeared with his changelings all those years ago, then he could have found the perfect way around our restriction upon leaving the valley. Jacks, and the kid, could *be* in Midheaven. So I bet that's what Warren had been referring to when he said the answer to fixing Jas—fixing our world—was in that one.

I was so taken by the thought that I almost missed Felix's whisper. "I think I hate him."

I looked at him sharply, taken aback. "Who? Warren?"

Jaw set, he nodded. I swallowed hard, then nodded back in return. I don't think Felix meant it, but he *thought* he did. I'd known, or at least suspected for a while, that Warren kept secrets from us. He so often wanted things his way, no questions asked, no explanation given. No wonder Felix was pissed. How often had Warren gotten what he wanted by omission? There was an entire world out there, sidled up next to our own, yet it had taken the destruction of our safe zones for him to even mention it.

Which meant he was probably hiding even more.

Not wanting to fuel an already volatile anger, I veered course a bit. "He didn't happen to tell you how to get to Midheaven, did he?"

Felix cursed under his breath. "You know Warren."

Yes. He wouldn't tell them anything he didn't think they needed to know. And here was Felix, powerless to do anything to help heal the one person he loved above all others, his impotence palpable. What he needed was an outlet for all that pent-up anger. He needed to feel like he could help her, even if after the fact. I'd seen the same look on my boyfriend's face years ago, right after I was assaulted, but in a way it was worse for Felix. After all, he was a super-hero.

I bit my lip and considered him. His cover identity as perpetual college student and playboy fit him perfectly. I remembered Vanessa once telling me that Felix had Neptune in his Eleventh House, which supposedly meant he was dreamy and irresponsible, basically the complete opposite of a normal Capricorn. At the time, though, she'd been on a rant about him forcing her to track a possible Shadow alone while he danced the night away at a new technobar. Never mind that he'd found the Shadow at the same club.

"He's impulsive, unreliable, and can't be depended upon to even tie his shoes!" Vanessa had fumed, not entirely wrong. He often left his shoes untied. "He has no work ethic beyond seducing coeds out of their clothing, and you would think that with the goat as his glyph he'd have some sort of ability to see things through, but nooo!"

While all her accusations were undeniably true, Felix also had a laugh as lithe as his body and mind, and he could sense—and even alter—the mood of a room with his playful energy. I suspected his much maligned mischievous nature, like the frat-boy persona, was exactly what had attracted the serious-minded Vanessa in the first place.

And it might come in handy at Xavier's. My view of the place was, after all, colored by familiarity and loathing. My energy would also be divided by having to hide that, so I could probably use an extra pair of eyes. Perhaps Felix would see something I could not.

Plus he was cute, a necessity for any of Olivia's romantic interests . . . or conquests. Riddick would've been a better match—his cover as a successful dentist satisfied Xavier's standards of suitability as a match for his beloved daughter—but Felix was the one standing in front of me. Xavier would probably just think Olivia was slumming again, the boy nothing more than another trivial pursuit.

Besides, it would be a good way for Felix to expel some of that pent-up fury.

"You'll do," I finally said, motioning him to the passenger side.

"Thanks," he said flatly as he angled around the nose of the car. "I'll do what?"

"I have to pay a visit to my other daddy. Or Olivia's, that is. You're going to come along as my plaything."

He said nothing, but his sigh was long and drawn, his mutterings incoherent. Clearly it wasn't exactly what he'd had in mind. I shot him a sweet smile as I settled in next to him. "Oh, and we'll go ahead and kill one of the Tulpa's most loyal Shadow agents while we're there."

Felix's head shot up then, and for the first time he looked like his old self.

I filled Felix in on the Archer household as we drove to the compound—the personnel, the layout . . . the strange little room shaped like a Tibetan burial mound.

He nodded impatiently before asking, "And Lindy Maguire? How do we get to her?"

Ah, Lindy. The woman who once massacred an ally's

entire family just because her leader said to. The Shadow so in love with the Tulpa that any woman seen as a threat met an inexplicable, early demise. If she'd known who I really was, she'd have killed me in my sleep years ago, and not just because I was one of the Light. Lindy Maguire and my mother had a well-documented, decades-old feud due to Lindy's infatuation with the Tulpa. I'd long wanted Lindy taken out because of this, among other things, but Warren's cooler head had prevailed.

"If we kill Lindy," he'd said, "the Tulpa might send someone more attentive to watch over Xavier and his assets. And 'Helen,'" he said, referencing her alter ego in the Archer household, "has never looked at Olivia as anything more than a dizzy airhead."

No, like Xavier, she'd always saved her pointed criticism for me, Joanna. If Xavier had made my young life a living hell, Lindy/Helen had aided and abetted. I obviously hadn't known then that she was an agent monitoring Xavier for the Tulpa, but I did now. And I was going to use that information to help bring down her beloved Tulpa.

But I'd go ahead and give the pleasure of killing her over to Felix.

"Age hasn't made her any less dangerous," I told Felix now. Shadows were scary enough when acting out of duty, or because they simply liked wreaking havoc, but Lindy was even more brutal because of her obsession. "But we have the advantage here, so just keep your eye out, your emotions dampened, and your hands hidden."

Felix glanced down at the shiny, smooth surface of his fingertips, where his prints were missing. "The biggest 'tell' in our paranormal identities, huh?"

"Yeah," I said with a wry smile. "And Lindy, 'Helen,' will be looking."

Once admitted through the guard gate, I cruised up the serpentine drive, kicking gravel as I skidded to a stop between the mansion and an eternally running fountain.

Excess, I thought, staring up at a matching marble staircase, was a word Xavier Archer defined. And why not? He'd literally sold his soul to attain all this. He should make the most of it.

It was surprisingly windy as we climbed from the car, reminding me of the powerful gusts that held the valley captive every spring. They bit into the flesh now that it was winter, and we rushed up the white marble steps, ducking beneath a portico to ring a bell that chimed for miles. I rubbed my arms through my T-shirt and gave Felix a closed-mouth smile, knowing he was wondering what it was like to be raised with all this space and falsely winking splendor.

It'd been an emotional haunted house.

How appropriate, then, that the door swung wide to reveal the woman of the hour . . . and one of the primary people who'd made it that way.

"Pulling butler duty now too, Helen?" I stepped inside quickly, hiding the way Felix stiffened beside me. Neither of us had expected the Shadow to open the door. "Where's Deluca?"

My voice bounced back from the ornate vaulted ceiling. It was important that I act as breezy and unaffected by my surroundings as Olivia always had. "Helen" caught and catalogued every action. At least now I knew why.

"He's taking some time off," she answered stiffly, nose high, skin sallow, and expression as disapproving as ever. All that was alive on her were those beady, assessing eyes. I met them openly. "I'm forced to take up his post."

"Didn't he recently take a vacation?" I asked, tilting my head so blond curls fell over my shoulder.

The visual cue that I was nothing more than a ditz, a nuisance, had her relaxing enough to shut the door behind us. She had yet to acknowledge Felix. Good. "This isn't a vacation. It's . . . a little more than that."

I raised a perfectly waxed brow. Ralphie Deluca hadn't taken a leave of absence in the twenty-odd years he'd been employed by the Archer estate. I paused long enough that

"Helen" registered my deliberately blank look as impossibly vacant.

"Ah, well. This is my boy—" I broke off, pretending to stumble. "This is my friend, Nathan." I took Felix by the arm, pulling him close. She'd think I was trying to pull a fast one on my father again by dating someone unsuitable, and would run to him with the news as soon as I left. Olivia's flighty, unstable reputation would remain unsullied. "Nate, this is Helen . . . um, So-and-so."

Helen surprised me by addressing Felix directly. "I anticipated your arrival, Mister . . . ?"

"Stewart. Nate Stewart. Nice to meet you, Mrs. So-and-so."

My laugh rang, genuinely. Felix liked getting his digs in too.

"But how'd you know I was coming?" he said before Helen could take offense. It was one of the traits that made him so likable, and it kept stoic, severe Helen off balance. "Olivia and I hooked up this afternoon rather . . . spontaneously."

He let the memory of something hidden and secret ring in his voice. I flushed at the intimation in it, shuffling my feet. Wow. Those coeds didn't have a chance.

Helen colored as well, before clearing her throat. "Well, it wasn't *you*, precisely. Our Olivia seems incapable of traveling anywhere solo . . . " She left the sentence incomplete as she motioned for us to follow her into the sitting room. "I've prepared refreshments. You may wait here for her business with her father to be concluded."

It didn't surprise me that she wasn't going to let my new friend near Xavier's office. The last time she had, a valuable mask had temporarily gone missing.

"Actually, Nathan is looking to find a job at Valhalla." I motioned toward the offices, and Felix half rose from the settee he'd just sunken down onto, his abject confusion perfect for the moment. "We want to ask Daddy if we can work in the gift shop together."

Xavier wouldn't concern himself with minor personnel decisions, but Olivia would have been able to get away with it.

"No, Olivia."

"But it'd be fun," I protested with a little foot stomp. "Nathan's great at getting people to buy things they don't need. He could sell shot glasses at an AA meeting."

"I mean, no, your friend must remain here."

"The office is big enough for all of us."

"Your father's not in his office."

My mouth snapped shut in surprise. At last, an emotion I didn't have to fake. Xavier might have turned into a recluse, but he lived in his office.

He siphoned away his soul there. I suppressed a shudder.

"So where is he?"

"His suites."

"He has suites?" Felix asked, picking up a scone and taking a bite. "Sweet."

I smirked. "She means his bedroom."

Felix turned on his heel. "I'll be with the cookies and tea."

Clown, I thought, letting my smile show. But what a clever clown. While I kept Xavier busy, he could take care of Helen. "Divide and conquer" I could practically hear him thinking as he kicked up his Pumas.

So I blew Felix an air kiss, and Helen guided me to the elevator reserved for Xavier's personal staff. Except there was no one bustling about, changing linens or dusting or vacuuming, and the secretary's wing was eerily quiet. What the hell was going on?

"Helen," I said, peering into one of the kitchens.

She kept walking.

"Helen!" I ran to keep up, my heels clacking off the Italian marble. "What's going on around here?"

"Mr. Archer is making changes." She punched the elevator button. The doors slid open silently. "These reductions in staff are just . . . preparations."

"For what?" I asked, joining her inside the steel box.

She spared me a glance through the mirrored doors as they closed. "For his death," she said, and the emotion of my genuine shock perfumed the air.

7

After the attack on my life when I was a teen, my mother's subsequent abandonment, and long after my early adolescent irreverence dried up into an ashy ball of hate and bitterness, the household staff of the Archer estate continued to treat me like one of the valuable antiques, to be looked at and cared for, but not touched. If the gardener or one of the maids asked how I was, it was done in that tone of disinterest reserved for strangers. I think it actually startled some of them when I moved.

And then there was Lindy.

I'd done some research since discovering my lifelong housekeeper was also a Shadow agent. At first I was merely awed that my mother had been able to live with a woman who could scent out the tiniest aberration in emotion. But then I realized that if Lindy had been here back then, my mother would have found a way to let Warren know, and get him to take care of her long ago. So somehow Lindy had taken over the life and identity of the original Helen, who *had* been a mortal . . . and was probably now dead.

One thing I knew for certain. Lindy McGuire loathed

Zoe Archer, and the hate that could fuel two women for decades could only have one thing at its molten core: a man.

Because in contrast to the apathy the Tulpa showed Lindy, he'd fallen for my mother like a felled oak. Twice. The first time had been twenty-seven years ago, when Zoe got close enough to ferret out the identity of his creator, then killed that man in the hopes that it would kill the Tulpa as well. This "closeness" had also led to my conception, another reason Zoe fled. As I grew in her womb, her body had begun recklessly kicking out the pheromones that would mark her as Light.

The second time she'd conned him was after giving up her near-immortal state in order to save me. I'd survived the attack on my life . . . and so had my baby. Premature, the infant clung to life like she knew herself the successor in a long line of stubborn women, but then she'd been abducted from her adoptive parents on the day she was born, almost lost to the Shadows. Zoe Archer—having given all her power to me, and more vulnerable to the Tulpa than she'd ever been before—went after her granddaughter, and reclaimed the child despite her mortal flesh, embarrassing the Tulpa in the process. Again.

This, I thought, was what burned the Tulpa the most. Not only did Zoe betray and dupe him, she'd done it as one of the mortals he scorned.

Yet in between those bookend betrayals, when my mother had lived under this roof, she'd been seen as nothing more than the trophy wife of a mortal casino magnate, with two daughters and an unbreakable Wednesday morning tennis mixer at the Las Vegas Country Club. This proved that most people saw only what they expected to see. Even archvillains.

As for Xavier, after she disappeared he gutted the rooms they'd shared and built a new wing with all new furnishings, one dramatically devoid of any feminine presence. Helen wasn't even allowed to put fresh flowers in the sitting area, which was why the half-dozen bouquets perfuming the foyer shocked me. I slowed, eyes lingering on the get-well cards sent by employees and acquaintances as we moved into the main bedroom's sitting area. There, a foursome of club chairs sat unimaginatively before a crackling fire, a peculiar scent rising from the flames, like herbs had been baked in with the kindling.

"Try not to upset him, Olivia," Helen said, ever imperious. "He needs his strength. Just nod and agree to everything he says."

"Don't I always?"

I let my placating expression fall as she led me into the recessed darkness, and hadn't taken three steps when the scent of sickness washed over me like a viscous wave. I fought not to gag, which would certainly give me away. Were I mortal, I wouldn't have smelled a thing beyond the scented fireplace and the battery of flowers fading outside this room. Helen, though, pulled a surgical mask over her mouth, explaining that it was to decrease the risk of additional illness.

I'd have asked why I didn't get one too, but it was too sharp a question to come from Olivia. My sister would be more concerned about her father, so I merely popped some chewing gum into my mouth to help manage the scent and quickly crossed the knee-deep carpet to the poster bed, where privacy screens were raised and a lamp was dimmed to low. I steeled myself to the task of having to suck up the hatred I felt for Xavier long enough to kiss him alongside his jutting jaw. It was one of the hardest parts of being Olivia.

Good thing Helen had allowed me to take the lead, because if she'd seen my face as I rounded that privacy screen, she would have noted not an ounce of love in the horror and shock and revulsion that swept through me. I put one hand to my mouth and another to my heart, consciously trying to still its pounding as Helen slipped up close beside me.

Quickly, I bent closer to the rank, and yes, rotting, human being instead.

"Daddy?" His chest was bird-bone frail, and rattling with the effort of wakefulness. I jerked my hand away, covering the movement by straightening the covers over shoulders gone gaunt.

"Helen," he rasped, making even that sole word seem laborious. "The lights, if you please."

Helen wordlessly twisted the knob on the table lamp and I steeled myself . . . but even anticipating it couldn't prepare me for the carnage that could be wracked upon the flesh of someone still living. He was all bony protrusions and cutting angles, concave where he should have been convex, and vice versa, with a sunken chest, a distended belly, and eyes that bulged within disappearing sockets. He was, I realized with a start, a Shadow clothed in mortality. A human unable to escape his flesh, even while rotting inside.

I swallowed hard and set my jaw. That's what happened when you siphoned off your soul to fuel unadulterated evil.

Unbeknownst to Xavier, I had walked in on him twice when he was performing a ritual that fed the Tulpa parts of his soul, an exchange for the paranormal leader's patronage—money and power, a network of allies, and a surprisingly diminished pool of rivals—so that they could each continue to rule their respective worlds. At first I'd thought it a willing exchange, and it probably was in the beginning. But the second time, I'd watched the woman beside me force Xavier to his knees, and the scent of his soul mingled with fear—burnt anise and rancid vanilla—so cloying and white-hot it cauterized the lining in my nose.

I returned my gaze to his, still locked on mine. When he caught sight of me chewing gum, I thought he was going to start in again about pedigree and class and the way even the tiniest public action was a direct reflection upon him. But the zeal that had always fired this particular tirade only sparked for a second before dying off in a sigh. He simply didn't have the energy.

"Daddy?" I said again, letting uncertainty coat my throat. It wasn't hard.

"Still ringing up T-shirts and polishing mugs?" His voice cracked, caught somewhere between a whisper and a growl.

I inclined my head. "Unless you're firing me."

"My own daughter? Not likely." He didn't like me working, but he had to maintain appearances as well. "Of course, quit now and I'll buy you a new car. Didn't you say you had your eye on that Aston Martin?"

I thought of the Vanquish, and sighed. "Thanks, Daddy, but I'm saving up for it myself."

Xavier stared. It would take decades to afford that car on my salary. He finally grunted and half turned on his pillow. Helen moved to help, but a low growl had her jerking back. I knew who was really in control here, but neither of them knew that I knew, so in front of me she had to at least pretend to be servile.

"Then this should help." Xavier pulled a giant wad of bills, wrapped in a rubber band, from behind his pillowcase. Laboriously, he reached back and followed it up with another. I clasped the bundles to my chest, barely able to get my hands around each.

"You sleep with your money?" I was unable to stop myself from asking.

At the same time, Helen asked, "Is this from the safe?"

A madman's fury bloomed behind his eyes, and I stepped back, more surprised than alarmed. "Don't question me about my own money! I've earned every cent!"

I scented the gaseous odor of her contempt, and knew she'd like to snap his neck like a matchstick. She wanted to do it in front of me. Instead she sucked in a deep breath, then let it out through her nose . . . a sliver of briny hate leaking like a noxious fume. Olivia would never scent it, so I gave no indication that I could, but Xavier immediately began hacking. It sounded like his heart was trying to climb through his throat. Helen chose that moment to leave.

"Shh, it's all right. Just be calm. And of course you've earned every cent," I said when he was comfortable again. My job now was to keep Xavier occupied while Felix took care of Helen . . . though I could see I needn't bother. Xavier couldn't even sit up on his own after that last attack. "And that's what I want to do too. Earn it myself. Make my own way in this world."

I held the bundles out, but he waved them away with an irritable grunt and knuckles too large for the rest of his hands. "Just take it. Use it as toilet paper. I don't care."

I stared at the money for a moment, then tossed it into my handbag. "Daddy, Helen says you're . . . " I hesitated, swallowing hard, and tried again. "Well, that you think you're . . . that you might be—"

"Dying. Jesus, Olivia, just say it!" Xavier's body jerked, the covers slipping down those nonexistent shoulders again. "I am dying. I'm scheduled for open-heart surgery the day after tomorrow. I won't live through it. I've known that for a while now."

"Is that why you let the household staff go?"

"They're not gone. They're temporarily released, with pay. I'm sure most will be happy to return to their positions, if you'll have them. My suggestion is that you allow it. This ship runs smoothly."

"Shh." I smoothed my hand over his brow, my cool flesh against his heated skin, remembering that Helen had said to keep him settled, and Olivia would endeavor to do just that. When he was reclined again, breath as settled as it was going to get, I straightened. "Okay, but Daddy, why did you release them?"

"Because I don't want an audience when I die." This time he merely sounded weary. "A man shouldn't have to worry about who's listening while he's in the throes of his last breath."

I opened my mouth to protest, some nonsense about how he wasn't dying and he couldn't give up, that the doctors were overreacting and he'd come out of it just fine.

He cut me off with a hard glance. "It's fine. The long illness has given me a chance to get my affairs in order. Including this."

He jerked his head at a thick black binder resting atop the bedside table. I flipped it open to find graphs and charts and things I really *didn't* understand.

"A log of all my businesses, properties, and acquisitions. There's another for pending developments. I'll have one of my lawyers go over those with you, but this is a good start."

I paged through the folder, grateful for the dim light that kept the smooth pads of my fingertips from gleaming unnaturally. "A start to what?"

"To taking over my empire. Someone needs to when I'm gone."

I lifted my head and audibly swallowed my gum. "No. You're going to get better."

He saw the lie in my eyes, and responded in kind. "Just in case, then."

I looked away, actually panicking, feeling far less at ease with this binder in my hands than my weapon. "Well, why can't someone else do it? Someone on the board? Maybe we could sell it to MGM?" God knew they owned practically everything else.

"Because you're my daughter. An Archer. And the only one I can truly trust." He didn't seem to notice when I looked away at that. "Besides, now that you've sold your illicit underground enterprise to one Maximus X, you won't have to divide your time."

My mouth fell open before I could stop it. "You know about that?"

His smile was self-satisfied and he looked himself for the first time since I'd entered the room. "I've known since you hacked into the Archer Enterprises database."

"Oh, that." I ducked my head, mind spinning. Olivia had done that at sixteen. She might have been built like a brick house, but it was her mind that was really mighty.

To chide me for it now, both the hacking and the interest in "indelicate activity" must have seemed senseless. He also glossed over the morality of the illegal activity. "So the timing is . . . convenient."

Selling it had been necessary. I didn't possess the facility with computers my sister had. Although Maximus hadn't been happy with his gorgeous debutante bailing on their covert plans to take over the world, he'd gotten a smokin' deal on the business.

For the first time, I wondered if Helen wasn't the only one in the household who'd been lulled into complacency. If Xavier had been keeping an eye on Olivia's secret life and I hadn't known it, what did that say about *my* powers of observation?

"Everything's in there," Xavier continued. "Just read it carefully, and call John if you have any questions. His card is up front. I've seen to it that you're the controlling investor. The board members value their positions . . . and they've also signed contracts that allow you to fire them on the spot. Even if they don't respect you at first, they'll respect your power."

"Power," I said airily. It always came down to that, didn't it? All of life's wars, from the bedroom to the battlefield, seemed to be fervent bids for power.

"Power," he repeated, all the strength in his body concentrated in that one word. It was like a spring trap in the air. "Promise me, though, whatever you do, whatever decisions you make—whether they affect one person or all of Archer, Inc.—you will remember to always put others *above* yourself."

I couldn't hide my surprise. This, coming from a man who lorded himself over the entire city? Someone who treated family like servants, servants like subjects, and subjects as pawns to be thrown about a boardroom according to his whim? Someone who'd literally sold his soul for power?

He heard all these thoughts in my hesitation. "True," he sighed, "it's something I paid little heed to in building this empire, but I've learned since then. When it comes to deciding between someone else's well being or your own, you must *always* choose the other person. It's the difference, you see."

"What difference?"

"Between you and them."

I sucked in a sharp breath, and glanced up at the security camera in the corner before I could stop myself. Helen had ostensibly placed it there in case Xavier needed help at night. I thought I saw Xavier glance at it too, but I couldn't be sure in the dim light. "Them, who?"

Xavier's labored breath ceased for so long that for a moment I wasn't sure he was still breathing at all. He was. Breathing and staring with the fearlessness borne from only one thing: the death of hope.

"Between you . . . and the plebeians, of course," he answered, and my disgust for him was renewed. "Between an Archer and someone who merely does what they're told."

And this time I was certain he glanced at the camera.

Then Xavier began hacking so badly that for a moment I didn't think he'd make it to the surgery. I angled him on his side, not knowing if I was helping or hurting him.

Meanwhile, I glanced back at the binder in my lap, realizing just how much power I suddenly held. When Xavier died, I would have complete control over Valhalla, all the Archer assets, and this household as well. I thought of the masks hanging on the walls just outside Xavier's home office, their magical properties, and the hidden room where he performed rituals that provided additional power to the Tulpa. Very suddenly I was on the precipice of all that my mother had spent years trying to get to—the heart of the Archer organization. Unexpected. Undetected.

Unstoppable.

And if Felix killed Helen, leaving a kill spot that any supernatural could read, it would all be undone in an instant. *Shit.*

."Okay, thanks for the family business, Daddy." I dropped a kiss on his forehead and turned. It was all I could do not to run to the door. Only that ever-present camera—and the ones I knew were positioned in every room—stopped me. "Take care."

"Olivia?" he said softly.

I turned impatiently.

"When I call you next . . . will you come?"

I knew then that he would die soon. He would die because of every contemptible little deed, each snarling thought, every mean intent. Such things built up, just as in business . . . compounding his sins, multiplying them, returning them with interest. But because of what he'd meant to my sister, and she to him, I didn't avert my eyes.

"Sure," I said, swallowing hard. "Of course."

I bypassed the elevator in favor of the stairs, having trouble keeping myself to a mortal pace. I sniffed at the air. No blood yet. *Please don't let it be too late.* Hitting the landing of the winding staircase, I heard Helen moving about in the sitting room, and whipped around the corner to find her bent over the tea set, the room awash in light and peaches and creams. She was arranging pastry.

Felix was poised behind her, boyish face gone fierce with hatred, double-edged boomerang fisted over his head.

"Scones!" I yelled, bounding into the room before he could decapitate her. Both their heads jerked my way. Felix's boomerang disappeared from sight. "I—I—I love scones with my tea. Oh, Helen. You remembered!"

I shot her a smile that felt too giant for my face. Then I jerked my head, causing Felix to back down and Helen to raise a brow. I turned the move into a shudder. "Is it cold in here? Are you guys cold? Tea sounds good. Doesn't it sound good, Nate? Join us, Helen?"

I was babbling, too loud and fast, but Helen fortunately begged off with the excuse of attending Xavier, and Felix and I sipped from tiny teacups in a protracted silence, remaining like that up until we were cocooned in my car and zipping down the gravel drive.

Once we hit the guard gate, Felix turned in his seat and ran a hand through his tousled hair. "What the hell was that?"

"I just inherited the family business."

I explained to him about the power we'd have upon Xavier's death to move about the mansion. How we could install agents and moles inside my familial home to unearth more of its paranormal secrets, and no one would dare question it. More importantly, we could do the same with Valhalla, and *that* might be key in finally uncovering a way to kill the Tulpa. I finished with an explanation of why I'd stopped him from decapitating Helen. "Leaving a kill spot in the mansion would have done away with all of that."

Felix immediately nodded his agreement, but I could tell he was disappointed as he gazed out the window. The adrenaline that would have allowed him to cleave Helen's head from her body in one strong swipe had dissipated, and he sunk into his seat, sighing heavily. "He really is dying."

"You heard that?"

"Dude, I *smelled* that." Facing forward again, legs splayed, he lowered the window, allowing fresh air to race through the car's cab. We both inhaled deeply. "The place reeks."

"I know."

He glanced at me sideways, wind warring with his hair. "How does it make you feel?"

"How should it?"

"You tell me."

I opened my mouth, prepped for the easy retort, then snapped it shut. "I feel nothing."

"Apathy," Felix said, nodding his head while his bald fingertips tapped out a tune only he could hear. "That's okay. He was never kind to you."

"No, I mean I'm not even apathetic. I'm not even numb. I feel nothing." I shot him a tense smile and changed the subject. I needed to drop him somewhere and get back to my search for Skamar. "So, back to Vanessa?"

He nodded, eyes downcast. The air in the car suddenly felt heavier—like a hot, wet blanket had been dropped over me. I shivered anyway.

"Where can I drop you?"

He shrugged one shoulder. It didn't matter. The warehouse was centrally located, so he'd reach it from any side of the valley within the hour.

"I thought she was dead, you know," he said suddenly, looking back up. "When we reached Chinatown? Right before we entered that bakery?" He shook his head, eyes fluttering shut. "For a few moments I had to live in a world without V . . . it was like the earth tilted again on its axis."

I knew what he meant. I'd felt the same shift when my mother left me. Again when Olivia died. That one was still unbalancing. And even though I'd chosen to let go of my past love, Ben Traina, his absence in my life had forced me to a different emotional plane as well. The dismantling of a dream was also a sort of death.

"I'm not really good at remembering things, not even birthdays and anniversaries," Felix said, shrugging as he looked out the window. We were back on the I-215 loop, nestled between banked, decorative walls that blended with the surrounding desert. "Stuff like that just doesn't seem important at the time. But then Vanessa? She'll talk about something, a time or place—a battle, a childhood memory—and with one small detail, like the season or what it smelled like or what we were wearing—I'm back there, and I remember it. And when I can remember," he added, voice unusually soft, "there's nothing at odds inside of me. Everything makes sense. Like every step in my life was consciously chosen to lead me to her, and now. Times like that, I'm perfectly balanced. I don't need anything else."

I tapped my fingers on the wheels. My chances of finding balance with *anyone* was hamstrung by a past where I'd had only myself to rely upon. Being as vulnerable as Felix was with Vanessa, even with an equal and someone I trusted, went against everything my instinct told me.

But I would have loved to feel exactly what Felix was talking about.

"I'm coming with you to the warehouse," I said before I could stop myself. Hunter was there, and I suddenly wanted to see him . . . though I didn't say that to Felix. Then again, from the way his attention was fixed on the scenery, I didn't need to. My fingers tightened on the wheel. Damn these super senses. "Hunter's been working on a replacement conduit for me," I explained.

"Mmm-hmmm."

"It might help me in Midheaven."

This time he said nothing.

"And I need to tell Warren about Xavier's plans for me."

Now Felix snorted bitterly. "If he doesn't already know."

I nodded at that, then bit my lip. "Do you think Vanessa would like to see me?"

He frowned over at me. "Of course."

I swallowed hard. "I just ask, you know, because they hurt her . . . "

He immediately began shaking his head. "They hurt her because she was doing her job—"

"Protecting the Kairos," I said softly.

"Protecting her friend." He put a hand on my arm, causing me to look over at him. "Not all of us see you as a weapon, Jo."

"Oh." I kept my eyes on the road, paused for a moment, then said, "Thank you, Felix."

He settled back and pretended not to notice the tears staining my eyes.

8

The troop's workshop, like most things in industrial Vegas, was hidden inside a windowless steel building that resembled a small airplane hangar. However, unlike the surrounding warehouses, this place was booby-trapped to the teeth. I suppose that as our weaponeer, Hunter considered it a moral imperative to keep the place properly secured, but every time I entered it I felt like Indiana Jones waiting for the boulder.

Felix beelined for the panic room, and I decided to give him and Vanessa a few minutes alone before joining them. But this left me alone with Hunter, who was half dressed in his Valhalla security uniform; dark pants, polished black shoes, and white undershirt that moved with his muscles. His moods lately had ranged from surly to sarcastic when dealing with me, so I only nodded in greeting, and waited to see what it would be today.

Felix's talk about Vanessa and balance had fortified my emotions. I decided that I could stand up to whatever Hunter threw at me. I'd absorb both his anger and indifference, and give him nothing to beat against. And maybe soon, I thought, tossing my bag on the concrete floor, he wouldn't feel the need to fight me at all.

Besides, I'd seen people and situations that were beyond fixing before—hell, I'd been one of them—and this wasn't it. Hunter wasn't broken. The possibility of *us* wasn't broken. The silence echoing around us was only weighty in comparison to the cries and murmurs and soft sighs that had once preceded it. If I remembered that, he did as well.

"I should throw you out," he said immediately, barely looking up from his drafting table. "Warren wouldn't want you here."

"Where is he?"

He lifted a shoulder. "You know Warren."

Yes. He demanded to know where we were at all times, but disappeared whenever he felt like it. But it was for "our own good."

"Vanessa?" I asked, jerking my head to the panic room.

"Better. You'll see." So he *wasn't* going to throw me out. Good.

I headed to the chair next to his drawing board, careful not to wrinkle the navy dress shirt draped along its back. Yet spotting the half-finished sketches, I stood almost before I'd sat down. A conduit, drawn in varying sizes and angles, was depicted on half a dozen sheets. I knew immediately that it was for me.

"Wow." All thoughts of romance, past wrongs, and other worlds, dropped away.

It was beautiful. Another crossbow, smaller than my original, and so sleek my palm itched to hold it. Vials of metal alloys were scattered along the table beside the drawing, along with a shiny lead crossbow bolt. Glancing around a plastic partition, I frowned across the length of the indoor firing range. The current target had bolts pinned to it as well. I gasped and turned toward Hunter.

"It's only a model, so don't try to take off with it. I'm still working out the kinks. Something's off with the balance, and the bolts are more like paintballs than missiles, so you'd only bruise a Shadow, at best." Though his tone was serious, a knowing half smile lit his face . . . and suddenly the sleek new conduit was in his hand. Any tension between us was immediately forgotten.

"Come to Mama," I said, beckoning him, and the weapon, forward.

A conduit was an extension of an agent's body and will, and once bequeathed or bestowed upon an agent, in a way became a part of the controlling agent . . . a fact that had been made painfully clear as soon as Regan snatched mine away. One of the few items my mother had left me in this brave new world, my conduit was perfect for the Archer sign, and its absence was almost a physical ache. Any other conduit, including this lovely little replacement, was a poor substitute—like pairing up with a partner you knew was wrong for you out of convenience, or until a better one came along—but I wasn't in any position to be picky.

Hunter made me follow him around the shielding plastic, but instead of handing the weapon to me, he motioned me still and took his place at the shooter's stand. Control freak, I thought, frowning, but stood back. He exaggerated his movements, demonstrating the proper stance—as if I needed to be shown—then stretched his arm to the side, one-handed, and aimed for a paper bull's-eye fifty feet away. I'd have said he was showing off, but his facility with any conduit—though especially his own barbed whip—was physical poetry. He was pure athlete, war his chosen sport, and when he finally fired three bolts in quick succession, I had to admit I couldn't have done any better.

The bolts dived for the target's center, splitting air in chill-inducing hisses, as straight as if they were being reeled in . . . until the last moment, when they redirected—one, two, three—and barreled the opposite way. Right at me.

I ducked and the first whizzed by my head, a deadly whisper of wind trailing in its wake. The second one burrowed into my side with a white-hot pain. I cried out and instinctively dove for cover.

"Not behind me!"

So, at the last moment, I dodged the bolt by jumping into Hunter's arms. His grunt against my neck let me know when it hit home. We froze there, both breathing hard for long moments, until I leaned back and looked into his pained face. "That didn't hit anything important, did it?"

Wincing, he shook his head, but didn't yet speak. When he finally caught his breath, he was succinct. "Oops."

I eased down from him, a slow slide that let me experience all his athletic contours. I didn't let the pleasure deter me. "You shot me."

"No."

I pointed at the iron dart sticking out between my ribs, the blood ruining my T-shirt, and raised my brows.

"The projectile was drawn to you. There's a difference."

"Well, the difference feels the same with a metal tip buried in my side." And it didn't feel like a mere bruise either.

"I told you I was still tweaking it," he said, but even he looked frustrated. Still wincing, I put my hand on his shoulders as I looked down. He held me there for a moment, letting me use his body to steady myself, but shifted his gaze when I looked back up into his eyes.

Disregarding his own small injury, he stalked toward his shooting stand, simultaneously yanking the bolt from his thigh, while I relearned how to breathe. Thank God it was only a mock-up. Had that been a real conduit, neither of us would heal.

"I just don't understand! I have the right metallic bonds . . . the frame is near identical. The bolts are slimmer, but that should make them more manageable, not less . . . fucking reactive, but I can't get the right fit!"

He turned on me, eyes blazing, and I held up my hands in mock surrender in case he was going to shoot again. He didn't, but he didn't smile either. He just gazed at me in a way that made him look diminished. "Why can't I get the right fit?"

I limped over to him, pain almost forgotten, and dropped the fired bolt on the shooting stand. "You're going to," I said, turning to him.

Hunter's shoulders slumped and, turning away, he threw the replicate on the steel table. "I'm gonna get you killed."

"You're so arrogant," I said, and he jerked his head up sharply to catch my smile. "Even I haven't managed that yet."

The tension disappeared, but the smile still didn't come. He ran his hand over his head, then fisted it there, muttering to himself. His hair was currently medium length, shaggy again after some unfathomable impulse had him shaving it down to nothing. He didn't look any softer now that it was growing back, though. I liked that.

"What?" he said as I continued to stare at him.

One of the things that had drawn me to photography was that the people and events framed through my camera lens were determined by my interest and discretion alone. There was no discussion about composition, no compromise on subject matter. I'd worked alone, and still had an instinctive preference for that. It was one of the hardest things to overcome upon joining the troop.

But Felix's earlier words about balance and need made me realize something I'd been trying to ignore. I didn't work with a camera and film and developer anymore, but I still fixated on the subjects that either interested me or mattered most. So, as I continued to stare up into Hunter's face, I was unsurprised by the way the rest of the warehouse, the sounds and smells and sights, slid out of focus, and he sharpened like wire.

"What?" he repeated when I only continued to stare.

"I want you to let me back in." It wasn't a question. Coy and guarded were for people like Suzanne and Cher. That wasn't how Hunter or I operated. We took what we wanted. Again, I liked that.

But Hunter's face slid into a marble smoothness. I sighed

and put my hand on his arm. And though he didn't respond, he didn't pull away either.

"I remember what you said about making a decision and not looking back, and I know I screwed up. I'm sorry. Give me a chance."

He opened his mouth, began to shake his head from side to side.

"Please," I said softly, stopping him cold, but I didn't see pleading as a weakness. On the contrary, desire was also a powerful strength. Couldn't he see that? I wondered, eyes searching his face.

He looked away, saying nothing.

I sighed. "Hunter, I don't know how to do this. I mean, I veered off the path to normal a long time ago, and never really quite found my way back. Everyone before Ben—"

"You don't have to tell me this."

The thought that he might not feel the same struck dread through me. The moment felt full and weighty, like this was my chance to step into a present so vital it could finally, once and for all, put all the tragedies in my past to bed. If I didn't go on, and quick, I'd definitely turn and walk out of there. And if I did that, I knew I'd never be back.

But I needed space to tell this story. Hunter's physicality wasn't just distracting, it was overwhelming. I searched for a place to sit, settling on the chair that held his shirt. Careful not to wrinkle it, I leaned back and looked at my hands. "Before last year I saw dating as a personal challenge rather than a relationship between two equals. I selected men to test my strength and determination and self-reliance. Most men instinctively ran from that—I mean, who likes feeling like an emotional litmus test?—and I'd congratulate myself when they did. I told myself they were weak. Wrong for me. Unworthy."

I ran my index finger around the tip of my opposing thumb, the printless pads rubbing against each other with an unnerving smoothness. I still hadn't gotten entirely used to the feeling.

"Ben was different because of our shared past, and because we'd loved each other first." We'd shared friendship, then love. There was no going back after that. Unfortunately, though we didn't realize it at the time, there was also no going forward.

I sighed, letting Hunter see this memory playing out in me, letting him feel it if he must. It was truth, and he should know it all. "So that's why it took me a while to realize I didn't know the man he'd become. The boy I'd loved a decade earlier didn't exist anymore. Nowhere but in my own mind, anyway."

I wondered how many relationships were like that. One person hanging on to a memory of what once was, the dream more alive than the reality had ever been . . . more real than the actual relationship, now wilting, unseen, on the vine.

Always one to see clearly, Hunter remained silent. I looked up at the ceiling, then realized I was doing it only to avoid his gaze. "I'm sorry. I'm sorry I took what I needed from you on a night I'd been left emotionally bankrupt—and that's not an excuse, just a fact—but mostly that I left you in the morning. That I left you at all."

I'd made a mistake and would take it back if I could, but that was something people said when they knew they could not. So I fell silent, watched him soak in the information, his brilliant mind whirring beneath the face I was starting to crave, the olive skin I longed to touch, the mouth that curved dangerously when considering some private, dangerous secret. I was addicted, I realized. One taste of this man and I'd become a junkie.

"I'm sorry too, Joanna," he said, and this time he was the one who looked away. "But I can't."

An invisible foot planted itself into my chest. I was actually surprised the air didn't whoosh from my chest. I shook my head. "But—"

Hunter held up a hand.

I thought about knocking that hand out of the air, controlled myself and only flinched instead. "You still want me. I can feel it. I can sense it like a second heartbeat."

"Yes." And, suddenly, it was there. The desire I'd been looking for bloomed so round and full I felt like I could take a bite from the air, come away with a mouthful of emotion that would warm my belly . . . and still be ravenous for more. I thought about kissing his eyelids until they softened, and took a step forward. I'd seen them that way before. That softness, ironically, accentuated his strength.

I bit my lip, narrowing my eyes at I watched him not watching me. "But there's something else, isn't there? Something you want more."

He hesitated. "Yes."

I flinched. "Someone?"

He sighed. "Joanna."

I didn't look away. "Does it have to do with that callboy identity?"

"I told you. I'm no longer doing that."

I tilted my head, studying him. So had he found her, then? Because he'd been looking for a woman, I was sure of that much. And she'd been dark-haired and dark-eyed. She'd been someone he didn't want anyone else to know about.

I should tell Warren.

But even as the thought visited, I showed it the door. I wouldn't. Hunter had kept the secret of my daughter—a girl destined to follow me as the troop's Archer; one Warren still didn't know about—and I owed him for that.

"Hey, Jo!" The voice shot across the warehouse, startling us both. I turned to find Felix motioning me from the doorway of the panic room. He looked much better, a flush in his cheeks and a familiar spark in his eye. "She wants to see you."

I nodded and he disappeared back inside. By the time I looked back, Hunter had turned away. I hesitated, then headed for Vanessa. I couldn't help wondering what would have occurred between Hunter and me if I'd been raised in the sanctuary too, safe from desert predators, with a knowledge of what and who I was. Would we have had an easier time forging a relationship without old griefs standing between us? Maybe not, I thought, glancing over my shoulder. We seemed destined to butt heads—one of us high when the other was low; one positive while the other nursed bitterness like an addictive brew. If only I could turn my mind from him altogether, I thought, swallowing hard.

But addictions, I knew, didn't work that way.

There were other places we could have taken Vanessa. Micah worked as a physician at one such hospital, where supernatural fallout wouldn't attract the attention of the mortal population. That's where they'd first taken me to alter my looks so I could live convincingly as my sister. Yet given the disappearance of our safe zones, we couldn't be certain the Shadows hadn't infiltrated the hospitals as well. Besides, precautions or not, if a person showed up with Vanessa's kind of injuries, *someone* was going to notice.

So in the small, windowless panic room of the secured warehouse—where Micah busied himself in the early hours with stabilizing Vanessa—Hunter and Felix had gathered the supplies needed to turn it into the strangest one-person, mini-E.R. I'd ever seen.

"Wow." I knew I should be more attentive to the room's sole patient, and possibly more discreet about my awe, but the giant, clear Plexiglas tank positioned in the center of the room wasn't like anything I'd ever seen. I bent over, peering inside, to see Vanessa's silhouette suspended in a baby blue substance more viscous than water, air bubbles caught mid-rise. The room's dim lighting couldn't filter fully through the thick gelatinous substance, but I could see well enough to follow the length of her left calf to where it abruptly ended in a stump. There were bones growing from it, but they were newly formed and too small for her body, more like the talons on a bird of prey. Obviously there was still a ways to go before the foot fully regenerated. Straightening, I turned my attention to her head, which had received most of the destruction.

She looked like she'd been hit by a wrecking ball, eyes so swollen her irises were almost rimmed in red, newly grown right ear and nose tomato red, so the pigment didn't yet match the rest of her face. This was actually preferable since the rest of her face was an unsightly mass of bruises and swollen tissue, and though she smiled, she did so with a mouth that looked overly stuffed with cotton.

Of course, the worst damage had been delivered to her skull. Drake had partially scalped her while cutting her hair, and though the skin was already healed, her entire head had to be shaved down to nothing so her beautiful mahogany curls could grow back in evenly. Though she couldn't move much, she tilted her head slightly on her neck cushion, and rolled her eyes in my direction. "I'm not quite there yet, though my tongue has grown back nicely."

No complaint, no anger, no blame. I clenched my jaw to hold back tears.

"More's the shame," Felix said, stroking the side of her head. It was the only part of her body not submerged in the gooey blue substance.

"Shut up, honey," she said lightly, then stuck out her tongue in demonstration. "No taste buds yet, though. It feels like I gargled with habaneros."

"That's because you're not drinking your reparative. I don't care if it does taste like moldy ash."

"Tekla!" I hugged our troop's Seer before either of us expected it. I couldn't help it. I hadn't seen her since the battle in Chinatown. "Oh my God, you made it. How'd you escape the Tulpa?"

She'd been so focused, I remembered now. Her small features drawn tight on her face, like a balloon pinched together in the center. Though I'd long learned not to underestimate Tekla due to her small stature—a bird's foot would fit better on *her* tidy frame—her ability to single-handedly hold off the Tulpa using nothing but her imagination and will had been outstanding.

"You were amazing," I said, indulging in a bit of my own hero worship.

She shrugged, but I could tell she was pleased, if surprised, by my reaction. Maybe she was just used to people who were used to her. I was still new enough to this world that I recognized unusual martial skill when I saw it.

"No, really." I touched her arm, forcing her to look at me. "You amaze me."

She actually blushed at that.

And speaking of amazing talents . . . "Where's Micah?"

"Resting in the crow's nest," Vanessa said, her swollen tongue giving her a bit of a lisp. "He's been working on me nonstop."

"And he'll have my hide if I don't continue to do the same." Holding a glass in one hand, Tekla cupped Vanessa's chin in the other and gently tilted it back. I sniffed. Water, herbs, and some sort of chalky substance I didn't recognize.

"Not too much," Tekla murmured, pulling the drink away. "You're still healing on the inside too."

"What exactly are you lying in?" I asked, bending over again.

"Sanative gel, shot with numbing cream. I'd never be able to sit still, much less manage lucidity without it."

Frowning, I straightened. "Vanessa, I'm so sorry."

She made a sound, halting me from speaking further. "Felix told me you'd say that. When are you going to learn? A battle-born death is always written in the stars, Jo."

Yeah, I thought wryly, but the handwriting had been a little sloppy this time. "Then I'm happy it wasn't meant to be."

"And speaking of fates," Tekla said, "Felix, if you'll excuse us?"

Felix and I stared at her, both surprised by this abrupt, and obvious, dismissal. His need to argue—to stay put and protect and just *be* with Vanessa—slipped from him in waves, almost as visible as a bright pulse from a lighthouse. But Tekla raised her brows, and he finally nodded and left.

"He's worried about you," I told Vanessa, her gaze following him until he disappeared.

"He's been so sweet." She lowered her eyes and swallowed hard. "I hate for him to see me this way."

I frowned. "You were ambushed by an entire Shadow troop. He's not going to think anything less of you for succumbing to that."

"No, I mean . . . " She ducked her head so it reminded me of a turtle retreating into its shell. In this case a very blue, viscous shell. "I mean, I look awful. Silly, huh?"

"Oh." I was taken aback but tried not to show it. "No. It makes sense."

She sniffed. "No, it doesn't. I mean, all the things they did to me, and you know what I keep thinking?"

I shook my head.

"When's my hair going to grow back?" Her voice cracked.

"It's only because you know it's going to take the longest to return to normal," Tekla said reasonably. Worrying about a haircut after surviving a brutal attack wasn't reasonable, but it was understandable.

"It's okay," I added, forcing a smile. "I would too, if I had your hair."

But watching her nod, I knew it wasn't okay. Like those men who threw acid in the faces of women who rejected them, this mutilation had been extremely personal, and of course it was designed to shame. However, unlike those mortal victims, Vanessa would blessedly heal from her injuries.

Even no-nonsense Tekla had to respond to the self-pity filling the room like waterlogged roses. At least, she tried.

"Micah can make you a gorgeous hairpiece in the meantime. Nobody will know the difference."

Vanessa closed her eyes, but a tear slipped out anyway. Sensing her embarrassment along with her sorrow, I changed the subject. It's what I would have wanted. "So, why did we just get rid of Felix?"

"Because there are some things you can explain over and again to a man," Tekla said, "and he still won't understand."

Vanessa sniffed. "Like the hair thing."

I nodded. Because a head understanding was different from a heart understanding. I expected there were times the reverse was true as well.

"Like how you need to arm yourself differently when entering a world where women rule." Tekla smiled as my head predictably shot up.

Even Vanessa managed a small grin. "Look, even threats of a scalping won't deter her," she said to Tekla, about me. "The girl does love a fight."

"There won't be any scalping in Midheaven. Women fight differently . . . in any world."

"You don't say," I said dryly, thinking of Regan DuPree. Shadow agent. Leo. Bitch.

Regan had most often eschewed a direct martial approach, at least in dealing with me, taking a circuitous path instead by attacking those I loved. Fortunately, she was no longer an issue. A rogue was utterly alone. She was also a walking advertisement for skin grafts gone bad, because when the Tulpa discovered the deception, he'd raked the skin from her body in wounds that would never heal. I might have felt bad about this except that she'd once gotten me captured, tortured, and nearly killed by my greatest enemy. She'd also slept with my boyfriend.

Tekla read my mind. "You think you know what I'm talking about, but hear me when I tell you: stealth and subtlety are the most powerful weapons in our world, but they were honed on the fires of Midheaven's core. If the myths bear out, you haven't encountered women like this before, so don't enter lightly. Don't be lulled by soft looks or voices, no matter how familiar or natural they may seem."

"Don't worry. Femininity has never felt normal to me." It was a joke, but it was also true. I hadn't been raised in a female-dominated culture. The honor and respect these two women took for granted was foreign to me. I'd always had to fight for my power.

Tekla shook her head. "Those are two different things. Normal is simply what you're accustomed to. Natural is what is, in spite of what you're used to."

"So, you're saying don't go in swinging?"

"It's a bit . . . obvious," she said diplomatically.

I tilted my head. "I think I'm offended."

"What Tekla is trying to say," Vanessa interceded quickly, "is don't be fooled into thinking you're not at war just because you're not blowing things up. Yet don't be intimidated by it either. You have the ability to utilize the more indirect tactics too."

I snorted. I had the ability to fake it until I made it. "So let me get this straight. You guys are worried I can't hold my own against, what, some chicks?"

"Chicks powerful enough to rule an entire world."

"With a glance alone," Tekla added.

"Looks that can kill?" I asked.

"No." She smiled. "Just stun. Or so that's the myth."

I didn't roll my eyes because that would earn me a stunning look in return. Instead, I blew out a long breath. "Well, I don't have to worry about it at all if I can't actually find the place. And even then I don't know how I'll find Jaden Jacks. I don't even know what he looks like."

All I had to go on were cryptic orders from Warren, part of a silly song, and useless advice about fighting like a woman instead of a man.

"I do," Tekla said. I looked at her sharply. Unsmiling, and suddenly too serious, she stepped forward and handed me a picture.

Whoa. Not a picture, I thought, studying the man on it. A ripped out page from a Shadow manual. "Damn, he's *huge*."

"You'll be fine," Vanessa said reassuringly. "You're the Kairos."

And I was getting tired of *that* being the one thing I had going for me. I sighed again as I tucked the folded page in my back pocket.

"By the way," Vanessa said, changing the subject, "Felix told us about Xavier's housekeeper, Lindy. Helen. Whatever. Thanks for stopping him. I'd hate for all that work to be undone just because of me."

Hiding my own disappointment at not having Helen out of the way for good, it was my turn to shrug. "We'll get another shot at Lindy. Plenty of them. In fact . . . maybe you'd like to do the honors?"

"Still fighting," Tekla muttered, returning to her chair in the corner, but Vanessa laughed, truly laughed for the first time since I'd seen her. It drew Felix into the room like a siren's call. Her smile remained as she caught his gaze. "I think maybe I would."

"Good. Then *when* I return from Midheaven," I said, smiling, "I'll hand you the keys to Archer castle myself."

9

My parting words to Vanessa sounded a lot more hopeful than I felt, both because I didn't want her worrying and because the question still remained: How was I to find Midheaven? All I had was a mishmashing of cryptic advice that, even together, still didn't form a complete picture. Yet with nothing else to go on, with no certain means of finding Skamar, and my troop leader's directive still weighing on my shoulders, I had no choice but to leave the security of the warehouse and keep searching. So after a shower and a quick bite to eat, I did what I'd always done when feeling restless and lost. I put on my steel-toed boots and began walking.

Okay, so first I drove. Right out to the military base, where chicken wire and sensors and cameras would serve as backup to my wanderings. Sure, none of it could actually stop a Shadow attack—Nellis's best hotshot flyboys couldn't do that, not in their biggest plane—but even the Light normally avoided attracting attention of this sort. We didn't like our body heat showing up on anyone's electrical charts, and we certainly didn't like to be caught on camera. Tonight, however, it was the lesser of two evils. The Shadows wouldn't be expecting it, and the only thing the Air Force would pick up on was a lone girl, hands shoved in the pockets of her own bomber jacket, hunched against the wind as she walked down the street.

What the hell did "walk the line" mean? I wondered, boots clanging across a metal grate. Stay in line like a good little girl? Surely not. Warren wouldn't waste his breath telling me that. Restless, I tapped on a metal lamppost and kept thinking. Okay, so what about Zane's ballad, then?

"Beneath the neon glowing bright here . . . lies a land of starry skies . . . " How could there be stars underneath Vegas? That didn't make any sense. I kicked a rock from the road as I crossed the street, watching it sail over the street until it disappeared down a sharp embankment. Oops. I glanced over my shoulder, wondering if the base's camera had caught that. Lone girl or not, I shouldn't be able to kick something with that density as easily as a soccer ball. Switching direction, I followed its trajectory to what looked like a bike path next to the nearest housing development. The homes had to be a good fifteen years old, but they clearly had a home association, because the common greens were pristine.

Look below, dear, not in the middle . . .

"The middle of what?" I muttered, lowering my eyes to the ground, following the gravel path as I slipped into the darkness. It was safer near the base, but the darkness of the bike path soothed me. I shook my head and sucked in a crisp breath of early winter and smog and mildew from the nearby drainage ditch.

And froze.

Then I leaned over the railing that lined the walkway and gazed twenty feet below where a scrubby and poorly landscaped embankment gave way to an underground tunnel. No, I thought, correcting myself. Not a tunnel. A pipeline that fed runoff away from the city.

I didn't know about a land of starry skies—maybe that was Midheaven itself—but if the city, and where I was standing, was considered the middle, then the storm drain leading underground could be considered below.

I ducked under the railing and half slid, half sidestepped down the embankment. I knew about the drainage system, of course. Fifty miles of serpentine concrete running water out of the city to the Las Vegas Wash. Las Vegas actually sat in a bowl rimmed in mountain ranges, and received a good deal of runoff from those jagged peaks. Unfortunately, we usually received it all on the same day. We had an annual monsoon season that could effectively flood the baked desert floor within minutes, so the underground system had been designed to rush these floodwaters from the surface streets into the scattered inlets dotting the valley.

The water department was constantly improving the drains, and though it was certainly better than when I was a kid—when the Charleston underpass regularly claimed the lives of the brave, unwary, and the just plain idiotic— every once in a while things that were washed away never turned up at all. Sometimes *people* were never seen again. And here was an inlet. Beneath the neon. A *line*, I thought, smiling to myself.

I began to walk it.

Twenty feet below the surface streets, I stood cradled in the curve of a tunnel that was eight feet in diameter and held a darkness so complete I'd have been blinded if I only possessed a mortal's sight. As it was, I could barely make out the shape of the slick, slanted walls, and unwilling to touch them for guidance—and even more unwilling to stand in a complete vacuum—I willed the glyph on my chest into a steady but muted glow. Cobwebs larger than my entire body hung in elegant tatters from mildewed concrete walls, and smells I'd already identified as algae and waste lay in a barely moving stream at my feet.

I walked a few feet toward the tunnel's heart, then looked back over my shoulder. I was supposed to wait for Skamar.

Warren had said she would tell me how to "walk the line." Then again, the troop was weakening, and a little girl was dying. I couldn't exactly wait around for some diva thought-form to make an appearance. Besides, I wasn't even sure this was the entrance I sought. If it was, then I'd gotten lucky. If not, I'd lose nothing by searching it. Right?

It was eerily still the farther I ventured in, the concrete corridor frigid as the city winked out behind me and the familiar dropped away. Unable to see even an inch in front of my face, I sent an extra pulse to strengthen the glyph on my chest. Seventy-five feet beyond that, the tunnel shrunk so that, hunching down, I felt buried alive. Sound was dampened, air thinned, vision blocked, and it was with a start that I realized I was the one doing the burying.

A hundred feet in, though, I began a steep vertical rise, like those winding staircases found in European castles. "Dammit," I muttered, and began to climb. Apparently I'd just gotten lucky.

I climbed so long I had to be well above street level by the time the tunnel sloped and swirled again. This time it angled deeper than seemingly possible, as if the concrete had accidentally been spilled there. Though there was no water this deep in, the surface was slick with algae, and it was uncomfortably warm, even humid. A sourceless gust rustled my hair, like the heat coming on in an old house, and I glanced straight up to find a passage narrow enough to admit only one body at a time.

"And for my next great feat . . . " I leapt to the opening just as I'd done at Master Comics earlier that day. Yet the distance lengthened while I was in flight, and I yelped in surprise, barely catching the edge's lip with my elbows. Shoulders straining under my weight, I grunted and pushed myself straight, glyph fully powered. I then found myself eye level with another concrete wall. It was studded with only one feature: a safe's dial.

Looking closer, I breathed a sigh of relief. The signs of the Zodiac fanned around its center, and I flipped it so the

Archer glyph lined up with the raised arrow, then yanked hard. There was a tumble of internal locks, and something growled deep inside the tunnel. Then a jagged seam began working its way down the wall, altering direction before moving vertically again to flip on itself with a depthless creak, ending where it began. I pulled on the dial, the seam took on hinges, and a tiny doorway swung open.

A rough-hewn shelf held a wrought-iron stand pinching a primitive, and burning, candle.

"What the hell?" Whatever I'd been expecting, it wasn't this.

Lifting the iron base to move the simple candle aside, I looked for a spring underneath. Maybe its removal would cause the wall to shift and open. Nothing happened. Thinking then that the wooden backing was false, I pushed, but it too remained intact. I wiped at my brow. Man, there was a lot of heat coming from one sole candle.

So no spring catch, I thought, and no lever. No other obvious purpose to the box. I blew out a hard breath, and the candle wavered . . . which made me wonder how it'd been lit in the first place. There were no matches or lighter, no person to perform the action, and no wax running down the long taper. So *When?* joined the question as to *How?* "Think, Jo," I said under my breath.

Well, obviously I had to take some sort of action. Something definitive that would ferry me from this world into Midheaven. Was I supposed to sing Zane's stupid song? Feeling like an idiot, I cleared my throat and gave it a try.

> *Beneath the neon glowing bright here*
> *Lies a land of starry skies*
> *Look below, dear, not in the middle*
> *And kill the rushlight in two tries.*

"Oh."

Rushlight. That was an old-fashioned word for a candle made of a plant, and grease or wax. One like the taper I was currently holding. Gingerly, like it was a snake writhing in my hand, I returned it to the rough-hewn shadow box. Gazing at the bright flame, I took a deep breath and felt my heartbeat thrum irregularly. Deciding it was probably best not to tempt the second try, I leaned forward and blew with all my might. Nothing happened.

Oh, God. Did that mean I only had one try left to me?

I blew again. Same results, but nothing else happened either. A third time . . . and no fucking charm. What was going on?

Finally, I was so annoyed and antsy about the whole situation that I grabbed hold of the candle's iron stick and with the taper only an inch from my mouth blew again.

Darkness attacked. My released breath was yanked from my chest, burning nausea rising with it. Blindly, I grabbed at my throat, but my mouth wouldn't close, and the outline of my glyph began tingling madly, like something with lots of legs was eating away at it. Oxygen bled from my mouth and pores, sucked from white and red blood cells so that I felt like a withering husk, dehydrated and dizzy.

Then the process flipped so suddenly I was encased like a brick in a kiln while unseen tendrils of smoke arrowed back into my mouth, prying my throat wide. Individual needles of pain splintered along that soft passageway, shredding my larynx and voice box, murdering my ability to scream. I didn't know what was worse, the literal breath-taking or the invasion of something foreign soaking into my bloodstream, muscle, tissue, and bone. Whatever it was, it was miasmic. The sulfuric stench of rotten eggs forced an inhalation, injecting me with a noxious, polluting drug. My nausea rose.

Then the air I was straining for pumped back into me, burning cold against the coppery tears like tiny icicles of blood were embedded in my throat. I staggered backward to hit my head against something hard. The sense of all physical matter being voided out lessened, my dizziness abated, but I still couldn't see. If not for the solid stamp of earth beneath me, I would have thought I'd passed out. Then the air gradually took on layers, and the smoke walling me in lessened.

I ran my tongue over my teeth, gritty, my mouth filled with a sandpaper scratch. I couldn't smell the festering poison anymore, but it was pumping in my veins, and that scared me more than the sightlessness or the stolen air.

As the haze lessened degree by degree, a light formed directly across from me. Please not another candle, I thought as it sharpened into a bright yellow eye. It acted as a hypnotist's pendulum, controlling my focus until the rest of the room—and I *was* now standing in a room—came into view. When it did, despite the breath having just been stolen from my body, my mouth fell open again.

I knew I was missing a million little details, but was so overwhelmed by what appeared to be an old western saloon that it took a moment longer to note the bartender blinking back at me. I did, however, notice the green felt tables fanning to my right, if only because they were the only truly familiar things in the room. Less familiar? An ornate door with a scrolled gilt handle and glossy red surface adorned with stylized coils and whipping bands—cones, balls, wedges, prisms, geometric bands, and disks—all overlapping each other in writhing detail, though I had no idea what any of it meant. It stood out not only for its lavish detail but for its splash of color, and the rim of light halo-ing its perimeter. Because even though the smoke was thinning, everything else was washed in a sepia haze.

I turned my attention back to the bar where the light I'd seen was revealed to be the reflection of a pagoda lantern attached to the wall behind me. The oval mirror showcasing it had a twin, like eyes holding my outline in their unblinking gaze. A third mirror, rectangular and centered between the first two, was split by an antique brass cash register, while a long bar sat before that, white towels pegged at each end, and spittoons spaced evenly along the base. A brass foot rail shone as brightly as the polished bar, matching the paneled oak crisscrossing every inch of wall space, giving the simple room an opulent feel. I glanced up at a ceiling of beautiful pressed tin, each intricate square cupping a constellation. Fans twirled lazily overhead, and an elegant staircase on the left rose to a split hallway.

I tried to shake the feeling of being watched. Hard, since my warrior's mind calculated almost two dozen men in straight-backed, unpainted chairs, who stopped cold as they stared directly at me. I had a sudden, desperate hankering for a six-shooter.

"Well . . . " I cleared my throat and resisted the urge to tip an imaginary hat. "Howdy."

Despite being born and raised in the Sierra Nevadas, at the southernmost tip of what was known as the Silver State, what I knew about the era where saloons had proliferated across the West was confined to Hollywood bastardizations of Wyatt Earp and Doc Holliday. I thought I'd been in over my head when I woke up to discover I was a twenty-first century superhero veiled in my sister's fleshly body. But at least then I'd had a cultural rope to grab onto and regain my equilibrium . . . and I don't mean a lasso.

There was nothing in this nineteenth-century-style saloon that looked vaguely familiar. Even the people were the sort that looked out at you, unsmiling, from black-and-white photos . . . like long-dead relatives with hard lives that leeched their personalities from their leathered skins. Ironically enough, it was the flash of a photographer's bulb that snapped the silence from the room, blinding me once again. Vulnerable, I braced for assault, but the worry dissolved under the trickling keys of a piano intro.

"You've gotta be kidding me," I muttered to no one, rubbing my eyes and squinting in the direction of the music.

> *Oh, many secrets does this girl have*
> *And she hides them in the light*
> *But the darkness may have the last laugh*
> *Because her temper has a bite.*

I was as surprised by the subject of the song as at the way it ended . . . or didn't. The piano player, a reed-thin man with a bowler hat, long fingers and a hook nose, cut off the jaunty song as abruptly as he'd begun, withering into himself like a skeleton sinking into his swivel stool. I raised my brows, waiting for some other random weirdness to occur—might as well get it all out at once, right?—and it obliged me in the form of a saloon girl appearing over the second floor's shining brass railing.

In a muted world of sepia tones and scratchy grays, she was saturated color, almost blinding in her brightness. She smiled down at me as I rubbed my eyes again, not moving, just letting the shock of her appearance amidst so much gray sink in. None of the men, I noted, could take their eyes off of her either. The only thing to rival her brilliance was that steady orange glow circling the bright red door next to the bar.

A world ruled by women.

Hitching a hip onto the left-hand railing, she crossed her arms beneath what these people probably referred to as her bosom.

"Sleepy Mack, I could just kiss you." Her laughter rang over the sunken room as musically as the piano had moments before. "I mean, finally. A new fuckin' song."

The slumped piano player didn't respond, his hands drooped lifelessly over his knees, the dusty bowler hat tipped low over his eyes. I finally moved—Yay, me—twisting to find another solid wall behind me. Gilt frames with oil paintings of women in various states of undress were interspersed with old-fashioned oil lanterns, but the small box with its candle and the tunnel leading back to modern-day Vegas was nowhere to be found.

I did, however, spot the cause of my earlier blindness. A nineteenth century daguerreotype camera sat next to me, a shiny box front and wooden tripod so pristine that my dormant photographer's heart went *boom-boom*. But anger rose along with my covetousness—two sins for the price of one—because the camera had clearly been set there for the purpose of catching people as they entered. I thought of what I knew about fairy tales, the way myth derived from fact and vice versa, and suddenly didn't like that someone had snapped my photograph at all. Some cultures believed capturing a person's image also enslaved their soul. I turned my head and narrowed eyes back to the bartender, and had the satisfaction of watching wariness overcome his handsome features as I headed his way.

"I want that picture back," I said, pounding my fist on the bar, though I shot a nervous glance at the red door, instinctively edging away from it. By now another woman had joined the first at the top of the stairs, and two more were heading out of a room as resplendent as they were—shimmering, shining, tasseled, bright, and *alive* in a way nothing downstairs was. Catching the direction of my gaze, a Latina with heels even sharper than my tongue swiftly pulled the door shut behind her, while the rest leaned in various states of repose along the railing. Eyes were shaped, lashed, and lined from corner to corner, black kohl apparently a girl's best friend over here, while lips fighting with nails to sport the greatest sheen. It was a rainbow-hued array of fringed and beaded and silken clothing, jewels sparking off their ears and fingers and arms, and even from the shawls pulled about their shoulders.

I wiped my brow with my free hand, unable to keep from comparing its ashen hue with the vibrancy and life perched above me. It was steaming hot down here, so maybe in this world color rose instead of heat.

Because the women above didn't look hot. The few holding fans were clearly doing so for effect, feathers swaying with the casual flick of their wrists, shots of light from bright gems gleaming from bone handles and gold wrist straps. There was nothing on or near them that wasn't adorned. Even Cher and Suzanne, using their entire feminine arsenal, couldn't compete with the show above.

I returned my attention to the bartender, who calmly reached over and lifted my hand, polishing the shining bar top beneath with his pristine white rag. "Been a long time since we had anyone come through that entrance, miss."

His voice was a sweetened drawl, and the "miss" melted me somewhat, so while I removed my hand from his grasp, I was careful not to touch the bar. He smiled his thanks. He was dressed in traditional barman garb, the collar on his white shirt pressed beneath the black vest, his white apron spotless. I didn't look, but I would have bet that his shit-kickers were polished to a glossy sheen. His hair would have been fashionable in my world if not for the handlebar mustache above his goatee and the generous helping of pomade slicking back the honey-blond strands. Honey blond, I thought grimly, if he hadn't been living in an achromatic world.

"My picture?" I demanded, holding out my hand. Meanwhile I sniffed, trying to scent out if he was Light or Shadow, for me or against, but I came up with the mental equivalent of a blank chalkboard, a big void, but even less than both of those things implied, because the molecules I inhaled were empty. I drew back, even warier.

The bartender shrugged. "All first-timers to the Rest House have their images taken. How 'bout a drink? First one's on the house."

The Rest House? I tilted my head. "And that's secret agent language for what?"

"No secret, ma'am." He jerked his chin, indicating a point over my shoulder, and I turned, ignoring the cluster of people—all men, I now noted—still eavesdropping. One man, dark-skinned even outside the monochromatic room, rose from his seat so slowly it looked like he was floating in space. He pointed to the wall where my image, or eventual one, sat nestled among dozens of others. I took my eyes off it long enough to watch him float back to his seat, wondering exactly how long *he'd* been drinking.

I knew from my photography classes that daguerreotype processing took time, and the hot mercury vapor used to develop the images was highly dangerous to the photographer. But there was no photographer, and the image hadn't been burned beneath a glass plate. It appeared directly onto a molding yellow piece of paper pinned to a giant board.

One with "Most Wanted" typed in bold across the top.

"Well," I said, turning back. "It's nice to be wanted, right?"

The bartender smiled amicably. "Everybody has one," he said consolingly, but I'd already noted that. The entire wall was filled with posters, most with full images and agent names scrawled beneath. Many of the represented agents were at the gaming tables—all wearing, interestingly enough, the same clothing they'd been photographed in—though there were far more posters than players, pinned atop and sideways, some even on the floor. I wondered what had happened to the agents underneath.

And that's when I spotted it, pinned to the top left corner of the board, hanging off the side, as if an afterthought. Not an agent, but the faded line drawing of a freckle-faced boy whose image Zane carried around in his wallet. Like many preteen boys, he'd been smiling uncertainly in the photo Zane had shown me. In this one he was screaming.

Jacks's missing changeling.

Not alive. Not healed. And he hadn't even been given the dignity of his name. All it said beneath the macabre drawing was, *Mortal.*

Bill mistook my gasp for one of self-concern.

"Don't worry, your full identity isn't revealed until you enter three times."

"Let me guess," I said, licking my dry lips, pulling my mind away from the changeling. I had to stay focused. New world. New rules. I looked at the musty men scattered around the room like litter. *Clearly.* "At which point I won't be able to leave?"

And kill the rushlight in two tries.

"You catch on quick." He smiled, and held out his hand this time. "I'm Bill."

"I'm—" I caught myself just in time—caught his calculated look too—but shook his hand anyway. "Pleased to meet you, Bill."

Bartenders, no matter how attractive, worked for the house. I shut my mouth and shoved my hands into my pockets, and he shrugged and turned back to his taps. That's when I caught my reflection in the bar's foggy back mirror. "Oh my God."

It was me. Though reflected in soft focus, there was no mistaking the dark blunt bob ending just below my chin, the athletic rather than amative frame. I glanced back over my shoulder, blinking away unexpected tears, to find my poster also seemed to be taking on my old, my original, my *true* form. I looked down at the longer, more sinewy muscles in my arms, patted my legs—tighter, my nose—wider . . . I couldn't help it, my breasts, smaller. Shoot, it was all I could do to keep from kissing myself.

"You're in the Rest House . . . but also the Tenth House," Bill explained, careful to stand aside as he slid an opulent glass in front of me. I curled my hand around it, surprised to find myself shaking so much the crystal cut against my smooth fingertips. Bill motioned to a picture pinned next to the bar, like a health inspector's card, which I recognized as part of a natal chart, the Tenth House and Midheaven centered in its frame. "The house in astrology where deeds reflect your purpose *and* your true self."

That's why I was seeing myself now. Wiping my brow, I sipped thoughtfully. The room was like a steamless sauna, wicking moisture from my pores, but the drink helped. Its finish was cloying, not the traditional firewater I'd expected, but the aftertaste washed away with the next cooling sip. I took another and studied the rest of the room. "So why is everyone moving so slowly?"

Bill shot me that affable smile. "Maybe you're just moving too fast."

My movements, natural though they were, did make me stand out. While most of the men had returned to their games, their movements were molasses-slow. Others continued to stare at me, unblinking, and lifting cut crystal glassware to their lips or murmuring to themselves in unending monologues. I could practically track their gazes as they swung my way. Shit, UPS could have tracked them. And one man—black Stetson low, leather vest extended over his giant belly, dark eyes hard on mine—didn't move at all.

The piano player might be catatonic, I thought, sipping again, but the rest of the room wasn't far behind.

Except for upstairs. I lifted my eyes back to the women lounging against the banister, and as if she'd been anticipating it, the first began making her way down the stairs.

A world ruled by women.

And one of those rulers was headed my way.

10

Her pace was normal, but calculated. A deeply tanned hand, bejeweled with heavy rings and shimmering red nails, trailed along the carved railing. I'd have described her clothes as old-fashioned, and matching the western decor, except that even to my untrained eye they possessed a modern sensibility.

Though her jade silk dress had a high neck and button front, it was embellished with a cinched leather sash, to match the black stockings and ankle boots. Her body was liquid beneath the shifting silk skirts, her face heart-shaped below dark hair and curls I'd last seen on *Little House on the Prairie*. Deep-stained rosebud lips were turned upward in a secret smile, and diamonds as big as my thumbnails sat like flat pancakes at her earlobes. Her gold chain would have been more at home in a rap video than a western flick, with an inverted horseshoe that actually shot sparks of light from its diamond facets, as if tiny disco balls were reeling inside. It seemed she was mocking her own disguise, poking fun at the era while taking part in it.

She paused at the last stair, a predator's smile on her budding lips, before jumping to the ground floor, both booted feet landing with a hard thwack. There was a collective inhalation as the room shot to life, suddenly brighter. A black man grinned the biggest, most beautifully blinding smile I'd ever seen, his ashy hue leached away. An Asian guy ran a hand over thick silky hair as he turned his head, thankfully, toward the heavens. The man who'd stared so unblinkingly at me now had his eyes shut in relief, and I didn't blame him. The air was suddenly alive, like a cooling breeze had swept through the building, and I wasn't as thirsty as I'd been even a moment earlier.

The fans directly above us stilled, punctuating the silence, and the woman reached for a gaunt man at the nearest table, her left hand a sinuous ribbon around his neck as she pulled him from his chair. She pretended not to notice when he shuddered, dragging him along as she advanced upon me. Though I felt color and sensation and *life* washing off of her in waves, I took advantage of my quicker movements to grasp her left wrist before it fell to my arm.

I didn't care how dead sexy and life-affirming she was, nobody touched me without permission.

The surprised dulcet tones of the women above told me I'd done something unexpected. I decided to keep on doing it.

"There's a man," I said without preamble.

"There's always a man." She smiled. I tightened my hold.

"This one came from my world." *And killed a child in doing so.*

"I know the lantern."

That didn't make sense to me, but I flagged that information for later too. "I need to find him."

Her eyes skirted to the board. "His name?"

"Jaden Jacks." I gave it freely. What did I care if they possessed, and used, the name of a Shadow?

"Don't know him," she said, too quickly, snatching her hand away. She held it out. The man rubbed it for her. "Why don't you ask Mackie?"

I glanced over at the comatose piano player. Yeah. He looked like he was going to be a big help.

"And what's your name again, honey? I didn't quite catch it the first time." She leaned toward me, dragging the man with her, though he only blew errant tendrils from his comb-over in a grateful sigh. Her breath was light, like sugar wafers. "Whisper it in my ear and I promise I won't tell a *soul*."

"Diana," Bill warned, gaze darting between us as he continued polishing glasses. They were all as elaborate as the one I held, shot through with refracted color now that Diana had gifted us with her presence. Mine was golden with a hint of emerald. As for Bill, Diana's arrival on the bottom floor had neither enhanced nor diminished him in any way.

"Shut up, Bill," the gaunt man said, languishing beneath Diana's arm. She laughed brightly, the sound accompanied by a fresh wave of breathable sugar.

"Yes, Bill. Do shut up," she said, batting lacquered lashes. "I just want to know her name."

The rest of the bar was quiet, their interest a tight pressure against my back. Diana's mouth twitched. I gave her a perfunctory smile. "It's Olivia."

She pushed from the bar so quickly the room seemed to tilt with her. The man stumbled, and I stepped away. Diana studied my poster, my face, and the poster again. No name, I realized. Not even the beginnings of one. I was telling the truth, though not the *true* truth, so the information wasn't being recorded on the wall. She took another step backward, and because the vitality in my own breast seemed to recede with her, I had no idea whether I preferred that she stay or go.

Or what I preferred less, I mused.

She did go, finally, turning her back amid the groans and pleas of those in the room, the man she'd left next to me looking close to tears. Diana ignored them all. And as soon as one booted heel hit the staircase, the color in the room snapped off like a light. Heat flooded back in. Breathing was instantly laborious. The fans above us started their slow spin once again, and the women giggled behind palms and fringed fans. A heat haze rolled off the red door in invisible waves. What the hell was behind that thing?

"You could have played along. Bought us time." I glanced over my shoulder. The giant man wearing the black Stetson had resumed his original position, arms folded over his great belly, eyes indistinguishable beneath the low hat brim. He was sweating profusely, beads rolling down his neck to disappear beneath the vest.

"Why don't you offer up your name, then?"

"I have. Freely. It's Harlan Tripp."

I frowned, and because the name was vaguely familiar, asked, "Do you know Jacks?"

Tripp scoffed. "Honey, you want information in the Rest House, you gotta play for it."

"No," called a woman from above. She was black, wiry, and tough, and her scent was as heavy and cloying on the air as the drink in my glass. "Don't waste time with the boys. Come on up here. I promise we won't bite."

"*I* make no promises," said a blonde with brows plucked so severely she looked permanently surprised. Spicy this time, with a bitter aftertaste.

"Leave her alone, girls. She'll come when she's ready."

This voice was liquid, thick and smooth. A shaft of light split the wall opposite the other women, a door opening enough to allow a single silhouette passage. And this scent, minty rose with a creamy heart, had me nearly lifting to my toes. I tried to inhale more, and glanced around to find every man in the room trying to do the same. Yearning blanketed every face, and most eyes had fallen half shut. The women, though not that far gone, were silent and nodding at one another. The first, smoky-skinned and dark eyes, turned away with a smile. "Yes, she'll come."

Don't be lulled . . . don't be intimidated.

Easy for Vanessa to say, I thought, swallowing hard. All she had was a thin myth, and a matriarchal legacy and culture, to guide her. I was suddenly face-to-face with that myth . . . face-to-face with Bill.

"Can I get a credit limit?" I asked him, pleased when his brows winged in surprise. He'd expected me to follow the voice upstairs. But I needed to find out about Jacks, and the women only seemed interested in playing mental games. At least with poker I knew the rules.

"Boyd?" Bill glanced at Tripp's dealer, who inclined his head. I picked up my glass and headed to the table.

"Do I need to sign for it?" I asked Boyd, taking the seat across from him. He motioned to the wall with my picture on it. So that was how they kept track of their debtors. "Fine. Deal 'em."

There were five men at the table, including Boyd, who shuffled cards so worn they'd never have seen a table at Valhalla. An albino with startling black eyes was to his left, while an Asian man, who had yet to look at me, sat between the two of us. To my right was a black man with sideburns that would have made John Shaft, the movie character, proud. Guess I didn't have to ask how long he'd been there. Tripp sat next to him.

"So what'll it be? Three-card monte, brag, faro?" I smiled, referring to the games that were popular way back when the West was originally won.

Boyd slipped his clay pipe from his lips, though oddly, his answer still flowed from the left side of his mouth. "A simple game of hold'em."

"More like strip poker," the albino said, and the other men chuckled. For a moment I thought they were messing with me, but their looks weren't lascivious, and everyone was fully clothed. The Asian next to me was the only one who remained unsmiling and serious. His arms were knotted, wiry with muscle as he gripped the edge of the table. "And you only get to ask questions when you win the hand."

At my surprised expression, Tripp nodded. "You gotta win to get what you want."

"We all want something . . . or we did," the albino said. "Once."

Boyd began picking at the different chips from his stacked racks, poring over each, which I could see were marked by symbols or words, as he puffed consideringly. The others seemed content to wait, and why not? It didn't seem they had any place to go. Besides, it was too hot to expend energy in pointless conversation. Like them, I sat back and decided to save it for the game. In fact, everyone other than Tripp was moving so slowly I could probably take a nap between hands.

"Interesting," the dealer said, still poring over his chips. "Never seen this one before . . . though this other's fairly common . . . now, I don't know what to think of that . . . "

A dozen chips filled his hands, and everyone watched as he racked and passed them to me. "That should get you started. And might I add," he said, with the courtesy shown to a player with loads to lose, "welcome to the Rest House."

I palmed a chip, wondering what he was so anxious to gain. It didn't take long to figure it out. As I stilled, gazing at the chips, a chuckle rimmed the table. Now I knew why the albino had said it was like strip poker. But instead of removing clothing when you lost a hand, you gave up something far more valuable.

"My powers?" I couldn't keep my horror from seeping into the question.

"Only if you lose," Tripp said, smile widening.

I swallowed hard and glanced back down at my chips. Everything I'd only begun to get used to having and controlling was represented there. Everything that made me special. Including what made me the Kairos.

I could start off small, I saw, biting my lower lip, bartering degrees of speed or strength—there were a number of those chips—though it wouldn't be too many losing hands before I'd have to wager more costly powers. There were chips for each of the five senses, another for the sixth, which I didn't even know I had.

What the hell was quintessence, anyway?

And what did the four triangles represent? I wondered. Two were inverted, and two had horizontal lines near the base.

There was the ability to erect shielding walls, and another that made living things erupt from the earth. Here was a surprise: I could regenerate?

Healing, dumbass. That's what that means.

And transmogrify? I thought of the way the Tulpa could take on entirely different appearances. That had to be a Shadow strength. Then again, what if my ability to so convincingly take on Olivia's physical form had more to do with *me* than Micah's surgeon's steel? Did all agents possess that power? Or had I inherited it from the man who'd been imagined into existence?

I was most surprised to see that emotions were represented on the chips, and that they were considered powers. Simple ones too, like love and hate and passion. The simplest, I realized, and the most valuable.

"Oh my God," I said, feeling all eyes on me. "All this time . . . "

I looked up, met Tripp's questioning gaze.

"I had no idea I was good at math." I smiled. He scowled, and slumped farther in his seat. Boyd snorted, clay pipe wobbling between his lips.

My sarcasm—also represented on a chip, and an apparent strength—hid my panic. How had they known all this? I wondered, looking around. Was there some sort of hidden camera?

Yeah Jo, I thought, turning the caustic strength on myself. A daguerreotype. One to reveal a person's internal landscape. It'd captured everything differentiating me from other agents, yet at the same time everything that added up to make anyone a fully functioning, healthy human being. And it was all stacked in front of me, ready to be parceled out in quantifiable bits. My hands began to shake.

Other than the full smile again splitting Tripp's face, a singular question sat in the gaze of every other player, as well as Boyd's assessing gaze. It was the same one, I thought, looking down at my chips, that I needed to ask myself.

Which power would I sacrifice first?

Boyd doled out the pocket cards, a face card and a nine, then smiled around his pipe. "Ante up."

At Boyd's left, Tripp opened the pot. He had dozens of chips stacked before him, indicating his skill.

Next came the black man, who stacked and restacked his chips before matching Tripp's bet. A soul chip for a soul chip.

My turn, then. So what essential part of me, what vital aspect that made me *super,* should I wager first? I was sure some people would be happy to see my sarcastic nature gone, but since it was oft-used, I'd rather keep it. What might affect me least? I clinked them in my hand for a good minute, but nobody rushed me.

I chose one of the triangles. I didn't know what they were, but I had three others left in my stack.

The Asian and the albino—which sounded like a poor title for a spaghetti western—had already chosen their chips and pushed them forward. Boyd presented the flop. Tripp frowned and folded outright, while the black man matched the blind. I didn't like the ace showing, but one more jack and I could have three of a kind. Not bad for a first hand.

Boyd flipped again. No help. A ten. Again the man to my right raised. The hand could go either way, but I couldn't win if I didn't play, right? And that's why I was there: to heal Jasmine, win freedom for my city, and bring to life the fourth sign of the Zodiac so my troop could get back to their regularly scheduled superhero programming. I threw in a portion of my speed.

The Chinese guy folded, the albino sipped nervously at his drink. I mentally dismissed him and focused on the black man while Boyd flipped the last card. A jack. I began to relax, but caught my opponent smiling as he raised again. Damn. Did he have a jack too?

I curled up the edge of my cards, peeking again at the nine. Fighting the need to swallow hard, I called again, giving another triangle, this one without a line parallel to the base. Boyd snorted as soon as I tossed it in the pot, which had me rethinking the move, but the chip was released. It was too late.

As I'd anticipated, the albino folded. Boyd tapped the table. The black man turned his cards. There was the last jack.

But his other card was a seven.

I had won.

I wiped a hand over the back of my neck, sighing as I raked the chips toward me. I'd won back all that I'd risked, and even had buffer chips for the next round. I took a fortifying sip from my glass, noting thankfully that it seemed to stay cool in the cup. Tripp was watching me hungrily, though whether it was due to my drink or my luck, I didn't know. I just tilted my cup in his direction before sipping some more.

"Wow. Haven't had my ass handed to me by a woman since I was on the bayou."

I shot a sidelong glance at Shaft. "You're from the South?"

"With this accent, where else? And it's not like everyone here doesn't already know that, so y'all can't barter with it." His laughter boomed, and the men joined in, so I knew I was missing something. At least their movements and words were a little more up to speed. They'd been obviously messing with me before, a group of friends ganging up on a dupe.

"Well, I didn't know. I'm from . . . " I was going to say Vegas, but remembered they might not know that. "A transient town. You could have relocated."

"Maybe," he said, as if he couldn't remember. "Which lantern marks your entrance?"

"That . . . one . . . " There were eight lanterns, all evenly spaced across the wall, all with identical frames, powder coat finishes, and evenly burning flames. *I know the lantern*, Diana had said. But I didn't.

The black man rattled his chips. "Yeah, that's what I thought."

They all laughed again.

And *How do I get out of here?* suddenly rose to the top of my question list.

Boyd dealt again. When it came my turn to sweeten the pot, I threw back the albino's chip. He was annoying me the least.

"You get to ask your question too," Boyd said, puffing lightly at his pipe, though his eyes were assessing.

I rattled my chips—my strengths—still thinking about that. Discovering a way out of here was clearly important, but I wanted to find Jaden Jacks *now*. To do that, I'd have to eliminate the men in this room, one by one. So, with a glance at the motionless piano player, I sipped at my drink. "What's Mackie's deal?"

Diana had said he might know who Jacks was, so I'd start with him.

The black guy's eyes went wide as he risked a glance at the pianist. He quickly looked away, though Mackie hadn't even twitched.

"Mackie ain't exactly one of us . . . but he's not one of them either." He jerked his head toward the dealer and Bill. Just as I'd thought. Working for the house. Boyd smiled unapologetically, and I wondered if they were tulpas like Skamar and my father. "He's reportedly the last of the Nez Perce. Hear of them?"

Not in recent years, of course. The Nez Indians had tribal lands north of Nevada, dating back five hundred years, but like most Native Americans, they'd been displaced. Had that resulted in Mackie's relocation this far south? And when? Because though I'd yet to fully see his face beneath that bowler, it looked like brown parchment had been fisted around his neck. I realized I was looking at a piece of living history.

Well, living-ish.

"He's been here the longest," the black man went on, throwing down a chip, still in. I'd have asked his name, but knew he wouldn't say, so I silently named him Hippie as I added my bet to the pile. "Nobody knows anything about him, beyond not to touch his piano."

"And that he keeps a knife on him at all times." This from the Asian, who didn't seem to have issues with revealing information that wasn't about himself. He continued play as well. "They say it's where he keeps the last ounce of his soul, transmogrified in the blade. He's been hanging onto it by refusing to say anything. Refusing to move unless he has to. Refusing to give up knowledge or energy or anything that will contribute to this world."

I glanced at Bill and Boyd, but they didn't seem to have a problem with him telling me this, and a skein of panic arrowed through my belly. Contribute to this world? Is that what we were doing?

"But you must communicate if you want to live here," Boyd added after the albino folded, and revealed the final of the three flop cards. My anxiety spiked again. No chance for a straight, but one more spade? *Flush.* "You have to allow your personal power to be used to fuel this world, or at least wager it."

Because even if you didn't lose, I realized as I matched and raised, the interaction kept the others wagering theirs.

Hippie jerked his head back at Mackie. "He was his tribe's storyteller, so his music is his payment—"

"Except now it is our stories he tells," the Asian put in

sourly. I wondered how long ago he'd thrown in his happiness chip.

Boyd sat up straighter. "Don't share that with her."

The albino turned his black eyes on Boyd and flipped him off so closely that Boyd went cross-eyed. "She asked about Mackie. She earned the right." He turned back to me and smiled. I bet he didn't get a lot of chances to flip Boyd the bird.

"The songs," I said, studying each man's face. "Like the one he began when I came in? That was my song, wasn't it?"

"The songs are what bind your ass here." Hippie slumped farther in his chair. "They keep this world going. Once completed, the Mother will know everything about you."

He said "the Mother" like one would say the Earth, or the World, or God. I swallowed hard.

"When the murder ballad is complete, the poster will be drawn. Your name—your *true* name—will be printed across the bottom."

The Asian cut in. "And once Mother knows everything about you—"

"She can draw from your energy reserves at will." Hippie pursed his lips as he studied his cards, finally folding. "She don't even have to wait for you to lose, if she don't want. Basically, we're all here on borrowed time."

So our powers literally fueled this world. We were energy. Little power plants with beating hearts. I fingered my chips idly, back and forth, until the one I'd won from the Asian caught my eye. His name was printed on one side, Shen, and his star sign and Zodiac troop was on the other.

"Pisces of Light?" I asked, twirling it absently, noting it because we'd been missing ours the entire time I'd been with my troop. I saw from Hippie's chip that he was a Capricorn and—

"Damn you!" My chair back and head cracked against the rough wooden floor and my vision went sparkly as

Shen's hands found my neck. Tinkling laughter, feminine and bright and amused, rang in the air.

"That was my secret to tell. *My* power!"

"Get off of her, Shen!" Bill yelled from behind the bar. "You're wasting energy. Yours and hers."

But he didn't waste any of his in helping me.

"You bartered my power. You rendered it useless!"

"I didn't do it on purpose!" I choked out. Shen squeezed harder. Then suddenly he was gone, lifted so high in the air I was looking directly up at the soles of his shoes.

"She didn't know, Shen," Boyd said calmly, and sat him back in his seat.

"I could have won it back! Now it's null! That part of me is voided out forever!"

"I'm sorry," I added, sitting up. I really was. I knew how I'd feel if someone had just nullified a power of mine. "I— I'll pay you back."

"One of your chips!" he yelled, spittle raining down on me. "My pick!"

"No." I didn't want to give him that, but I felt bad about the loss. I looked at the dealer. "Can I give him someone else's chip?"

Boyd scratched his head. "No one's ever asked that before."

"Because no one's that stupid," Tripp said, and chuckled darkly.

"No. Hers alone. It's only fair." Shen crossed his arms. The other men nodded.

"Fine." I wasn't going to win this argument. I'd just have to win the hand. I smirked at Tripp as I found my feet. "Any other ground rules before we resume the game?"

"Yes," Shen yelled, still angry, though he was already rifling through my chips. He palmed a chip before I could see which he'd taken. Ungrateful friggin' *Pisces*. "Keep your hole shut!"

I sat again and counted my powers, unable to figure out what was missing since I didn't even know everything I'd had, but from Shen's smug expression, and the sudden interest in his pile, I knew I'd just lost something big.

Preoccupied with this, and really feeling the relentless heat, it was unsurprising when I also lost the next hand. To be fair, it was probably just bad luck—Hippie had the next best hand and he didn't win either—but Tripp's satisfied expression as he flipped my two original chips between his fingers irritated me, like he was rubbing raw a patch of my skin. Why couldn't it have been anyone but him?

"What are you going to do with those?" I asked, wondering what I was missing without those triangles.

"Same as anyone. I'm going to buy something with it."

I realized then that we were like a bunch of magpies hoarding our goods, scavenging from others, and pillaging whatever we could. Some things didn't change, I thought, with a slow shake of my head. No matter what world you lived in.

"Bill," he called out, without looking away from me. "Kindly call up to Solange and see if she'll accept my company for the evening?"

"Miss Solange hasn't taken your calls in . . . a while, Tripp." He'd barely kept from referencing the time again, and I wondered why. And asking a working girl if she was willing to accept your company? Another mind-boggling, interworldly twist.

"Well, now I have something she might want."

I swallowed hard. Bill nodded at Boyd. He stared straight ahead at the wall, then his eyes rolled. "Hold, please."

And those eyes kept on rolling. Actually they spun, tiny globes that refracted light as they whirled faster and faster. His eyelids pulsed with the movement and his lips began to move, almost like an incantation, though from the way they paused—as if waiting for reply—I recognized it as his side of a conversation. Sure enough, a few seconds later the spinning slowed, he blinked his irises into focus, and tilted his head at Tripp. "Go on up."

The Shadow agent pushed back his chair, and pulled at

his belt buckle, though there was no way it could rise beneath the girth of his belly. I clenched my teeth when he resumed flipping my chips between his fingers, whistling as his boots sounded hollowly over the scarred wooden floor. He was moving again in frames, herky-jerky, like a badly cut movie.

"Enjoy your soiled dove," I snapped.

He faced me without my seeing him pivot. "Enjoy your drink."

Fear streamed through me, washing right over my face so that Tripp laughed as he headed toward those stairs. I reached out to stop him, but my arm was heavy and he was gone too quickly. Flying up the stairs and whizzing to the right before I could even open my mouth. Oh my God. The *drink.*

The others hadn't sped up, I realized now. I had slowed down. I looked down at my still brimming—my ever-brimming—glass.

Solange, I thought as color and light spilled again into the hallway above. Tripp's shadow elongated, then snapped as the door swung shut behind him. No matter what, I had to remember that.

I didn't know how long I sat there, staring, but I gradually became aware of everyone watching me. I no longer had any sense of time, but I met all their gazes one by one—Shen's still-malevolent one, Hippie's understanding one, the albino, calculating, and finally the dealer's. Boyd merely gave me a professional nod, his spinning eyes still once again.

"Ante up," he said in an elongated drawl that had to be put on. The sound emanated as though from a tunnel. I wavered in its wake.

11

It was all so obvious now. It was a *bar*, the heat was unbearable, and the bartender had offered the first one "on the house," presumably to get me hooked. I realized from the way my fellow players watched me that they'd each come to these same conclusions, and that none of them were fighting it. I can do this, I thought, trying to shake my head of the drink. I succeeded only in making myself dizzy.

With Tripp gone, I starting winning easily. I had to be the most "sober" person at the table, though every time someone sipped from their eternally full glasses, every time they licked their lips or swallowed hard, I greedily followed the movement. Even the wasteful beads of sweat on their foreheads were suddenly as enticing as a cold spring in summer. I quickly grew a begrudging respect for Tripp. I was dying of thirst, and I'd only been fighting it for . . . how long?

But I was also cleaning up at power poker.

Shen finally had enough.

"Why don't you go up where you belong," he spat when I raked a pile of chips toward me that included his sense of smell. He bet that power instead of the one he'd taken

from me, which told me how valuable mine was, and that I
definitely wanted it back.

If possible, my movements slowed even further because
what Shen meant was up with the whores. Too bad for
him I hadn't handed over the chip containing my temper,
because I'd had far less to drink than he, and had the re-
flexes to prove it. Yet even before I could swing, Boyd was
pushing me back into my chair. The effort it'd taken just
to get up drained me.

"That's the second fight you've been involved with at
this table today!" He shook his finger in my face like he
was scolding a child.

"He insinuated I was a whore!"

Boyd's eyes did a full rotation. "He insinuated you were
a *woman*, though it's hard to believe given your color."

"You can go upstairs at any time," the albino said, finally revealing the source of his obvious resentment. "Not
like us."

"How about another drink to calm yourself, sweetie?"
I turned at the voice that bloomed beside me, and Bill
gifted me with that deadly hot smile. Yet it was the sweet-
smelling liquor in his hand that had my heart racing. Light
refracted off the gold liquid, and sweat poured down my
face.

God, I wanted it. Even knowing what it was and did, I
couldn't help it; I was literally dying of thirst.

I reached for my bag, and the wallet inside. Xavier's
money was still in there. If I could go upstairs—get away
from these men and heat and drink long enough to clear
my head—surely this Solange woman would accept a pile
of bills as payment for those chips. I'd make the trade and
find my way out after that. Maybe I'd be strong enough to
play Shen for my last chip, though more likely I'd have to
leave it. I knew not to chase my losses.

But my wallet wasn't there. I emptied the entire contents
of my satchel onto the table, not caring that I was holding
up the game, that Shen looked like he wanted to lunge at

me again, or that Boyd was nervously eyeing his felt. I'd had the money when I entered . . .

My gaze rose slowly to the top of the staircase. Diana, who'd bumped against me at the bar, was there, smiling. And fanning herself with a small stack of bills.

Pushing from the table, I fumbled at my belongings as she disappeared from sight. I had to go up there, and not merely for money. Whether I learned Jaden Jacks's secrets or not, I wasn't leaving pieces of myself lying around this so-called Rest House.

Though my trek to the staircase was almost painfully slow, no one tried to stop me, and I was steadier when I hit the second floor landing. Aged floorboards creaked beneath my weight in the silent, empty hallway. Tired and on edge, I wiped the back of my neck, trying to recall a time when I'd been so exhausted. Not to mention this afraid of the heat. I looked down at the saloon, and the red door with its glowing frame. I'd grown up in the desert, and knew its dangers, but this was different. It was as if fire was being held back behind it, and chasing me up the stairway too.

The men below stared at me with hollow eyes, envy warring with their curiosity as they wondered which woman—Diana or Solange—I'd go after first. Mackie remained slumped over on his piano stool, and from this angle I could see the layer of dust coating the instrument, the keys, and even the wide lapels of his dark jacket. The whole room, I thought, looked like a living museum, a reenactment of the Wild West where visitors could pay to walk into the past. The difference? Those people paid with coin, not power . . . and they could walk back out into their proper reality whenever they chose.

Bill, ever solicitous, nodded up at me, and Boyd remained granite-faced while puffing on his pipe. I'd drawn the attention of the other half-dozen dealers, and returned their nods as if doing nothing more than taking in the scenery. In reality, as I regained my strength, I surveyed the room like a map.

The most direct path to the poster board was through the center of all those dealers. I counted the steps it would take me to get from the stairs to the wall of lanterns, then did it again from the poster board across the room. If I could risk the energy, which seemed unlikely since I'd barely made it up here, that would be my next stop in looking for Jacks. I shuddered, though, as my gaze fell on my poster. Its half-finished state made my features appear erased rather than the reverse.

That was a worry for later. First Tripp, my powers . . . and Solange.

I gave the other side of the hallway a cursory glance, needing to know what was at my back. All of the women had disappeared, though their muted voices sounded like cooing doves behind a trio of closed wooden doors. Unlike the red door downstairs, each of these sported only one symbol: a triangle like those on the gaming chips I'd been given downstairs. So they represented powers of some sort . . . but what?

I turned back to the solo door at the other end of the hall, expecting—and finding—the fourth triangle. I didn't know why it was set apart from the rest, or why Solange was either, but it irked me that the very woman who'd told the others I'd come to them in such a husky, self-assured voice was the one I most needed to see. I rapped on the door hard, and, after a few silent moments, pushed it open.

"Hello?" I strained to see into a surprisingly complete darkness. "Solange? Tripp?"

I had to brace a hand against the wall to maintain equilibrium in the absolute dark. Everywhere I gazed—up, straight ahead, down—was inky depthlessness so complete I couldn't tell if I was entering a space spanning the width of my arms or one the size of a state. No way was I letting that door shut behind me.

There has to be a light switch somewhere, I thought, just as my fingers fumbled across one. It was a flip switch, and when powered on, lit twelve small squares along the remaining three walls. The glow from those palm-sized windows was enough to allow me my bearings . . . and reveal that this was neither a small space nor vast. It was simply a modest-sized square room, containing only those tiny, eye-level windows.

And a woman centered in the middle.

At first I wasn't sure this was Solange. From the way the men spoke of her, the way the women listened, I'd expected a lethal beauty, and hers was not. She bore little ornamentation, only fragile gold hoops with colored gem drops and intricate scrollwork at her ears. Beautiful, but not ostentatious.

Her hair was an unremarkable brown, parted simply down the middle to fall past her shoulders in uneven lengths, her attire simple; a fitted silk dress running from neck to ankles, shoulders to wrists, in a dual pattern of chocolate hues that played off the depth of her hair. A lace inset drew the eye to a slashing V-neck that ended snugly at her navel, but the silk was so sheer her every curve was revealed. The eye even strained toward it beneath the fluctuating pattern, and I realized that was its allure. It showed nothing and everything at once.

"Hello." She stood before a wooden cart with iron-rimmed wheels. It was lined in unrelieved black silk, pillows and cushions and throws all dangerously soft and smooth. A rope that disappeared into the depthless ceiling hooked to a bar across the middle, and other than the silken interior, the entire contraption looked like it belonged in a mine shaft. "I'm Solange."

That she greeted me so openly both eased and alarmed me.

"Where's Tripp?" I asked as she perched a hip on the cart.

She stared at one of the small square windows, studying it with solemn focus. "Did you really come here to ask that question?"

"Well, it wasn't for the pleasures of the flesh," I shot back, jaw clenched.

Solange sighed, and gave me a quick once-over, pursing her lips in what was either disgust or distaste.

"I don't know what to do about the color, okay?" And I chafed at the idea that someone could look at my body—*mine*, Joanna Archer's, in its strength and truth and perfect imperfections—and find something lacking. Perhaps I'd once done the same, but that was before it'd been so abruptly taken from me.

"No, you don't," she agreed, and my mouth was already open for a rebuke when she added, "but that's not what I was observing."

She climbed into the cart in a slide of chocolate silk, holding up her shift as she settled. Crossing the room in a much clumsier fashion, I grabbed her arm, forcing her to look at me. There was, I noted, even a glamour to the narrowing of her eyes. I didn't care. "I want my power back."

"Of course you do." Her voice was unstrained, and she didn't pull away, just sunk back until she was leaning upon the pillows. Feeling too aggressive against that pretty passiveness, I let her go. "What do you have to barter for it?"

I started to answer, but Solange tilted her head. "And don't say money either. The only use we have for that wad of paper is in the lavatory."

I knew. Diana had been fucking with me, drawing me upstairs. But why?

"I can tell you're not stupid, honey, so don't make me treat you as if you are. You now know what we trade in here."

I finally nodded.

Solange crossed her legs at her knees. "Tripp doesn't like you. He told me you're not to be trusted."

"Tripp and I are natural enemies."

"So you're of the Light."

"Not exactly."

She tilted her head. "Come," she said after a bit, and motioned for me to join her. "I have something to show you."

"Is it a poker chip embossed with my powers?"

"You are persistent," she said, shifting to make room. "I'll give you that."

And that was it. No asking, begging, threats, or yelling. She just watched me expectantly with those great dark eyes. Seeing no other choice, I climbed in. Whatever she wanted to show me couldn't be more shocking than everything I'd already experienced.

I hoped.

I'd expected to be nestled snugly beside Solange, but the interior of the cart expanded as I settled in, and I found myself sinking backward on a sea of smooth, limitless silk. Every muscle in my body relaxed, fatigue dogging me after the heat from downstairs. If I could just close my eyes . . .

Solange struck a match, the small sound an exaggerated zip that had my eyes flipping back open, but she was only lighting a small tea light in a cutout obviously designed for the purpose. She then pushed a button, leaning back as machinery above us kicked into gear. We rose in a slow wave, the light from the twelve tiny windows dropping away until they sparked out altogether. The pitch-dark coupled with my fatigue to make me feel stationary, so the sound of those grinding gears drawing closer was all that let me know I was still rising.

Our halt was jarring, and my melting limbs flew outward involuntarily. Solange murmured an apology. The light from her tea candle continued to burn stick-straight, as it had on our entire ascent, as if the flame too was being pulled upward, but other than that, and her delicate outline, there was nothing more to see.

Of course, maybe that was the purpose. Because the more I stared at Solange, the prettier she appeared. Some women were like that. I knew from living in Olivia's skin that her effect on others was also instantaneous. However, Solange's growing appeal was different. It was like the removal of blinders, or scales falling from the eyes. Even in the continual dimness her beauty grew more defined. She had delicate fingers and wrists, poised now over a tiny wheel, and her hair glowed softer than the silk surrounding me. Her half-lit silhouette was honeyed, her long neck as smooth as fragile ceramic. I suddenly found myself wondering how I ever could have believed her plain, and the thought that she'd need any ornamentation was so laughable I actually snorted.

Gripping that small steel wheel, she began twisting it. I felt like I was levitating. I'd once seen a man thrown into a black hole—a created one, sure, but a black hole nonetheless—and I felt as he'd looked then; rotating, softly spinning in space, my body pulled in unnatural and strange directions. I leaned my head back and couldn't tell if my eyes were open or closed, and just as I decided I didn't care, hundreds of stars burst to life around me.

I sat up on an awed exhalation. My rational mind told me I was at the center of a hollowed-out sphere, that the heaven engulfing me, embracing me as if I'd long been lost, was actually a metallic ceiling, and a bevy of mechanisms worked behind the scenes. But the sensation of being cradled in the pinpricked firmament was like a clap of thunder in my breast.

My God. Did I really identify this closely with the constellations? Because it felt like bloodline and lineage were rearing their heads, letting me know that for all my careful control, I was still very much at the mercy of the planets. I let my gaze wander, mentally crisscrossing lines to link the stunning little orbs into patterns of familiar constellations. It was a perfect diorama of the night sky. And yet, the stars . . .

"Are those . . . ?" I leaned forward, squinting as I focused on the constellations winging overhead.

"Yes." She sighed, like she was window shopping at Tiffany's. "Minerals and some organics. No synthetics."

"Gems?" There had to be millions of dollars worth splayed out above me.

"Jewelry befitting the sky," Solange confirmed. "I've been collecting them for years."

Unlike the others in my troop, I hadn't been raised observing and adoring the natural night sky. Sure, I'd thought it cool and all, but pretty much the only thing I could pick out with any certainty was the Big Dipper, which I did now. "There are some missing," I said, noting that the Little Dipper was shot through with pinpoints of light, but had no gems.

"Typical of someone with your coloring. Missing what is there and finding fault with what's not."

Surprised, I drew back at the venom in Solange's voice. "No, I was just—"

"It doesn't matter!" she snapped, eyes suddenly as fiery and fierce as the jewels above. "I'll fill the entire sky soon enough, and then I'll be the First." She tilted her head sharply. "You don't have a problem with that, do you?"

"What?" I didn't know what she was talking about, and I was taken aback by her sudden anger. "No."

Leaning back, she resettled silk over her knees. "Good."

I tried to relax or at least look like I was relaxed. I didn't trust her, especially after that little outburst, but I had a hard time pushing back the peace I felt amidst all this beauty. The cloud of pillows was soft at my back, and still spinning, the air a mere whisper against my skin. I wished I could undress just to feel more of it. My eyes began fluttering shut again.

"In the past, the constellations were what brought people the nightly news." Solange's voice arose beside me, closer than I thought she'd be, but I didn't open my eyes. "A person ignored the heavens at their own risk."

"Couldn't be any less accurate than modern-day meteorologists," I murmured before catching myself, but when

I looked at Solange, she only nodded. I sighed. She might not know where I was from, but surely she knew *when* I was from. My dress, my speech, even my hair and deportment, all modern. Her, however? She could have been from just about anywhere, any place. Any time.

"Because meteorologists study maps and currents and calculations. They neglect to look up. They forget that the word cosmos means 'harmonious order.'" Her dark eyes glittered. "The heavens are as ordered as the western calendar. Vikings sailed by it. Pilots used it to train in night navigation. If you read the skies correctly, you can even anticipate what will happen next. Nothing drawn upon the sky is by mistake."

I tilted my head back to the ceiling, quietly sharing her awe if not her knowledge. "Are you like Bill or Boyd?"

What else could she be, I thought, but some sort of supernatural being? A phenomenon, I thought, looking at her. One as breathtaking as a shooting star. "No. I am my own."

Her pursed lips and flat response made me feel like I'd failed a test.

She sat back, nearly disappearing into the shadows. "You're looking for Jaden."

That brought me to full alert. "You know him?"

"You could say." The shrug was in her voice. "Is he still a romantic at heart? Belief in the individual, in choice, et-cetera and so on?"

"I don't know. I mean, I don't know him at all."

Solange shifted her attention away from the sky. "Then why are you looking for him?"

"I broke something. That Shadow knows how to fix it." Except that he hadn't fixed the changeling, I now knew. Jacks had killed him.

"He is good with his hands," she said wistfully, and it was clear she wasn't talking about tools. "But I haven't seen JJ in years. Your lantern's been locked."

I shook my head. "I didn't have any problems getting in."

She shrugged. "Then someone unlocked it."

"So . . . " Jacks wasn't in Midheaven? I'd lost power, and he'd been in Vegas all along? "Well, do you know where he might be?"

"Is Warren Clarke still the leader of Light?"

That surprised me into momentary silence. "Yes."

"Then I suggest you ask him."

"How would . . . " I never finished the thought. My mind raced, searching for a time when a manual or even Warren had mentioned *Jacks* and *Shadow agent* in the same sentence. Coming up blank, I realized I had just assumed, and Warren had let me. "You mean . . . "

"Jaden is Light, dear."

My dizzy-headedness wasn't due to heat or drink or spinning stars. Everything I'd believed had just realigned into a different, unrecognizable pattern. I could understand Zane not telling me—he was the record keeper and had a cosmic obligation to remain a neutral force between Shadow and Light—but Warren . . .

All this time he'd let me act on the assumption that Jacks was a Shadow. "This is making me sick to my stomach."

Solange immediately sat up, pushing the button so our slow spinning came to a stop. The heavens above ceased their movement.

"It's that god-awful drink," she muttered, and bent over, returning quickly with a simple gold flask. "Here. Wash it away."

I sniffed. Water. I took one sip, then found myself guzzling it. The cloying finish of the drink downstairs disappeared, and my head cleared. Sheepish, I pulled the flask away before I emptied it. Solange smiled and waved at me to hold onto it. "It's okay. I have more."

By the time I finished the water, the nausea had faded.

"Warren hasn't told you anything, has he?" she said softly as I closed my eyes. "He just sent you into a whole new world without even mentioning what this place is and does."

I whimpered. She leaned me back again, like I was a child.

"You've spent many years at war with yourself. That's why you're gray." She pressed a finger to my skin, looking at it like she expected to come away with soot on the shiny tips. "Toxins ooze from your pores. You doubt who you are and your place in that world. But here, you can embrace all your contradictions."

"Like you do?"

She nodded as she leaned back, shutting her eyes, beautiful in repose. "I choose to be. Myself. In the moment. With the person I'm with. It's simple, really. Anyone can do it."

And there *was* something about Solange that was authentic. Maybe that's why she was so beautiful. Maybe I was looking at the best *her*, the *most* her. That sort of comfort with oneself was rare.

I certainly wasn't there yet.

Which reminded me . . . "I need my power back."

"Why?" To her credit, Solange only cracked an eyelid. "No, really. Why?"

"Because it's a part of me. I entered the world wholly and I want to leave the same way."

"Nobody can walk through the world unchanged." She nestled farther into the inky darkness. "Besides, the moment is all that matters. Control that and you control all. That's true power."

I found her lack of sentiment unnerving, and her dismissal of the people and events that marked and made a person was ruthless. Yet her eyes were soft when she turned her face back to mine.

"You look tired," she said, voice honey-rich. "Maybe you're coming down with something?"

That's certainly what it felt like. My head pounded and my limbs were heavy. My skin ached and the nausea from before threatened again. Even Solange's soft hand stroking my forearm was an irritant. Only the enveloping silk was welcome. A thought visited me: *But superheroes don't get sick.*

"The water . . . "

The water . . . drugged . . . too late . . .

My eyelids were heavy, my limbs numb. "Oh, no . . . "

"Oh, yes." Her words were sharp, her fingertips silken as she stroked my cheek. My eyes fluttered shut.

"I drank . . . "

"What you were given. Silly girl."

And I nose-dived into sleep, the universe pulsing around me.

Fire greeted me on the other side of wakefulness; innocuous flames dancing atop a tiered cake, twenty-six candles burning in celebration. There were symbols on the cake, ones I should recognize, but my knowledge of them lay like words on the tip of my tongue; both there and not until their meaning dissolved. I panned backward, as you do in dreams, to find myself standing in Saturn's Orchard, the training room and dojo in my troop's sanctuary. Pink and white paper streamers hung fifty feet from the pyramid's hollowed apex, and the mirrored walls that normally flashed star signs across their surfaces picked up the girly color, lightly hued at the tip, depth graduating in degree until reaching a toothaching fuchsia at the base. It was clear I'd walked in on a birthday celebration, and from the plastic crown nestled atop her head, and the wide, clownlike grin stretching Chandra's face, I knew it was hers.

This, I realized with a start, was her twenty-sixth birthday. More than a quarter century spent in our troop, but with no star sign to inherit, and still no metamorphosis to make her "super." I looked for any sign of bitterness or resentment, because as long as I was in the troop, Chandra would always be relegated to sidekick status, no matter how old she grew. Her dark eyes landed on me, and though they remained blank and unseeing, the too-red lips of that clown smile widened. She gave me a "howdy-do" wave, then turned to mill with her guests.

My entire troop was there, and though no one else wore a painted-on smile, they were all grinning and silly, and had been celebrating for a while. Shot glasses littered the glasstop table holding Chandra's cake, and a full Scotch bottle was being passed from hand to hand, though it never seemed to empty. As with most drunken social gatherings, it wasn't long before the universal, and unanswerable, questions began to fly.

Is there a God? Who's right, the Creationists or Darwin? What is the human position in the Universe?

"What is it," shouted Micah, staggering dangerously from his seven-foot height, "that makes the world go round?"

People began blurting their answers like they were blowing on party horns.

"Money!" Kimber said, and threw a wad into the air.

"Not true!" said Tekla, pointing a stern finger at her before toppling into a chair and passing out.

"Spoken like someone who has it," Warren put in, slurring every syllable. He was dressed in his undercover bum attire, which he rarely wore in the sanctuary. He raised his arm in a silent toast when he saw me looking. He wasn't holding a glass, though, because he didn't have a hand.

I jumped, mouth falling open, but he shrugged and found a shot glass with his other hand. Draining whiskey, he then offered his own answer to the question. "Power runs this world, of course. People will spend their last dime to acquire it. Just look at me," he said, spinning to show off his tattered trench.

"Power won't satisfy you when you're lying alone at night," Felix said, one arm draped over Kimber's shoulder, the other over Vanessa's. "Sex rules the world, my friends. That's why people want power. People want different sex, better sex, more sex. It's the only valid reason to acquire money in the first place."

"You're all wrong."

The place fell silent. A spotlight landed on Hunter. He was completely naked and totally aroused. Nobody commented, or even seemed to notice. They were as attentive as a roomful of reporters at a press conference, heads cocked in concentration as they tried to decipher his meaning. Vanessa had even taken out her pocket notebook, pen poised at the ready. But Hunter was staring straight at me, and he walked my way in a warrior's beat, stopping so close I felt the heat of his breath on my lips.

"Love," he said, putting a hand to my cheek, "is what makes this crazy world go round."

Again, awareness that this was a dream washed over me—Hunter would never say that—but the kiss that followed certainly made my head spin. I reached out—wanting deeper, longer, more—but Hunter pulled back, palm on his lips, blinking rapidly as he looked back at me. Shocked, he whirled on his heel without another word, and the spotlight faded.

"What do you think, Jo-livia?"

I was still gazing after Hunter, who walked right through the pyramid wall and disappeared, and I had to work to turn my attention to Felix, and his unanswerable question. After a minute I shook my head. "I can't remember."

"That's okay, babe," he said, and he was suddenly standing before me, as near as Hunter had been when kissing me. I backed away. Felix and I weren't close like that. We were only friends, and he knew it. One side of his mouth tilted in understanding. "Memories are just silent promises you once made to yourself. The moment is all that matters. Here."

Chandra's birthday cake suddenly appeared between us, Felix struggling to steady it on a silver platter more appropriate for medieval feasts and giant banquets. We balanced it between us, and approached Chandra, now seated on a throne and dais, the plastic silver crown lopsided on her head. When we came to a stop in front of her, she tilted her head to the other side, the soullessly blank eyes remaining fixed on me, that obscene smile never wavering.

"Make a wish," she said, screwing up her lines . . . and doing it in the Tulpa's voice. Then, just as I realized they were really sticks of dynamite, she extinguished those twenty-six candles. Blood coated my face and body, and with the heat of my father's scorched laughter raining down on my shoulders, my dream blew up. I woke.

Screaming.

Sweating, I sat straight up in the rickety mine cart. My mouth was sandpaper dry, probably from breathing hard, though at least it was still dark and cool. I was back on the second floor, no longer lost in the stars.

"That's odd." Solange's voice was tight. I swiveled to find her seated at a rough wood table, tweezers in one hand, a loupe in the other. She was frozen over a microscope, a bright lamp hanging from a ceiling rope and casting her honeyed skin lighter. The windows along the wall were muted, notable only against the inky blackness of the wall.

She still stared at me with dark, liquid eyes, though she'd changed into a pale strapless dress a shade lighter than her skin tone. Her feet were bare, toes peeking from beneath the silk folds, and her only adornment was still the gold earrings hanging like petite chandeliers, winking from her ears. She was also wearing a deep frown. "Diana was supposed to check for protective charms."

And she rose like she was going to battle.

I scrambled to my feet, suddenly not wanting to be anywhere near her.

"I have to go." I also had to pause to be sure my knees were steady before stepping over the cart's side. Then I had to pause to be sure they were *my* knees. My unreasonable, if instinctive, fear was suddenly eclipsed. "What the . . . why the hell am I wearing chaps?"

"Shit-hot leather chaps," Solange corrected, a smile broad in her voice. They were shit-hot. That and skin-tight, with studs securing them to my sides, and a woven belt with thick silver meshing that caught even the meager light. The mesh overlaid a batik-stamped pattern like a tiny chain-linked fence, and the result—though two-toned—was a complicated pattern that was both fierce and feminine.

It was echoed in the halter top.

I don't *do* halter tops, I thought, though my cold dismay melded into horror as my eyes turned to my jewelry. I'd been wearing none upon entering the Rest House, but now I looked like some sort of Bedouin experiment gone bad. It wasn't that the jewelry was ugly . . . there was just so much of it; armbands like thick silver snakes and wrists cuffed as if fettered with aged, thick silver and secured with a pin closure. I fingered heavy hoop earrings with a row of teardrops, and a choker that felt like a shackle. Rings studded every other finger in sharp points, more brass knuckles than ornamentation. I turned toward one of the windows to study my superimposed image . . . and found an entirely different person looking back at me.

My short black hair was slicked back and secured at the nape, with a single cornrow framing my face and threaded with silver. A rose the size of my palm was tucked behind my right ear, a bloodred punch against all the monochromatic costuming. It matched only my lips, currently drawn into a frown. The tar black shadow edging my eyes winged to my brow line.

Which also mirrored the black henna sunburst flaring from my now-pierced belly button. How long had I been out?

At least I still had my boots, I thought, sniffing. And the chaps were perfect for my knife harnesses. I caught myself halfway through this last thought and shook my head. A bell, apparently woven into my cornrow, jangled, further clearing my senses. "Where are my clothes?"

"By now? Probably incinerated. Don't look at me," Solange said when I spun back around. "Diana paid a visit while I was changing. There's your wallet, by the way. Tell me, how do you feel?"

Like an odalisque escapee from a goth harem, I thought, gingerly touching my belly ring. But I had a feeling she wasn't merely interested in my health. I was just happy she seemed to have calmed. Picking up my wallet, I returned it to my bag. Studying the rifled contents, I muttered, "They went through it."

"Of course. They knew you wouldn't just tell them who you are."

I flipped the bag over my shoulder and fumbled for the door at the sole blank wall, hands searching for the knob.

"Who armored you?"

I turned back. "What?"

She went from sitting at that table to standing in front of me, and I swore I hadn't blinked. "Who. Armored. You?"

"I don't know what—"

Something slapped me. But Solange never moved. "Who armored you?"

"Please," I said before I could help it . . .

"Who, who, who—"

She flanked my every side but I still hadn't seen her move. Then she was gone and I knew she was behind me. The scent of whipped rose wafted over my shoulder, and I stood so still I stopped breathing.

"Who the fuck is protecting your soul?"

Only my lips moved. "Y-You're like Boyd and Bill, aren't you? You work for the house?"

Suddenly in front of me again, she smiled, and it was beautiful. "More like Mackie."

Where, I thought, backing up, was the fucking door?

"Calm down. I'll let you leave." Solange took a small step toward me. "But when you find JJ, you're going to tell him Sola says hello. You're going to make sure that door remains unlocked." She licked her lips before smiling, and while alluring, there was also something feral in it. "And *when* you return, you'll bring him along so I can string both your souls in my sky."

Souls. That was why her gems were so beautiful. I thought of the men downstairs, ashy and drawn. The women, bright and alive. I shook my head even as the horror of that— all those colorful stones!—sunk in. "You can't force me to barter my soul."

"Of course not." She was suddenly back at her desk, loupe in hand, hair swinging over her face as she studied a bloodred gem. After what she'd just done, the distance didn't make me feel any safer. "Besides, you've already given up a third of it up for free."

I frowned, swallowing hard. She had no reason to lie, but I didn't know what she meant.

To clarify, she held up the precious gem between her tweezers and smiled. "Yours is the second lantern on the right."

Your full identity isn't revealed until you enter three times.

Giving someone your name gave her control over your soul.

And kill the rushlight in two tries . . .

That was what had been stripped from my body upon my passage here. I hadn't just given up air in blowing out that candle . . . I'd given up a third of my soul. But how on earth had Solange gotten hold of it?

I didn't know, but suddenly she didn't look so beautiful. She was a spider, weaving a web of stolen gems, and I was being spun into its design. But I didn't fight her. I didn't know how. And I'd need all the energy I had left to me once I hit the staircase outside this door.

Women fight differently . . . in any world.

Oh Tekla, I thought, backing from the room. If only you knew.

12

Heat assailed me even before I hit the landing. Everything, I suddenly realized as I resettled my bag behind my back, from wacky Mackie at the piano to the potent drinks the bartender served, was meant to reinforce this world and keep it fueled. As for the men used as that fuel? Well, let's just say I had a change of heart regarding their POW status when I reached the top of the landing to find every chair pushed back, every man standing, and every hard gaze turned my way.

Well, almost every man was standing.

Tripp remained seated, either unable to move due to the heat or merely unwilling to waste his energy on me. But from the way he watched me, his amusement honed, I could tell he was thinking wistfully of a world where Shadow and Light were all that mattered. Here he was content to let everyone else do the work for him.

And why wouldn't they try to stop me? I thought, swallowing hard. By leaving now, and possessing nearly everything I'd entered with, I was robbing the men of the opportunity to skin my powers from me, and the women from using my soul to reinforce their pretty realities.

I returned my attention to the crowd, knowing I couldn't

take them all on. The players didn't scare me. Each had been here far longer than I had, and I knew the extent of the lethargy one suffered under the influence of that drink. I'd be past them and at my lantern before any could shuffle from their seats.

Bill was more of a concern. He kept casting glances up at me, showing unnatural consideration as he ran his rag over the bar in small controlled circles. Moving normally, he could be over that bar top in one solid leap. Question was, how far could I get before he reached me?

Not far enough, I decided, especially if the dealers were in on the action. Though still seated, they too were operating on full cylinders. What bothered me were the things I *didn't* know about them. Did they have weapons? What would they do if they caught me? How soon would they rise from their seats?

I took the stairs slowly, ring-studded fingers and black lacquered nails trailing over mysterious symbols carved into the banister, and by the time I hit the bottom stair my thirst was back in full force, like moisture was being wicked from my body from the inside out. The dry heat pulsed against me, and I knew standing and fighting would deplete all my energy reserves. Working together, these men would easily wear me down, and even if all they did was deliver me back upstairs, I wouldn't be in any state to resist. I'd drink whatever those women put to my lips, fall asleep in the sky, and awake to someone studying my pretty soul.

So, bag on my back, I ran.

Closest to me, fittest, Bill moved first. I turned away from the rest of the room to focus on him. I felt the men moving behind me, but they were still like ants in molasses, so I was free to concentrate on the bartender. He was taller than me, wider too, with the extra mass and density afforded his sex. Everyone here was or had been agents raised and trained in battle, but it'd been a while since any of them had bothered to use their skills. Surprise rippled over his smooth features when I squared on him.

I shook my head. Pretty boys. Thought they could do whatever they wanted.

"Sit down, honey," he said, circling like a hawk on prey. "Have a drink on the house."

"The last man who called me honey," I said, circling back, "spent the rest of his very short life sitting down."

He remained cautious, knowing I had skills. Yet I doubted he'd ever encountered a woman exactly like me before; one who'd been born to mortality, never relying upon strength beyond what she'd built up herself. And what I'd built was a quick mind and a mean jab. Just because this was the house where "deeds reflected our true selves" didn't mean our actions couldn't lie. I drew him into a boxing stance by setting up my own, anticipated the one-two combination that was automatic in most fighters, and timed my double jab to rock his head straight back on his neck. I finished it with my own cross, and his eyes rolled back, much like Boyd's had when calling Solange, before he hit the floor.

I smiled. If I didn't know how good I was, I would have said he hadn't even tried.

A tinkle of laughter had accompanied Bill's fall, and I glanced up to find the women gathered again on the landing, though Solange was notably absent. Her mention of the second lantern on the right was what pulled my gaze from the light and life and color above, and I turned . . .

Just in time to dodge Boyd's cruel uppercut.

Dodge it, but not avoid it completely. He too knew what he was doing, and grazed my kidney, the impact stealing breath I could ill afford to lose. The bell and bloodred rose in my hair fell to the ground. I coughed, a rasp that kept building, and almost got hit again because of it. Wheeling away, I instinctively backed toward the bar because that's where all the liquid was. My throat was parched. It was like suffocating, but through lack of moisture instead of air. I squinted, noting with a mounting panic that my lids were beginning to stick to my eyeballs. If I didn't leave soon, I'd dehydrate where I stood.

"Boyd," I rasped, bracing myself against the bar, my tongue fat in my mouth. "I didn't like you before, but now you've pissed me off." The words stuck to the insides of my cheeks, one syllable hiccuping into the next, but he caught my meaning okay. Maybe it was the accompanying straight kick into his gut.

He managed to grab my foot as he toppled forward, but I closed the space between us, balancing my weight on his shoulders as my kneecap collided with his nose. From there, I just hammered the back of his neck until Boyd joined Bill in la-la-land.

Above me, Diana laughed. She'd changed into pink tulle and fishnets, but was still channeling a music hall version of Raj Barbie, looking like a neon ornament in the muted branching of the stark hallway. "Two down, Olivia. Only five more to go."

I whirled to find the remaining half-dozen dealers lined up, single file, the ones near the front popping their knuckles and rolling their necks. They knew what I could do now, so I'd lost the element of surprise. However, the dealers near the back looked bored, the final one even glancing at his table to making sure his pot was safe while he stepped away. Meanwhile the players—men who'd once been both agents of Light and Shadow—had shuffled to the wall of lanterns, four and five bodies deep, a wall of flesh and muscle to overcome on my way home.

Okay, I thought, first things first. I returned my attention to the men who worked for the house.

The last dealer was right to be unconcerned, of course. Even fresh, it would have been a challenge, but as it was, I'd expire from dehydration and exhaustion long before reaching him. So I held up my hands in surrender. The first dealer, severely pock-faced with odd silvery eyes, shot a smile at the guy behind him, and I hit the floor, yanking the lighter from Boyd's shirt pocket. Then I grabbed

Bill's ever-brimming liquor bottle and prayed the liquid
that extinguished the will to fight would ignite like gas in
the pretty green bottle.

It flared like a torch gun, and for the briefest of moments
I considered throwing it in the direction of the beautiful,
carefree laughter still raining from above, but the dealers
were closer, faster, and rightly alarmed. I hurtled it forward, my body swinging with the movement.

I am a great fighter, but my pitching arm has always
been shit, and the improvised bomb landed to the right of
where I'd intended, directly between the lined dealers and
huddled players . . . and atop one of the poker tables.

Felt and cards went up in a searing conflagration, the
dry air hungry for fuel. Fire uncoiled across the table like
a whip, and within seconds a handful of men guarding the
wall started screaming, breaking rank in the tight forma-
tion. For once they moved at a normal speed, yanking at
their clothes, clenching their throats, and scraping at their
chest and necks.

Every eye gaped at that table and at the flaming little
disks sparking with color, tiny tabletop fireworks of vibrant
blues and yellows, greens, golds, and violet. Those men's
powers popped and sizzled like Roman candles and stunted
sparklers, but the air wasn't scented with sulfur or barium
or black powder. Even the dealers leaned toward the in-
ferno, inhaling deeply of toasted cinnamon and warmed
coconut. The women upstairs started crying out, some
weeping, some running their hands along their bodies in
pleasure as power floated up to them.

As horrified as I was by what I'd inadvertently done, I
couldn't help inhaling the tiny bits of lost power wafting my
way. They whetted my tongue, revived my energy, but also
stirred the unconscious men at my feet. Before they could
rise, or the dealers stopped getting off on someone else's
destroyed power, I sprang toward the wall of men, focusing
on the holes left by those I'd inadvertently attacked.

I plowed through the remaining agents like they were

bowling pins. Indeed, pushing them aside wasn't much different than a gym workout; they did nothing to resist me, because they couldn't. Their sole purpose was to form a wall of flesh, and my job was to dismantle it . . . body by body.

I took the most direct approach, because even with the added distraction of the flaming chips, my limbs were growing heavy and weak. I wanted to drop to my knees, put my cheek to the splintered floor and cry. But I was almost there. One last big bastard to plow through, a sandy-haired man with empty button eyes and outstretched hands, and then I could yank the cover off that second lantern and go home.

The thought spurred my strength. I barreled into him and delivered an elbow that caught him in the larynx, a little extreme, but I'd feel guilty over it later. Hell, I'd go to confession if it meant returning to a patriarchal society.

Not everybody felt the same. At the end of the line, while the dealers were still leaning over the burning poker table like kids beneath a broken piñata, and the rogue agents littered the floor like discarded toy soldiers, there was one man left standing. He had a dusty bowler hat on his head and a knife in his hand.

It was Mackie, the piano player. He stood erect, like he'd been pulled straight by levers and strings. Twisting the knife like a butcher would, I saw that he moved as quickly as I did, but my attention was on his face as he lifted his chin, his leather skin rearranging itself over his frame. Creepy when still, he was terrifying when animate. His eyes were missing altogether, black sockets empty as craters. His teeth were rotted away, mouth caught in an eternal grimace.

"Sleepy Mack," I said slowly, licking my lips as I kept an eye on that deadly blade. The only indication he heard me was a wide-lipped snarl. *Great*. I took a step back. "That chip thing was an accident. I wasn't really aiming for the table."

Obviously a man who cared about results, not intentions, his arm arced through the air in a full-forced swing. Training took over as I stood beneath that falling blade, and I defended and countered at the same time. I thrust my left arm up to connect with his wrist, shifting my weight with it despite my instinct to recoil. At the same time, I burst forward, delivering a straight punch to his jaw, which I envisioned disappearing through the back of his head.

The blade allegedly holding the last of Mackie's soul flew from his hands. There was a collective gasp, and the look on his face was more like I'd severed a limb than disarmed a weapon. I kept moving forward, knowing but ignoring that he'd nicked my left forearm, and attacked with everything I had left. My goal was to imprint his final expression of bereft surprise upon my knuckles.

The next few seconds were so fast I'd remember them forever. Mackie was stronger than the others, as dense and tough as jerky, almost petrified from living so long in a room that was also a kiln. No wonder he had no conscience. His brain was probably as rotted as the meat of a walnut. So I was guilt-free as I hit him again on the button. As good a shot as it was, it only popped his head straight back. He was reaching for me even as it snapped forward again.

And now the fucker was starting to growl, a high-pitched whining that intensified as he returned to offense. I sprang, my knee exploding into his temple, into his ribs so he'd buckle, again and again, and still he didn't go down. I kept pummeling him, but it wasn't until I picked up his piano stool and whipped it across his face that he fell to the ground and stayed there.

Mackie was down. Bill was up. And Boyd was charging.

But it was too late. I still had breath in my body, and with two steps and an overhead stretch, I also had the lantern off its hook and in my hand. A stunned cry drowned out even the rushing feet, and as my gaze met Diana's shocked one above, I took an extra moment to smile and blow her a kiss.

In doing so, I extinguished the flame.

Smoke carried me. I was familiar with the sensation now, the weightlessness accompanying the obscured sight, the gritty vapor so paralyzing it was almost heavy. The cries and yells and voices I left behind blurred like streaming colors outside a speeding vehicle, and after I'd outrun them, there was a moment of supreme silence in which I was flipped vertically and diagonally and horizontally all at the same time. It was a whipping motion, strange because I never even moved, but this, I now understood, was a worlds-crossing. There both was and wasn't ground beneath my feet, and though breathing, I hadn't taken in air since extinguishing that lantern. And while nothing and everything changed, I had enough consciousness to recognize the shift when it occurred, like tectonic plates were grinding against one another. The sound made my teeth ache at their roots, though I eventually realized I was grating my lower jaw against the upper. I stopped, the aching ceased, and the smoke gradually cleared.

Don't fight it, I thought, taking my first real breath of cool winter air. Yet that was like telling a driver not to tense before a car accident. My knee-jerk reaction was to try to control the situation, but it was release that I needed. Remember, I told myself, in a head-on collision it was the careless ones, those already out of control, who came out fine.

Then a sphere began to take shape in front of me. It grew larger, flipping over itself and expanding to the size of my head, doubling again on the next rotation to become a large mirror.

Catching my reflection, it froze. Cleopatra eyes, ruby lips, leather halter, cuffs and hoops, winking silver. I had a single moment to take it all in.

Then the mirror began ripping away the powers I'd lost in a game of chance.

I'd once been cold-cocked in a sparring match with a guy who didn't take well to being beaten by a girl. It had been a controlled situation—in a dojo, on a mat—but none of that meant a thing once the blow met my jaw. Tingling launched through my limbs to pool in my fingertips, while my eyes rolled into my head. Numbness had me crumpling like a wad of paper instead of catching myself, and I felt that now, except it was concentrated on the inside of my skull, shot like novocaine upward through my spinal cord.

My eyes remained unblinking upon the reflection that locked me immobile against my wishes. My scream was silent, rebounding off the vacated places in my mind where three powers were methodically ripped away. I tried to protest, but my mouth wouldn't move. The mirrored eyes shot to silver and then black, like they were catching light from a dark sun. Numbness ran through my mind like maggots over meat. Bitterness drained down my throat as infection was introduced, then cauterized.

And for one last, brief moment my bartered power was reflected back at me, beauty being torn away like pages from a book. And without them, I suddenly realized, the rest of the story wouldn't make sense.

You can't have it! I thought, staring back into eyes that were and were not mine. But those black eyes only winked to silver.

You have to leave me something.

The silver began to fade.

No, I thought. I'll keep it for myself.

I fought then. I didn't need to move to will every nerve and neuron into fighting for the information. *Don't you know who I am, what I've done? I'm the Kairos, I've survived attack before, I've adapted to other bodies and worlds. I've always fought for what's mine. And . . .*

And I didn't know who I was without my power. I didn't

want to be incomplete. I wanted to run with my troop, battle the Shadows and defeat the Tulpa. I needed these powers because they were the foundation for so much more! Returning home without them would be like standing on pockets of air. Without them, I'd be less than Kimber, or even Chandra—relegated to an auxiliary role. If Warren even allowed that, I thought, panicked. I wouldn't be permitted, or even able, to fight. Not for myself, and not for people as injured as I'd once been.

And who was I, if I wasn't a fighter?

So I used all my strength of will to mentally hold onto the powers that had been taken from me. Suddenly I knew these losses would shape my future happiness more than any other.

No, I stated again, still holding tight.

And I continued to hold tight until their last precious tendrils slipped away.

My reflection winked. The mirror began spiraling back into the mist, shrinking in size as it went, until it was no larger than a mere gaming chip. I blinked and it snapped from sight, and I was again alone in the dark.

13

Taking a shaky step forward to be sure my legs were working properly, I realized too late that I was back where I'd started before entering Midheaven. The candle was burning again, but behind me, so it didn't light the gaping hole directly before me . . . one that I dropped through with an amazing lack of grace.

My left ankle twisted over on itself as I dropped, but the short fall—and my pained grunt—was quickly followed by a joyous squeal. *I'd escaped!* Olivia's curves now burst from the halter and chaps that had been merely snug on my athletic frame, another physical sign my return to Vegas had been successful. Checking for injury, I was dismayed to find a small new scar on my left forearm from Mackie's knife, and though healed over, the fact that it'd scarred at all told me that blade was the equivalent of a conduit. I'd been lucky not to suffer a direct hit. Of course, there was also . . .

"The friggin' belly ring," I muttered, touching the stupid thing, voice resonating softly through the tunnel.

A surprised grunt echoed back at me. I froze. There was a charred growl, like something awakened from slumber, and a heavy exhalation . . . and a scent I immediately recognized over the stink of the tunnel. I froze like a doe, but instead of headlights, found myself staring down the concrete corridor of inked-out darkness. The serpentine tunnel system, so spacious moments ago, shrunk in on itself. It was only perception, not an adjustment of time or space the way the passage to Midheaven had been, but I suddenly felt small, and all too vulnerable. I even thought of vaulting back up into that vertical shaft, grabbing that candle by the base and giving it another good puff.

After all, I thought, what was worse? A fight against the Tulpa or a return to Mackie and his soul-infused knife? A gamble with my life or with my soul?

Damned. Hard. Call.

And in a few more moments, I thought as the scuffling sounds drew nearer, the decision wouldn't be mine to make.

"Who's there?" The breath was gurgled, labored and pained.

My glyph began to pulse with heat, and the *drip-drip* of the drain's befouled water joined it in syncopation, as if marking off seconds of my life.

"Come out, come out, wherever you are."

Instinct screamed to retreat, but I forced myself to inch forward instead. It was the first rule of combat, one my trainer, Asaf, had drilled into me. Always move forward. Through. Advance. Attack. It lent physical momentum, mental courage, and took your opponent off guard. Unless, I thought swallowing hard, your opponent was never off guard. In that case, the rule meant advance, attack, and if you were going to die, do it on your feet.

I could see, via my glyph, another three hundred feet of drain before it trended right. The shuffling sounds had ceased, which gave me hope as I inched past a lateral pipe, the source of that sulfuric dripping. That's when I spotted rungs. I tested them, looking straight up into a concave hollow. If I hid there, the Tulpa might pass right beneath me. Then my path to Vegas would be open, and I'd be free. It was preferable to the head-on collision I was currently facing, Asaf's instructions be damned. So I climbed. Once there, I used shaking hands to yank on my identity-shielding mask, then wrapped my shoulder bag around the highest rung. The chips inside clinked softly, like tiny cymbals.

I sank into the concrete pocket and widened my stance. Though tight, my costuming allowed for movement as I stretched for the other side of the drop inlet. Rock climbers stemmed from improbable places all the time; all I had to do was calm myself enough that I didn't fall on the Tulpa as he passed beneath me.

That could give me away, I thought, and extinguished my glyph.

Even in the void, I knew when he'd gained the corner. The air was instantly harder to breathe, infused with a carbon burn and a soured hook. Stinging at my tear ducts through my mask, at my mouth, even my ears, it was as if a poisonous cloud wafted from the man, infecting and defiling anything within range. The darkness, nuanced before, was now absolute in its opaqueness. I couldn't see the titan he became when no one was looking, or his sheer bulk, but I felt it. It was like an airplane slipping into a private hangar. Too late, I wondered if the tunnel was large enough for both of us, or if I'd soon feel the osseous scrape of horns across my naked belly.

I pushed the thought from my mind before it bloomed into emotion.

"Show yourself now . . . or I might just get angry." Heat accompanied the warning, one that burned rather than warmed.

I considered revealing myself—I'd fought toe-to-claw with him before—and I itched with the need for action. I opened my mouth, but another voice startled us both.

"I'm over here." An audible swallow. "Sir."

A swishing, the Tulpa's tail whipping around in the dark, and then, "You . . . "

"I didn't think you'd want to see me. I thought you'd want to repair . . . alone." The words ran together in a half-swallowed hiss, even without the sibilant sounds. *Oh, shit.*

"Regan."

The source of her speech impediment? Fractured vocal cords and a sliced tongue, courtesy of the Tulpa. Those things, combined with her banishment and what amounted to a paranormal fatwa on her head, were supposed to keep this situation—her talking to him now—from ever happening.

"Sir. I don't mean to intrude. I'll wait. Until you're more fully recovered."

A growl. "I'm not—"

"It's okay." There was a slap and slide as she stepped closer, and the briny scent of her nervousness covered my own growing panic. "You need to regenerate. It was a hell of a battle."

"The biggest yet." I'd never heard the Tulpa sound fatigued. And I didn't understand what they were talking about. The last battle between the Tulpa and Skamar had left razored clouds in the sky, but that wasn't unusual. Not anymore, anyway.

"Your senses are blunted . . . otherwise you'd have discerned me before. I've been down here since my . . . banishment."

Of course.

It made perfect sense. Regan hadn't been seen since her exile, and as she'd disappeared with my conduit, I'd looked. The general stench and decay of things washed into the tunnels would help cover Regan's stench, if anyone bothered coming in this far, which made it the perfect place for her to hide . . . though it couldn't be doing much for her open wounds. I was so busy thinking of her languishing for weeks in the fetid underground that it was another moment before I realized the Tulpa hadn't contradicted her about what *he* was doing here.

Oh, my God. He came here to reform, to regenerate.

And that made sense too. Skamar had taken on her own identity and features when given a name. But the Tulpa lacked a name and thus that power, so his features regularly shifted, mutated, wobbled on his face. It had always appeared to be a strength. He could evade reach, elongate his limbs, disappear altogether . . . but that took power. Which, right now, he apparently didn't have.

But he also hadn't slain Regan on the spot, as he'd promised he would if he ever saw her again. Panic joined the awe that'd wedged its way into my belly. The two beings that hated me most were blocking my exit. I had no doubt that together they could cobble together a very creative lesson in payback. I strengthened my hold.

"You're still alive. Despite my punishment. Despite the pain." He hadn't thought she would be. Being flayed was a hard way to die, but an even harder way to live.

"I'm . . . brave."

It was obvious even the words pained her.

"Come here."

Yeah, do that, Regan. Because brave and stupid are exactly the same thing.

Apparently Regan was of the same mind, because there was no answer or movement. It would take a good deal of energy, which the Tulpa was clearly trying to amass, to reach out and touch her by magical means. But to step within reach? Even a glancing swipe of those claws could cleave her in half.

"You betrayed my trust, brought the third sign of the Zodiac to life, and now you're going to cower in the dark like you even have a right to be standing there? Come here," he repeated, and there was nothing tired in the command, "Or I'll come and get you."

An immediate scuffling followed. "I want only to serve."

A little late for that, I thought . . . which is what the Tulpa said. "But I suppose banishment has given you a change of heart."

No, her heart had changed the moment his index finger plowed through it.

I kept my grip strong.

Knowing the Tulpa demanded absolute loyalty from his troop, and that she'd failed him, Regan didn't defend herself. She switched subjects. "I have a gift."

Something metal and weighty scraped across the concrete floor, followed by a sharp click as it came to rest against what was probably a honed talon.

"As you're the Shadow Archer, this should be just as powerful in your hands."

And *now* I was trapped in a hole with my two greatest enemies and the one weapon that could totally obliterate my existence. I teetered, my knees and elbows wanting to buckle.

"This *is* handy," he said, nails clacking against my conduit. I grimaced, swallowing hard as he pulled back on the crossbow. It felt like he was pawing one of my internal organs.

"I've also been following your daughter, gathering intel on her haunts and friends, her habits. May I share them?"

She waited, and so did I, heart slamming, a lump closing my throat. The news that she'd been following me was a surprise, but it was a concern I shunted aside for later. Because consent *now* would mean forgiveness, and would make Regan dangerous again. The Tulpa took a long time before delivering his verdict.

"Speak."

I closed my eyes and fought not to sag. And Regan began telling him about the real me, the one the rest of the world thought dead, the one he knew was alive . . . but not how or where.

"She's a woman of surprising regularity, coming and going from her residence like clockwork. Admittedly one with a skewed sense of time, but regular for someone who abides by the rules of two realities."

"Where is it?"

"The Greenspun Residences. Do you know it?"

Of course he did. His main mortal ally's daughter, Olivia Archer, lived in the same building. Crafty, I thought. Regan both was and was not telling him my identity. Her ass was in tatters and yet she was still covering it.

"You think she'd know better," Regan was saying, "but hubris is her greatest fault."

The Tulpa let the useless remark pass. "What else?"

The effort to speak was paining her, and as Regan swallowed, I imagined congealing blood clots sliding down her tattered throat. She might be substantially more helpless than she'd been as a Shadow agent, but her determination was still terrifying. "She visits Master Comics with shocking regularity."

"As you said. Hubris." His voice was noncommittal, but that he was allowing her to continue spoke volumes.

"She's no longer in contact with her mortal boyfriend, and as far as I can tell, cares nothing for him. He has no memory of their relationship beyond their dalliance as teens."

The romance between Ben Traina and me had popped up in the Shadow manuals over the last few weeks, now that the information couldn't be used against me. Still, I tensed.

"Rewiring," the Tulpa said.

"Complete."

I couldn't afford a sigh of relief, but the confirmation that Ben had been eliminated from the Tulpa's mental radar was nice. A month ago he might have still gone after him. These days he had bigger fish to fry.

"She's in constant search for a way to heal the changeling of Light—"

"That is not news." He said it like she was wasting his time.

"And she has a daughter."

A gasp escaped me before I could stop it. Particularly loud in the wake of the Tulpa's shocked silence, it was no surprise that the next sound was again talons scrambling against concrete. I envisioned his tail jerking from that barbed spine as the growl slipped from his throat. His eyes pulsed in a red strobe, expending some of that precious energy to light the tunnel before him. I held as still as a corpse . . . exactly what I'd be if either of them saw me hanging there like a big blond bat. My eyes were closed—I couldn't risk them reflecting that red—but through the thin lids I made out his methodical scan, like a tiny searchlight slipping along the slick walls. It paused on algae and graffiti, caught light from water crystals hanging like stalactites from the ceiling, but I remained tucked into that inverted basin, silently praying nothing of my clothing or self hung tellingly from above.

"It was probably just a rat. They're as large as cats down here."

"And if it wasn't?" A step forward. I swallowed hard.

"I've been in this tunnel almost a week. I'd have heard anyone entering or exiting."

Or not, I thought with smug relief as the Tulpa's attention returned to her. Perhaps Regan had mistaken me for a very large rat that morning.

The light relented. "So where is this daughter of my daughter's?"

"I don't know," Regan admitted, "but her name is Ashlyn."

"Surname?"

"Still working on that, sir."

I did sag then. I couldn't help it. This was salvageable. Warren and Micah could amend Ashlyn's birth records. They could convince her adoptive parents to move, as they'd done once before. Of course, that was when Warren had believed she was only a mortal infant targeted by the Shadow side.

I'd have to tell him, I realized. That she was my daughter. A future Archer. And Warren—a man who'd told me to venture into a soul- and power-stealing world in search of a

Shadow who was really Light—would take Ashlyn, almost ten and completely oblivious of her paranormal future, away from everything she'd ever known.

"And Joanna's new identity?" His voice was deadly soft now, like snow falling. "Who is she now, while freely roaming my city?"

Regan hesitated. "Allow me to return to the Shadow troop, and I'll tell you."

A soft sulfuric sigh. "Your sign has already been filled by a new Leo."

"Kill him," she replied without hesitation. No, destroyed body or not, Regan hadn't changed at all.

"Tell me Joanna's cover identity," the Tulpa countered.

"No."

Smoke—instant, hot and venomous—roiled in the tunnel. I fought not to cough. Fortunately, Regan's pained hacking covered my own small sounds. The toxic smoke had to burn against those raw, festering wounds. Had it been anyone else, I'd have felt sorry for them.

"You insufferable little—"

"Kill me now," she coughed, "and you'll never know."

Silence. A moment where his emotions could have tipped either way. "Clever, Regan."

"You've no use for anyone who is not." Relief oozed around the sibilant hiss of her shredded tongue. She sounded, I thought, like a different species altogether.

"True. But if this information isn't entirely correct, I'll make sure the rest of your days are spent as nothing more than a beating heart encased in bone."

"But if any small bit leads to her capture," she negotiated, "from her residence to her associates, then I'll be allowed to return. And repair."

A moment's hesitation, coupled with a considering breath. "I can do that."

I closed my eyes, head drooping.

"Additionally, I promise this: I'll deliver her to you alive."

"How?" The noxious scent had receded, like the Tulpa had pulled it back into his pores, but a puff of it returned in that one disbelieving word. "You can't go out in public. Even at night she'll scent you out."

A shrug seeped into her voice. "Except I have a new friend."

"A goat?" the Tulpa asked, referring derisively to our mortal helpers. "Another changeling?"

"Better. An agent of Light."

The Tulpa sucked in a surprised breath. And I couldn't breathe at all.

"Do we have a deal?"

There was no hesitation now, just another sharp scraping along the floor. "Take back her conduit. Use it as bait and leverage in leading her to me. She's desperate for it."

"Unfortunately for you both," said another, new flowing voice, an unexpected bloom. "It has absolutely no effect on me."

Skamar charged. Wind lit through the tunnel like a match thrown on gasoline. The two tulpas careened past me, clawing and snarling as they rolled over one another before slamming into the dead end. The impact shook the entire pipeline, and dislodged me from my hidey-hole. My feet swung down, one hand slipping from its rung.

Spotting the movement, Regan gasped.

"Oops." My glyph burst to life.

She fired.

Too late to drop, I swung. The bolt clipped my chaps and pinned my left leg to the wall.

"No!" Skamar barreled into Regan so quickly the Shadow ricocheted off her, bounced against a wall and fell still.

I whipped my head the other way. The Tulpa's eyes, literally, lit on me.

"Got him!" Skamar pinballed back the other way. "Go!"

As the tulpas again collided, I yanked the bolt from

where it was embedded in the wall and dropped to a crouch on the fetid floor. Ahead of me, Regan was rising. Flipping the crossbow bolt in my hand, I wound up like hometown hero Greg Maddox and let it fly.

My pitching arm was no better over here than it'd been in the Rest House. I didn't hit Regan's torso . . . but I did nick her arm, and she screamed as her flesh endured yet more injury. Then she ran.

"I like these odds better." And leaving my bag tied to the rungs, and the tulpas battling like rabid wolves behind me, I gave chase.

14

Though I could no longer see Regan, I tracked her scent easily. It wound through the pipeline like a rancid ribbon, her fear and pain so heightened there might as well have been a bloody arrow pointing in her direction. Sure, she had my crossbow, but I'd appeared out of nowhere, and she couldn't be sure I was alone.

Her instinct to play it safe married well with my pent-up need to hunt.

One last slithering corner and the tunnel's mouth came into view. I burst into a full sprint because I knew that once outside, Regan's scent would scatter. If she moved fast enough, she could disappear in the shifting wind. I slowed into a quick sidestep as I neared the entrance, but still managed to barrel square into the figure who pivoted into my path, like a shadow eclipsing the sun.

I immediately began swinging. Strong arms absorbed, deflected, and eventually held mine. "God! You're here!"

I looked up. "Hunter?"

His eyes searched mine wildly. "Geez, are you okay?"

"Move." I pushed him aside, sniffing as I risked a peek from the tunnel. Though still dark, the sky was a night-light compared to the pitch of the pipeline behind me. "Which way did she go?"

"Who? What?"

"Regan! She was here—can't you smell her?"

"I smell tunnel water and blood, and most of it's coming off you. Uh, why are you dressed like that?"

I reeled, and almost pushed him out of frustration. "She came out this way!"

He held up a hand, shaking his head. "Jo, I've been standing watch all night. We've been scouring the pipeline ever since Warren told us he thought you'd gone into Midheaven. No one even came near this entrance."

"But the Tulpa—"

The Tulpa rocketed into the sky in a wheeling screech of power that had me cringing even from a distance. His ascent was followed by a comet, Skamar, burning a bright rainbow on the night sky.

I sighed and let my body sag. "The Tulpa was down there."

And Regan had been as well. I tried not to sulk over the lost opportunity. Maybe this had flushed her from the pipeline. She'd be easier to find out in the open.

"Holy hell." Hunter was still watching the rupturing sky, the tulpas in the distance now, cutting a path like a black rainbow. "Are you okay?"

"Yeah, he didn't see me until it was too late. I had my mask on the whole time."

I removed it now and ran a hand over my damp forehead. Hunter ordered me to wait while he looked around, though I could tell he still didn't believe me about Regan.

This was a different drain than the one I'd entered, I saw, and I took in a deep breath along with the view of an abandoned cardboard shelter, blissing out as an icy breeze caressed my chapped skin. It was colder than when I'd breached Midheaven, like the temperature had dropped twenty degrees in the hours I'd been gone—though it was probably only in contrast to the relentless heat of that other world.

"Like returning from a trip to the moon," I murmured, letting my eyes fall shut. I was happy I'd returned at all.

"Nothing," Hunter said, dropping into the tunnel from the ledge above. I wasn't surprised. Regan had probably already planned for this eventuality.

"She's been following me," I murmured, knowing he could hear, though my head was bowed. "She knows about my daughter. She told the Tulpa about Ashlyn."

Shock kept him silent for long seconds, and I kept my face hidden. I didn't want to see the disbelief and blame in that gaze. "But you haven't gone near Ashlyn . . . have you?"

I shook my head before daring a glance up. "Someone's been helping Regan. She says it's an agent of Light."

He stared for a long moment to see if I was serious. Then he pulled out his cell phone. "We have to tell Warren."

"Wait."

His eyes flicked to me under brows that furrowed, but he punched his speed dial and put the phone to his ear. I spoke faster, knowing Warren would come on the line soon.

"Hunter, no. Please. He knows things." *He knew what that place would take from me and let me go anyway.* "He's kept secrets from us . . . Jaden Jacks, he was Light."

I could tell the second Warren came on the line. Hunter stiffened, wide eyes searching my face. "I have her."

Knowing Warren would hear if I even made a sound, I pleaded with my expression alone. Hunter threw up a hand. He didn't know what to do.

"Yes," he said, to Warren's inquiry. I held my breath. "Yes. At dawn."

He put his phone away without saying good-bye . . . or anything about Regan's alleged ally. "Your explanation had better be damned good."

I slumped, grateful for the reprieve. I needed time to reorder my thoughts, not just soak in everything that'd happened to me in Midheaven, but what I'd learned of Warren, of Regan . . . and to figure out what do to now that the Tulpa knew of Ashlyn too.

Oh my God. The Tulpa knew about Ashlyn.

"What the hell happened to you over there?" Hunter meant Midheaven but he gestured at me like I was in a full body cast. I glanced down at the halter, the bangles and armbands, the rings like industrial screws, the chaps now overtight at my hips, then flattened him with my own hard look.

"You can't possibly think this was my idea."

"I'm not talking about that. You're bleeding."

"No, it's . . . " Regan's, I was going to say as he lifted my hands. My palms were only lightly scraped, but it was easy to scent the blood with our magnified senses. The larger injury was where the cross bolt had grazed my thigh. If not for the leather chaps, I'd certainly have noted it sooner.

But I shouldn't be noting my palms at all.

"Midheaven," I lied breathlessly. I couldn't say why, but I didn't want him to know that I'd gotten these injuries after I'd returned. My shocked suspicion about what they were, and why, was unwanted, even now while it was still forming. "Um . . . you heal like a mortal if you're injured over there."

Hunter's fingers slid gently but firmly up my arm. "And this one?"

The scar from Mackie's knife. Leave it to Hunter to catch everything. "I got it first. So, it's healing first."

"That makes sense." His baffled expression cleared and he nodded. "Even mortals begin healing in a week."

An involuntary shudder racketed my spine. "Sorry?"

Hunter's eyes swirled with the same dark confusion, and even when they cleared I felt lost in their pooling depths. I staggered. His firm touch grew supporting. "Whoa there. Easy."

A week? As in seven whole *days*?

"What day is it?" I managed.

"Thursday," he said haltingly. "The twelfth."

The words swirled, making me dizzy, causing my knees to buckle for the second time that night. I'd left on the third. *Over* a week ago. Well, at least that explained why Regan hadn't seen me enter the pipeline when she claimed to have been there for days.

Dazed, I pushed past Hunter, fully exiting the tunnel this time to study the landscape. Sunk between two concrete slopes, there wasn't much to see, but the tunnel water was frozen in slick and shallow rivers, brackish weeds trapped between crevasses crunchy with ice. That never happened in early November. Not in Vegas.

Hunter had joined me, again with a supporting hand on my arm, but I jerked away and looked straight up . . . into a blistered sky. "What *happened*?"

He tore his gaze from me long enough to join me studying the sky. A liquid cobalt haze, threaded through with a shock of violent green, had replaced the pewter gray that had been swirling when I left. Lightning flashed behind bulging clouds, infusing the vivid colors with a solid core of pure electricity. It would have been pretty if it hadn't looked like it was going to fall down around the city's shoulders.

"It's the result of the tulpas' battles," Hunter explained. "All their expended energy is being released over the city, but as long as neither side wins, it has no place to go. It can't hold for much longer."

An electrical storm created directly above the most powerfully lit city on the planet. The atmosphere burning so violently it couldn't help but cave in. Great.

"Jo?" He edged in to block my view of the sky. "Midheaven?"

"Yeah, okay." I blew out a breath. Focusing on the facts would give me a mental foothold. I'd just have to come to terms with losing a week of my life step by step. "Ruled by women. Crazy ones." I gestured at my body again, and blew at a strand of hair escaped from ribbon and braid.

"I don't know. They seem all right to me."

I smirked, but the humor settled me. I remembered everything; the pain of the passage over there, the daguerreotype and the wall of Most Wanted posters, the poker game and what it cost. Thirst and heat, and how they were used against you. The women drawn in watercolor, the men in charcoal. Yet when I opened my mouth, every one of those images snaked away. It was irritating how tangible everything was until I tried to voice it. As soon as I tried to speak, something would shift inside, and the words would slide away.

I shrugged, and shook my head. "It won't let me."

"What?"

I threw up my hands. "I mean, I remember everything, but I can't tell you about it. Silence like that has to be some sort of . . . I don't know, fail-safe." And I wondered if Warren knew that too. Still, I'd been able to mention what I learned about Jacks to Hunter. I looked at him and pursed my lips.

"Jaden Jacks. Solange. Harlan Tripp."

"What?"

I nodded to myself. So I couldn't speak of what happened over there, but I could talk about the people there. Those were the only ones, though. Shen was only a wisp of a memory, Boyd was a lump in my throat. Mackie disappeared the fastest. "Wow, okay. So only people who came from this world."

Hunter gave me the appropriate look for someone who'd taken to conversing with herself, and again took me by the arm. "Let's go. You can try to recall more when we're somewhere safe."

I glanced up at the sky, fought the impulse to duck, and wondered exactly where that would be. Because I'd returned to a scarred world, an embattled troop, and a leader who—if my intuition was right—was turning out to be as ruthless as the enemies we fought.

Worst of all, I had an unwanted suspicion about what

gaming chip Shen had stolen from my pile. Shaking my head, I followed Hunter out into the open night.

Forced to wait until dawn to cross back into the boneyard, we returned to the warehouse. Without our safe zones, it was still the most secure place on this side of reality. The Shadows could theoretically get to us there, but they'd have to go through a hell of a lot of artillery to do so. We were quiet on the drive over, Hunter still furtively studying my appearance from the corner of his eye, and me staring out the window like a moody teenager. Maybe it was psychosomatic—the shocking knowledge that I'd lost a week of my life to another world slowly sinking in—but Las Vegas was suddenly what appeared unreal. It was like returning to a childhood home. Though I had an intimate knowledge of the terrain, I no longer felt a part of it.

I glanced up when we whizzed past Valhalla, the fountains out front reflecting the eerie colors of the sky. It looked like I could stand atop the giant hotel and reach my hand straight through the swirling clouds to take hold of the bolts being flung from one side of the valley to the other. As disconcerting as that was, I had more pressing problems. So while Hunter pondered the tattoo on my belly, I turned my mind to the surprise subject of Regan's new "friend."

An agent of Light betraying one of their own. I shook my head and blew out a hard breath. It wouldn't be the first time. When I first came to the Zodiac, the troop had unknowingly harbored a mole. But it was hard to see any of the current star signs—most of whom had endured that betrayal—doing what that traitor had, marking an ally and sending them out in the world toward certain death. And everyone knew someone who died before she'd been stopped.

All but Kimber, I thought grimly. She was from our sister troop in Arizona, where we sent our initiates for fostering prior to metamorphosis, when they were still free to leave the city. Despite our allied status, Kimber had disliked me from the moment she arrived, but she had greater reason to hate me now that I'd cost her power. Warren had shunted her aside since then, rarely inviting her out of the sanctuary. She blamed me for that too. Never mind that it'd been an accident, I thought grimly. Or that I'd saved her life. So if I had to take bets, my money would have been on her as the one to betray me to Regan.

But what about Chandra? My emergence a year ago had usurped her place within the troop. She'd backed off from the more overt hostility—and seemingly accepted her auxiliary role in the troop, since we'd worked so well together in October—but was her reluctant acceptance actually a front? Could it be her way—a devious, better way—of dealing with me? Did she have it in her to work with a Shadow agent, a rogue agent even, in order to set up my fall?

I pondered it a bit longer before dismissing the possibility. My capture and death would certainly free up the Archer sign for her, but it would also weaken the troop, possibly annihilating it altogether. Her feelings toward me might be ambivalent, but she was committed to the agents of Light with every cell of her being.

Besides, Regan might have been lying. If the Tulpa thought she had a source that would lead him to me, he'd be likelier to reinstate her in his troop. No, I couldn't peg any of my allies—my *friends*—as betrayers, unless something drastic had happened in the week I'd been gone. So I'd report the conversation to Warren and let him figure out a way to deal with it. We'd figure it out together.

But will you tell him about Ashlyn?

I let out a sigh, running a hand over my face.

"Are you sure you're okay?"

I let my head loll Hunter's way. "I'm hennaed, pierced, and just found out I lost an entire week of my life. What do you think?"

"Ah, but your sparkling personality is still intact."

"Lucky for you," I muttered. He snorted, and turned his attention back to the road. I searched his face a moment longer before saying, "Listen, thank you for not saying anything to Warren about a possible mole just yet. Something isn't adding up. It's like he knows things but isn't sharing them with us."

"Warren does what he thinks is right for the troop." Meaning it wasn't for us to know those reasons, just to obey them.

I shook my head and turned back to the window. "He's ruthless."

"We're all ruthless, Joanna." He said it like it disgusted him.

I looked back at his silhouette etched against the night, wondering what he meant. Then I pushed the wonder away, refocusing on Warren. "I think he locked people over there, Hunter. I don't care if they were Shadows or rogues or the devil incarnate. He knew what that world was even if he didn't know exactly what it did." Maybe he'd even been there, and returned. Little would surprise me about Warren's machinations anymore. "And, knowing it, he still sent me over there."

As Hunter said, Warren did what he thought best for the troop. But how was it best to send me to a place he knew would steal time from my life? My powers? My *soul*? "And why wouldn't he tell us that Jaden Jacks was Light?"

Hunter looked upset by that too, but raised his brows to erase the worry. "Also in our best interests?"

"Devil's advocate," I spat, annoyed with his automatic need to defend Warren. "Jaden killed that changeling. I saw proof enough of that . . . and I bet Warren knows it."

Hunter's breath stuttered from him. "Are you sure?"

"Yes," I said, pleased he was finally listening to me. "So don't argue just for the sake of arguing."

"I'm not." He gripped the steering wheel more tightly. "But if we're going to go to Warren with accusations of moles in our troop and secrets kept from us all, then we'd better have thought it through."

His use of the word "we" pacified me, and I blew out a breath. I waited until he'd relaxed, then said more calmly, "Do you know what it would take for our entire troop to be unaware that Jacks was Light? I mean, how could we not know one of our own? By my calculations, Jaden is only a few years older than me. That means Felix and Jewell and Vanessa should know him. It means you should."

Hunter gave me the most unamused smile I'd ever seen. "Rewiring."

I shook my head. "Would Warren do that to all of you?"

"I told you. He'd do anything if he thought it right for the troop."

So, again, *why*? I tilted my head, looked again at the pressurized webbing of the sky threatening to spill its contents all over the city. "Maybe he's protecting Jaden?"

Hunter scowled at me. "Protecting a guy who killed a changeling?"

"Well, I don't know! You come up with a better idea."

He studied the road, then finally shook his head. "I can't."

And that was the problem. No one could say exactly what Warren was doing and thinking, or why. As I thought about that, the pocket of night untouched by the neon or the strange night sky seemed to reach into the car and deepen. I shifted my eyes to Hunter's face and set my jaw. "I'm not telling him about Ashlyn. It's not that I don't trust him. It's just that . . . "

Hunter finally finished the sentence for me. "You don't trust him."

I didn't say anything. The silence was so elongated, I thought it was going to snap.

Finally, Hunter said, "I didn't tell him about Lola either."

I breathed a sigh of relief.

Because what we both knew about Warren, and had no need to say, was that while he continued to do what he thought best for the troop, he ignored the implication of those actions on the individual troop members. I didn't know what Hunter had endured at his hands, or exactly why he didn't want Warren knowing about his own daughter, but Warren's past actions made him a bit of a ticking bomb. He'd known, for instance, about Skamar long before I did, that the doppelgänger was an evolutionary precursor to a tulpa, and that my mother had been the one creating her. He hadn't told me any of that, making me instead discover it on my own. He'd then admitted he would have taken Ben from me, deleting me from the mortal's mind and life, except for fear it would interfere with my focus. With his plans. What had Warren said at the time?

I didn't want you distracted.

"He always knows more than he lets on."

"His right as troop leader," Hunter muttered, and I could practically hear the addendum. *Or so he thinks.*

I angled myself toward Hunter then, chaps squeaking against the seat. He would have made a smart remark about that except he caught sight of my face first. "You're wrong. I do trust Warren. I trust him to do what he wants regardless of what it means to us. I trust him to run my emotions down if it's the most direct path to his goals. I trust him to take what he wants without asking, without care, and without guilt."

Hunter ran a hand along the hair at his temple. "Oh, he'll ask."

"Then demand that I agree."

He said nothing, which told me everything. I relaxed . . . until his next question. "Is that why you let go of Ben?"

He was studiously not looking at me.

And that was the sign *I'd* been waiting for. I didn't need five fingers to count the number of times in the year I'd known Hunter that he'd begun a revealing, personal conversation. I wasn't sure exactly why he was doing so now, but the vulnerability it exposed was so raw I both wanted to protect it and look away at the same time. And I had to tread softly, I knew, or he'd turn away.

"You know why I did that," I said softly.

"Because Ben chose wrongly."

"Partly." And I wouldn't apologize. Ben should have known he was bedding down with Regan, not mistaken her for me. Sure, I understood she'd tricked him. And that life was complicated . . . I think I got it more acutely than most. But that was precisely why I wanted my most intimate relationship to be simple. I opened my mouth to say that, but we were already pulling into the workshop bay, and Hunter shoved the gear into park. He told me to wait in the car while he disengaged the alarms.

I sighed at the slamming of his door. I'd waited too long to speak. Other than a few intermittent beeps from within the warehouse, complete silence enveloped me. Hunter disappeared inside. The bay door lowered to encase me in darkness.

I leaned back my head, closed my eyes, and sighed again.

15

↗ While Hunter busied himself putting space between us, I again cursed the timing of our return to the warehouse. He'd opened up to me for a moment there, like the dappled edging of the sun through the trees, the first real opportunity at intimacy since I'd left his bed in this very warehouse more than a month earlier. I knew even before stepping from the car that the precious sliver of vulnerability, like the sun, would be clouded over again by the time I joined him inside. Again I wondered why it couldn't be simple.

No, not simple, I silently clarified, but true. Undivided. Decisive. A woman wants to be chosen, after all, the one deemed precious above all others. The thought made me think of Hunter's eyes fixed on the road as he asked about Ben. Could that be what he wanted as well?

"Wow. I'm always leaving, aren't I?" I laughed, a small, unamused puff trapped in the cab of the car. How ironic that I could do so much *leaving* while trapped in Vegas, in this body, in this life. How ironic also that my return from another world was what emphasized all those little departures.

Before I could think, or back out of it, I went inside and said that same thing to Hunter.

"What are you talking about?" He was occupied at his drawing board, shuffling papers and tossing foam pieces into an open bin. He looked like he wanted to shrug off my words but couldn't quite. He knew exactly what I was talking about.

I just smiled. "I mean, I left Ben . . . actually, I left him a note. In a mailbox." I shook my head at the stupidity of thinking that was somehow acceptable. "Then I left you for him . . . then him again. But you helped me return from Midheaven, do you know that?"

He swallowed hard and shrugged. His actions were jerky, not at all his usual lithe, catlike movements.

I leaned against the table, toward him. He turned, disappearing behind the clouded plastic screen separating the workshop from the shooting range. I raised my voice. "You did. I was . . . trapped there. It would have been easy just to . . . " *Give up. Die.* The words slipped away. "Anyway, it would have been easy. But I remembered you once talking about my strength, how you thought it was beautiful, and that memory made me want to fight."

It'd been in this very workshop, the sole time we'd made love. I'd left him then too. I edged around the hanging plastic sheet to find him standing before it, unseeing, motionless. He licked his lip, still not looking at me. "Not now," he whispered. "Please."

I didn't know what he meant by that.

"You also said it was okay to change, to want something new. To admit you made a mistake and then make a new choice. For a new person. In a moment."

I thought of what Solange had said as we were spinning in her planetarium, that I doubted my place in the world.

But I didn't doubt this.

Sure, I wasn't Solange, with her confidence and authenticity—her powers—but I was certainly the best *me* I'd ever been. I put my hand on his arm, hoping he'd choose this moment too. That he'd choose this new me. Hunter lowered his head for a moment.

Then he turned away.

It hurt. I closed my eyes. Yet I still wanted him. I opened them again.

And when he strode off to clear the target, I followed. A firing range, I thought. How appropriate.

"What are you doing?" he said, stopping in front of the first bull's-eye, feeling me behind him.

Keeping my expression pleasant, I inched closer. "Sticking," I said shortly, slipping my smile into the word.

"No, you're being obnoxious." He yanked on the old bull's-eye, crumpling it in his hands. "Not to mention aggressive."

"I know." I rolled my eyes. "It's *so* unattractive."

He loved my strength. He loved my stubbornness. I stepped closer.

Hunter moved away, not looking at me. "We tried this before."

His resolve was so firm it made me ache to shatter it. I smiled. "And we're going to do it again."

He whirled. *"No."*

"Yes." I snorted. He was right. It was obnoxious. "What, *hero*? Nobody and nothing touches you just because you're bulletproof?"

He lifted his chin. "That's right."

I tilted my shoulder and batted my lashes. "C'mere, Bulletproof."

His mouth actually twitched at that.

"See. You're going to start liking this." I let my glance fall to his mouth. "I promise."

He swallowed hard, serious again. "Stop."

Maybe I would have. If his gaze hadn't slid over my halter top, lingered on the belly ring, caught on the zipper of my chaps. My smile widened, he took another step back . . . and I picked him up.

"What the—"

I threw him into the sidewall ten feet away, hard enough to knock some sense into him without causing injury. He was a big boy. He could tell the difference.

He was already on his feet as I advanced again, looking at me like my body had been taken over by aliens while I'd been visiting another world.

"You're thinking too much," I said, closing in. The thick silver encircling my wrists jingled. My leather pants rubbed when I walked. Hunter watched me warily. All combined? It was a huge turn-on. "It's starting to annoy me."

He swallowed when I stopped before him, body tensed, ready to deflect another shot if he had to. "One of us has to."

I feigned turning away . . . and pitched him across the room extra hard for that.

"Joanna!" Now he was really pissed. I wanted to throw back my head and laugh.

I stalked him again, took the shooting stand he was keeping between us in an underhanded grip and flipped it across the room too. Steel clattered against concrete to send my blood soaring. I knew Hunter scented it. He inhaled deeply and his dark eyes dilated. I was hunting, I realized. Still hunting, still fighting, and—oh, look—damned feminine while doing it. God, this felt good. "Don't say my name if you're going to say it like that."

I reached him, and he caught my wrists so I couldn't pitch him again. I stepped closer. He angled his body, shielding choice body parts. Not a bit of trust in the boy. "How should I say it?" he asked.

"Like this." And, gently, I lifted to my toes and breathed the syllables into his mouth.

It was a reluctant enfolding, his mouth closing so gently over mine that I might have missed it were it not for the accompanying warmth. I moved my lips, opening to him further, and his hands gentled on my skin, but he didn't let go.

"I won't leave again," I murmured, leaning into him. The warmth spread to all the places my body met his—lips, arms, breasts. I pressed. "I won't leave *you* again."

He swallowed hard and I knew I'd hit on a fear too deeply felt to even voice. Even the next one, which he did murmur, had him averting his eyes. "Looking back is a form of leaving."

"Hunter." I took his face in my palms, so gently you would have never known I'd thrown down only minutes before. "My mother is MIA, my sister's dead, my ex has no idea who I am, and I can't even revisit the last week of my life because I never lived it. If any of that is an issue between you and me, then, Hunt? I'm not the one looking back."

"That's not fair." He drew back from my touch, though he didn't let go. "Look, you've had time to think this through—"

I moved in again, eyes on his lips. "Just thought of it, actually."

"And right now you might be confusing what you think you want—"

"I want you."

His jaw clenched. "You have to give me time."

"You've got thirty seconds."

His eyes went wide.

I shrugged. "Thirty seconds and either these chaps come off or I walk away forever. Twenty, now."

"You can't expect me to make that sort of—"

"Fifteen. C'mon, Hunter. I'm keeping it simple."

"Jo!"

"I told you. Don't say my name like that." I slid my gaze down his body, lids going heavy with what I saw. Damn, this man spoke to me. "What do you want?"

"What exactly do *you* want?"

I smiled, my gaze flipping back up on his, warming once there. "I want to know what you crave and need and desire in the next . . . " I looked at my bangled wrist. "Five seconds."

"I want you to stop throwing me around!"

And he also wanted to take the words back as soon as they were out of his mouth, because we both froze in their wake. He meant physically, but the accompanying scent said it was his emotions that were battered. As did the way his brows furrowed, as if pained.

"Oh." I drew back and swallowed hard, my amusement fleeing. What was I doing to this poor guy? I thought, eyes wildly searching his face. He was right to want time and space. He had a right to his feelings, and to take as much time as he needed to come around to them. I could wait for him to come to me . . . if he chose.

"Phew." I ran a hand over my head as I turned away. "Okay."

Thank God for the wall, because my back was against it so fast it was like the earth came unhinged from its axis. Hunter's mouth brought everything swimming into its proper place again, and I thought, Yes. This is right. This is fate. This is mine.

He pulled back long enough to catch his breath. "I still had two seconds left."

"Three cheers for time management." I flipped on him again, not throwing him around this time, but rolling with him. We pushed each other in tandem, working together now, mouths and hands frantic, until I halted it with a leg snaking up his side. I wrapped it around the back of his left thigh as he pressed, then shuddered. I smiled. "So you *do* like the chaps."

"Not so much." He hooked his thumbs into the waistband, I lowered my leg and braced. Diana's chaps ripped free, attached silver studs tinkling as they hit the floor. Hunter quirked a brow.

I rolled my eyes. "I know, they're like wind chimes. I have no idea . . . "

How I was going to finish that sentence, I thought as his mouth recaptured mine. I wrapped my legs around his waist, and he braced me with his core, hand fisted in my hair as he pushed me higher.

I winced as my lower back took most of the impact. "Ow."

"What?" He pulled back, brows drawn.

I grabbed him again. "Nothing."

A month ago we'd been tentative, uncertain, gentle and giving. This time we were ravenous in our demands, active and punishing. I didn't feel bad about raking my fingers over his back as I stripped his shirt from him, because his knuckles dug into my hips as he tore off my briefs. So I bit his shoulder until he growled and redirected my mouth. He kissed me so long and hard my heartbeat actually slowed.

Flipping my hair to one side, he dove for my neck. I countered, angling for his, and we tussled until he created space enough to flip me, remaining behind this time. My protest stuttered off as he angled my palms on the wall, higher than I'd have chosen, exposing me more, before his hands pushed aside my leather halter, pinching as he again captured my neck with his mouth.

I arched back on a moan, arms spreading, and he wrapped one forearm around my chest, bracing me there. There was the slide of a zipper, and my breath quickened from expectation alone. Nothing happened. I held still. Still nothing. I bit my lip, whimpering some wordless plea, but there was only that one bracing arm around my core. Frustrated, I angled a look back. "Hunt—"

He plunged, a gorgeous, solid stroke that set off the first of my orgasms. I wasn't even letting him take me, instead arching, reaching back with every sense to demand more, wanting friction and heat, his strength in return for mine. I wanted him to go on forever. I wanted . . . I wanted . . . I wanted . . .

He wanted too. Hands returning to my breasts, he hooked his thumbs beneath my arms, nipples captured beneath long, strong fingers. I continued to open to him, luxuriating in his demand, and when I thought I couldn't open any further, I gave some more. I wanted to pull him into me. I wanted to disappear into him. I wanted the one person who knew me to find shelter inside of me so I could do the same.

And right when I felt I was giving and getting just that, the magic of the aureole whipped across us. It was like the cresting tide of a monsoon, and having experienced it twice before, we each braced for the flash of color and knowledge to soak our senses, we both cried out as our minds intertwined. The energy gathering like a cosmic disaster in the sky was nothing compared to what arrowed between us. Our individual minds and thoughts slipped past skin and bone so that Hunter's memories took root in my head, he took ownership of mine, and the separately lived moments merged as one.

His worry as he'd realized I'd disappeared into the pipeline a week earlier was an ache in my chest, like a fist squeezing my heart. I felt it now just as he had then.

The pain that had assailed me in the crossing between worlds reached out like an ice cream scoop to hollow his middle, and I actually heard his breath stutter.

After that I had a vision of him hunched over papers in the map room attached to the warehouse, making connections, his determination fueling long hours. In return, the memory plucked from me was of staring down Harlan Tripp across a pile of poker chips, and of sweeping those chips into my bag. The bag, connecting memories, was next seen hanging around a pipe as I huddled, barely breathing, feet away from the Tulpa and Regan in the dark.

The linear connection broke then, and we were flung back in time where a slash of stark moonlight lit Hunter's face as he spoke the words I'd last read in a Shadow manual.

Everyone should have their greatest desire.

I wanted to turn to him, to question that, but the pain of the rejection he'd just endured, because of me, ran through me like a guillotine. To escape it, I squeezed my eyes . . .

And recalled for us both Solange in silhouette, stars spinning around her.

Hunter and I gasped together as the power arching between us reached its apex then, a shuddering pause before the coaster of emotion thundered downhill, picking up speed as we found our bodies again, renewed our rhythm, regained the present, and came together as one. Hunter's aura, a gold spinning behind my closed lids, burst through me like a rocket. My red aura was weak, but my emotion was concentrated, and it spun from my mouth on that final cry.

It took minutes for the world to right itself, our breaths interloping to tug us back, together, inhale by exhale. I pressed my cheek against the cool concrete wall, spotted a bull's-eye across the distance of the shooting range, and still breathless, I smiled.

We dropped to the platform bed tucked in the crow's nest after that . . . it was either that or fall over, but the rightness that had slid over me upon climax enveloped me again as I nestled in next to Hunter. I was sore from the give and take, the aggressiveness and the surprising desperation in our lovemaking. I was also feeling the effects of my fight in Midheaven, and the passage both there and back, but nestled into the crook of his left arm, staring up at a ceiling of faux stars, I sighed, and every muscle relaxed.

Unlike Solange's planetarium, this ceiling offered up a faulty version of the night sky. Hunter didn't only track constellations, but "frozen stars," dead ones, black holes. I'd wondered at that once, thinking it strange, but right now I had no energy to even care. I fit so well at his side, and was so relieved to be safe and home—not to mention out of those chaps—that I immediately began to drift off.

"How do you feel?" Hunter's voice reached out to me like a breeze, hesitant and shifting. It was a similar question to the one he'd asked the last time we'd been tented beneath this improbable sky.

What do I make you feel?

*At war with myself, like there's something lacking . . .
and violence . . .*

I knew my answer had been hurtful, but at the time it
had also been my truest reaction to the shock and sadness
of having witnessed Ben and Regan together. Though re-
phrased, by asking the question now, Hunter was again
opening himself to that hard answer, obviously hoping it'd
changed.

My hesitation spooked him. He edged away, turning his
back to me, but I caught his hip with my palm and spooned
his body with my own, feet and knees and hips and chest
an echo of his male strength. So complimentary, I thought,
drawing closer. It made me honestly wonder why we were
so often at odds.

While he remained silent, waiting, I traced the tattoo on
his back with my fingers, trailing the shadowed side of the
yin/yang symbol before running my index finger along the
dueling words on each side: fear and desire.

"You make me feel . . . "

*You make me feel like touching myself in the dark. You
make me feel like whispering your name for no reason.
You make me wish to put need and lack and violence
behind me.*

He turned to me, determined to face whatever I was
going to say.

I offered up a watery smile, my fingers going tentative
on his arm. I whispered, "I feel like me."

Like I could be me—the good and the bad, the fabled
and fallible, the Light and the Shadow—and still look in
the mirror without shame. The jerk of his head revealed
his surprise, but his relieved sigh told me it was the answer
he'd been seeking. I stroked his arms, feeling the fine hairs
there, the soft skin, the hard muscle underneath. I'd go
back to Midheaven, I thought, like he could still hear it,
and risk soul and powers and life for you alone.

He shifted toward me again, taking me in his arms. "It
hurt." It wasn't a question. He knew, through the aure-

ole. Still, the words made me feel small. I recalled what memory the aureole had shared, and closed my eyes.

"Yes," I whispered.

"Was it . . . that woman? The one in the aureole memory?" He was going to say "the beautiful one." The hesitation was in his voice. I suppose it was indiscreet to say something like that when another woman was in your arms. But it was my memory . . . and Solange *was* beautiful.

"It was all of them." They'd all been working together there, I now realized, as much of a troop as we were over here.

"What did they take?"

Now I really wanted to hide. How was I supposed to know? I hadn't even had time to catch a second breath upon extinguishing that candle, much less worry about the triangles I'd so freely gambled away, what they represented, what I'd lost. I remembered the personality traits, stubbornness and fear, things that made people irrational—freeze when they should act, act when they should be still—yet they were also tools that could save a person's life. Each trait on the human spectrum overlapped to zigzag like the locked pieces of a unique puzzle.

Then again, what about Solange's words? *Who armored you? Who is protecting your soul?* Was someone protecting me? Had I possessed some sort of armor while there? I honestly didn't know—not that, or what my passage to Midheaven had cost me. I just hoped it wasn't a corner piece.

"I don't know," I finally sighed, so softly it disappeared into the black space between the winking stars.

"I'm sorry."

And somehow that made it better. Not okay, I thought, turning into him again. But better.

Sleep visited in a series of images, none of them as pleasant as the reality that fatigue had me leaving behind. The first time I'd endured scorching heat and twisted poker games it was because I'd been trapped in another world. This time they were only bearable because even in unconsciousness I was aware of Hunter's solid form next to me, that I was safe in my world, that I was home. I tossed during the next few hours, murmuring the names of men so washed out they looked made of dust, until Mackie's skeletal visage, stretched in a furious scream, had me startling into full awareness. Hunter's lips at my temples slowed my breathing to a normal rate, but when I turned to him again, limbs and lips seeking, it sped up in short time.

He entered me slowly this time, a calmness that hadn't been there before riding over the both of us like we were still dreaming. Buoyed by it, we rode the waves of sliding limbs and twining tongues, and our long, slow climaxes were like ripples from stones dropped deep inside of us. He fell asleep, still inside, muscle gone lax atop me, transferring his strength to my bone. I lay there for a quarter of an hour, enjoying the weight, then shifted so we fell apart, again two separate people.

Hunter didn't stir. His attention to me throughout the previous hours, plus whatever he'd endured in the days before that, had exhausted him. I ran my hand along the length of his body as I watched him breathe, and swore to never return to those tunnels. Entering them was like inviting in oblivion. One step in and you were enfolded in darkness. Much safer to stay on the outside, I thought, even with faux neon lighting up beneath a bulging sky.

He slept on his side, facing me, head resting on one arm, the other flung out as if reaching for something. I trailed my fingertips along his jaw. I loved the ability men possessed to expend all their energy in sex, and drop off like the dead directly after. I envied it a bit, but it also made me smile. I smoothed the dark hair from his forehead, feeling the silkiness rub, ghostlike, against the marble smoothness of my fingertips, and let myself begin to drift again as well.

Pounding at the steel bay door brought us both lurching upright.

"It's Warren," Hunter muttered, climbing over me so he was momentarily tenting my body with his own. I had a flashback of him lingering there, but by the time the slick, white-hot thought took hold, he was already pulling on his jeans and running a hand through his tousled hair.

"How do you know?" My voice was scratchy and raw. I cleared it and reached for the bottled water on the floor.

"That's his knock. Here." He threw me a sweatshirt, rolling his eyes when I put it to my nose and sniffed. "It's fine. Don't turn on a light until you're dressed. Unless you want to be showcased like a burlesque dancer."

It was early, predawn, and I nodded groggily as he rejected the ladder in favor of leaping directly to the floor twenty feet below. I groaned, feeling stiff and achy as I swung my legs over the side of the bed. My briefs and chaps were still downstairs in the firing range, but no way was I putting those back on. I fumbled about until I found an extra pair of sweats in a basket under the bed, answering Warren with a grunt as he yelled for me to meet them in the panic room. There was a metal desk lamp across from the bed, and I flipped it on once dressed to begin the hopeless task of trying to untangle my hair as I stretched. Gawd, I was stiff.

I felt the belly ring pull as I lifted my arms, and lifted my shirt to make sure it was okay. It was . . . but bruises surrounded it.

Bruises. "Oh my God."

Fingertips dotted my skin in angry red brands, the memory of rough embraces marking every rib. I shot a glance downstairs, but the light was on beneath the panic room door, the two men already engaged in conversation. I twisted around to find my lower back already deepening in color, more places littered with livid color than not.

And this had resulted from a little charged, consensual sex? Okay, a *lot* of charged, consensual sex. At least now I knew which power Shen had taken. I dropped back to the edge of the bed.

"Regeneration," I whispered. My ability to heal. I lowered my head to my palms, my palms to my knees. And now, like any human, I could be injured if struck by a bullet, sliced by a knife, hit by a car. Forget conduits. A mere slap from a Shadow agent would be dangerous.

All of a sudden, in a world of near immortals, the tiniest thing could kill me.

16

The panic room was entirely different than the last time I'd seen it. Obviously Vanessa was long gone, but the tank with the healing gel was also absent, along with all the hospital equipment. Pushing the door open, I blinked against the bright light, and at the weighty silence. I'd been too preoccupied by the chinks in my paranormal armor to note the hissing murmurs that'd accompanied my careful climb down the crow's nest ladder—to be honest, I was on the verge of tears—and I wiped my eyes, pretending to rub sleep from them and acclimate to the fluorescent light. I knew the moment Warren and Hunter scented my mood. I couldn't contain it fully. My grief at this lost power, the stolen ability to heal, was felt as keenly as if someone had died.

I silently admonished myself to pull it together, and studied my surroundings—not looking at the men—hoping that would ground me. The small, sterile room was suddenly depressing in its austerity, and though not normally claustrophobic, I knew that if I were trapped in here, I'd be begging for someone to kill me within days. The cure that was worse than the proverbial disease.

There were rations tucked away, additional sources of

heat and light, although sieges meant something different to Zodiac agents than they did to even a mortal paramilitary troop. Those could last weeks, not mere days. Back in the late nineties, New York's agents of Light had endured one lasting longer than the time it took to conceive, gestate, and birth a squalling child. Learning from that, our troop had installed a side bathroom with a small shower while constructing this one.

Hunter's memory, which the aureole gifted me with earlier, had shown scattered papers, and there were indeed two maps lying side by side over the centered drawing tables. I tucked my hair behind my ear and bent over them, rubbing my arms, aware that Warren and Hunter were still eyeing me. The maps turned out to be identical, the original pristine but its twin copy marked up in a completely nonsensical fashion. What the maps detailed, however, was clear.

"The flood system?" I said as Hunter came to stand at my side. I heard his deep inhalation as he tried to ferret out my mood. I held my own breath and didn't look at him. Instead I wondered how long he'd been studying this. Multicolored markings zigzagged and crosshatched the second drawing like an enthusiastic toddler's art project.

"This is it in full." I did look up then. His hair was disheveled, and bare-chested, he looked warm, but his eyes were shadowed. Not at all the sinking softness he'd turned on me hours before. I couldn't tell if it was in reaction to my shuttered mood or in response to whatever he and Warren had been discussing. "Joanna was helping me chart her path into Midheaven."

Warren gave him a look that said he knew exactly what I'd been helping him with, and we both shifted our gazes to the floor like teens caught after curfew.

"Where the hell did you get it?"

"The Flood Control District."

Warren quirked a wiry brow. "They just handed you a map of the entire underground system?"

"I told them I was doing a story on the homeless living in the tunnels. Do you know that floodwaters can rise in there at the rate of a foot per minute?" When Warren only stared, Hunter shrugged and went to sit on a corner stool. "What? Your undercover identity is what gave me the idea."

The strained silence between the men elongated, and I glanced back at the maps.

He's already mapped the place out.

This was what I'd seen him working on in the shared aureole. The emotion accompanying it had been exhaustion and determination. But exactly what was he doing? The bright intersecting lines gave no clue.

Warren took Hunter's place at my side, using a fingernail to trace the entrance I'd emerged from all the way to its intersecting point. All lines, I noted, met in the middle. So there really was only one entrance to Midheaven. "Did you make sure everything was as you found it?" Warren asked me.

"Sure," I said sarcastically. "I even dusted. Right after I lost my powers and before being ambushed by Regan and the Tulpa."

Warren's head slowly swiveled my way. "Powers?"

I scrambled to think, before deciding to turn the blame on him. "Well, something was jerked from me upon entry, and it felt pretty powerful. What else could it be?"

I stared at him, daring him to tell me he knew he was sending me to a place that would strip my soul in three tries.

His gaze lingered on my face, and then he ran a hand over his spiky hair. "Well, it won't be as bad the second time."

I look at him like he was stoned.

He gave me the same once-over.

"Uh-uh." I shook my head and backed up until I was leaning into Hunter's knees. He opened them, giving me harbor in between, and I nestled in tight. Warren's eyes flickered at the intimacy, but he said nothing. Both things gave me courage. "Not me. No way. That place is evil. The passage alone felt like it was going to kill me."

"But it didn't, and that which doesn't kill you . . ."

It took all my self-control not to roll my eyes. I'd collected quotes as a teen, mental touchstones, wise words in an unpredictable world. But I hated clichés, and I certainly wasn't going to spout empty bravado. I nestled in more tightly to the pocket Hunter created for me. I wasn't feeling particularly brave. "Makes you weaker?"

"Leaves loose ends," Hunter muttered, his voice stirring my hair. Despite my worry, it stirred other things as well. Sick, I thought, shaking my head slightly, but every bruise had been worth it.

Warren scowled, crossing his arms as his eyes darted between the two of us. "Might be a second chance at redemption."

Something niggled at me, like a secret whispered in the dark. Someone had just told me something, but who? I leaned against Hunter and remembered his silhouette in sleep. I looked at Warren and the whisper echoed faintly.

"Why would I go back?"

Warren glanced at the maps beside him, then back at Hunter. There was something vaguely threatening in the action. "Hunter, would you mind leaving the two of us alone?" It wasn't a question.

Hunter remained where he was for about a year under Warren's direct gaze, before gently easing me forward to stand. A light brush of his fingertips trailed my belly as he crossed in front of me, and then he was gone. Warren and I said nothing for a long time; he allowing no indication of what he thought of this new development, and me making it clear I didn't care either way.

Finally he leaned back on his elbows, crossing tattered boots at the ankles. "Hunter caught me up on what happened to you in Midheaven. As much as he could, that is. Is it true that it felt like you were gone only hours?"

While a week had passed here. Nodding, I pushed myself up on the stool. I recounted the conversation I'd overheard in the pipeline, that though still broken, Regan was once again back in the Tulpa's good graces. That she'd been hiding in the pipeline, she still had my conduit, and that she was going to try to bring me to the Shadow leader alive. "She's been following me everywhere, in both my daily life as Olivia and as the Archer. I know she followed me to Master Comics."

He watched me with dull eyes, looking less surprised by this knowledge than I thought it warranted. *How about this, then, Warren . . .*

"She also claims to be tracking me with the help of someone in the troop. An agent of Light."

"A bluff." Warren shrugged, immediately dismissing the claim. "Not possible."

He let that, and the surety with which he said it, sink in. His tone said he was in charge and I should be glad that he was. He must have realized how imperious it was because he shrugged one shoulder and smiled. "Tell me what you can about Midheaven."

What I could. He knew, then, that I couldn't tell him everything. But I frowned anyway, wanting to accommodate him. I saw a skeleton with a bowler hat. I saw inky masculine shapes and bright feminine ones. Images zipped by, a very few lingering like mental balloons in my frontal lobe, but when I opened my mouth, they slid away, leaving me with nothing but a fleeting sensory reminder. I shook my head apologetically.

"It's okay," Warren said, like he'd been expecting it. "You only remember the people and things linked to your own time and place. Like the man and woman you mentioned to Hunter. Harlan Tripp and Solange?"

I'd figured that out for myself, but I still shook my head. "I remember more than just them. I remember it all. But trying to verbalize it is like trying to tell a story without a subject or object or any linking verbage." I sighed. "But you already knew that too, didn't you?"

He shrugged again. There were worlds to interpret in that one movement. "Midheaven's vibration doesn't register over here. It's why the place is considered myth and why Zane can't write about it in manuals. It's a place that becomes known to you only when it's time for you to know it."

Warren hasn't told you anything, has he?

I couldn't shake Solange's taunt from my head. He hadn't. And I'd lost a third of my soul, power, time, and nearly my life. For what? To learn things he already knew? To feel like I was going crazy in my own mind? Or crazier?

Since I was having trouble voicing my own thoughts, I decided to pry out his. "Let's play a little game, Warren. I'm going to start a sentence, and since I can't finish any thought that contains knowledge gleaned in Midheaven, you're going to finish it for me."

Before he could protest, I started.

"Jaden Jacks is . . . "

"In Midheaven."

The answer I was looking for was *Light*. I shook my head. "Jaden Jacks is . . . "

"A rogue agent like Harlan Tripp, who has also been gone a very long time."

"Jaden Jacks is . . . "

Warren sighed. "Watch your temper—"

"Jaden Jacks is!" I pounded the wall so hard I felt the reverberation through my fist. Shit. I was going to have to relearn how to walk through this world as a mortal. I closed my eyes, fought not to rub my hand or wince, and calmed myself.

When I opened my eyes, Warren was watching me like I was crazy. "I should have known this would happen."

"What, Warren? That I'd come back with a tattoo of the sun hennaed on my belly?" I asked bitingly, coming off my stool, pissed because he could have prevented all my losses. And because they'd been for absolutely nothing. "Or that I'd return with more questions about Jaden Jacks, agent of . . . "

I didn't complete the sentence, I refused, but its start let him know exactly what I was driving at. *Light.*

"Jaden Jacks is in Midheaven," he repeated. "And Harlan Tripp can help you find him."

"That's not what I hear."

"Then someone is lying to you." He straightened at my arch look. "And, no, it's not me. Because I'm the one who put him there."

I shuddered involuntarily at that, both at the way he said it and the thought of being forced through that passage. Of having to remain in that heat with Boyd and Bill and Mackie and a drink that slowed your senses to an impossible crawl. All because Jacks had broken a changeling?

I had broken a changeling.

I shook the thought free. Jacks had knowingly killed one. "You put a lock on the entrance, didn't you?"

That indeterminable shrug again. He'd known that changeling was dead and he'd sent me in anyway!

"Goddamn it, Warren—"

"I do *not* have to explain myself to you!" he roared with such force that it rocked from the small room, and I imagined it ping-ponging off the warehouse walls. "Do you understand me? You may be the Kairos, but I am the leader of this troop!"

I swallowed hard, clenching my jaw. "Nothing short of death will make me go back there."

"We need to heal our changeling. Our troop. Our world."

There was hope in his eyes when I searched their dark depths again, a rabid hope that I'd do this thing without arguing, and the manuals would be written, Jasmine would move on, Li would be whole. Like my disappearance was a magic wand waved over the landscape of all these lives, making everything all right.

"Jacks killed that kid."

"By choice. Which means he knows an alternative."

"Then *you* go." I sighed again, not caring if fear and exhaustion perfumed the room like the fields of Grasse.

Warren's scuffed boots appeared in my sightline, and I raised my head. His deep brown eyes bore into mine. "How do you feel now?"

"Fine," I said through clenched teeth.

"Jo."

"It feels like there's a piece of me missing here," I put a hand over the sweatshirt, the hennaed sun beneath and what a more metaphysically inclined person would call my sacrum. My other hand, just my fingertips, went to my head, touching gently like it was an open wound. I didn't know why—it didn't make sense—but I softly added, "And here."

"But do you feel lighter? Like something has been yanked up by the root?"

I swallowed hard. "How do you know that?"

One side of his mouth lifted. "Your scent, Jo. You smell lighter. There's less Shadow there. That's all it took from you, don't you see? Your Shadow side."

Is that what Solange had meant by me being armored, then? Was my Light side somehow being protected? But she'd talked about my *soul* . . .

"I don't want to go." Even if he was right.

"Then Li will die."

"Don't lay that on me!" I yelled, even knowing that it was true, and that was my fault. "There has to be another way."

"And we'll be working to find it while you're there." He was composed again; my rising emotion seemed to calm him. He put a hand on my bruised shoulder. "Do it for your troop."

I shook it off. "Your troop," I muttered, because that much was clear.

Warren looked away, sighed, then paced to the door. Did he deem me a lost cause? Not quite yet. He turned, hope still alive in his eyes. "We still have a little time. Keep thinking and you'll see I'm right. For now, it's good to have you back. Chandra has been working in your stead. Kimber has been trying . . . not that she can do much." He shook his head, almost in disgust. "I'd send her back to her family if I could. She's miserable, and we need someone stronger."

Of course Kimber was miserable. Warren was horrible at hiding his feelings. He wanted to throw her away because of her weaknesses, get someone else to fill her sign. I self-consciously tugged Hunter's sweatshirt over my bruised wrists.

"Meanwhile, stay away from Regan. No matter what she's told the Tulpa, she may kill you out of spite."

I sighed in relief. So he wasn't going to push me into Midheaven, and he wouldn't lock me in the sanctuary either. Giving me a choice might be an obvious ploy at slowly gaining my acquiescence, but it was the least of all evils. Still, he'd admitted to locking Jacks in Midheaven, and he'd sent me in as well, knowing what the passage would demand of me. He had his reasons—he was the troop leader; he was Light—but both decisions tasted of pure, uncut ruthlessness. So was it true that he believed I'd given up nothing but my Shadow side? Again, how could I tell? How could he?

"Who else have you seen since your return?"

"Just Hunter."

He bit his bottom lip, mind working like a calculator. I could practically hear it clicking away.

I raised a brow. "Is that a problem?"

"Of course not."

I nodded, then looked at the ground. "Look, about this . . . about Hunter—"

He held up a hand. "Please. The less I know, the better."

My thoughts exactly.

"As for the others . . ." He just shrugged. "They probably won't be as . . . incurious."

I wanted to tell him that the others didn't need to know of my relationship with Hunter yet, if ever, but then a shout sounded throughout the warehouse, Felix's unmistakable whoop as he scented out the where, who, and most of the what of the previous night's events. I closed my eyes with a low groan. When I opened them again, Warren was wearing an ill-concealed smile.

"You might want to put on something a little more appropriate," he said, taking in Hunter's crumpled sweats. I couldn't really see the point as I could still hear Felix, now grilling Hunter in a playful tone. Even Warren rolled his eyes as he turned away. "Besides, it's time to train."

I wavered on my feet, and had to brace myself against the wall. I couldn't train with these people! They'd kill me just deflecting one of my blows! But Warren left the room before I could think of an excuse, and almost immediately, Hunter stood in the doorway, looking more hesitant than I was used to.

I straightened, rubbing a hand over my face as I shot him a distant smile.

"What did he say?" He asked.

"He wants me to go back to Midheaven. He says Harlan Tripp can tell me how to find Jaden Jacks."

Hunter stiffened as he eased toward me.

"I told him no."

Surprise froze on his face. "And he was okay with that?"

I tried for bravado, hoping the effort would actually lend me some. "What's he going to do, force me to give up pieces of my soul?"

"Good for you, Joanna." But as he reached for me, I could tell what he meant was, *Good for us.* I'd told Hunter I wouldn't leave again, and though I'd meant emotionally, I decided now that it would hold true for this world too.

And I definitely wasn't going to tell Warren about Ashlyn now. Even if the Tulpa did know of her. Don't ask me why, but it somehow seemed the lesser danger. How messed up was that?

"Hunt, about these maps . . . " I pulled back, wanting to ask what he was doing or planning, and what he so clearly didn't want Warren to know. What they were arguing about. Why?

"It's not clear?" he finally asked in the wake of all these unasked questions. I shook my head. "I was trying to find my way to you, Joanna. Once it was clear where you'd gone, I decided to come get you. I wanted you back. Safe and sound."

His hands fell again over my back, reminding me of the bruises there. *Sound.* I closed my eyes and leaned my head against his chest. I wasn't that . . . but as he pulled me close, dropping a kiss to my temple, smoothing back my hair with his smooth fingertips, I almost felt safe.

Then he spoke again. "C'mon. Let's train."

And he pulled me to the door, not knowing that what awaited me on the other side was the exact opposite of safe and sound.

"We have to drop back ten and punt, my friends," Warren was saying as Hunter and I joined the rest of the troop in the shooting range. I scanned the cavernous room, quickly noting who was there and who wasn't. Vanessa was absent, of course, probably given over to Chandra's care since Micah was here, and a quick scan told me that Kimber had been omitted again. Dammit. My first thought had been to stick close to her, the weakest in our troop, during this training session. Though perhaps her absence was for the best. Her dislike of me had shifted into unconcealed hatred, and she would have probably used the opportunity to settle scores.

Not, I thought, something I could currently afford.

I turned back to Warren as I leaned against the plastic

screen Felix, Jewell, and Riddick were clustered in front of, and fought to keep my thudding heart in check. It was beating too fast, and, though they didn't seem to notice, I glanced back to find Hunter—arms crossed, one brow lifted—staring right at me. I jerked my head and turned away. Tekla was to the right of him and, though she had her eyes closed, she was always aware of her surroundings. Shit, we could probably communicate by mental telepathy, and she'd still know it.

Of course, our appearance together—and mine in particular—was also noted. Micah and Gregor managed to nod and merely look away, though Felix wiggled his brows, and Jewell blushed for me. Riddick looked more like he wanted to question me about Midheaven—they all probably did—but Warren had obviously already filled them in or told them to drop it until later. Probably both.

I crossed my arms self-consciously, and pulled Hunter's sweatshirt tighter about me. Warren ignored the curious undercurrent and knowing glances that met our joint arrival, returning the group's focus to the point at hand.

"Safe zones," he said, positioning himself in the cavernous room's center, "have now become the least safe places for us in this city. Therefore, we need to rethink our place in this valley—indeed, in our entire world."

"You mean now that there's no place for us to hide outside of the sanctuary."

I automatically cringed. Gregor hadn't meant it as criticism, but I still felt it as such.

Warren, though, uncharacteristically shrugged it off. "It doesn't matter."

I tilted my head, unsure that I'd heard him right. "What?"

Warren fisted one hand on his hip, the other raking through his short, choppy hair. "Obviously I'd prefer if the Shadows were the ones hamstrung by a lack of safe zones, but we feel it as a loss only because we've known the alternative. This is what I mean by reconceptualizing our world. We must now reimagine our territory."

"I'm sorry. Are you telling us to . . . think cheery thoughts?" Felix clearly hadn't forgiven him for keeping them in the dark about Midheaven's existence. "What? And it will all go away?"

"I'm saying check the attitude, son. Change your mind, and you can—"

"Change the world. Yeah, yeah. Got that memo." Felix crossed his arms. "And we still have no safe zones." He shot me an apologetic look when I ducked my head again, because his anger wasn't for me. But Warren was too obtuse and stubborn and focused to note it, or care. "So what's your suggestion, hide out in our sanctuary?"

"I suggest," Warren said coldly, "that we don't hide at all."

An appropriately dead silence met that proclamation.

Warren's mouth lifted at one side. "Inside the safe zones, we are vulnerable to our enemies' weapons—"

"While they remain impervious to our own," Tekla added, opening her eyes. I realized she already knew what Warren was going to say. However, the rest of us were still in the dark.

"But *outside* of those zones . . ."

Warren trailed off, waiting. And, slowly, one by one, understanding crept over each face. Outside of those zones, our weapons still worked. We could still fight. Hunter was the first to voice the new thought. "We just don't enter the safe zones. We meet them, only and always, in *our* city."

"That's where we take our stand," Riddick added, punching a fist into his opposite palm. "On the streets."

"That's our even ground," Jewell added, with a lift of her chin.

"But we don't do it alone. We do it back to back. In teams." Warren jerked his head at our surgeon . . . and scientist. "Micah."

Micah had moved to a table containing what looked like a fire extinguisher, and we all watched as he pointed the hose and nozzle toward himself. "This is a fortifying preservative. Chandra and I have been working on it for some time now. It defends against attack."

He demonstrated by spraying his thigh with a mist that fell like a spider's web over his frame before disappearing. Then he whipped his conduit, a pristine scalpel that caught light as if drawing it in . . . and plunged it into his leg.

Jewell screamed.

The scalpel bounced off of him . . . and the webbing rippled with the after-effects, then fell away, dissolving on the floor.

"And now I can be injured again."

"So it's a shield?" Gregor asked, touching the nozzle. A shimmering strand adhered to its tip like a piece of chewing gum as he pulled his finger away.

"More like a fire retardant over clothing. You're safeguarded for exactly one strike."

"I don't understand," I said. "I mean, I can see its use if we're ambushed, but why do we need a protective layer in training?"

"For the same reason Tekla just walled in the entire warehouse," Warren cut in, joining Micah, and crossing his arms. "We're in an all-out war, but right now the stakes are higher for us than for them. Right now we're off-balance."

"And in order to regain our footing," Micah said, motioning with his reclaimed scalpel, "we need to train harder than they do."

I was happy to don all the protective layering I could—I'd wear a hazmat suit everywhere but the shower if it meant unconditional safety—still, I was missing something. "But we've never worn protection while training before."

"Because we've never done a live-fire exercise before." He gestured to Micah and smiled. "Suit up."

The others lined up to be sprayed like bugs, but I just stood there. *Live fire*. That meant full force. And *that* meant training with the intent to kill.

Friendly fire, live fire, playing with fire . . . I couldn't afford any of it. So while everyone else crowded Micah like they were being crop-dusted, I slipped behind the plastic partitions and joined Warren. "I don't have a conduit."

He shrugged as he busied himself with what looked like a brand new iPhone. He hadn't missed a beat in dropping his hobo cover. For some reason, it made me want to iSmack him. "Then work on your defense."

Sure, no big deal to him. Throwing walls up into the air, like Tekla had when covering my retreat in Chinatown, was as important as remembering to hold your breath underwater. But if I missed? If I threw something up even a nanosecond late? Bye-bye defense, and bye-bye Jo.

"Jo! C'mon, it's your turn!"

Warren turned his back to make a call, effectively shutting me out. So I trudged over to Micah, still searching for a way out of this without letting on that I wasn't much more than a fast, bitchy mortal. "How protective is this coating?" I asked, as he sprayed my skin, clothing and hair. It felt like roll-on antiperspirant gliding over my entire body. I sniffed, expecting to smell powdery.

"It'll deflect any conduit once, no matter how hard the impact. Don't worry."

"Can I have two layers?"

He gazed down at me from his seven-foot height, and gave a fatherly sigh. "Now that'd be cheating, wouldn't it?"

"But I'm the only one without a conduit," I argued. "Two layers will even the playing field . . . and it'll be better for my partner, too."

"Nice try. But your partner can take care of him- or herself."

He looked less sure of this when Warren named *him* as my partner, but it was too late. The preservative was back on the other side of the partitions. Meanwhile, Gregor and Jewell had paired up—a senior agent with a junior—as had Tekla and Riddick. Hunter was paired with Felix . . . two senior agents, and the strongest team here.

Warren, as usual, took the center spot in our huddle. "I

want full force contact here, kids. Don't hold back. These are Shadow agents. They're trying to kill you, weaken your troop, and overtake *your* city." He made eye contact with each of us before turning away. "Tekla will run the drill."

"Wait," I said, stepping forward. "Where will you be?"

"Back in the panic room."

"Why?" Hunter asked, sounding wary.

Warren's answer was a flat look. Without another word, he turned and walked away.

Riddick twirled his conduit, a pencil-thin steel rod with hooks on the end, and everybody cringed. Dental tools. Fuck, they were scary. "So, um . . . once the protective layer's breached, stop attacking?"

Tekla smirked, as she pulled out a weapon similar to my crossbow, though with a retracting chain and anchor. I'd seen her remove hearts with that, leaving behind a warm body, still standing. "We're battling Shadow agents for the welfare of our city. A little reminder of what a conduit can do under controlled conditions won't hurt anyone. Just be sure to pull that punch."

A pulled punch, I thought with a sigh. Just a little something that could maim me. I dropped my head to my hands as I thought about battling my allies . . . for my life.

"What's wrong with you?" Hunter asked, coming up behind me as I tried to decide if I was going to center myself so that I could fight effectively . . . or run for my life.

"Nothing. Why?"

"You're tense all of a sudden." He dropped a hand to my shoulder and I flinched, underlining his point. "You look worried about something."

I glanced around. "No one else seems to think so."

He leaned so close his breath stirred my hair. "No one else was living inside you a few hours ago."

I swallowed hard, and looked away. Not just my body. My bloodstream and marrow. My heart and soul. We could all intuit moods more easily than mortals—with most people it was as simple as reading a magazine. Flip a page and the emotion was simply revealed there. Agents had the ability to disguise their emotions more easily too, synthetic compounds and strong wills helped with that—but he was right. I could still feel his warmth inside me, and I didn't doubt it was the same for him.

"That's why I wanted to be partnered with you."

"Micah will have your back."

Micah didn't know my life was in his hands. Hunter felt my anxiety spike again at the thought.

"Why are you suddenly so afraid?"

Just tell him.

Tell him that I could now be injured and killed? And then he'd report it to Warren, who'd lock me away and treat me as shittily as he did Kimber. Like a nuisance, something that gave drag, deadweight to be discarded at the first given opportunity. And in spite of my wishes and the soft feelings Hunter had for me—perhaps even because of them—he'd support it. *No, thank you.*

I shrugged, but the movement was too jerky. "I just wish I had a conduit, you know?"

"The best offense is a good defense," he said, unfurling a black, barbed whip. It was as wicked looking as the other conduits, though it gave Hunter a reach they didn't have. Great. Now I had to keep from getting killed by my lover.

"Then a good offense," I muttered, as he left to confer with Felix, "is massive artillery."

We paired up, taking on cross-angles in the giant room, and I worked on settling myself. I could do this. This was *training.* Not remotely as difficult or dangerous as the battles I'd survived over the past year. I'd fight, deflect, and gain ground for Micah, and if it looked like I was going to be hit or overpowered, I'd either duck behind the giant man, or call the match. None of my allies was going to keep pounding at me if I called a truce, right?

We turned our back to the others, and Micah stretched,

lifting his arms over his head. I looked straight up at ten feet of agent of Light. And Hunter thought *he* had reach.

"You've just gotta cover me," Micah reassured, as if I didn't know.

I gave him an obvious once over, from head to toe. "That's a big fucking wall."

We turned, looking at Tekla, as did the others. She remained supremely still, waiting until everyone was steeled in their stances, conduits palmed.

"Make the walls invisible," Micah muttered from the side of his mouth. "That should buy us some time, and an advantage."

Tekla jerked her head, a short nod, and we were off. Suddenly bodies whipped through the air, sticking in pairs as Warren decreed, individual strength doubled. As the weakest team, Micah and I were the biggest targets but this surprisingly worked to our advantage. Two of the three teams collided on their way to beat me down, which left Gregor and Jewell for us. I timed my first invisible wall perfectly and Gregor face-planted like a cartoon character. Micah actually laughed before lunging at the junior agent.

You had to give it to Jewell. Seven feet of big, mean motherfucker coming at her, and she only flinched a little. She had to wait until he got in close; her cover in the mortal world was that of a schoolteacher . . . and a party girl. In both instances, a set of fisted keys were not out of place . . . but Jewell's keys locked around her knuckles once laced together, and each was honed to a lethal point. It still wasn't an even match, not with Micah's experience making his blade work extra dangerous, but she was fortunate enough to also be considered paranoid in the mortal world. So she had two sets of keys, one for each fist, in contrast to Micah's sole weapon. In his mind, this clearly made them even. He swiped.

But by this time Gregor had ducked my wall, and his eyes flicked from Micah to me, first assessing . . . then knowing. Knock me out, and Micah would be his. Fortunately, Riddick came from nowhere to cut Gregor off with a leap and an agile slash of his hooked blade, which connected . . . and pulled Gregor's web of protection free. It shimmered as it stretched from his body . . . then fell. Gregor leapt to safety, calling out his apologies as he left Jewell alone, and I turned my attention to Riddick.

"Box him in!" Micah called, as Jewell backed up. Riddick heard Micah's orders, of course, but it was still a good idea. He, too, had to get in close, as his conduit wasn't anything he could risk throwing.

The biggest problem now was Riddick's partner, Tekla. Sure, this aptly illustrated the effectiveness of working in teams, but I was too busy trying to stay alive to appreciate it. She pointed her weapon at me, and the anchor imbedded in my wall so fast I was surprised I managed to raise it in time. She retracted the anchor, my wall fell, and we countered again. My wall shook this time. Fuck, she was strong. I doubled up, bent and crossed over my own body to shield Micah from Riddick . . . and that's when I hit my groove.

If you've trained hard enough—and if you last long enough—there's a point in every altercation where muscle memory takes over. It's like a pilot getting everything set, then giving the plane over to autopilot. Make the right move at the right time and suddenly your whole being—body and thought and will—snaps into alignment. It's the same feeling athletes get when they're "in the zone." I whirled, feinted, and suddenly my body was singing.

My stance was wide, arms extended full length, and I circled Micah, keeping close as I deflected left and then right, crossing arms, and at times, not even glancing in the direction of my deflections. I put up a wall so strong Tekla's anchor got stuck. I held it, and another, while delivering a back kick that sent Jewell barreling into Hunter's range. I erected walls that were both vertical and horizontal, climbing them, leaping twenty feet in the air . . . certainly no longer the weakest link.

Riddick decided to follow my lead, and drove up a

wall between himself and Micah, then dropped it before charging the bigger, slower man. I raised another at the last second, buying Micah time and space to fall back, and when Tekla tried to do the same for Riddick, I flipped my wrist so that my wall spread horizontally, splicing her visible one so that it rose only to waist height. She gasped and turned on me, wide-eyed. Micah leapt, I kept the surface as strong as a table, and he dispatched Riddick with a single, deft slice.

Then Hunter's whip appeared out of nowhere, and I screamed. The reaction was inappropriate—I was nowhere near the conduit, but had yelled as if I were—so Hunter's head jerked my way, but it was already too late. The whip snapped and Micah's protectant went down. Hunter, seeing the vulnerability, stood down so that Micah could clear the floor without mortal injury. Micah leapt, dropping f-bombs as he soared from the battle area, and Felix—Hunter's partner—immediately began advancing upon me.

"Shit." I backed up, knowing my fear was pumping out pheromones inappropriate for a training exercise, but I wasted no energy trying to stop them. Felix scented it, and like a Viking berserker in the throes of battle-lust, his eyes glazed over with martial fury. I slammed up three vertical walls in quick succession, which was a drain on my energy, and with every additional shield, the previous ones weakened. I whimpered.

"Jo?"

It was only a murmur, but Hunter's concern cost him. He should have been covering Felix—and his own ass—but Jewell saw it and struck.

She caught him at his wrist, following up quickly, clearly expecting to miss. But she didn't miss, and his whip dropped, skittering behind us like a sidewinder. That was enough to pull his web of coating away . . . and the followup nicked his arm. Jewell blanched as blood bloomed in the room, and looked as if she wanted to apologize. Someone gasped on the sidelines. But Hunter's gaze was for me.

He couldn't stay, of course. Live fire was now as dangerous for him as it was for me, and Tekla and Felix, battling hard, probably hadn't seen his disarmament.

By the time Hunter was gone, so was Felix, shot through with an anchor in his side, and cursing Tekla with a bald lack of respect. Meanwhile, she'd also woven between my three walls, and I created a fourth on the fly, just to buy myself time. I was too tired to make it invisible, but my mind was still clicking at warp speed, and that gave me an idea.

My next one was opaque, black as a Shadow's heart and as wide as the room. I pivoted and ducked behind it . . . then realized I was three feet from the warehouse wall and running out of space.

"Tekla . . . I give up!"

"Push yourself, Jo." She answered, and the wall behind me shook.

Shit. "No, I can't—"

"Agents of Light don't ever quit!" And her anchor plunged through the concrete barrier at my back, barely missing my shoulder.

Yelping, I ducked. She wasn't going to stop. So I pleaded. "Tekla, I can't be hit!"

"Oh, I bet I can hit you," Jewell said, from my other side. I whipped my left arm out just in time. My wall didn't rise to full height—it was too hurried for that— but it halted her momentum and she tumbled over its top. By the time she somersaulted into a standing position, I had another wall erected. I couldn't see the impact, but I heard her groan.

And then back to Tekla. Dammit! I was too unfocused now. I was getting tired, my eyes darting around as quickly as my thoughts, and I wondered why these bitches weren't taking each other out instead of closing in on *me*.

That's when I saw it. Lunging without hesitation, I grabbed Hunter's barbed whip—the conduit of an ally who was still alive—and squeezed its handle. Its weight felt awkward as I whirled it around, but it lashed out like a lightning rod, and took down Jewell with a resounding snap. She screamed, though whether from pain or surprise, I couldn't tell . . . or care. I whirled and again, the whip responded as if it was my own.

Maybe it was due to the aureole Hunter and I had recently shared again. Maybe it was because, as he mentioned earlier, he'd lived inside of me only a short time before. But I wasn't just holding his weapon, I was using it effectively, and the more I moved—erecting walls with the torque of my palm, leaping atop them, now hunting Tekla—the more I reveled in the ease of my armament, even while I wondered at it.

Hunter was alive. This conduit was an extension of his body. And yet it was responding agilely to my touch.

I let out a battle cry and leapt to the rafters, whip hissing from my palm.

"Kairos!" Someone yelled from the sidelines, and I thought, yes. Maybe *that* was it. I was the Kairos. I couldn't replace my own conduit—not with the original still out there, still a part of me, and still yearning to be united with me as I did with it—but I could use those of my allies. Because as I caught air, I felt the way Hunter looked in battle: confident and lithe . . . and scary as shit.

"That's bullshit!" Someone else said, echoing my next fleeting thought. So I pivoted at the apex of my flight, took the whip's handle in both hands, and wheeled it around like a discus. I caught Tekla's anchor right at its release, and pulled, yanking her from her feet . . .

"Stop!"

The cry rocked the building, rippling in the air like a physical blow. Tekla, still sprawled on her stomach, cursed under her breath—a rarity for her—and shut her eyes, probably to reinforce the mental walls she'd put up around the building. I dropped to the ground with a soft bend of my knees, breathing hard, but smiling inside. I was still fast. My wall work was improving. *Keep that bitchy edge,*

I thought as I straightened and turned to the others, and I might be okay yet.

But Warren was not smiling. "Jo, you're with me. Bring the whip. The rest of you, clean this place up." And he stalked back to the panic room while the others continued silently staring at me.

"Why's he pissed at us?" Riddick muttered, kicking at the debris of one of my walls that had collapsed under Warren's cry. It ricocheted into another, and both disappeared in a puff of smoke.

"How did you do that?" Jewell asked as I passed. I shrugged and swallowed hard, risking a glance at Hunter who, ominously, hadn't moved. He just stared as he held his bloodied forearm tight to his side, eyes flicking to his whip before winging back up at me. I kept walking . . . and once inside the panic room, Warren posed the same question.

"How *did* you do that?"

I shrugged uncomfortably as he shut the door behind me. "I—I don't know. I wasn't able to use the replacement conduit that he was making me at all."

"Because yours still exists." Warren nodded impatiently, already knowing that. "Have you used or practiced with this whip before?"

I shook my head. "Never."

He frowned. "So maybe it's this bond between you two. Maybe because you just—"

"Okay!" I held up a hand just to keep the thought from passing his lips. I hated my relationships, or my emotions, being displayed so openly. Still . . . could that be it? Were Hunter and I somehow linked now? Share a body and bed . . . share a soul and conduit?

A quick rap at the door and Hunter peeked in, still looking disturbed, and I could understand why. Touching someone else's conduit—using it as your own—that was like reaching inside a body and shifting around a person's organs. An apology was already on my lips when Warren snapped.

"Not now, Hunter." He waved him away and motioned for him to shut the door.

"There's a call—"

"Ignore it!"

"It can't be ignored!" Hunter held out the phone, his good arm steady in the air, eyes leveled on his troop leader's face. Warren frowned at the text on the screen, then crossed the room for a closer look. Once there, he stilled altogether. "Oh."

Hunter's gaze shifted to me.

"What?" My first thought was that Vanessa had been captured again . . . or maybe one of the others. But Vanessa was safe in our underground lair, and everyone else was here. So . . . "What?" I said louder.

Warren finally looked back at me. "I don't know whether to tell you that I'm sorry or not."

"Why? What happened?"

"It's your father, Joanna. Or . . . not your father, but Xavier." He swallowed hard.

"What about him?" I stepped closer.

"He died, Jo," Hunter said, stilling me again. "In the middle of the night."

17

    "I'm sorry for your loss."
    My loss, I thought, staring at the suit of yet another man smiling placatingly in front of me. I'd arrived at Xavier's compound directly from the warehouse, and had to push aside the thoughts of my relationships with Hunter and my ability to use his conduit as if it were my own, for the time being. But the fact was, all my thoughts seemed to be sluggish right now, and I finally gave up on trying to remember this man's name—or even care—and simply nodded. This pattern repeated itself as I moved on through the sitting room, the family room, the living room . . . all the misnamed rooms in Xavier Archer's house, while I avoided the sympathetic gazes of the strangers around me and thought about my *loss*.

    The man who'd despised me practically since birth was dead. The man who blamed me for my mother's abandonment was dead. The man who treated people as usable objects, and siphoned his soul to the Tulpa in return for unlimited power and money was, finally, dead. I looked around at all that remained.

    I'd lost nothing.

But strangely, I didn't feel I'd gained anything either.

"My condolences, Ms. Archer." I did recognize this man. This was John, Xavier's closest confidant, and a man who moved like an offensive lineman instead of a lawyer. He'd never given either Olivia or me a second glance, but that had changed now. I could see him developing plays as he looked at me, looking for weaknesses, figuring out if I needed to be double-teamed, trapped, or cross-blocked. And why not? Once a Playmate, a plaything—arm candy to be given a second glance but not a thought—Olivia Archer was no longer simply an heiress. She was a mogul. John, I knew, had strategies for dealing with moguls.

I made my way to the winding staircase and the upstairs corridor under the watchful eye of John and the army of sycophants Xavier had left leaderless, though I knew I wouldn't be followed. They thought I was in shock. Xavier's personal physician had already offered me soothing sedatives, so I'd take the path of least resistance and play the part of the frail princess until I could get out of there and back to searching for Jaden Jacks. I didn't feel bad about the hypocrisy, pretending to care when I knew I did not. Xavier had gotten what was coming to him. He was an ass, he was greedy, and I'd never loved him.

So why was my heart heavy, as if I did?

I dodged two maids who averted their eyes, arms filled with linens, their Spanish whispered once they thought I could no longer hear. The household staff had returned upon Helen's orders, and were putting things back to order, dusting and scrubbing and wondering what I was going to do with all this space and belongings, with their paychecks and all their lives. Their gazes were just as assessing as John's, which was probably how I ended up in Xavier's vacant wing. There was no other reason to be there. But it was quiet, and with Xavier's body still in residence, no one seemed ready to tread there yet.

Exactly what I needed.

Yet I hesitated until the soft dulcet tones of Spanish arose again behind me, then pushed the door open and slipped inside.

The first thing I noticed was that the flowers sent by well-wishers were no longer moldering in lukewarm water, the table once holding them now a bald spot among the rest of the ornate tableaus of the sitting room. I crossed to the window where thick curtain blotted out the sunlight and shoved it open. Xavier was dead. He couldn't say a thing about it.

As if approving of this belated rebellion, the storm clouds that'd been dogging the valley last night had thinned and parted, revealing a tender blue sky and a sharp morning sun. I saw John step outside on the patio below me, the bald spot on his head a perfect O from directly above, a phone to his ear as he lit a cigarillo. Unlocking the window, I slid it open an inch, all I'd need to hear his end of the conversation even though I was thirty feet above him.

"Of course she's incompetent," he scoffed on a thin stream of smoke. "A figurehead is all . . . with the emphasis on her figure . . . "

He laughed, and so did the person on the other end of the line. I did not.

" . . . an easy mark for anyone with the intelligence above that of a soybean. I've called an emergency meeting with the board of directors. Yes, we'll handle that now. And her . . . "

He disappeared under the back portico, totally unaware that I was there . . . and I was a woman who disliked being handled. Guessing he was going to take this conversation into the inner courtyard, I crossed into the bedroom, where I could watch and hear him from Xavier's window. I was so preoccupied by listening in that I forgot about Xavier's body, lying like an empty shell on the linen shore of his crisp bedsheets. I was also halfway through the room before I realized I wasn't alone.

"He underestimates you." The voice was strong and low. Charbroiled.

My gut reaction was to run. I jolted, automatically reaching for the mask in my bag, though the reaction could be attributed to the shock of finding someone else in the room. I played it off that way . . . and turned around to face the Tulpa.

He was seated in a straight-backed chair next to Xavier's bed, looking neither large nor small, not overdressed or under, but as comfortable in this clothing and body as he was in any other. The skin he lived in today was pale, but a blank-slate pale, without a freckle to mar the entire canvas. It made him look as lifeless as the corpse next to him, and made me wonder if he'd hidden in the dark long enough to gather enough power to willingly take on these features, or if they'd been superimposed upon him by the mind and expectation of one of his followers. Perhaps Lindy—or Helen—as she was downstairs? I forced myself to calm. My scent was masked; I'd injected the pheromones before leaving the warehouse. I was here as Olivia, so Olivia I would be.

Still, I couldn't help a fleeting wish for a layer or two of Micah's protective webbing. "Y-You heard what he was saying?"

Of course he had. His hearing was sharper than a jungle cat's.

The Tulpa shrugged. "Don't worry about John. He'll come at you head-on, full-force, like he's in a demolition derby. I, on the other hand, learned long ago to be more circumspect around beautiful women."

His smile widened, dimples appeared, as if that was supposed to be a compliment. Knowing what I did of his past, how it intertwined with my mother's, I remained on guard. "Who are you?" I asked. Like I didn't know.

"You mean Helen hasn't mentioned me?" He tsk-tsked at the shake of my head. "I was a mentor of sorts to your father. A benefactor, if you will."

But he still didn't say his name. I tilted my head, frowning. "Daddy never mentioned you either."

"I was a sort of fairy godfather, if you will. There when he needed me. Behind the scenes the rest of the time." He stood, unnaturally unwrinkled. I took a step back, and he smiled benignly. "I could do the same for you."

"I—I don't know what you mean."

"You'll need help running this empire." He gestured to the window, then folded his hands in front of him. "Navigating men like John who see only dollar signs when they look at you. They'll see you as someone to run down on their way to a financial utopia. But I could teach you how to nullify his greed while using his skills for your own gain. I've known many such men myself."

He was the archetype for such men.

I bit my lip, nodding, then changed the subject lest he think me too smart. "So what are you doing here now?"

"Paying my respects, of course." He sighed heavily, looking over at Xavier. "Saying good-bye."

Seeing if there was anything left of Xavier's soul to drain, I thought wryly. Maybe I should offer him a straw.

"Well," he said in the wake of my silence, "at least promise me you'll think about it."

He held out his hand. I looked at it as shock struck me like a bolt. He'd know who and what I was as soon as I touched him. He'd feel my too-smooth fingertips. And from the narrow, assessing look in his eyes, that was the point. He wasn't here for Xavier, he was here because he knew Olivia Archer would be also. He was testing the waters of this relationship, beginning to build trust on both sides.

Shit, shit, shit.

I swallowed hard, making damned sure to keep the scent of my emotions dampened, and took a step forward. But I let my gaze veer to Xavier's lifeless body, willed my face into a teary frown, and ran right into the footstool that'd been pushed thoughtlessly aside.

"Ow!" I leaned down, rubbing at my shin.

"Are you okay?" Though buried beneath layers of control, the annoyance was sharp in his voice. I glanced up and gave him one of Olivia's most sheepish and sweetest smiles.

"I'm such a klutz. I mean, I fell down half a staircase just yesterday. See?"

I pushed up my shirt to reveal the marks I'd received from Hunter. Most men would focus on the petal smooth belly and curve of my hip. The Tulpa, I knew, was only seeing the bruises. He relaxed further into the shadows, no longer interested in touching, testing me. Why should he? I was clearly mortal. "You should be more careful."

"That's so true," I said, pulling my shirt down. I nodded vigorously, then looked again at Xavier.

"Oh . . . " The Tulpa stood fluidly. "How rude of me. Of course you want a few moments alone to say good-bye."

"Yes." I lowered my head, pretending not to see his outstretched hand. Fortunately, he dropped it. "Thank you."

He slid by so smoothly I expected to hear a rattler's tail. I stepped to Xavier's bedside to ward off my shudder, and bit my lip as I looked at Xavier's body.

"You may call me if you need anything at all. Helen knows how to get ahold of me."

I nodded but didn't look up, not wanting to give him too much deference, too early. Olivia would have no idea who he was, so this first impression wouldn't leave much of a visible mark. But he would be back, I now knew, hearing the sitting room door snap shut. The Tulpa was going to try and use me. The Archer dynasty was too vast and strong to allow a little lost soul to get in the way.

I lifted my gaze to Xavier's face, wondering how he'd feel about that. Again I was shocked from thought by his appearance. He was hardly much more than a skeleton with skin, a thin, brittle covering that would be decomposed by week's end. I will not feel sorry for him, I thought, clenching my jaw as my gaze drifted down his once-great frame, snagging on the fingers that had once curled in cast-iron fists. They were pencil thin now. I could reach out and snap them like twigs.

No, I'd waste no sorrow on Xavier. The man had willingly sold his soul for status. He'd given the Tulpa a front of respectability, and a base from which to operate. Xavier, more than any other person, had helped the Tulpa actualize in this world.

And he'd treated me like refuse.

"Don't think of that," I muttered to myself, wiping at my eyes. There must have been pollen or dander or dust mites thick in the room. "Just focus on facts."

And the fact was, it made no difference that someone else would have taken up the mantle if Xavier had refused—there was no shortage of people who'd abandon morals for money—because it *had* been him. All through my youth. Even while I suffered, I thought, sniffling, he continued to fuel and feed that limitless evil.

So Xavier hadn't died from something practical, like a disease that had forgotten to question his station and power and status before creeping up to strangle his arteries. He hadn't even died from something as dramatic as a broken heart. No, he'd finally expired because there was so little left inside of him that was still human. This physical shell, which looked like it would blow away in the faintest of winds, was simply the last of him to fall to rot.

"I should dance on your grave," I said, a tear from the allergens falling down my cheek. But there was no snapped comeback, no sense of being heard, now or ever. Xavier's soul was finally, utterly depleted, and now the hollow shell his wealth had created could finally be put to rest.

I wiped my eyes and left the room.

There were twenty-eight messages of condolence waiting for me by the time I left Xavier's home—now mine, I supposed—and twelve of them were from Cher alone. I cursed silently, but knew I'd have to visit her before I did anything else. That's what Olivia would do, and people were certainly watching now.

By the time I reached the sprawling ranch house where Cher lived with her mother, the sun was once again blocked in by barren clouds, and a chilled wind whipped over the ground, causing me to think of Northern Lights instead of neon ones. What was going on with the weather? I gazed heavenward, but didn't have much time to dwell on it. The door flew open almost as soon as I knocked, and I was swept up into an all-encompassing hug.

"Hey, Suz," I said, sounding strangled. She loosened her hold. She was wearing thin fleece sweats, her gray zip-top making it clear she wore nothing underneath, and her hair was piled atop her head, dark roots visible at the base of her neck. It was still early morning, so her face was barer than I'd ever seen it, but it was creamy and smooth, still silky perfection at forty-something. She never spoke of her age. She considered it bad juju.

"Oh, darlin'," she began, and it was all I could do not to sigh. She tilted her head, soft errant strands falling around her face as I turned to her. "We only just heard. It's terrible. I'm so sorry for your loss. Are you okay?"

Pulling me through the threshold, she simultaneously answered her own question. "Silly. Of course you're not. If anyone should know that, it's me." From all appearances, she was the typical Vegas trophy wife. She'd married someone far older than she, yet by all accounts she'd truly loved Cher's father, something that'd been questioned in the recent spate of articles and gossip surrounding her new engagement . . . and that meant we really didn't share the same loss. I did not love the man who had died in the night. Still, I appreciated her effort and knew Olivia would be grateful for it.

"Thank you." Wanting to distract her, I said, "Where's Cher?"

"She went to Xavier's to find you, of course. You two probably drove right by each other on the way over. We should call." As she picked up the cordless phone, I tossed my bag down on the cream sofa, immediately relaxing. It was nice to be in a safe, estrogen-filled environment that wouldn't actually kill me. Thick white candles dotted nearly every surface, their sheer numbers and smooth melted shapes making them art all on their own. Their scent lingered among the silk and brocades of the pillows and throws, and softened the stark collage of photos blanketing an entire wall. My sister was a significant part of that collage, and in the past year I'd been incorporated as well . . . though, of course, in Olivia's softly smiling, beautiful form.

Suzanne turned to me after she'd hung up with Cher, who promised to be right home, and gave me a watery smile. "Is there anything at all I can do to help?"

"You're doing it," I told her, and blew out a long sigh. And I did feel better. Lighter, though I had no reason to be down. "But what are you doing here? I thought Arun moved you into Asgard?"

Apparently the roomy but modest home wasn't good enough for a future princess, and Arun had chosen the palatial suites at Valhalla as his bride's new residence until he could have his own compound built. He knew she liked living in Vegas, and was indulging her desire to have a fourth home here. Or was it fifth?

At any rate, Cher would have the sprawling, if slightly aged, home to herself from now on, and for some reason that brought on my melancholy again. A home without the two of them in it, I realized with some surprise, wouldn't feel like much of a home at all.

"I think I'm doing the same thing here that you are," she said quietly, looking up at me as she lowered her head. "Escaping."

I winced. "That bad, huh?"

She shook her head, too quickly. "Not bad at all, actually. But . . . different."

"Well, why don't you talk to Arun about it? He seems like he'd move the world for you."

Her smile brightened and she actually blushed at that. "Maybe I will when he gets back."

"Back?"

"He went to Scottsdale for meetings. He's a bit superstitious. Says the weather here is unlucky, and that it looks like the sky is falling."

I eyed the bulging nest of power through the decorative glass of the front door. It *did* look like it was falling. "So he left you under it?"

"I told him I didn't want to go. It's my home." She leaned against the back of the sofa and crossed her bare feet at the ankles. "Besides, Thanksgiving is coming up soon. You're still spending it with us, right?"

"Of course."

"Are you injured?"

"Wha . . . ?" I glanced down in the direction of her gaze and saw the dried blood from where I'd run into the footstool. *Damn it.* I was going to have to get used to moving around differently again. "It's just a scratch," I said sadly.

"Sit here," Suzanne said, pointing at an overstuffed ottoman. "I'll get the Bactine."

I sighed as I sat. Bactine today . . . a full body cast tomorrow.

She returned with the medicine and a whole bag of cotton balls. "What happened?" she asked, dabbing lightly.

"Dark club," I lied. "Too much to drink. Late night. I fell down some stairs."

"Ouch," she said, and I watched the cool liquid bubble on my skin. I couldn't believe I was going to have to get used to this again. How the hell was I going to tell Warren?

"Well, that which doesn't kill you, right?" I said, quoting him now.

Suzanne grimaced. "I've always hated that saying."

"Yeah, me too."

"There, that should do it." She sat back on her heels and blew hair from her eyes. "Want pancakes while we wait?" she asked, looking up at me.

"Oh, is that what you're burning?"

She leapt to her feet. "Shit!"

I followed her to the kitchen, where she was, indeed, enthusiastically burning pancakes. While she went to scrape those into the trash and start over, I looked around.

The View played on in the background, some pseudo-Thanksgiving show reminding me that in this world—despite being camped out over another one, despite Xavier's death—celebration was only days away. I eyed the tiny TV mounted beneath the shiny beech cabinets, the light granite countertops, the collection of ceramic roosters and pigs, and sighed. Sometimes I wished I had Suzanne's life. And that was without the prince.

I leaned on the counter across from her and watched as she poured more pancakes into the skillet.

All this, I thought with a grimace, and she couldn't flip a pancake for crap.

"Here," I said, nudging her aside. "Let me."

I took the spatula and turned down the heat. Suzanne dropped onto a bar stool and sighed in relief. If only taking over pancake duty was the most tasking of my heroic duties. I added some butter to the pan and poured the batter, glancing at her as she blithely sipped from her tiny espresso cup.

"Let's talk about something cheery, shall we?" she said. "What about you? How's your pursuit of pleasure and bliss going?"

It took me a moment to recall our conversation at the lingerie trunk show, right after Madeleine and Lena had turned on her. That seemed a lifetime ago now—before Vanessa, before Midheaven, and before I'd knew real goddesses existed—so I'd forgotten all about it. That was the problem with lying. Remembering what you were lying about was often harder than telling the truth.

"Not great." I thought about Solange languishing beneath her stars, fashioning precious jewels out of other people's souls—beautiful and strong . . . and more deadly than I'd ever be. "Um, I met a woman who showed me I have a long way to go."

"Bitch," Suzanne said shortly, which caused me to bark out in laughter. "The Olivia Archer I know and love would go head-to-head with her."

The thought was laughable, and I actually snorted. It would take me weeks alone just to learn how to walk in Diana's spiked shoes. But what really got me was the women's amplified power. I'd doubted a lot of things about myself in the past, but I'd never doubted my strength. Yet Solange's power made me feel like the Karate Kid.

"I'm afraid I'm out of my league there." I shrugged, a move that betrayed my self-consciousness. "It's easy most of the time here. Vegas, I mean. Big fish, small pond. But this other woman is . . . formidable." I handed Suzanne a plate and slid her the syrup.

She put off answering long enough to cut into her food, groaning with the first bite, taking a second as I poured more batter. She spoke with a full mouth. "You still don't get it, do you? Want me to spell out for you what a real man finds most attractive?"

I was talking about might, not men, but I nodded for her to continue. She lived, very simply, in another world.

"An authentic woman. Someone who walks through this world following her own whim. He'll see her, he'll watch her, and he'll continue to stare, unblinking, as if mesmerized by the tail of a kite soaring and tossing about on the wind. For the right man, one who's ready, just watching his woman move around scores new patterns on his retina, creates new pathways in his mind—or, for the first time, lights up the ancient ones—about what a real woman is."

I tapped my spatula on the side of the pan, sharply, and put a hand on my hip. "Really? So what about all that lingerie and . . . " *Shit.* " . . . stuff?"

"Oh." She sat up straighter, popped another bite into her mouth. "That's not for a man. That's for me."

I stared.

She stabbed some more cooked batter. "These are really good."

I glanced down, realized it was time to flip over another. "My sister showed me how to make them," I said softly, moving another pancake to a plate.

Suzanne reached over the countertop and touched my arm. Her fingertips were cool and light, almost like she could float away. "You look tired, honey. Do you want to lie down in the guest room after breakfast? Just for a bit?"

I was exhausted, flipping the last pancake. But my mind was wired, and I still had too much to figure out about Jasmine and Warren. Solange and Jacks. Hunter and me, I thought, returning to Suzanne's words. *An authentic woman?* I frowned, pouring the syrup.

"Suz," I said hesitantly, not looking at her. "You know when you told me that women were the color of the world? That we were the life and—"

"The beauty." She nodded, sighing to herself. "It's so true. It's our natural state. It's—"

"I'm not," I said suddenly, and I didn't know why, but I wanted to cry at the statement. I swallowed hard. "I'm gray."

"Has someone been telling you that? Who? That woman?" She was suddenly at my side, soft blue eyes burrowing into my own. I looked down. Solange had *shown* me. But Warren, I now realized, was the one treating me that way. And it wasn't in words, but specifically in what he didn't tell me, in the things he kept close to his chest. He claimed that he wanted me close, but then he'd sent me away. He said he valued me, but he continually put me at risk.

"Nah." I shook myself, realizing I was frowning and staring into space, and that I hadn't yet answered Suzanne. "A man, actually."

"Then you don't want him in your life. A man like that is poison, do you understand?"

A man, sure. A mortal, and I'd agree. But I wasn't sure the same held true of a powerful and overbearing superhero. I also wasn't so sure that "want" had anything to do with it. I took a bite of my own pancakes just to avoid answering, when a movement at the back door window caught my eye. I froze, fork halfway to my mouth, as I was caught in the gaze of a tulpa.

Suzanne, seeing my stricken look, whirled. Of course, there was nothing there but the strangely blotted sky, and a small dust devil blowing up debris behind her pool. She turned back around and I raised my brows.

"Just had a thought. Gotta go."

She lifted her brows as high as the Botox would allow. "What?"

"Yeah, um . . . funeral plans. Gotta get it done. But the pancakes fortified me." I patted my tummy before dropping a hand on her arm. "And so did the chat. Thank you."

She rolled her eyes and shook off my hand. "Well, sheesh. Just hold on."

I did, tapping my foot impatiently as she disappeared at the back of the house. Skamar popped up again, and I made a face, waving her away. Suzanne rounded the corner again, and I turned the gesture into a smooth patting of my hair, smiling grimly.

"Here," she said, holding out her hands.

"What is it?"

"A necklace given to me by my first husband. Actually, it was the first gift he ever gave me. Said it shields you from the evil eye. It's Asian, so Arun will most certainly know what it is . . . and he wouldn't understand if I hung onto it. I want you to have it."

I frowned, and stared at her, Skamar forgotten. "What about Cher?"

Why me? Though, too late, I remembered Suzanne

didn't differentiate between the two of us. We were both daughters to her.

She rolled her eyes as she circled behind me. I lifted my hair and she slid the necklace over my neck. "She's the one who thought of it. Actually, she wanted to give it to you herself."

I looked down. It was a solid pendant of intricate scroll-work and bright gold. There were seven places for precious stones, all different colors, though I noticed there were a couple missing. I attributed that to age, which meant it was all the more valuable. "It's beautiful. But I can't possibly accept it. It means so much to you both."

She nodded, like she'd been expecting that, and folded my fingers over it. "Then just wear it to your father's funeral."

"Okay," I said, deeming it easier not to argue. "Thank you."

She followed me to the door. "Cher's going to be upset that she missed you."

"I'll see her at Thanksgiving. Tell her I'm doing okay." I stepped from the patio and into a gust of whipping wind as I headed down the drive.

"Olivia!" Half out the door, Suz shook her head. "You're not gray. You're a fuckin' rainbow. Got it?"

I could only smile and wave . . . and hope that she was right.

18

"Yo, Rainbow Brite," Skamar said, meeting me around the corner. I hoped we looked like two neighbors swapping recipes on the street corner. Or, from the way Skamar had her hands fisted on her hips, at least like two women fighting over the same man. That, at least, wasn't too out of the ordinary. "What the fuck are you doing?"

"Don't criticize her," I said, ignoring the latter half of her question. I walked a bit farther so we could duck beneath the concealing shade of a giant plum tree. "I'm being Olivia. What the fuck are *you* doing?"

"Oh, just dodging the Tulpa."

"You mean he's here?" I couldn't keep the panic from bleeding into my voice, and I cleared my throat, remembering that revealed emotion normally caused my troubles.

"Not yet. But he'll find me. He always does."

I wanted to tell her that *I'd* been trying to find her, but the fatigue in her voice had me softening toward her, as did her explanation. It couldn't be easy. She'd only come into full being a month ago, and had been fighting nonstop ever since. Not exactly the homecoming most newborns were given in this world.

"Look, I'm sorry for showing up here. I had to get you alone."

My full attention narrowed back on her, along with my hard gaze. "You're not going to try to eat any of my vital organs again, are you?"

She gave me a tight smile. "It no longer appeals, no."

Good. Devouring the organs, and particularly the heart of the person whose face and life a doppelgänger mirrored—and I mean that in a twisted, funhouse sort of way—was the fastest, most efficient means of becoming a fully realized entity. Fortunately, I'd satisfied her greed for life with something even stronger than my flesh: her name. Skamar meant *star* in the Tibetan tongue. I'd thought it apropos for someone who'd begun life as a mere thought-form constructed out of the myth and meditation so critical to the eastern culture.

"You look different."

What I meant was she didn't look like me.

When we'd first met, Skamar was a doppelgänger, the evolutionary precursor to a full-fledged tulpa. Sporting a body of ripples and waves, one as malleable as tensile foam, she'd shone with a light that made her skin snap with every movement, like a diamond in the sun. Intent upon killing me and taking over my life, that bubble and light had solidified into a body mirroring mine so closely in both physical aspect and mannerism that even I wasn't able to discern the difference. However, in the weeks since I'd last seen her, Skamar had taken on an identity of her own.

Thin and small and pale, she'd have been plain too, were her features not so sharp. Her short hair was blunt and red, her matching lashes so light she looked bald-eyed, but her lips were defined even without color, and her nose arrowed between cheekbones you could hang laundry from, wide and high. I'd have commented about one of Jane Austen's characters inadvertently wandering into an action flick, but I didn't think she'd appreciate it.

Her clothes were dark, but silk and lightweight, obviously chosen for comfort and mobility rather than warmth. Not remotely appropriate for a chilled winter day, I thought, but from the looks of them—tattered and bloodied—she'd been wearing them awhile.

For a moment I wondered what I'd choose to look like were I given physical creative carte blanche. As much as I loved my sister, and had come to accept my transformation into her, I wouldn't have been a buxom, blond socialite who needed a calendar just to keep up with her physical maintenance.

"I need more power, Joanna. The energy from the name-giving is no longer enough."

"What? You want a middle one? Fine. Matilda. Take it." I flicked my hands at her, more of a nervous gesture than a dismissive one. "Be merry."

That almost earned a smile. "Skamar is sufficient, thanks. But a true live birth in this world is always recorded in written form. Mine still hasn't been."

I drew back at that. "Like a birth certificate?"

"Exactly."

"Dude. You were born of thought and, like, bubbles." She'd been practically see-through when we first met. "No offense, but the drones down at County probably won't certify someone who could have once passed as a bath product."

"The manuals, Joanna. My name must be made public in the manuals of Light."

Again, the manuals. But the sharpness in her voice obliterated my sarcasm. A chill passed through me as she glared, and I checked my attitude. It was a good idea to remember that the creature in front of me wasn't an ordinary woman. In fact, one got the idea that she could take over my troop if she wanted to, the same way the Tulpa had waltzed into the top position with the Shadow agents. Right now, however, she was focused on one thing.

"It's the only way I can harness that." She was pointing at the sky.

I looked up and winced. "Ozone? Smog? Unusual cloud coverage?"

"Power."

So that was what was spinning behind those wispy layers, just as Hunter claimed on my recent return from the underground. The sky now appeared blown up with fog that glowed with soft blues and greens, which bounced off each other, making them appear alive.

"That's the unclaimed power given off every time the two of us fight but don't win. Neither of us can lay claim to it."

"So stop fighting." *That* seemed kinda obvious.

"And let him just kill you instead?"

"Oh."

Her expression said *I told you so.* I swallowed hard, looking with renewed respect at the sky. The unclaimed power of two tulpas whipping above like an energetic freeway. "So what happens if all that energy is funneled into either of you?"

"If I get it? I'll reduce him to ash. If he does?" She swallowed hard. "He'll knock me from the globe like a figure from a chessboard."

"But you're beating him! I heard him in those tunnels. He was gasping for breath. He needed to be encased in total darkness just to heal."

In solitude and silence. Safe from eyes that might impose expectation upon his figure and form, which would siphon off the very energy he was trying to recoup. So now that we knew his lack of permeability was a weakness, why weren't we trying to exploit it?

"Speaking of the tunnels. Your mother was not happy to learn you'd been in there."

"Then tell her to take it up with me herself," I said smartly. "Besides, I tried to find you. Warren wanted me to ask you about walking the line. I just got lucky and found it myself first."

"You didn't get lucky, Jo. Quite the opposite." And she looked at me like I'd lost something irreplaceable.

Please don't let it be irreplaceable.

I hid my fear under a thin layer of bravado. "Well, I think we should all go back in together. Ambush the Tulpa after one of his battles with you. He'll be alone, his energy at its lowest."

"Let me worry about the Tulpa. You fix that changeling. And get those manuals written. But stay away from Midheaven. I haven't shown you—" She whirled in response to something I could neither see nor feel. "Fuck. He's on the move again."

"But—"

Turning back, she grabbed my shoulders and shook me hard. "I'm doing my best to keep him away from you, Joanna! Now, please. Fix those manuals."

An explosive gust thrust me backward, and I was alone in the expanse of a breath. My shoulder angled awkwardly into the tree trunk, but my grunt was drowned out by Skamar's battle cry. A second later the two tulpas reengaged, the sound like a rocket firing across the valley.

Save the life of a little girl, restore safety for my troop, not to mention power to both the agents of Light and Skamar. And now, I thought, cringing as I looked above, keep the sky from falling in and crushing the entire city. It would've seemed like a full plate but for one thing. It all hinged on healing one little girl.

I needed to find her now.

I ducked into dark pockets created by the low-lying blue haze and slowly made my way to the modest development where the Chans had their home, keeping to side streets and dusty lots. Unfortunately, Midheaven was actually the second-to-last place I wanted to go. The very last was the Chan household, where an eight-year-old little girl, Jasmine's sister, was suffering because of something I'd done.

In a newer section of town, their tract home was virtually indistinguishable from those around it, but the small figure reclining on the gentle slope of terra cotta tiles helped me locate it, as did her scent: dried berries, Bonnie Bell, and Bubblicious. Slipping into the concealing shadows offered up by the cloud haze and the overgrown fronds of a giant pepper tree, I leapt to the roof as quietly and quickly as I could.

Even so, Jasmine didn't look surprised when I dropped down five feet from her. She only waited, as I did, to see if anyone else in the household had heard. When it was clear no one had, she turned her great dark eyes up to me. "I knew you were coming."

"See me?"

She frowned, hesitating, then shook her head.

"Smell?" I asked, because ever since I'd displaced a portion of her *chi* with my own, she'd been gaining some of my more desirable abilities. This was part of the problem. Jasmine thought she was becoming a superhero and she refused to give up those powers.

"Not until you got close," she admitted, tucking a lock of black hair behind her ear, the color shiny and rich even in the fractured light.

"Then how?"

"I felt it. Like I . . . sensed you." She put a hand to her belly. "Do you know what I mean?"

I did. The second I'd reached her side I'd felt a corporeal recognition, like my veins ran in her body, my blood pumping in her heart.

I dropped next to her, huddling close in the cool air as clouds began to roil and pop in the distance. Neither of us was immune to the elements, so I was relieved when she didn't object, and not just because of her body heat. She'd been prickly with me since we'd butted heads over her unwillingness to pass on her changeling status to her younger sister.

Her appearance had altered since I'd last seen her, though.

Her dark hair now graduated sharply into an uneven bob, and was streaked on the left side with pink and blond. Her clothes were equally chaotic, blacks and plaids with thick military boots, and she had her backpack next to her, like she regularly waited on the rooftop for her bus. It was still Hello Kitty pink, but the cute icon's eyes had been taped over by dual X's, making the round mouth more resemble a scream.

The scent of eastern herbs and western medicines wafted from her open window, but I didn't look her over for signs of injury. Jasmine hadn't suffered physical injury when I'd failed to give her back the whole of her borrowed aura. No, it was her younger sister, Li, who was living proof that I truly had screwed it all up.

I bent my head to my knees, resting for a moment.

"Where have you been?" she finally asked. "I felt weak, like when you have the flu and can't lift your limbs . . . but I felt it in my mind too."

That made sense. The link between us probably didn't extend to different words. Entering Midheaven must have severed the connection between us, halving both her *chi* and mine. "I had to go somewhere else."

I explained to her about Midheaven and the pipeline, that I was searching for Jacks and a way to heal her, though I skipped the part about the dead changeling. I ended with an account of my return, including that Regan was again in the Tulpa's good graces. "Skamar has kept the Tulpa too busy for him to get to you, but Regan has been following me everywhere. It's not inconceivable that she might end up here."

Her round face scrunched up. "So what are you doing now? Dropping the bread crumbs?"

"I've changed up my routine, smartass," I said tightly. "And I was thinking you could go somewhere safe until all of this is over."

She wrapped her arms around her knobby knees, turning away. "I can take care of myself."

I shifted, crouched in front of her and waited until she met my eye. "Jas, I can't protect you. I have no conduit, half my natural power is being filtered into you, and there's no safe zone for me on this side of reality. That means if Regan gets tired of trying to pick up my trail, she's going to come after the people closest to me, and hello *chi*-sharing superhero-wannabe, that's you."

She said nothing, just stared straight ahead with her jaw clenched stubbornly, expression unreadable.

I tried again. "Look, I just wanted to come check on you and Li. Make sure . . . "

Jasmine read the fear in my hesitation, and swooped in for the kill. "Make sure she's not dead?"

I ran my hand over my face. "Jesus, Jas."

She scoffed, then jerked her head in the direction of the lighted window. "See for yourself."

I hesitated. "Parental units?"

"Both at work. They need the insurance." She stared up at me, her gaze challenging. "Go on. *Superhero*."

I glanced at the window almost fearfully, but dusted myself off and stood. Jas was right; I needed to look for myself. To prove I could look in the bedroom of a dying child as clear-eyed as I could face down a rotting Shadow agent. I'd look, even if it scorched my soul.

But peering into that room wasn't at all like facing fire. It was like dropping into an endless pool of water without first taking a breath.

She lay facing away from the window, tiny body outlined beneath her pile of blankets. Her dark hair was a black hole against the white pillow, tangled strands that had once been glossy with good health now dulled. Her breathing appeared even but indistinguishable over the machines monitoring her vital stats, and though hidden behind privacy screens, they were like another presence in the room.

I was just breaching the surface of seeing all this for the first time, and aching for breath, when she turned.

Her eyes, so similar to Jasmine's—if you didn't count the blood vessels weaving over the whites—found mine like she knew I'd be there. As if she'd been waiting. The hope in that gaze, displaced in a face that was little more than skin smoothed over bone, crashed over me like a wave. The vessels seemed to have dried up inside her body, the percentage of water needed to fuel a human being half what it should have been. The three marks across her charcoal cheek, where she'd taken a hit from the Tulpa on my behalf, were jet black. Her lashes had all fallen out. The weave of hair tangled across that pillow shifted . . . a wig.

Li didn't have the strength to wave—the tiny hand faltered on its way up—but she smiled and it was achingly beautiful.

The strike of a match behind me sounded like an arrow slicking through the dim sky, and I flinched before I saw Jas's amused profile outlined behind cupped hands. She deliberately didn't look at me, and I grabbed at that momentary privacy, letting my face crumble as I bent my head. This was an image I'd never be able to erase, no matter how many worlds I hitchhiked my way into.

Mind stunned, I moved away from the window. Jasmine silently handed me the cigarette as I hunched next to her, even closer this time, as if she could warm me. I sucked in smoke, before handing it back to Jas. She took another drag, her smooth features lighting up prettily behind the orange glow.

"Jasmine—"

"No."

I wanted to wring her scrawny preteen neck. "Why? Just pass on your post to Li! Give her changeling status. Move on as nature intended."

She whipped her gaze to mine so fast I jerked back. "Because passing the post on to Li isn't the cure-all you think it is. Your *chi* will still be divided, just in her body instead of mine. The Zodiac will still be unbalanced. Your manuals will still unwritten."

"Jas—"

"I said no. And don't ask me again either. I don't want to be that, okay?" She motioned to Li's window, scattering ash. "I want to live."

I glanced at the sky. The day was strong enough now that rays of light had crept through the cloud breaks to find our bodies. They trailed out in stingy pockets, shifted, and tried again. "You don't know that maturing will kill you."

"You don't know that it won't."

True. But if I didn't come through, one of these sisters was going to die a death that would accomplish nothing. It might buy the agents of Light a little more time. Maybe slow the downward spiral in power that so aptly mirrored Li's deteriorating health. But it wouldn't get the manuals written, or transfer a vast amount of power to Skamar. It wouldn't save my shiny, irreverent city from what amounted to a cataclysmic electrical storm raining down like God's wrath. Only one thing would do all that.

We fell silent again. Jas smoked and brooded. I bit my lip and worried. Clouds roiled and moved across the sky like scattered gray silk; beautiful, if you didn't know it was the result of massive cosmic destruction.

After another moment, Jasmine flicked the spent cigarette over the roofline. "Look, it's not that I don't want to help her, okay? I want Li to get better . . . "

But if Jasmine gave over the split *chi* that would enable Li to heal and take her place as the changeling of Light, she might break in turn.

"Would you switch with *your* sister?" she asked suddenly, voice rising with emotion. "Be dead in her place, if it means she would live?"

"Yes."

I wasn't trying for a politically correct answer, or even to convince Jasmine that she should do the same. But yes, I would have done that for Olivia. In an instant. I would do it still.

"That's because her death was quick," Jasmine scoffed, flipping her backpack over her shoulder. "It was violent, yeah, but it was a moment's choice. Not a choice moment after moment."

I saw what she meant. She was envisioning herself lying ashen against those white linens, sweating out her body's nutrients, being drained of her vitality.

"You're saying it would have been easy for me?"

"I'm saying take a look at all the good things you've experienced since then, and then wipe them from your mind. I'm watching Li, and as much as I love her, my mind keeps drifting to the things I don't know—the people I'll never meet, the career and maybe family I'll never have. I don't . . . I don't want to die a virgin."

"The first time sucks anyway."

She shook her head, unamused. "What about all my other firsts? Don't I have a right to those either?"

I glanced up at her. Sometimes I forgot I was talking to a girl whose prom was still years away. It was easy to forget that these kids were as divided in their lives as we were . . . at least up until it was time for them to grow and age and live as mortals. But . . . "What about Li's?"

"Why are hers any more important than mine?"

I looked at her with her crossed arms and forced pout, and remembered what it was like to be that age. Not long after that I would be attacked, and my life as irreparably damaged as Li's. But at Jasmine's exact age I had lived for the day, by the day, my future unwinding in front of me like a long hopeful road. "Look, Jas, I'm working on it."

She turned to me. "So let me help."

"It's mostly grunt work," I lied. "Not even any fighting," I lied some more. "Just hours of sitting there, staring at nothing. Like a stakeout. You'll be happier waiting here."

"But I've never been on a stakeout before!"

"That's because you're thirteen. You need to survive a few slumber parties first." She turned away again, and I sighed. "Look, I just don't want you to return to your mother with pieces missing, you know?" One Chan sister down was enough.

"Then protect me. You can move faster than a speeding bullet, right?"

"I can move faster than a speeding softball. I haven't really tested the bullet theory yet." *And I could barely protect myself.*

"Oh."

"Look, just watch out for oddities or, you know, walking corpses. Stay safe."

She blew out a breath that lifted her hair from her forehead. "Don't talk to strangers, yeah, yeah. Got that memo . . ."

My cell phone vibrated in my pocket, and I pulled it out, hoping to see a message from Hunter. I didn't recognize the number. The voice, though? That was unforgettable. I rose to my feet on the slanted rooftop, staring off into the blue haze. "What do you want?"

"You. On your knees before me. Your skin shredded so finely it looks like angel hair."

I motioned for Jas to get behind me, get inside, get away, and scanned the perimeter of the house. Everything and nothing moved beneath the roiling, mobile sky. Yet Regan couldn't openly walk the streets in her condition. "So you want to be twins?"

"That's right. Except for your sense of humor. I fucking hate that."

I started to reply.

"I have to wonder, though, if it's something little Ashlyn inherited."

I drew a blank, my mouth stuttering shut. I decided to wait to see where she was going with this.

"Ah, that finally shut you up. Now . . . " She took a breath so deep it gurgled in her cracked chest. "Sit back down so we can talk."

I angled my head, squinting at the house across from us. "Where are you?"

"Sit your ass down."

I checked to make sure Jasmine was back inside, and sat. How traumatized would the kid be, I wondered, if I took an arrow to the heart on her rooftop?

"That's better." Regan paused, letting me wonder how she could see me, obviously enjoying the attention. "I was wondering when you'd check on your changeling. Nice of you to care."

Her admonition, and her ability to see me, made me want to leap from the roof. I kept my voice even with great effort. "Your point, Regan? Because the cloud cover seems to be clearing up, and you're not going to be able to catch a cab in your condition this far past Halloween."

There was no way she could be there. Unless she'd arrived in full dark and planned to exit the same way. In a neighboring house? Looking out through a window? In that box tree hedge across the street?

"I'm tired of waiting for you to return to your penthouse, *Olivia*. Or show up at Valhalla for your shift—nice touch there, by the way—or to stop by and check on your former mortal lover."

"That will never happen," I said, which was true enough. Let her think I didn't care. As long as I stayed away from Ben Traina, he was safe.

"Which is why I've had to come to you."

"Changelings are out of bounds. You can't touch Jasmine."

"Oh, dear. You are fucking retarded." Laughter wheezed from her again, and I clenched my jaw. "Your little 'Wonder Twin' doesn't interest me. After all, there's another little girl out there, with little bits of Joanna floating through her bloodstream."

Icy fear kept me quiet now.

"What do you think?" Regan had no such problem. "A few choice slices with a butcher's knife and she and I might be able to pass for mother and daughter."

"She knows nothing about me," I said flatly.

"Ah, but you know about her." And that was all she'd ever cared about. How whatever she did to those I loved would affect me.

"So, what? I do as you say, and you won't hurt her?"

"Oh, you'd think so, wouldn't you? But predictability is also where you and I differ. See, I've already carved her up."

The air left my body in one fell whoosh. I teetered on the rooftop as I stood, and took two quick steps before I caught myself. Regan giggled. I closed my eyes and took a deep breath.

"Well, you almost fell for it," she said, her sliced tongue doing a strange dance over the words. "But for future reference, would *you* like to find her little corpse first, or just hear about it on the five o'clock news?"

Now her laughter dug, as sharp and deep as that butcher's knife.

"If you hurt her . . ." I couldn't finish the sentence. *God. Ashlyn. My daughter . . . and Ben's. Because of me . . .*

"If I hurt her, I've hurt you," she finished succinctly, and the line went dead.

I stood for a long while with the phone still pressed to my ear. Then I vaulted to the pepper tree, scurrying down it as quickly as I could without hurting myself, and studied the wide open road with all of my senses. Despite Regan's words, there was no one, mortal or otherwise, on the street. I allowed myself one betraying sigh—infused with a relief that anyone with heightened senses could sniff—then pulled out my cell again and dialed Hunter's number.

I looked back up at Li's window as the phone rang. Jasmine's silhouette was visible in the corner. Inside lay an innocent little girl, dying because she'd taken a wound belonging to me. On the outside—not close, but getting closer to me—was Regan. Her threats toward Ashlyn were horrifying because she'd do exactly as she said, no remorse, no second thought—just like the Tulpa, she'd injure a child in an attempt to get to me.

Not only that, I thought, as I began to walk, but that child would be eleven in a fistful of days—on my birthday, actually, like all the first daughters in the Zodiac—which wasn't too early for a girl to start puberty. Once she did, her second life cycle would begin, her pheromones would flare, and everyone—Shadow and Light—would know of her existence. Then Regan and Warren would be the least of my worries. And her mortal mother wouldn't be remotely able to protect her.

No, she'd need a superhero for that.

So, despite Skamar's warning, was the soul sliver required to enter another world in search of a man who knew how to fix a changeling worth ensuring Ashlyn's safety in this one? Damn straight, I thought, along with Jasmine's and the little girl huddled in her bed above like a tiny mummy. I squared my shoulders and, with a final glance behind me, left a voice mail with the one person I trusted more than anyone else in this world. I didn't want to see him. Hunter had sensed a vulnerability about me during the live-fire exercise at the warehouse, and perhaps even before it. If he knew I could be injured as easily as a mortal, he'd physically restrain me from crossing into Midheaven again. So I kept it short, telling him only what he needed to know in order for us both to keep moving forward. "Hunter. Tell Warren I'm going in."

19

I dressed for the crossing like I was prepping for war, in a black leather jacket with a Mandarin collar, matching boot-cut pants cut low for movement, and thick-soled boots . . . perfect for ass-kicking. What can I say? Though I knew what the women in Midheaven considered feminine—I left on the necklace Suzanne had given me in deference to that—I was going to stick with the tried and true: I'd go in fists flying, assuming guilt before innocence, and take what I wanted by force if that was the only way to get it done. Sure, beneath all this armor was a spray-on tan, and breasts that had a serial number stamped on a silicone shell, but I still felt most powerful when strong, limber, and packing an attitude I could fire like an Uzi.

"Putting the 'bomb' in bombshell," I muttered, side-stepping down the storm drain's embankment. I'd brought a giant bottle of ice water, and was wearing the mesh belt again, with one important addition: a knife to rival Mackie's, in case it came down to another duel, mano a mano. My goal was to remain downstairs—talk to Tripp, look for Jacks, scan the Most Wanted board, before fighting my way back to my lantern. Whatever happened, I did not want to go upstairs.

If it was cold outside, it was going to be absolutely frigid in the catacombs of the Las Vegas underground. Ice, milkweed, and escaped bahai grass crackled underfoot as I approached the tunnels, all hidden beneath a wreathing mist that trailed ominously into the concrete drain. I stole a final glance at my glittering hometown as a wind gust raced across the entrance, its chill fingers reaching out to beckon me back. In the distance, the Strip was as brilliant and bold as an ice floe, snapping back at the inclement weather with LID billboards, pastel spotlights, and heated gas that blistered the air. I smiled, then softened my gaze so it all blurred; the colorful ice floe melting as I turned away.

I found the shoulder bag I'd looped around the drain, and shoved all the gaming chips with the remaining bits of my power into my pockets before I dumped my cell phone inside. I'd leave the bag here, but I was going to keep the chips on me from now on . . . no matter what world I was in.

As I was using the same storm drain as the first time I'd accessed Midheaven, I was surprised when it veered in an altogether different direction than I remembered. But I figured as long as the pipeline wound over unfamiliar terrain and looped improbably around on itself, as long as everything remained abnormal, all was normal, right?

So I found my way back to the concrete cupboard simply by putting one foot in front of the other, careful all the while to watch and listen for Regan. I could tell by the fractious sounds emanating from the south end of the valley—rumbling belches and ear-splitting squeals—that Skamar was keeping the Tulpa occupied. I'd heard on the car radio that some the mortal weathermen were beginning to make dire predictions about the bulging sky, and even an evangelical diehard had picked up on it, spouting his apocalyptic predictions. I would have liked to stick around long enough to hear someone blast back that an apocalypse generally included the *entirety* of humanity and not just a city built on gaming tables and dancing girls, but I couldn't wait any longer. Even if the sky didn't fall, Li wouldn't last much longer, and very possibly, neither would Skamar. So with their faces fueling my resolve, I again spun the dial on the lock, and lined up the Archer glyph so the combination tumbled like fates falling into place.

"In and out, Archer. Make it fast," I murmured, licking my lips as I focused on the candle. Dread washed through my body at the sight of that pinched taper, and I couldn't help wondering how many days or weeks of my life I'd lose this time around. At least now I knew what to expect. I also had something to look forward to—or back at—once I was there. Hunter would get my message and be waiting for me upon my return. So, shaking, I leaned forward and blew. Nothing. I'd forgotten to grasp it at its base, linking my energy and—I now knew—my soul to it. I did so, blew again, and this time the candle snuffed out.

Smoke wrapped around my body, somehow managing to be both insistent and light. I heard a sound, faint chaos stirring inside me so that my thoughts bolted and scattered. Then my mouth was pried open. My soul screamed. And my world disappeared once more.

I was shaking as the Rest House revealed itself, smoke and vision clearing gradually to reveal the bar like a mahogany snake across from me. My hands were empty; the water bottle hadn't made it over. The knife in my belt was gone too. Dammit. I frowned as Bill gave me a little wave from behind the bar. The silver-eyed dealers just stared, and the torpid denizens merely shifted their eyes before turning back to their cards. Mackie's acknowledgment extended only to a tip of his hat and, of course, the second verse of my personal song. The murder ballad, I realized, that he'd begun on my initial visit here.

> *When that temper bursts to life, dear*
> *Her pretty eyes, they flare to red*

*But that black heart has its own fear
Which may strike her down instead.*

"Cheery," I deadpanned. His head swiveled my way, as if on a hinge, and he grinned that skeletal smile, adding an extra flourish to the song's finish.

I turned my eyes to the wall with the Most Wanted posters, gaze locking on my yellowed sheet in time to see more features being burned into the fraying paper. The whole of my surname was now visible, and the *O* and *A* clearly outlined in the first. One more entry and they'd have my portrait in full. I'd be stuck there forever.

Bullshit. I wasn't going to return here, ever. I was going to find Jacks—ask, force, coerce, convince, *kill* him, if it meant getting what I wanted—and then take the information back home, save my world, a child's life, fix the manuals of Light, strengthen my troop, keep Ashlyn safe, and live up to the designation of superhero and Kairos.

In that order.

For now, I searched out that asshole, Tripp. My eyes landed on Shen.

"How you healin' over there, Miss Olivia?"

"Better than you would if I laid hands on you," I shot back. "In any world."

He grinned, and despite my words I knew I'd be in trouble if I took one threatening step toward him, so I dismissed him and went back to searching for Tripp.

He was actually at the bar, and it was clear he was suffering, the teetotaler giving in to temptation. I smiled as our eyes met, his weakness invigorating me. I wanted to tip his head back and pour that cloying liquid down his throat. I wanted it to permeate his every cell and slow his movements like sap running down a tree trunk. I wanted his power stolen from him as thoroughly as mine had been ripped from me. I strode across the room, boots reporting off the hard pine floor. The feeling of all eyes on me made me feel powerful, even as the heat seeping in from behind that bright red door began its invisible assault.

"Welcome back, Miss Olivia," Bill said, with his easy friendliness. I fought the urge to stuff the bar rag down his throat.

"Bill." I angled my head his way. I caught my reflection in the mirror. Old Joanna—dark-haired and dark-eyed, pissed. "Hello, beautiful," I said to myself, then turned. "Tripp."

Tripp licked his bottom lip, his mustache twitching with a knowing smile. "Told you you'd be back. One taste of the power afforded women in this world, and the other is easily abandoned. Especially irresistible to Shadows too."

"I'm not back to stay, and for the last time, I'm not a Shadow agent."

He scoffed, and leaned his elbows on the bar, addressing me though the back mirror. "Well I am, on both counts apparently," he muttered, but got over his bitterness quickly enough to shoot me a dark look. "And I recognize one of my own. You are Shadow. Look at your fucking eyes in that picture."

He jerked his head toward the wall, but I didn't follow his gaze. I'd already seen my father's eyes staring back at me, and I shrugged away the comparison.

"In any case, why not return to a place where you're untouchable?"

I raised a brow.

Tripp scoffed at my arch look. "Your exit didn't count. You destroyed gaming chips. You wasted valuable fuel when there's too little of it to begin with. Besides, first rule in the Rest House: don't piss off the piano player."

"And speaking of our homicidal little entertainer," I said, glancing over at the man who'd fallen still and silent again, like a giant mechanical doll. "When do you think Mackie's going to come after you?"

Tripp jolted at that. "Why would he? I play by the rules."

"You don't drink, which allows you to win all of the hands—"

"Have you seen how long it takes these fuckers to finish a hand?"

Good point. "But you don't give up any powers that way. In fact, you haven't given up much beyond the initial soul energy it took to cross, have you? The people running this show are bound to get sick of that after a while. Even the freebies in Vegas dry up when you don't play."

He snarled, resettled his cowboy hat over his head, and swirled his drink. "It's a game to them. A novelty. They want to see how hard they can push me. How long I can withstand their temptations."

"But, Harlan, you've already been here a *very* long time."

His eyes snapped back to mine, and I let knowledge shine through in my smile. I'd looked him up after Warren's mention. My ability to read the Shadow manuals was still coming in handy.

"I'm willing to tell you how long . . . for information that can help me bring down your old master, the Tulpa."

He looked away, but there'd been hesitation in his gaze. "You got the wrong Shadow agent."

I looked around the room like I didn't care, wiping my brow as I watched slow hands being dealt. The soles of my feet were starting to burn. Tripp didn't move. Time for a different approach. "Why didn't you ever try to escape?"

He looked surprised at the question, but shrugged stiffly after a moment. "I did. Right after I first arrived. The dealers tried to stop me, same as you. Every time I made a move toward our lantern, Mackie would raise that knife. Then they stopped trying. They realized before I did that someone had locked the entrance from the other side."

The memory blanketed his face like a fever. There'd probably been a moment of exhilaration, where he thought he'd had them all bested, only to be followed by a dizzying plummet as he realized he had nowhere to go. I swallowed hard, and told myself to remember who this guy was. He destroyed mortal lives . . . and once belonged to the troop that most wanted me dead.

"And now? Why don't you try again? Why didn't you attempt to come with me? Follow me? Help me?"

"You've only been gone half an hour," he said, and glanced back down at the glass in his hand. He tipped it to one side, watching the liquid run down the sides of the glass, and missed the way I goggled. A half an hour on this side of the candle? My God, time wasn't just altered over here. It was turned inside out. "But I was thinking about it."

"And yet you hold a glass of death in your hands."

He pursed his lips and shook his head. "Lady, I may not know how long I've been here, but I can tell it's long enough that I have no place left back home. You think I'm not a part of this world just because I haven't sipped from this glass, but I am. As much as I've fought against it, my energy has been bleeding out of me in a slow trickle. I am a leaky faucet."

He looked me up and down, and frowned. "I don't know who you are, and can't even guess at your lineage and sign, but I know this: whatever I had in that world is long gone."

We didn't say anything for a long time. I knew what Warren would say about Tripp's ennui. *Good riddance.* And before this conversation I would have thought the same. But knowing how long he'd been holding out the hope to return, I couldn't help but admire his fight.

Tripp mistook my silence as implicit agreement. "See? I told you you'd like this place."

"You're wrong, Tripp. I chafe at certain things that go on in our world," and I made sure to include him in that equation, recognizing him as more than just a thread in the fabric of this one, "but I don't want anyone else to feel lesser just so I can feel more."

Harlan looked at me like he was seeing me for the first time.

"Well, isn't this a peach," Bill interrupted, grin wide as he looked over our shoulders. Tripp and I turned together. "Two new songs in one day."

The first thing I saw was Mackie lifting his head and arms. The second was a cloud of smoke billowing from my lantern in lapping waves, building an opaque wall as an acrid scent rolled across the room and threatened to make me sneeze. A bright flash, the daguerreotype capturing a new image, and suddenly a figure began taking shape before our eyes. It was obviously a man, broad-shouldered and thick-necked, tall, though his features were obscured in the swelling haze. I glanced over at the wall of posters to see a delicate image burning through a new page, the angles tapered, and drawn so finely that it almost looked feminine.

Because it's the first pass, I thought, turning my attention to the most assuredly *not* feminine form solidifying before us. The smoke abated and the man lifted his head. My jaw dropped as he scanned the room. It snapped shut as his gaze stilled on mine. He smiled.

"Oh, my God."

Here's an agent, his story epic
Because he's a ghost, even in plain sight
He's Machiavellian, his life a grand trick
But he grounds it with his might.

Jaden Jacks, I thought, swallowing hard, was in the Rest House.

I don't know whether the heat was finally sinking into my pores, or if the shock at seeing the man whom many in my world considered a ghost taking shape in front of me was what kept me immobile, but I didn't move for what felt like a long time. Yet Jaden Jacks was clearly real, though at first no more than a blurry silhouette backlit by the wall of lanterns. His form solidified as the smoke from the snuffed candle cleared, and I got my first good look at the man I'd previously only known from Tekla's ripped-up manual.

His skin was dark, the color of brewed tea, though light compared to the black clothes he sported. Battle wear, I saw, similar to mine. His hair was cropped close, so white-blond it was obviously bleached, which would have been funny except that it worked. Everything about him was daring and in-your-face. His musculature was dense beneath his fitted shirt, like tendons and marrow and bone had been baked, brick-hard. He flexed his fingers and the movement shot up the length of his arm in a fast twitch, so that even his shoulder moved. He was a force even at rest, and probably the strongest human being I'd ever seen.

But his eyes, I thought, inhaling sharply. His eyes were pure layers of sunlit amber.

Nostrils flaring, he took in the scent of the room as assessingly as his eyes took in the sights, both senses thrown out like weapons. He scanned the division of washed-out men at the poker tables, the women leaning over the banisters like colorful banners, and when he finished—and had determined no one was going to attack—he said one word only. "Solange."

The deep voice rumbled through the room, through my body, spiking in my nerve endings to shake me from my numbness. I looked to Bill, whom Jacks had intuitively, and rightly, addressed, and saw the bartender's lips thin to a narrow line, his rag moving in slow circles on the bar. A smile slipped onto my face before I could stop it.

Behold, dear viewers, this world's male species reacting under threat.

"Miss Solange doesn't take unsolicited guests," Bill replied shortly, eyes cutting to Mackie. Jacks caught the look and swiveled his head, but Mackie remained slumped, unresponsive and detached.

"Recognize him?" I whispered to Tripp.

He shook his head, and Jacks caught the movement, setting the full force of his attention on Tripp, who swallowed audibly, as recognition flashed in Jacks's bright gaze. But shouldn't Tripp recognize him as well? And how could this be the first pass on his Most Wanted poster? Warren said Jacks was, and had been, over here for some time now.

Except, I suddenly realized, his energy wouldn't register here if he'd used someone else's soul for the crossing. I glanced back at the brand new Most Wanted poster, and decided I'd been right the first time. It really was a woman featured there. He was using another innocent to gain entry. Just as he'd used the changeling's the first time.

So he'd murdered a woman simply for an audience with Solange.

"Tell her Jaden Jacks is here," he said to Bill, and without waiting for a reply or even glancing at me, he made his way to the staircase. I moved to stop him, but Bill's eyes flipped in their sockets, and I braced, just in case he was reacting to me. His head did, indeed, turn my way, but then he grimaced, like he'd bit into a lemon, before the expression smoothed out into a smile. He gestured, magnanimously, up the staircase. "She already knows."

The other men began to grumble. Bill bent his head, muttering as he scrubbed at the bar. Mackie remained immobile. I expected someone to stop Jacks, but nobody even tried, and he took the stairs two at a time, stance wide as he paused at the top, head tilted as he wondered which way to go.

No, not wondered. *Determined.*

"Wait!" I yelled, but he only nodded to himself and cut right, utterly ignoring me.

"Shit." I sighed. The last thing I wanted to do was head up those stairs. The real-time sink was there. I knew it. Everything was slowed on the lower level of the rest house, the life energy of the men conserved by as little movement or thought as possible. But up where the women moved in color, adornment, fluidly, easily . . . weeks could be lost just exchanging pleasantries. Yet I couldn't return home without any means of helping Li or Skamar or my troop.

Better a quick, or even slow, death here—lost trying—than returning to fight a helpless battle.

The predicament made me hate Jacks all the more. I pushed from the bar without another word and headed up the stairs.

20

The air was cooler on the landing, and seemingly less dense, as if the molecules were fat and inflated to dizzying effect. I'd been weighed down under the influence of drink upon my last ascension, and I wondered if this was how the women upstairs felt all the time, like they were tropical breezes off an island, the cool of a Caribbean drink in the palm. Breathing up here, I decided on my next woozy breath, was a bit like learning to walk on the moon.

The door leading to Solange's observatory stood ajar, and its hinges squeaked as I pushed it open, letting Jacks know I was there. He remained as he was, back turned as he gazed out one of the tiny windows, a strong hand pressed to the glass so the sheen of his smooth fingertips was reflected there. Those twelve squares emitted the only light in the room, which was otherwise empty—no mine cart, no Solange.

As I approached the first bright square, Jacks shifted, moving away like he didn't want me too near, but never fully turning my way. Attention still on him, I glanced out the first small, shining pane to see what he was studying. It was obviously another room, though fogged, with dull shapes weaving in and out of the wispy layers. None drew close enough to identify, and though obviously human, the movement reminded me of fish in an aquarium. Odd, I thought, as the shimmering landscape rippled, gray where it was nearest, melting into opacity farther away.

I moved to the next window, thinking maybe this was why he was here. Maybe there was something else he was searching for . . . plus, it had the added benefit of bringing me closer to him. But I halted when I discovered this was a different scene entirely. A bustling cityscape I didn't recognize until I spotted the triangular, Art Deco building looming across from me. There was only one early-century building like that and it was in Manhattan. The stairwell I was peering from was obviously a subway station, and a steady stream of people barreled by in a full-throttle thrust before disappearing underground.

The next window, still closer to Jacks, offered up a half view of an ornate mosque, and in the following one I immediately recognized Buckingham Palace, the guards immobile like human statues. I had no cultural moorings on which to plant myself for the one after that, except to know that the concave tiles and dramatic, sweeping eaves meant it was somewhere in Asia. But if those exotic sights perplexed me, I was absolutely astonished by what I saw next, though not because it was unfamiliar.

This, I thought with a gaping mouth, was a cityscape I recognized all too well. As if through the lens of a periscope, I found myself peering out on the faux settings of New York, Monte Carlo, and a make-believe castle. It was unmistakably Vegas.

"The pipeline," I whispered, making out the spot where I'd entered minutes before. I leaned heavily against the wall, my thoughts of Jacks momentarily diverted. What were these things? Pipelines from around the world? "Oh my God."

I'd been right. Midheaven was a way around the restriction about leaving the Las Vegas valley once we were full-fledged troop members. This, I was suddenly certain, was what Warren had been keeping from us. This was what the Shadow agents, and Jacks, had long known. This was why there were so many lanterns spaced along the wall below.

Which explained the varied agents in the Rest House, the full bloom of women behind lacquered doors, their differing races and colors and backgrounds . . . yet other questions bloomed in their place. What was at the other end of each pipeline? A candle, as it was for me? And while the Old West was appropriate for Vegas, it didn't hold for Asia or London. So was it hypothetically possible for me to get to London this way? To China?

Jacks had taken the opportunity of my distraction to place himself between the exit and me, and he smiled when I glanced sharply at him. We began to circle one another in that way, each keeping our back to the wall.

"Pretty from a distance, huh?" he said, jerking his head toward the Vegas window.

"Pretty from up close," I corrected.

"You think?" He pursed his lips in disagreement. "I've always thought it looks like an old lady who went to bed without taking off her makeup. A bit sad, and in need of a good scrubbing."

I tilted my head, continued my careful sidestep. "That why you came here? Take a little vacation from it all, play some poker . . . strip away part of your soul?"

I was looking for a reaction . . . but all I got was an admission.

"All but the last part," he said coldly.

My heart rate snapped to attention as I stared, but I tried to play it cool, though it was taking all of my formidable acting abilities to stand in the same room as him and not swing. "She's making you wait," I said, like I wasn't thinking of planting a boot—or a grenade—in his chest.

"It's what women do." The shrug was in his voice. He was looking at me, waiting for her, and standing in a world where he was a second-class citizen, yet he didn't look a bit concerned. He'd killed at least two mortals so he could bounce between worlds, and it weighed upon him like cigarette ash. I inhaled, expecting to find a deadened rot, similar to a Shadow's, but the scent emanating from his giant body was green, like money or opportunity, and so round on the air it was almost three-dimensional.

Not like the men downstairs, I thought, breathing in deeply again. Scent appeared to be attached to energy here; maybe the others had bartered away too much of both, and what was left had been watered down into an imitation of its former odor. This man's blood was rich, like elixir, and it didn't seem fair. It was also probably vain of me to wonder in that moment what exactly I smelled like, and if it was this heady and dizzying too.

But Jacks was here to see Solange. Beautiful, dangerous Solange, who had knowledge of the stars, who smelled sweet and frosty like ice wine, and who was also of our world.

Which reminded me. "I have a question for you."

He began to smile, already knowing I was going to ask how to fix the changeling. Everyone in my world knew what was happening there. "And you'll give what for the answer?"

"Your life," I answered coolly.

He laughed, but I couldn't tell if it was because or in spite of the threat. "And if I want yours in exchange?"

I thought of the sky falling over Vegas.

Skamar's desperate plea for power.

An unstoppable infection festering on Li's ravaged baby face.

It wasn't an entirely unreasonable request.

I swallowed hard.

Jacks began circling again, and this time I stood my ground. He folded his arms when he drew to a stop in front of me, so close his body heat lapped at my skin. His rich eyes had darkened in the depths of the dim room and now resembled dry sap, with life still caught within. "Here's what we'll do," he said, voice so low only the rumble escaped his throat. "We'll trade answers for answers. But I get to ask as many questions as I want. You only get the one."

I opened my mouth to agree, but hesitated again. What if Jacks returned to Vegas and used whatever information I'd given him against my troop? What if he asked who I really was, and my Olivia Archer cover was blown? What if he returned and told the Tulpa everything Regan was still holding close to her shredded chest?

What if I went back with nothing and the sky fell, and Li Chan died at the age of eight?

I leaned against the London window, where it was—surprise—raining. "A dance for information, then?"

"A tango," he replied with a twist of his lips, "for things we can use to harm one another later."

"How dysfunctional," I remarked lightly.

"Most relationships are." Another light sparked in his beautiful eyes. "Note, I saved you the trouble of falling in love with me first."

"Only because you know the separation will be a bitch." I gave him a broad smile. "Did you have an actual question?"

He cocked his head to the left. "I'd like to know what you think you're fighting for?"

I drew back before I could stop myself. "What kind of question is that?"

His grin was an unnecessary reminder of our agreement. "One that will tell me what you risked to get here."

It was clever. Big guy. Body like a weapon. Yet Jacks already knew, as I was learning, that not every battle was fought with bow-and-arrow, or fists. "You should be able to guess at that if you've done your homework. I mean, don't you know who I am?"

"You sure that's the question you want to ask?"

"No," I said immediately, retracting it.

He raised his brows, then shrugged, so I'd continue wondering just how much he knew. "I know why you're here. That's different, though, than why *you* think you're here."

"Boring superhero crap." I waved a hand through the air. "Save the world, all that. You wouldn't understand."

"Ah, but I understand that no one acts without some deep internal motivation. So why is this personal for you? What would you cross worlds to save?"

I bit my lip and stared at him so long that hours probably passed in Vegas. I don't know what I was searching for. Maybe some inkling that the agent of Light he'd once been was still living inside that bulging frame, some show of remorse. Something I could connect to.

But the more I stared, the more I saw our differences. We'd switched lives, I realized. I'd become an accepted part of the troop he'd left. He now worked alone, and the self-will that had gotten him thrown out so long ago had calcified into unwavering self-preservation. It was all he knew, all that made sense. So trying to explain why I'd give up my very soul for the chance to save someone else was like trying to explain chocolate to a caveman. It was a decadence he'd never live to know.

"You're morally bankrupt," I said instead.

"Untrue. I'm as honest as a person can be while impersonating two people at the same time." The intimation being that I was not. "Now answer the question."

I backed up to where he'd been standing when I'd entered, and looked out on a wind-whipped Vegas. She was taking a beating on the other side of the peaceful pane. I tapped my smooth fingertips off the glass, and they chinked unnaturally. "That," I finally answered, pointing. "I'm doing this for my home."

"I already told you, that answer isn't going to cut it. You can't tell me you feel for all of Vegas. It's not personal enough."

I shook my head. See? I knew he wouldn't understand. "I didn't say Vegas. I said home." I swallowed hard, and continued to stare out that bleak window. "It's a place . . . borne out in a person."

An awkward silence bloomed as he waited for me to

continue. I lifted my hand to the window, thinking of Ben—because I'd once told him he was my home—and of Jasmine and Li, of my troop and Cher and the mortals I felt a kinship with because I'd been one once. And though I was here for all that, it was Jacks's question that made me realize I'd come primarily for *me*. I wanted my city saved for me. I wanted my troop secured so I'd have security. I'd finally found a place where I fit in, felt whole, and saw—for the first time—an actual future. It included being a twenty-first century superhero. And, getting really personal, it included Hunter.

Hunter, who made my mouth dry up just by walking away. Who made it water when he came back, like I was anticipating the best meal of my life. I thought of how my fingers involuntarily twitched when I caught sight of him, how I reached for him without even realizing. Around Hunter, all my senses came to life. Not dormant ones, not long-lost ones, but present ones, brightly alive.

"I was with him just before I left." I thought of the night we'd spent together, the madness in our lovemaking, the awareness of how fleeting precious things could be. The need to consume and rage and hold on all at the same time. I sucked in a deep breath, and the memory wrapped around my heart like a shell protecting the life within. I smiled. "Yeah. He's why I'm really here."

"Don't tell me that the prophesied savior of our world is willing to forego destiny for a mere man? I mean, what *is* this world coming to?"

Guess I didn't have to worry about hiding who I was.

"Don't make fun of this." I turned on him slowly, like a mountain lion on an elk. He'd do well to remember I wasn't without claws. "You asked, and I'm being as honest as I possibly can. That's how much this means to me." That's how much *Hunter* means, I realized. I'd have made the trip over here, risking soul and life and personal power, for him alone. That was about as personal as it got.

Jacks's nostrils flared again, and I knew my discovery

was pouring from me in some sort of perfumed scent. I briefly wondered what love newly realized smelled like, and was instantly frustrated by the thought that this foul being was the one to scent it for the first time instead of Hunter.

Nicely done, I silently berated myself. Taking the moment from the man it belongs to and giving it to another. To a child-killer, I thought derisively. A soul-stealer. The idea of it, though repulsive, gave me another.

I stepped closer. My voice too became more intimate as I neared him. The chasm between the man before me and the one I was thinking of was wider than Red Rock Canyon, but I could use the emotion to get what I wanted. A world ruled by women, right? So could it be as easy as Solange said? Just embrace the contradiction. Be comfortable with myself . . . and lull Jacks into doing the same. I licked my upper lip, tilting my head so I was gazing directly into his eyes. "How do I fix the changeling of Light?"

Jacks's eyes flickered, watching my tongue. "You can't."

"I have to," I said, stepping closer. "Otherwise the Tulpa will win. The Light will snuff out. The world will collapse."

"Only part of it." He lifted a shoulder, but otherwise remained still. I continued my advance.

"My world," I said as blithely. I was so close that had I still been encased in Olivia's flesh, my breasts would have been brushing his chest. "My home. Tell me how to fix her."

He swallowed hard. "Haven't you figured it out yet, Archer? Human beings are fragile creatures. What do you think happened to that girl's *chi* the very moment yours invaded?"

I drew back a tad at that. "Invaded? My powers have been funneling into her, making her stronger."

"Yeah, and if you pull them back now, there'll be nothing to keep her upright. It'll be like removing her etheric spine. Her soul energy is long gone, departed for deep outer space. Not destroyed, of course, but reabsorbed, re-imagined into the fabric of the Universe."

"No." I shook my head and swallowed hard. "Her death is not an option." Nor was Li's. Nor the city's.

That careless shrug again, and he moved in, suddenly taking me up on my advances. I stiffened, wanting to vomit on his shoes. "It all depends on what you think of as death. Energy is always transmuted, and used for something new."

I jerked away from his hand on mine, pulling back again when his index finger trailed my wrist. "Is that how you justify murdering that changeling? A child? And the woman, whomever she was, whose soul power you used for passage this time?"

He grinned, and it wasn't at all handsome. "I was wondering how long it'd be before you snapped. It takes a lot of energy to pretend to be something you're not. To feign being in love with someone you're not."

As if I could ever love a poison like you. "What would a murderer like you know about love?"

"Because that's why I crossed over too."

And as if on cue, the door opposite the entrance swung wide. Solange stood in silhouette, delicately draped in deep-plunging, sophisticated black, posed like Erté's muse.

She stepped forward so that her features took focus just in time for me to catch the narrowing of her eyes. She scanned Jacks, me, the way our bodies were angled toward each other's. She inhaled deeply . . . and her features grew even more pointed.

"What the hell is going on here?" Her arms dropped to her side. She advanced upon me, the seductress suddenly replaced by a warrior princess, and I stepped back even though I had nothing to feel guilty about. "You're not supposed to be here."

"Well, Jacks and I—"

Her earrings, the same fine fragile hoops as before, swung at her lobes as she jerked her head. "Jacks and you *nothing*! He's here to see me, and it took him long enough."

I held up my hands. "No. I mean, yes. I just—"

"Get out." She pointed one slender arm at the door, black silk pooling to the ground.

"But—"

Jacks was suddenly by her side. "My wife wishes for you to leave."

"Wife?" Shock made my voice too loud.

"Out!" Solange repeated, matching the tone.

"Not now," he said, and there was nothing seductive left in his touch as he dragged me to the door.

"But you didn't answer my question!" I jerked my arm away, and he grabbed it again. "I need to fix the changeling of Light and only you can tell me how."

He spun me toward him after depositing me on the other side of the doorway, and still holding tight, leaned close. "You can't. All you can do is take back your own energy."

"What?"

"Kill her, Archer. It's the only way to save everything you love."

And he slammed the door in my face.

Only a moment of stunned silence passed, perhaps two, before I was pounding on the locked door, demanding re-entry. I didn't care who heard, what sort of energy I was expending, or who wanted it for their own. I was so desperate to get back in that room that I was only marginally aware of the women gathering to watch me at the other end of the banister. Meanwhile, my mind whirled.

Kill Jasmine? That couldn't be the only way.

I continued pounding and yelling, therefore missed the rapid footsteps approaching from the other side, though that also could have been because they belonged to the smaller of the two persons who'd thrown me out. The door jerked wide, and I briefly saw Jacks's silhouette by Las Vegas's viewing window, but then Solange thrust her face in mine, her features contorted with fury.

I was clearly ruining her long-anticipated reunion with her husband.

Jacks was Solange's husband!

She pushed into my space until she was halfway out the door, and I didn't think I'd ever seen a woman so close to a blinding rage. Not Regan, when I'd taken the life of the last person who meant anything to her, and not even me when my bones baked closely to the surface of my skin, eyes glowing in a crimson replica of the Tulpa's.

Because I was only *part* Shadow, I thought, swallowing hard. And for the first time I saw past Solange's borrowed beauty—the adornment she put on using everyone else's life energy—to the woman, the *Shadow*, that lay beneath.

Her bones were liquid, and rolled beneath her flesh. Her gaze was so white-hot it nearly sliced open the air on the way to me. Solange, I suddenly realized, was not left alone in this room and deferred to because she was especially beautiful. She owned it because she was especially dangerous. Power pooled around her like an electrical current, and I instinctively took another step back. She'd amassed more energy for herself in this world than I'd ever possessed, and it looked like she was about to unleash it all upon me.

Seeing my retreat for what it was, she inhaled sharply to rein in her anger. Clenching her jaw, those liquid bones rearranged themselves again, and she blew out a breath as hot as the air drying out the men below. It scared me more than if she'd screamed. "I'll tell you what you want to know if you promise to leave. Immediately."

Gladly, I thought, sighing as well. I nodded.

"To fix a displaced aura, to mend a broken human being, you must merely hold fast to one basic tenet. It's both simple and hard. It's also essential to your changeling's— and your troop's—continued existence." She licked her lips, formulating words that I knew would be truth . . . but as slight and obscure as she could make it. I waited. "Put her, always, physically and otherwise, above yourself."

I swallowed and shook my head. "I don't know what that means."

"That's not my problem." She began to shut the door again.

No, I thought, jamming my foot inside. I was too close to just leave now. "Just tell me—"

"Nobody gets anything for free here!" Her eyes fired again, like light catching on the facets of diamonds. "Now, leave!"

She thrust out a palm in my direction, and though it never touched me, a bolt sliced through my solar plexus, the shove staggering pieces inside me like a puzzle coming undone. A breeze swept over places air should never touch, and my mind, my emotion, my thoughts, and all the intangibles that made me *me* were pushed from my body. It was nauseating to both be there and not, and while my feet were bolted to the ground, everything that truly animated me flew backward, whistling against the wind, tumbling down the staircase to end up in a heap at the bottom of the stairs.

My body arrived a moment later. I sat up quickly—too quickly—and heard an audible snap. Sure enough, I wobbled, hesitated, then leaned over and puked on the floor. Still dizzy, room spinning, I remained on my hands and knees long after the howls of laughter and groans of disgust faded away. My vision was blurred and I had to pinpoint a solid object in order for it to clear, though when it finally did, I was sad to discover the object on the scarred wooden floor was the pendant Suzanne had given me, now broken down into four separate pieces. Slowly I gathered them up in my palm, and by the time I finally looked up, the women who'd gathered along the banister were gone, and most of the men had returned to their cards.

Not the dealers. They'd created a tight circle around me, eyes spinning like silver reels.

I used the curved banister to help gain my feet, letting go as soon as my knees would hold. It looked like I was about to get my ass kicked, because no way was I going back up those stairs. I was still dizzy, but the heat wasn't going to make it any better, so I pocketed the jewelry, widened my stance, and readied myself to take on a handful of angry dealers.

Eyes still whirling, Boyd only held out his hand.

I glanced over at Bill. He was stroking his chin, looking amused. I took a testing step in the direction of my lantern. The circle shifted around me. Bill leaned his elbows on the bar and gave me a small shake of his head. "Solange says you aren't to be touched."

I took another testing step to the side, and swallowed back a second bout of nausea as the ring of men shifted with me. "Then what's up with the dealers o'death?"

My words were sharp, but my voice was tinny and echoed in my ears. My spirit or soul or whatever it was that Solange had loosened from within me was back, but I wasn't sure it had all settled in the right place. For the first time I became aware of a high ringing in my ears. I'd have shaken my head, but I didn't want to be sick again.

"She wants you to leave, but she wants to teach you a lesson as well. And Solange generally gets what she wants." He shrugged as I thought, No kidding. "One of your gaming chips will gain you passage home."

I swallowed hard. *Nobody gets anything for free here.*

Despite Solange's parting words, and being outnumbered, I might have fought it. It was the heat that decided things for me, though. I could either hand one over, or wait until I was too weak to stop them from picking my pockets clean, and though I hated the way the fight drained from me, intuition told me not to choose this battle. "Can I pick it?"

"She didn't specify, but if you sit down for a game with the boys, I'll throw it in the pot." Giving me a chance to gain this chip back, along with the others.

I sighed, pulling my chips from my pocket, shaking my head as I looked them over. "I grew up in a gambling town,

Bill. I know not to chase my losses." And I needed to get out of here quickly. Thirst and heat fueled desperation, and desperation led to bad decisions.

"That's okay." Boyd dropped the chip I handed him into his front pocket. "Next time."

Still wary, I sidestepped toward my lantern, surrounded by my own personal retinue. The ringing in my head pounded like a heartbeat with every step. "No. I'm never coming back."

I'd faced multiple attacks on my life, the most recent at the hands of both the Tulpa and Skamar, but I'd never faced anything as intrinsically frightening as what Solange had just done. And that, I thought with my raised hand shaking, had only been her warning.

Bill began his endless round of polishing pretty crystal glasses again, unconcerned. "You will. Then Mackie will finish his ballad, your other name will be revealed, and we'll own you."

"You've caused us a lot of trouble, Olivia," Boyd said, his strange eyes fixed like lasers on me. "Maybe we'll just kill you upon your next passage and give your power over to Midheaven in one big bump. Use it to create something interesting for ourselves."

"You mean the women will create something for themselves." Harlan Tripp had returned to his seat, his hands empty of all but playing cards. Apparently my words had provided him with the resolve he needed to resist that drink. For now.

Boyd ignored him, and simply raised his bushy black brows above those still spinning eyes. Apparently he was in a hurry to return to his table, to slice away bits of other people's souls one sliver at a time.

Shen, one of the divided souls, grinned. "And then Mackie will slit your throat."

My eyes darted to Mackie, but he was motionless and slumped like a sack of bones. I paused at my lantern to take one last look over the Rest House. Why had the First

Mother, that dark twin, created this place? What need compelled a person—thing, goddess, monster, whatever she was—to take human energy to fuel a world where men were forced to languish in their vices? Because though none of the men down here could voice their objections, I could feel them, restless as ghosts, in my mind. Like a city of souls, I thought with a shiver, all the emotion bottled up. Inside, though? They were screaming like banshees.

As for me? I might be the Kairos in my world, but over here I was as expendable as a wad of tissue. I felt that in my cells, a knowledge as instinctive as flight or fight. Today I chose flight.

Boyd pulled my chip from his pocket again, holding it up so the etched denomination caught light. I looked at it regretfully, and he smiled. "Not bad. I'll have your line of credit waiting when you return."

I shook my head, but said nothing, already mute with dread, anticipating that power being ripped from me. Fortunately, the heat dried the moisture welling in my eyes before it could give me away. At least I was still keeping up the *appearance* of being tough.

I was just about to blow the wick out, already bracing myself for the pain of the passage home, when I caught the gaze of the one man down there that was from my time. A Shadow agent, yes, but the only one fighting the effects of this place as fully as I. It was enough to make me feel he was a sort of ally.

"Hey, Tripp," I said, lifting to my toes. He blinked, lifting his eyes from the cards. "Eighteen years."

There was only his shocked gasp before the smoke from my extinguished lantern billowed and built, solid enough to ferry me back to my world, thick enough to dampen my scream.

21

I arrived back in the pipeline, fists clenched, trying to hang onto the intangible. But by the time I recognized the deep well of curving concrete beneath my booted feet, the chip I'd given Boyd—my ability to create walls from thin air—was gone. Alone, there was only my breathing, shallow and uncertain. And thank God, because the last time this tunnel had been peopled with enemies. As I calmed, I sucked in the silence and cried, just a little, in the dark.

Pushing past that inconveniently timed weakness, I then went in search of my shoulder bag. The depthless black of the pipeline enveloped me as if I were going farther in, rather than out, but after retrieving the bag—and dumping my remaining, dwindling chips inside—I continued to inch along in the darkness, unwilling to light the glyph on my chest and turn myself into a walking target. I knew where I was, but not *when*.

Disoriented, I dug in the bag and turned on my phone. There were another dozen messages from Cher, which I skipped, but what was really important was the date. Three days after I'd left. Not too bad. I'd traveled to a whole new world and still made it back in time for Thanksgiving. I called Hunter, still got his voice mail, and realized he'd probably be "working" at Valhalla, so left a message for him to call me back on his break.

Not trusting that I was steady enough yet to drive, I caught a cab. I didn't care what Warren said, after dying from thirst, I needed a cool glass of water at my side; after Solange's separation of my body from my soul, I needed refuge; after days where I'd had nothing but worry, and a heated night of passion, I needed to be in a place where nothing was required of me but to *be*. In short, I needed the sanctuary.

It was downtown, buried beneath the discarded remains of our city, in the Neon Boneyard. The entrance sat kitty-corner to the restored La Concha Motel lobby, a mid-mod building with a wavy roof I used to point and laugh at as a kid, but was now considered historic. My, how things change. Our lair was surrounded by a brick wall, which also divided two parallel realities.

The exact split between dawn and dusk lasted the scant moments it took the sun to evenly split the sky, and in that time the wall surrounding the Neon Boneyard became a murky, swirling coagulation of liquefied matter. If you knew how to look, you could see parts of it thinning, the discarded signage of Las Vegas's yesteryear visible through shifting patches on the other side.

Still, you'd think the booming crash of a three thousand pound vehicle regularly hitting concrete would attract the Neighborhood Watch, but despite the explosion of cinder block and debris, and the squealing crunch of metal meeting wall, the dust acted as a sort of buffer. It didn't absorb the sound as much as it sucked it in.

Even with erratic, supernatural winds buffering this cab, and with four of my powers stripped away—the two odd triangles I'd lost at the tables, the power to heal taken by Shen, and the one I'd just given over to escape a second time—the thought gave me peace. Entering the sanctuary would be like stepping back into the womb, so with every mile gained, Midheaven faded like a nightmare, something I'd endured mentally but not physically. The soul slices and abilities taken from me had yet to show their effects, but I imagined this was what a surprise cancer diagnosis was like; the sudden, dark knowledge that something was wrong inside of you warring with a feeling of familiar, if not perfect, health. The awareness that the worst was soon to come.

As for those beings peopling the twisted magical kingdom, I was happy to have escaped them. Jacks and Solange deserved one another . . . though her sudden show of jealousy had thrown me. How a woman like that could see me as a threat was boggling. Yet since Jacks himself claimed he'd returned for love, I was sure they had it all straightened out by now.

And still no real way to fix Jasmine. I sighed heavily. Solange's advice was to put her above myself, something I didn't really need to be told. I'd gone there, hadn't I? Risked my soul. Lost my powers. I had no idea what else "put her above yourself" could mean.

"But I've heard that somewhere before," I muttered as we pulled onto Flamingo. We passed Money Plays, the neon green sign reminding me of half-yard beers and games of table shuffleboard. Maybe the advice had come from Hunter, I thought, glancing wistfully at Money's attached pizzeria. Possibly Warren.

Warren, who'd lied.

Because *he'd* told me Jacks was already in Midheaven, and Warren didn't make mistakes that big. So why lie? What would be his true motive in sending me to a place where the cost of entry was a third of my soul, where women ruled ruthlessly, and where my powers were risked in games of chance? I decided to ask him as soon as I entered the sanctuary.

Meanwhile, Jacks had been even less helpful. He told me to kill Jasmine so that my *chi* could return to me. It was shocking that a former agent of Light could think such a thing, much less say it. If he were a Shadow agent, or worse, if he were the Tulpa . . .

What would he do if he were the Tulpa? What would I do?

I sat up so straight in the backseat that the cab actually rocked and the driver cursed.

"Strong winds," I muttered, but he only frowned at me in the rearview mirror. I fumbled for my phone, again dialing Hunter's number.

"The Tulpa doesn't want me dead," I said as soon as his voice mail allowed. "He needs me alive. If I die, my *chi* will unite again. In Jasmine."

The energy would be reabsorbed in Jasmine's body, the same way the energy of the people Jaden Jacks used for crossing into Midheaven was absorbed into that world.

"But the Tulpa can't let that happen. Because then the manuals would be written again." Our troop would be strong again. Skamar would have her recorded name. Li would be healed. Sure, he wanted Regan to bring me to him, he probably even wanted to punish me for all the trouble I'd caused him this past year—especially for siccing Skamar on him—but he didn't want me dead. Yet.

"He needs me alive. He can't touch me." And I hung up without saying good-bye. There was a sonic boom in the distance, the tulpas warring over the black mountains, but I smiled grimly at the embattled sky. My powers had been taken from me, but I could walk freely on this side of reality, a power in itself. I'd cross over for now, work with the others to figure out how to use this knowledge to best the Tulpa, and we could all heal the Zodiac together.

After that, I thought, leaning my head back, I could truly rest.

I had the driver drop me at Town Square, a likely destination for Olivia Archer, with its upscale shopping and dining and nightlife. It was a straight shot down the Strip to the Peppermill, but also far enough away that I could approach by stealth. With my speed, one of the super strengths I'd managed to retain, I'd make it to the old-school Vegas lounge well in time for the dusk crossing.

But the low ceiling of cloud cover was throwing off my senses. The sun and sky were still there, somewhere, but the razored sheets of bulging gray obscured both. Gregor would have to sense the moment rather than using the light. I wasn't worried. For us, the splitting of dawn and dusk was like the dissection of a vein. It might be a small thing, but we felt it when it happened.

I dodged onto Koval Lane, where a cluster of kids was hanging around outside a run-down apartment complex. They were bundled in clothing more suited to the East Coast than anything I'd ever thought to see in the desert, and one greasy-haired punk glanced up from blowing on his knuckles and hooted, obviously recognizing me as Olivia Archer. Grumbling, I rounded the corner and yanked a hooded sweatshirt from my bag—it would conceal my hair if not my shape—and slipped my mask on as well.

I cut through the parking lot of the Guardian Angel Cathedral, an unlikely dome created in the fifties, where visitors to the valley could go get their Catholic on before the day's gambling began, and was just edging by the giant, and odd, odalisque out front when I heard the first whisper.

"Such a good day to die . . . "

The glyph on my chest shot to life, but when I whirled around I saw nothing.

"Over here . . . Archer."

Shit, shit, shit . . . The scent was that of Shadows . . . but I saw nothing. *They're on the flip side.* Concealed behind a portal.

I backed up in a swift skipping beat, blinked once, then softened my gaze as if looking through the air in front of me.

He was so close I could kiss him. He was especially white, with flat black freckles dotting his cheeks, and looked like he'd be a redhead on this side of reality. I back up more . . . straight into another Shadow. That one would have grabbed me but for my speed. I raked my heel down his shin on the way to stomping on his foot. My elbow connected with his jaw as he fell. After that I backed up more quickly. The first Shadow continued advancing, not letting me escape, but in no great hurry either.

"The Tulpa wants me alive," I blurted, expecting to feel another pair of hands on me at any minute. I had no way of knowing how many there were.

The would-be redhead shrugged. "There are lots of ways to hurt an agent and still keep them alive."

Not for me. I couldn't easily heal from anything more dangerous than a paper cut . . . but I had yet to tell my allies that, never mind my enemies. And I wasn't going to try to stand toe-to-toe and exchange blows. I could barely see the guy, much less guard against him.

I decided to put my formidable speed to the test. Letting a smile I didn't feel bloom on my face, I looked over the almost see-through shoulder. Sometimes the simplest plans worked best. I bolted even as he turned, on guard for an attack, and shouts sounded behind me. God, there *were* others. The pounding of their feet in reality's flip side was as loud and insistent as my own.

I hit Cathedral Way like I was late for mass, but put the skids on as soon as I saw a souped-up Honda wheeling in my direction. Instinct was to run the other way, but instead I backed up to the building's corner and ducked low. The Shadow chasing me was already turning as fast as I had, and he flipped over the top of my crouched body like he was auditioning for Cirque du Soleil. I was pretty sure that was the only reason the car didn't immediately run me down. But the Shadow driving it revved the engine in warning.

Obviously I was expected to turn and run. They were herding me away from Gregor's cab, I realized, which was behind the Honda. I could see its headlights on the other side of the Peppermill and wondered if he saw what was going on not two hundred yards away.

The Tulpa wants me alive.

They were trying to capture me.

I took advantage of my unlikely savior's prone form and bolted across his body—making sure to land one solid boot heel into his skull as I vaulted over the top of the Honda. It started backing up immediately, but the driver had to shift gears first and that bought me time. I waved my arms as I ran, and Gregor's headlights flashed in response. He saw me. The cab pulled out, barreled toward me, and swerved at the last moment. I flung open the back door, catapulted myself into the backseat, and yelled from a prone position, "Go, go, go!"

The door swung wide as he smoked rubber to get us going, and I anticipated another attack. Sure enough, an outlined hand clawed its way onto the frame of my open door. Stomping again with my feet, I heard the Shadow scream before falling away, and I pulled up into my seat to yank the door shut. Swiveling, I saw the Honda bounce over two parking blocks and mow down a handicapped sign as it flipped around to follow. Even as we fishtailed in front of the giant Stripside mall, I knew we wouldn't last long on the boulevard. It was a near straight shot from there to the boneyard, and the street was totally deserted in the wild night. Both things left the faster Honda free to rear-end us.

"We're too exposed," I yelled, reeling around to face Gregor. "We'll never make it all the way to—"

I stuttered off because the long-lashed eyes that met mine in the rearview mirror were most certainly not Gregor's. The manicured fingers tightening on the wheel were on the right hand, and Gregor only possessed his left. More than anything, the skull burning through the layers of muscle and tissue and skin to skim the surface could only belong to a senior Shadow agent.

"To the boneyard?" the Shadow finished for me, and suddenly I knew what they were doing. She smiled as my eyes widened. "Don't worry. We'll still make it."

The redhead had been the muscle. The other car was just an escort. *One filled with Shadows.* This one, the lead one, held me. Why? Because I was the only one who could get through the additional security measures Warren had implemented after the last time the Shadows infiltrated the boneyard. Similar to the light that attacked all Shadows if they tried to enter our sanctuary inside the boneyard, this system had to detect Light in order to allow passage.

"Shit."

The Shadow tapped on the Plexiglas dividing us, letting me know it was unbreakable . . . even for us. "That's one way to put it."

And another way to put it was to say I was surrounded—no, trapped—by my enemies, in a speeding car, without the ability to heal even from the impact of the crash through the wall dividing our realities. The Tulpa might not wish me dead, but chances were, I would still end up that way. It almost made me wish I'd remained in Midheaven. Almost.

Okay, so I didn't possess any weapons to help me combat the Shadows. I had no allies, no power to heal, no ability to erect walls to shield me from assault, and I was missing something else represented by two mysterious triangles.

I really needed to figure out what those were, I thought, holding tight to the bag holding my remaining powers as we hurtled down Washington Avenue. If I got out of this alive. It was a big *if*.

The now confirmed fact that the Tulpa did indeed want me alive could be seen as a positive, but as the redheaded Shadow had said, there were a lot of ways to hurt an agent and still keep them alive. So was it good news or bad, I wondered, that I wouldn't survive the impact of the cab hurtling through cinder block?

Yet the second car couldn't even attempt that. There were no agents of Light in the Honda, so it would have to stop . . . which meant we would too. My best guess was that they'd climb in with me before the driver took a run at the wall, like a bull spotting the matador. God, I thought, swallowing hard, I needed more time!

Question was, time for what?

Well, there was enough time to pray, I thought as the car whizzed under the freeway. I guess I could start doing that. Though if God were a cynic, he probably wouldn't appreciate my last minute scramble.

Time to say good-bye. *Thanks for the memories, everyone, it's been a nice ride . . . wish I could have stayed around to fulfill my destiny as the savior of the paranormal realm, but you know how these things go.* Yeah, I thought, clenching my fists. That was so me. Going gently into the night.

Time to think of dwindling options. Regret not getting another shower of Micah's fortifying preservative.

Nah, that was just depressing.

Time to imagine something new.

That thought snagged my attention. I tilted my head as the driver smiled at me through the rearview mirror and went back to that thought again.

It was true that I could no longer form the concrete walls from mere thought in order to shield me from the Shadows, but with a mortal's flesh, concrete wasn't my best friend right now anyway. Yet there was another option. Another risky, long shot of an option since I'd only succeeded in creating it on a small scale before. But it too was an ability only afforded the Light. Shadows couldn't do it because it involved a sort of birthing, and beings that were essentially dead inside couldn't bring something outside of themselves to life. But this meant they wouldn't be expecting it, I thought, closing my eyes. It was chancy, but that—along with the element of surprise—was pretty much all that was left in my paranormal arsenal.

"Hey. Hey! What are you doing?" I felt the weight of the Shadow's gaze as we barreled past Bunkers Mortuary, but kept my own eyes closed. I settled my senses and mind as much as possible, and began imagining the softest, most succulent, most enormous cactus buried below the dusty earth in front of the Neon Boneyard's entrance. It was a Joshua tree, native to the area—which was important—and I pictured its fibers as being silk-soft, airy, and far less dense than a tree grown from seed. That would absorb the impact of the vehicle. I conceived it, and more importantly, I believed in it—which was key to its creation.

Joshua trees are normally top-heavy with a shallow root, so I reinforced the base of this one—I didn't want it toppling to allow access into the wall just beyond—and then I visualized the branches lower, to match the driver's height. As I continued to imagine this, the car veered to a halt. I needed to have most of the cactus conceptualized before the others clambered in. Once there, they'd never let me continue my meditation. The driver was already yelling obscenities at me, knowing I was up to something but not sure what. How could she? She didn't have the capacity to even imagine what my Light side could create.

One final tweak: already naturally and conveniently bayonet-shaped, I reinforced the tapered leaves with iron, and made the spiraling clusters dense and tight and unyielding even under the full impact of a speeding car. As I finished off the last cluster, the Honda's doors slammed behind us. I opened my eyes and stared straight ahead. I could make out the boneyard wall in the distance. It was still solid, and I took another moment to give the underground cactus an extra energy pulse, mentally softening the ground above it. Had any of the Shadows been looking, the shift in the wide swath of earth could be attributed to the wind, but the backseat doors were winging open, and the driver was already yelling.

"She's doing something!" the woman screeched as sharp elbows and toxic breath suddenly hemmed me in. I knew them all, either from previous run-ins or, in the case of the newbies, from reading the Shadow manuals, an ability I possessed because I was half Shadow. I dampened my responding cough to their scent, forcing down bile, and continued staring straight ahead as Harrison slid in beside the driver. He shot me a little finger wave. The driver, still in animate cadaver mode, was like a snake spitting venom. "She's up to something!"

"She's trapped in a car with five Shadow agents and no conduit." Harrison was talking to her but still smirking at me. I carefully envisioned an extra sharp barb arrowing into his skull. "Now watch the wall."

Tariq leaned so close, his dump-site breath stirred my hair. "We're going to cross over to the boneyard's flip side and cut your troop down as they exit your sanctuary."

"Looks that way," I said woodenly, hoping no one would notice how much I was sweating beneath my hoodie and mask. It was harder to concentrate on creation with my eyes open. I'd never tried it that way before.

Sloane, next to me, was apparently looking for a greater reaction. She slapped my face so hard her nails raked the skin beneath the mask. Fortunately, she was too close to use her full power. I felt a tooth loosen at the back of my mouth and winced, which made her laugh. And that made my face burn.

"Don't sit there like a statue," she said as I lifted my chin and continued to stare at the wall. Dusk was splitting. The only good thing about this was that it divided and diverted their full attention from me. "You've gotta at least be getting excited."

I lifted one brow. "Because murder and destruction are so thrilling?"

She slapped me again. I really hated being slapped. "You're gonna lose that fucking hand," I muttered.

She slapped me again. Now I had matching red cheeks . . . and matching red eyes.

"Wow, she looks just like—"

"Him," Harrison said, and pointed at the sky.

The Tulpa was barreling toward us like a bull on acid. Damn it! The Shadows looked surprised to see him, so I knew it was my anger that had led him to us. He leveled out, going at least eighty miles an hour, swooping over the top of the car so it shook beneath his thundering cry. "Go!"

But it wasn't yet time. The boneyard wall was beginning to ripple, like the shimmer of sun off asphalt, but it hadn't softened yet. Impatient, the driver revved the engine, and everyone stared straight ahead, except for Tariq. He was watching the Tulpa behind us.

"Here it comes."

"Gotta time it right, Adele."

"I know what I'm doing, assholes."

Sloane hit the Plexiglas in reply. At least she was no longer hitting me. I took a deep breath and waited. The softened concrete shimmied to wrap around the barrier like a ribbon, minute undulations making room for air, softening the wall enough to allow passage. As the motion slid along the final corner, the cab's wheels spun against gravel before catching, and the car lurched forward. The Shadows were still looking at the slow wave as we sped forward, like it was a tsunami we wanted to meet head-on. I concentrated on the target, narrowing my eyes at the ground in front of the wall. That's why none of us saw the Tulpa that dropped between the cab and the wall until it was too late. Dropped down to save me, I realized at the last, like an angel, like a martyr . . . like a fly caught between a flat surface and a swatter.

The cab impaled Skamar on the silver-edged tip of the cactus that had shot up from nowhere, its spongy base absorbing the cab's impact but impaling its occupants on the barbed leaves. I barely had time to duck, much less gasp, but the screams of the Shadows around me joined the images from just before that: Skamar's mouth going wide with pain, Adele's blood coating the Plexiglas, the green and brown trunk of the Joshua tree folding like a marshmallow to cushion the impact.

The cab would have bounced backward on its wheels,

but the bodies of the Shadows around me were pulled forward, and it merely shuddered as it jarred to a halt, lifting slightly off its wheelbase. I was bleeding; too numb to feel it, but I could smell it. Damn I was fragile! And the Shadows were still alive. They were momentarily struggling like worms on hooks, but they'd survive this. I leaned forward, kicking up at the soft flesh of cactus limb that would have impaled me had I still been sitting up. Careful not to let the barbed cluster fall atop me, I swung it around, burying it in Tariq's back. As he screamed, I braced a foot on the seat and kicked out the back window. I kept kicking until the hole was big enough for me to climb through, and—making sure I had my bag with those valuable soul chips with me—I had nearly done so when I paused. Surely one second more wouldn't kill me.

I leaned back and slapped Sloane across her bloodied face. She had a barbed leaf through her windpipe, so she didn't have too much to say about it.

The Tulpa, however, laughed so loudly it again shook the car. He rocketed past us, skeletal smile wide as I ducked, but he ignored me to drop in front of all the destruction. Then, rabidly, he began pulling at Skamar's body. Her screams were like scissors on silk, too breathless to hold any weight but telling of destruction. She was lanced through the stomach, so his formidable strength widened the already impressive hole.

The Shadows stilled, their pain nothing compared to Skamar's agony. I froze, limbs gone numb, then shook my head and found my wits enough to will the Joshua tree gone. My emotions were nowhere near under control, and as I'd only discovered this ability the month before, it took some time. And I had to bolt as soon as the cactus dissolved; the Shadows stirred immediately. But it would take time for them to heal enough to give chase. I sprinted half a block, braced for the Tulpa's pursuit, but when I glanced over my shoulder, he merely shot me a thumbs-up. With a now-freed and limp Skamar scuffed like a kitten in one claw, he shot into the air like a bottle rocket, screaming with wild glee, and after another moment, disappeared into the night.

I ran . . . and kept running. I ran until I'd left the city proper and was somewhere in the middle of the desert, panting hard, tears dried on my face. Glancing back, I saw Vegas glittering stubbornly beneath the bright hornet's nest that was its sky, and I waited. I stood, slumped, waiting. I sat, and waited. But there were no storms or gales or howling winds that night. I sat for hours in the middle of a blackened void, and though the sky didn't clear above the city, it also didn't worsen. At one point I closed my eyes, bent my head, and sobbed for Skamar, cries slicing the air like razors, so the scorpions and snakes and lizards didn't bother me, sensing the sharp pain. My sorrow was palpable, a heavy cloud marking my location. But the Tulpa didn't come for me.

No one did.

The story spilled from me as soon as Warren answered his phone. My words tumbled over themselves like dice, cut up and spit out, but rolling up snake eyes anyway. With tears in my own I told him about how the Shadows had ambushed me and made a play for the boneyard, how Skamar had intercepted them, and how my created cactus had led to her capture.

"The Tulpa has her," I sniffed. "I don't know where."

"Okay, calm down." Warren's voice was tight and wooden, but he wasn't yelling. A part of me wished he would. I wiped at my nose and sniffed again. "Where are you now?"

Alone, was my first thought.

"I came back to the warehouse. To wait." For anything. For anyone.

"So you and Hunter stay put. The rest of us will cross at dawn. Keep the alarms on until we get there."

But I was still caught on the first thing he'd said. "Hunter?"

Warren paused. "Yes. Isn't he with you?"

"No."

Another beat of silence, then a soft curse. "I should have known this would happen."

"What?" My heart skipped full beats before speeding up abnormally, and my knees actually buckled. Eyes wide, I looked around the outside of the building as if that would bring Hunter into view. Instead I saw visions of him bent over his drawing board, Hunter working, Hunter fighting . . . Hunter approaching me. "What happened?" I croaked, shaking off the images.

"Due to the lack of safe zones, I ordered the troop into the sanctuary as soon as I'd learned you left for Midheaven. I didn't know when you'd be back," he added, almost apologetically. "That's why the Shadows attacked the boneyard. But Jasmine Chan went missing two days ago, and Hunter left the sanctuary right after that. I think he's gone to find her."

"So he's missing too?"

"They both are."

And now so was Skamar. "Oh my God." This time my legs did buckle. The sky was still holding overhead, if barely, and yet my world was still falling apart. I sat hard on the asphalt, slumped against the warehouse wall.

"Just stay where you are, okay? Do you know how to get in?" He raised his voice when I didn't answer. "Joanna?"

"Okay. Yes." I lifted a hand and covered my eyes. "Yes, Hunter showed me."

"Hm," Warren said, and I knew what he was thinking. Hunter never showed anyone how to deactivate his complicated system of codes and alarms.

We hung up and I let both my hands drop. My head lolled on the wall. Tears pricked my eyes again. Then after a long moment of silence, and before I went inside, I picked up my bag and ran my finger over the soul chips inside like they were a rosary. I revisited the first option I'd rejected when trapped in a cab surrounded by Shadows.

I prayed.

22

Exhaustion was a formidable opponent. As worried as I was, it pulled me into sleep again, even though I was slumped on the warehouse's cold concrete floor. I watched peacefully as my mind played out my worries in a dream. Skamar was leading Jasmine away from me. I yelled for them to come back, but Skamar only lifted the young girl to her toes and began floating, faster, so that Jasmine had to run to keep up. Finally, the young girl put on a sudden burst, the speed provided by my swiped powers, and took the lead enough to turn back and look at me as she ran. The pink and white streaks in her dark hair flew around her face like zigzagging neon, and she shot me a sheepish smile before waving through the hole in Skamar's stomach.

"It will still be okay," she said, pivoting to jump through that gaping hole like a circus performer. She somersaulted and came to her feet with her hands in the air. "If you put me above yourself."

I woke to a sharp pounding on the steel bay door. Jasmine's sweet voice still lingered as I clamored to my feet. I checked three different peepholes to make sure there were no Shadows outside before turning off the alarms.

"You look like crap," Vanessa told me with a weak smile. But despite the worry cutting lines around her eyes, she looked much better than the last time I'd seen her. She wore a black scarf around her head, pinned to one side with a silver broach. That was the only remaining sign of the Shadows' handiwork. Her speech was perfect, her ear and thumb and nose regrown, unmarred. I looked down, and she wiggled her left foot. Good as new.

Nice to know someone could heal, I thought, rubbing at my eyes. "Where is everyone?"

"Warren doesn't want to meet here anymore. It's counterintuitive, I know, but this warehouse is our safest place on this side of reality. He wants to guard its location for as long as possible."

So he thought the Shadows would find it eventually.

"Are you okay?" Vanessa asked as I sighed. She put a hand on my arm and I covered it with my own.

"Yeah, I just had a strange dream."

She grunted. "Not surprised. Do you know how to lock this place up?"

I nodded. "Hold on."

Deciding it would be safer to leave my bag and the soul chips in the warehouse, I tucked it in the bottom drawer of a standing toolbox, before running through the series of codes Hunter had shown me. I held my breath, hoping I remembered them correctly. Otherwise the whole place would blow. Vanessa and I backed a safe distance away, but nothing happened. I gave a quick prayer of thanks. I seemed to be praying a lot all of a sudden.

"What time is it?" I asked, knowing only that it was early morning. I never wore a watch. The kind Olivia Archer would wear would be a dead giveaway on the Kairos's arm.

"Almost seven. Not that you'd know it by this weather." Keeping half a step in front of me, she motioned me south. "Um . . . Happy Birthday, for what it's worth."

"Oh. Yeah." I was twenty-six now, and a bit surprised

at the fact. A part of me, it seemed, hadn't expected to make it a year. And Ashlyn, my daughter, was now eleven. "Thanks."

The sky was lumpy gravy, gray and badly stirred. Behind the shifting clouds, though, was a riot of flashing color, red and oranges battling with that strange liquid blue and green strain, like the most elaborate production show to hit town was being rehearsed on that side of the sooty curtain. I ducked my head as thunder ripped across the valley, like it was wired in surround sound. The grand finale, I thought worriedly, couldn't be far off.

Vanessa saw me looking and followed the trail of thunder across the sky. "Warren's concerned too."

Finally, I thought, shaking my head. "So where are we meeting?"

"Shapiro's Kitchen," she said, talking about the latest celebrity chef to be lured to town. "It's not open yet, so it'll be private, and because it's so new, no one could have tracked any of us there."

It was a stand-alone restaurant, a risky business move in a town where the most successful restaurants were backed with the seemingly endless cash flow and street traffic from an attached casino or hotel. Word was, though, that Sam Shapiro's name would be enough to draw a crowd. That's not why I remembered it, though. "Wasn't that supposed to be a safe zone?"

Vanessa shrugged, but the stiffness of worry was caught in the movement. "In another life."

We trudged on in silence after that, stuck with this one.

The places we were safe in this city—this world—had shrunk shockingly fast. Since Shapiro's Kitchen was supposed to have been a designated safe zone, meeting there was a calculated risk because the Shadows knew about it. Yet Warren obviously felt comfortable with the plan, and because of that, I tried to push my own worry away. Something about it didn't feel right, but I was exhausted, and needed to trust that his judgment was better than mine. So Vanessa and I stuck to the surface streets, burying ourselves in pockets of darkness whenever a lone car would pass, until we finally reached the sleek round building. Not until then did I realize how worried she'd been as well. At Shapiro's Kitchen she melted into Felix's arms and he buried her in his embrace. I swallowed hard, thinking that should be me with Hunter. Yet because I'd screwed up so badly, he was caught out somewhere beneath a threatening sky, searching for a girl I had broken.

I didn't have much time to give in to regret. Warren met me at the hostess podium. "You're okay?"

"For now," I muttered, but his gaze was flat and disinterested, and he was already turning away. I tried to tell myself that he was preoccupied with thoughts of saving the world, but I couldn't help a final glance back at Vanessa and Felix, dissolving as one into the alcove of a coat check, whispering so softly that even I couldn't hear.

I sighed and followed Warren through a mahogany paneled hallway and into the main dining room. The tables were already spaced, the floor laid out the way it would be on opening night. Stacks of linens threatened to topple in one corner, and a cart of glassware was totally out of place on the opulent floor, but you could already see that the dining room was going to be magnificent. The focal point, however, was the glass-encased kitchen, where—for the viewing pleasure of a gastronomically appreciative audience—Sam Shapiro himself would direct his crew like he was conducting an orchestra.

It was in this fragile interior that the troop was huddled, and they were battered. Not physically, not like me. But Iraqi War battered, like they'd been fighting for years and there was still no end in sight. Battered like they sometimes lost sight of what they were fighting for but kept on doing it anyway. Battered like people who had to keep taking orders, because left to their own devices, they might float away.

They greeted me when I entered, but the curiosity and enthusiasm that had met me after my first return from Midheaven wasn't there. They knew I couldn't tell them anything about the place, and the loss of Hunter and Jasmine—and now Skamar—weighed heavily upon them.

It was in that weighty silence that my eyes fell on the object in the middle of the stainless steel table. I blinked. "What's that?"

"We got you cake."

I felt my brows wing up to my hairline. "Cake?"

"For your birthday," Warren said, coming to stand at my side. He was the only one who sounded even remotely enthused about it. "You didn't think we were going to let our Kairos's big day pass without notice, did you?"

"Cake," I repeated dumbly, thinking I might puke if I tried to take a bite.

"You can say thank you," he muttered, pushing past me. I watched him go, frowning, then met Micah's eyes. He rolled his. Good to know I wasn't the only one who didn't feel like celebrating.

"Thank you," I muttered, following him around the table to join Gregor on the other side. Gregor put his good arm around me and kissed the top of my head. I felt a little better after that.

But almost immediately Vanessa appeared in the doorway, eyes wide, and face ghost white. Though her mouth worked open and shut, nothing came out. Warren quirked his head and took a step forward. "Van—"

"Vanessa! Get in there!"

A whimper escaped her throat and her fear hit us all with the full force of a cyclone. Felix yelled again behind her and I drew back at the strain in it, so different than the reunion I'd witnessed only moments before.

Warren headed that way. "Felix? What is it?"

Felix came into the room so slowly it looked like he was freeze-framed. Vanessa whimpered again. A gurgling laugh sounded somewhere behind him.

"Um, Warren?" Felix inched to the side once he'd breached the glass threshold to reveal my conduit shoved into the small of his back. Behind it was Regan DuPree. And behind *that*, I thought, mouth going dry, shuffled Hunter Lorenzo, wrapped tight in his own whip.

Regan pushed Felix through the doorway, and Vanessa jolted like she was going to leap forward, but she held herself, knowing an arrow would pierce either her or Felix before she could take a single step.

Regan looked much the way she had the last time I'd seen her, skin unraveled in vertical strips from head to toe, blackened at the edges, revealing bone. She was wrapped in dirty gauze from neck to ankle, thrift shop clothing donned atop that, but neither concealed the thinning of her ribboned skin. The flesh had corroded, and the stink I'd been tracking all over this city was worse. In the confines of the kitchen, it made bile stick in my throat.

She gave us all a tattered smile, her mouth winging upward in jigsawed pieces to reveal spaces of gum, oozing and receding from the bone. She knew how macabre she was, how grotesque, and she played it up under the full glare of the fluorescent lights. "And what are the agents of Light celebrating tonight, huh? I mean, what could you all possibly have to celebrate?"

Nobody answered or moved. She was dead, the knowledge of her inability to escape this room now that she was in it drawn across her gaze like a toddler's scrawl, but she was suicide-bomber dead. The question was, who did she intend to take with her?

That scribbled gaze fell on me.

"Just tell us what you want," Hunter said, again showing why—though he was the one closest to death—he was the one everyone looked up to. Warren might be troop leader, but it was Hunter who acted when the rest of us wouldn't. He spoke while everyone else remained mute. He'd been out there canvassing the city for Jasmine while we huddled in safety.

And what did he get for his troubles? A mummy-worthy wrapping in his own conduit, barbed spears from the whip burrowing into his flesh.

Regan's head swiveled unsteadily on her neck as she turned to look at him, her smile opening up, red-tinted pus oozing to stain her lips.

"Oh, I believe I want the same thing you do, my friend. Some good, old sat-is-fac-tion." She drew out the word, like in the song, and pushed Felix with the tip of my crossbow. He backed away slowly because she still had Hunter, and she pulled him along behind her as she sauntered into the center of the room. Crossbow still aimed at Felix's heart, finger on the trigger, her gaze fell down. "Mmm. Cake."

"How did you—"

The weapon swung Riddick's way, so close it crossed his eyes and his mouth fell shut.

"Shh," Regan said, reaching forward. "I like cake."

Felix took a step back, toward Vanessa. Regan sensed the movement—the tiniest breeze probably felt like a sandstorm when you'd been skinned—and directed the bow back his way.

Warren held up his hands. "Everyone hold still."

Keeping her hands steady, Regan leaned down. Her tongue was divided in four separate slices, but each found a bit of birthday cake, and though the white frosting disappeared in her mouth, I was able to follow its journey down her throat.

"Mmm," she hummed, straightening. "See, now that's satisfying." It was unclear whether she meant the cake or having the entire troop at her mercy. She turned back to Hunter. "Have you tried this yet, my friend?"

Why did she keep calling him that? *My friend.* It was the exact phrase she'd used in the pipeline with the Tulpa . . .

My new friend.

My sharp inhalation brought Regan's gaze back my way. "Ah," she said, sounding satisfied. "And now you see."

She was the person he'd been meeting with in the

Shadow manuals, the hidden contact lurking in the dark. The one he'd been talking to weeks ago when he said everyone should be allowed their greatest desire.

And her desire, her satisfaction, was in seeing me realize it. Me, also, on a hook. Betrayed. Brokenhearted. All of the above. Regan was only satisfied when destroying other people's loves, their futures, their *possibilities*. Her mother had done this with her father, turning him into the worst sort of criminal. Regan had tried to do the same with Ben.

And she had apparently succeeded with Hunter.

Suddenly, little incongruities began to add up: how Regan had slipped past Hunter during the chase in the pipeline. How, in her current state, she'd ever managed to get her hands on him now.

Oh my God, I thought, the realization hitting me afresh. He'd been *working* with my greatest personal enemy for weeks! And he still made love to me. I let him lay his head on my shoulder, find rest in my arms. We were lovers, and friends . . . and now enemies too.

"Joanna."

I shook my head. I couldn't even look at him.

Regan laughed, a tattered chortle, and dug my conduit into the cake, licked frosting from the tip.

"I see nothing," Warren interrupted, brow furrowed. "I see a rogue agent trying to bargain her way into a better situation."

"Then let me elucidate." Regan chuckled, and yanked on Hunter's whip. "Your star superhero here has been working with me. I give him what he wants, he gives me what I want."

"Bull." Riddick looked at Hunter with the same sure expression he always had.

Hunter gazed straight ahead, looking at no one.

"It's true," Regan continued, shrugging so the flesh on her shoulder wobbled. "How else have I eluded you for this amount of time? I mean, *fuck*!" Her face went wide with the enraged word, and literally split. Part of her tongue darted out to lick the blood on the side of her mouth. "Even I can smell myself. Yet I continue to get away. Slip through holes in your defenses. Disappear into the wild night."

Still staring at Hunter, Riddick finally winced, like it was painful. He clenched his jaw when he saw me looking, and turned to face Warren.

I didn't blame him. Even I, having long known that Hunter was up to something, that he was meeting with someone he shouldn't be, that he had a secret identity and agenda, had never fathomed that his contact had been Regan.

And he'd slept with me after what she'd done to me, to Ben. He entered me while helping this . . . . this walking carcass. This being I hated so very much.

The shock sizzled in my brain, clouding it, making it heavy on my shoulders. I felt the additional weight of Hunter's gaze. He knew that with every passing minute I was putting more and more of his betrayal together. Right now it seemed endless. A long road, and I was riding in a car that would never stop.

"Is this true?" Tekla spoke up from the far corner of the room, and though her arms were folded across her body as usual, the wall looked like it was holding her up.

"I had reasons," he told them all, still looking at me. "Good ones."

"Your reasons are *my* reasons!" Warren pounded at his chest, and we all jolted as if from a stupor. Tekla straightened. Everyone else looked at the floor.

Regan tucked my conduit beneath her right armpit and stuck her index finger directly in the center of my cake, swirling it, blood mingling with the white frosting.

Hunter glanced at me and I wanted to shake him. Instead I looked away. But Warren had words enough for us both.

"Hunter, did you help this—this—" He finally gestured at the center of the room, the former Shadow now smashing the cake between her fingers, a child in her own sandbox, "—*this,* escape us? Even knowing she had Jo's conduit?"

I cleared my throat before Hunter could answer. "Hey, Regan."

Her sugarcoated hand stilled.

"How'd you know we were here?"

Vanessa was shaking her head. "You told her about this place too, didn't you, Hunter? Damn it, I used this safehouse *last week*!"

"We did," Felix said flatly, stepping to her side. Regan tilted her head at the couple, another considering smile growing on her face.

"Stop looking at them and get your hand out of my fucking cake."

"Shut up, Jo!" Warren's eyes were on my conduit. Regan's were again on me. "This is about Hunter."

"I never put Jo in danger," Hunter said stiffly. She yanked on his conduit in warning. His mouth snapped shut.

"Except that Regan is still alive," Warren said.

Hunter glared at him.

"And here now," Regan added, still focused on me.

"How did you get here?" I wanted to know. I knew I was probably in shock, but something just wasn't adding up.

"By trusting nobody but myself." She pointed my conduit at my heart. "Now get your ass up over here. You and I are going for a walk. Bring the cake."

Hunter frowned, and beneath his brows I saw shock and fear and shame, and possibly even the need to keep me from walking out that door.

But he couldn't move. Because Regan, his "friend," had turned to watch his reaction.

And that was when Warren moved. Not to the Shadow—no, that would have been certain death for me, him . . . maybe both—but in front of me, using his body as a shield and with a bargain on his tongue.

"Not her." He said it calmly, as though bartering.

"Her," Regan insisted.

"*Not* her," he repeated. "Hunter."

"No," I said without hesitation.

Regan laughed so hard her guts tore through, shining and pink among the blood and shredded flesh. She used an elbow, grunting as she pushed them back in, but kept laughing. "What is this? Puppy love? Could you really care for a man who made a deal over your flesh?"

"I did not—"

She yanked on his whip. Hunter winced involuntarily.

"In return for what?" I wanted to know. What was so important that it would cause Hunter to betray me? All of us?

"It doesn't matter," said Warren, Mr. Black-and-White. But it mattered to me.

Regan licked her lips, her tongue darting out in four different directions. "Come with me and I'll tell you everything."

I nodded for a moment, then took a step forward. Felix stepped in front of me, beside Warren, creating a wall. Then Tekla was there. They were lined up like ducks, waiting for Regan to pick them off. She began to laugh again.

I too saw what they were doing. Sacrificing themselves for me, their Kairos, if need be. Regan could squeeze off one shot before someone tackled her. But the one agent she shot, they'd all determined, wouldn't be me.

"Fine," she finally said, dropping back from the table. "It's better this way anyhow. As long as I'm alive, I'll find her. For now, I'll take her lust-puppy."

She began backing up, crossbow pointed straight ahead.

"No—"

"Jo, let him go!"

"In return for what?" I demanded again, looking at Hunter now. "What were you going to give me over for?"

"I wasn't. Not ever."

Regan answered for him. "A free trip to Midheaven. A few ounces of my soul. About all that's left."

"If that," I snarled. She laughed again and bled some more.

"Why would you do that?" Warren was as incredulous as I. "After I expressly ordered no one to go there."

I frowned. No one but *me.*

"After the measures I took to keep this troop safe from that evil place." Warren shook his head, disbelief oozing from his pores. "You would go against that, after I've practically raised you, after all I've taught you, after I gave you a home and a place and a name in this troop? You put our Kairos at risk? You put this troop at risk!"

Hunter's jaw clenched. "I was only going after what was mine."

Warren's chin lifted at that. "So go. Because what's here is yours no longer."

Regan sighed happily. "Guess you won't need this," she said, and let Hunter's whip go slack before giving it a momentous yank with an enthusiastic growl. The torque jerked him from his feet, each barb in the whip's length ripping from his torso and taking skin with it. I think it was the first time most of us had ever seen Hunter injured, and it was like something had been defiled. Regan tossed his conduit in the corner, took a bow in the wake of our collective gasp, then picked him up in a headlock, the tip of my conduit buried in his forehead. A line of blood began to trail between his eyes. His level gaze remained fixed on Warren.

"Wait," I said, voice cracking. Things were happening too fast. I couldn't begin to guess what was held in those heavy glances passing back and forth between Warren and Hunter, what had happened in their shared past, but somehow I knew I couldn't let Regan's appearance here break the alliance between these two men. I couldn't let her break Hunter.

But Warren had made up his mind. Everyone else recognized his characteristic stubbornness, and they closed rank, filing in front of me until only Hunter and Regan stood across from us.

Hunter, bloodied and hunched over, said to Warren, "Don't do this."

"I said go."

"Wait!" I tried to push past Warren. He pushed back.

"This is pathetic." And Regan Dupree pistol-whipped Hunter with the butt of my crossbow, flipping the weapon around in her palm as he fell, before centering back in on Warren. Her physical destruction hadn't taken away any of her speed.

"Go," he told her.

"What?" My voice came out in a feeble shriek, but no one else made a sound or a move, and Regan began a slow, backward retreat, dragging Hunter's dead weight with her.

"Happy Birthday," she said to me, winking as she pulled him through the doorway. Through the glass enclosure I could see his limbs bumping against table legs and chairs, and then—as suddenly as she'd arrived—both of them were gone.

23

Nobody moved for so long it was as if the entire room had been paralyzed. When someone finally breathed—Gregor or Micah or Riddick letting a curse loose on the air—everyone else seemed to deflate. Whatever it was that'd been holding them up seconds before disappeared, and the entire troop sunk to the nearest surface—wall, tables, floor—looking more like rag dolls than superheroes.

I stared at them all, but my incredulity was met by blank stares. I spoke so loudly in the dumbed silence it was like a slap in the face. "We have to go after him!"

Warren, slumped in the corner, put his head in his hands. He shook it mournfully. "Joanna. He's gone."

My eyes winged so wide they felt like flying saucers. "What do you mean gone? He's right outside those doors!"

I pointed, but Warren said nothing.

I spun on the others, letting my arm fall. "Riddick, Vanessa?" Neither of them looked at me. I goggled again. "It's *Hunter*!"

Micah pushed himself into a standing position. He was so tall and wide it looked like a chunk of the wall was moving. I almost sighed in relief, but before he could take even one step forward, Warren rose as well.

"He betrayed you, Jo." Warren shook his head sorrowfully. "He betrayed us all."

Micah paused . . . then bent his head.

No arguing, Warren was right. Betrayal lay everywhere, but I'd seen the look in Hunter's eyes, and I knew that in some way he'd also betrayed himself. I needed to find out why. "So that erases all the good he's done before that. His friendship? His past deeds?"

"Yes," he said simply.

I shook my head. "So then *we* deal with him!" I looked around, but nobody would meet my eye. "All of us. Not Regan."

"We just did. Jo—"

"No!" I was so tired of Warren speaking for the rest of us—there was no way everyone in the room felt like that! No way had kinship and brotherhood and the absolute *love* these people felt for Hunter been so suddenly replaced by indifference. Not in mere moments. Not just because Warren said so. "So we take a vote or something, right? Isn't that what you were going to do when I first came in the troop?"

It was supposed to be a democratic gesture. Suddenly it felt more like a popularity contest.

Tekla finally stirred, her whisper full of grief. "That was different."

"He knew better," Warren added, like that made a difference. "He's known from birth."

Because unlike me, he'd been born and raised in a troop of superheroes, taught not to question his duty or his troop leader. He'd kept secrets from Warren too, but . . .

"Maybe he just made a mistake."

It sounded hollow even to me. A mistake was something done once, not over again and again. He'd been meeting with Regan repeatedly, if not regularly. It was inexcusable, but I still wanted to find out *why*.

"Some mistakes are irreparable."

I shook my head, staring at my troop leader. He sounded like a religious fanatic. One of the fundamentalists intent on spreading the Word to new places and people, and once the natives heard it, they had better heed it or burn. A year ago today I had been one of those natives.

So it wasn't my fault, I thought, crossing to pick up Hunter's whip, if things were getting a little hot in this kitchen.

From the corner of my eye I saw Tekla making her way to me, using the voice she reserved for her most troublesome pupils. "Archer, Warren is—"

She was going to tell me Warren was right. She was going to tell me to drop the conduit, fall into ranks, and do as I was told. But that was before I turned the whip on her.

"Get back, bitch."

Vanessa gasped. "Joanna!"

Now the troop came to life, and that pissed me off even more. They'd stir for Tekla, but not for Hunter? Was this how easily a valued member of the troop could be thrust on the outside? How much easier, then, would they do the same to me? The bad pupil, I thought, feeling Tekla's considering gaze. The wild native, I decided, catching Warren's.

My anger began simmering. I might not have had Tekla's control or Warren's ruthlessness, Shen may have taken my ability to heal, and I'd had to give over my ability to construct walls from thin air to Boyd on my last escape from Midheaven . . . but I still had my temper.

My father's temper.

"One step toward me, one wall set up to box me in . . . " I looked pointedly at Tekla. " . . . one move to stop me, and I'll let it go. My eyes will burn so red they'll serve as a beacon for the Tulpa. He'll dive-bomb your new hidey-hole. He'll flatten us all."

"Think about what you're doing, Joanna." Tekla's gaze was ice cold in comparison to my heated one.

Gregor, then, a man who'd never been anything but kind to me. "Don't betray us too."

"I'm not. But we're stronger with him." I turned back to Warren. "You know it."

Warren's jaw clenched and he swallowed hard, but he remained unmoved. I shook my head and started to back up, just as Regan had minutes earlier.

Vanessa, perhaps closer to me than anyone there, tried, her voice imploring. "Joanna, please—"

"No, let her go." Warren crossed his arms and leaned against a stainless steel rack. I wasn't fooled. The last thing he felt with his beloved Kairos walking out the door was in control. His tight smile kept me from feeling remotely bad about it. "But we won't help. We won't risk ourselves by going after him."

"Some friends," I spat, looking at each of them in turn. Felix was cross-legged on the floor, almost in a ball, and his fists were clenched so tight his knuckles were white. Good. I hoped his inaction sliced like a knife. Riddick had his eyes closed, head back, like he was thinking of pounding it through concrete—I hoped that hurt too—and though Micah had returned to his position up against the wall, he and Gregor were shooting uncertain glances at each other behind Warren's back. I shook my head. Hunter hurt me too, but outrage on his behalf momentarily helped keep that at bay. If there was one thing I knew, it was how to prioritize.

But so did Warren. He tried again. "He betrayed *you*."

Because Hunter had taken me to his bed, in his arms, while meeting with Regan. Knowing how I felt about her, I thought. Knowing she'd do anything to get to me. But it was the magnitude of those offenses that made me want to know why. "Well, I'm not going to lower myself by doing the same."

I felt something close to hatred then; not for Hunter, but for Warren. Because he *could* just wash his hands of Hunter, even after he'd dutifully served this troop for so many years. Hunter was still that same person, and he was out there, still alive . . . though not destined to stay that way for long. I sneered at Warren. I scoffed at them all.

"Stay safe, *heroes*." I looked pointedly at each of them, and found that none of them were willing to meet my eye. "Enjoy the fucking cake."

Doubts crept in once I was out on the apocalyptic streets with the strange hovering sky and eerie silence, with the Shadows lurking and my troop in hiding. I even had the urge to turn around a couple of times, but images of Hunter kept flashing through my mind: the whip that I was holding licking air as he battled the Shadows, his eyes going soft as caramel as he moved inside of me. Betrayed me? Okay, yes. He'd done that. But betray the rest of the troop? His family? It just didn't hold.

I wasn't far behind. Though she had a head start, Regan was weighted down with injury, Hunter, and the need for stealth. I had only the third issue to worry over, and that was nothing new. So I followed the scent of blood—both old and new; tainted and fresh, fouled and that of the recently ruined hope—and thought, Oh, Hunter. What have you done?

Grieve later, I told myself, and headed into the core of the city.

I wasn't surprised when the trail led to the nearest pipeline entrance. I hadn't been in this one before, but it didn't matter. All roads led home. It didn't take a genius to figure out where Regan was headed. She was going to the entrance to Midheaven. It was symbolic, since he'd apparently engaged her in order use her soul energy for access. It was mean and meant especially for me.

I picked up my pace inside the tunnel's depths. I could now move unseen, and I counted on Hunter to make enough noise so I was also unheard. The first tunnel emptied into a ninety-degree turn, but I stopped keeping track after that. The turns and whorls it took were impossible, part of a magic system rather than any clever planning on the city's part. After the first few, which I navigated by touch, the air became stifling, and the blood I'd smelled earlier intensified.

Just as I was wondering how much farther this particular rabbit hole went, I heard Regan's voice. It was closer than I expected, and I froze.

"They won't come after you," I heard her say, and a sharp *thwack!* told me she had just slapped his face. What was it with these Shadow women and face slapping? Did they take classes in it or something?

"I know." His flat, annoyed response told me it wasn't the first time he'd been hit. It was probably how she'd brought him back around. It was hard to carry someone heavier than yourself while trudging through a damp tunnel.

"Great, so be a good boy and leap onto that ledge. I'll tear off a huge chunk of flesh if I try throwing you, and it takes forever for that shit to grow back."

Eww. A part of Regan's personal hygiene routine that I really didn't need to know about.

"Nah," Hunter replied, and I could practically see the shoulder shrug that went with it. "Go ahead and kill me here."

"No. I want your kill spot to shine forever just outside Midheaven's entrance." By killing Hunter at the entrance to Midheaven, anyone who tried to access that world in the future would scent the olfactory chalk outline that was his kill spot, basically paranormal graffiti that said, *Regan was here.*

"I know," he said in a way that meant he wasn't budging.

She hesitated, thinking. "You know there are lots of ways to seriously injure you before killing you, and believe me, I'm familiar with most of them. This crossbow makes a particularly effective edged weapon."

"Try burying it just beneath his Adam's apple," I said, and sent a thought pulse to bring my glyph to full blast. "That's always been my favorite."

Both Hunter and Regan cringed, eyes closed. "Uh-uh-uh," I said when she swung my conduit my way. "You'd better watch where you point that."

She notched an iron bolt.

"You can't kill me, remember? The Tulpa wants me alive."

"No, but I can kill your boyfriend here." She pointed the bow exactly where I'd told her. Hunter gave me a dead stare. I grimaced apologetically. "Oops. I mean, *ex*."

"Geez, my memory must be bad." I put one hand on my hip, the other behind my back. "Regan, weren't you supposed to bring me to the Tulpa at the first given chance?"

Hunter made a warning sound, knowing I was baiting her. "Jo—"

We both ignored him, though Regan kept my conduit trained on his throat. Kill spot or not, she'd murder him there if she had to. He stilled again.

"So what if I tell Daddy Dearest that you traded me for Hunter? That, once again, you put your desires above your leader's?" I shook my head and heaved a sigh. "Then you'll never heal. You'll never be reinstated into the troop. You certainly won't ever sit at his right hand side . . . not unless it's as a knickknack on his side table."

"And what? *You're* going to tell him? Hunter is? Like I'll let either of you out of this tunnel." She laughed, but even in the empty tunnels it rang more hollowly than it should have. I smiled.

"He'll be happy to come to me. All I have to do is let the fury I'm feeling unfurl like a giant red banner. It's actually quite easy. Probably because it's so close to the surface."

She weighed her options, notching the arrow a little tighter in Hunter's throat, just to feel in control. "You're going to do that anyway."

I lifted one shoulder. "Not necessarily. Not if we can strike a deal."

"No," Hunter said, as I knew he would, drawing Regan's attention. "No more deals."

"Let the woman talk," she told him, before turning back to me. "What kind of deal? Your life for his?"

"Actually, I had something else in mind." And I pulled Hunter's whip from behind my back. Lashing like a rattler's tongue, I wrapped it around my conduit. Hunter—feeling the same attraction for his conduit that I felt for mine—ducked so the barbs nearest his face licked air. Regan misfired, and I jerked my crossbow from her palm.

But she didn't let go. She stumbled forward, instinct telling her release meant death, so I simultaneously pulled and delivered a front kick to her chest. My boot sank clear into its center, splitting ribs and separating muscle, and threatened to lodge there. I'm ashamed to say I squealed, but I'd have defied even Hunter to plow through someone else's chest without a groan.

"Yuck," he said now. I couldn't agree more.

"So here's the deal I was thinking of," I said once my foot was free. I was breathing hard, kinda grossed out, but I didn't miss a beat. Too bad Regan couldn't say the same. She was sprawled on the concrete floor, bloodied and stinkier than ever, and alternating squeals of pain with gulps of breath. I'd displaced her heart, which had to be unbelievably painful . . . especially when you couldn't die that way. Now via conduit was another matter, I thought, flipping mine around in my hand to point at her, and throwing Hunter his whip. "How about your soul in exchange for his passage into Midheaven? But wait—there's more! You get absolutely nothing out of it except more excruciating pain. Do we have a deal?"

"Fuck no, you—"

"Shh . . . I wasn't asking your permission." I shot Hunter a tentative smile, but he was standing flat-footed, arms at his sides, like he couldn't believe what he was seeing, that I'd come for him after what he'd done and what I now knew. I swallowed hard and shrugged. "Come on, let's hoist her up. I have a feeling we won't be alone for long."

He hesitated, but bent after another moment to grab an

arm and a leg. Well, what else was he going to do? He was a rogue agent now. He had nowhere else to go. Plus, Midheaven was obviously where he wanted to be.

"You think the Tulpa's really coming?" he said.

"Nah, I didn't work up my mad yet. Besides, he's captured Skamar." Hunter looked surprised. That even caught Regan's attention. I privately marveled at how natural it was to be working together, talking together, over the body of the one he'd betrayed me for. "I have a feeling he'll be busy for a while."

I didn't even want to know what kind of madness one tulpa could inflict on another.

"Warren, then." Hunter grimaced, and the niggling I'd felt in the kitchen was back. I was still angrier with Warren than Hunter, but he shouldn't get *too* comfortable.

"Of course." We both knew Warren wasn't going to just let me walk away. I was, after all, his precious Kairos.

We got Regan up on the ledge, then stood, staring at each other. Conscious of her eyes on us, I put my boot over her face. I resisted the urge to stomp, but only because we needed her breath.

"So," I finally said. "In return for what?"

"I didn't betray you, Jo. This," he said, motioning to Regan down at our feet, "this had nothing to do with you."

But it should have. Because we were lovers. Because I trusted you. That should have played into whether he teamed up with the trash we were standing on now. I let my silence speak for me. Hunter rubbed a hand over his face.

"This is so stupid," Regan muttered, knowing she was finished anyway.

"Shut. Up."

"Lovers are retarded."

I kicked her in the head.

"I don't know what you're looking for over there," I told Hunter softly, "but I hope it's worth it."

It was probably the dim lighting, but tears may have sparkled in his eyes. I looked at the small rips dotting his flesh like a new constellation. They'd scar, I thought, putting my finger to one and wiping the blood away. Injury from conduits always did. "Jo—"

I sniffed, and cleared my voice, focusing on the safe's dial instead of him. I lined it up with the Leo glyph, Regan's sign. I wanted to be sure it took her soul and not Hunter's. "You'll skip the worst of it by using Regan's soul in lieu of your own. I guess you figured that out."

And only now did I realize that was why Warren initially sent me to find Skamar. She'd originated in Midheaven, so she knew how to enter, and what it cost. Ah, well. At least I'd lived long enough to learn that. I sniffed. "So, that's good, because it really hurts. But you need to know about the drink. Hunter, the drink. You'll be dying of thirst, literally, but the minute you sip from that shot glass, you become a part of that world. Do you understand?"

He nodded, and that possible tear fell.

"And don't play poker," I said, voice cracking. I cleared my throat. "It'll remove bits of your power, and you won't have them when you return." If he returned. I felt tears starting to well suddenly too. Everything was happening so fast! How could this be good-bye? A year ago I'd been outside of the troop and he'd been firmly planted within. How could our fortunes have reversed so suddenly?

I wanted to ask, but his expression had sharpened. "Wait, you played? You *lost*?"

"It doesn't matter now." I paused, thinking I heard something far away, closer to the mouth of the tunnel than our placement there at the core. Far off, but not far enough. *Warren*. But there was so much more! "Watch out for Mackie, he's the piano player, I promise you can't miss him. There's also Harlan Tripp, you probably heard of him—"

"Harlan doesn't worry me." He wiped sweat from his brow, let his hand trail down his face.

I nodded, and though my throat was tight, I thought, I

can do this. I could let this man go. Everyone should have their greatest desires, right?

But what if he is yours?

I pushed the thought away by pulling on the concrete window. The candle was there, still burning, still appearing newly lit. "But the person you have to be most careful of, Hunter, is the woman you saw when we . . . when we . . . " I couldn't reference the way we'd made love, so instead I referenced our other connection. "In the aureole. She's beautiful, yes, but so dangerous. Her name is—"

"Solange."

"That's right." My brows drew down. Had that been in the aureole too? "And Jacks will be with her. He's a big motherfucker, and he's from here too. He'll know of you, of course. Solange and he are—"

"Married," he said softly. "He's her husband."

"Yes, he—" I froze, mouth open, all the blood in my body pooling in my toes. Hunter steadied me when I swayed. Regan snorted under my feet. Jaden Jacks . . .

Is standing right in front of me.

And despite the unearthing of that knowledge, the easy click of nonsensical pieces falling into place, a part of me felt numbed, dumbed. I didn't believe. "H-How am I able to talk to you about Midheaven? How can I provide all these details now, and not before. I haven't been able to tell anyone else. How—"

An undercover identity to lure women. One woman in particular. Dark-haired. Dark-eyed. A type. *Just like Solange.*

"Oh, my God." He'd returned to her as soon as Warren opened Midheaven, but he'd been plotting it long before that. Woodenly, I looked down. And Regan had been a part of that plot. And despite both those women . . .

He still made love to you.

"Oh my God," Regan mimicked, voice muffled. "It just keeps getting better and better." Hunter kicked her this time. She grunted.

Hunter was Jaden Jacks. Hunter had already been in Midheaven. And I finally knew Hunter's greatest desire.

Solange.

Had Warren known this?

Solange.

"Look, I've been searching for Sola for a long time . . . "

Sola?

"But I'd changed my mind. I wasn't going to go. And then last month. You chose Ben."

I tilted my head, not understanding.

Hunter squinted like he was in pain. "I asked you to forget. To be present and stay with me, and when you left . . . "

He'd made a deal with this she-devil.

The realization must have blanketed my face. I know the scent of my distress had to be reverberating like aftershocks against the walls of the confined space. Hunter's head jerked from side to side. "No, it's not what you think. There's more. So much more that you don't know—"

I held up a hand and laughed without humor. "Please, I don't want to hear any more. And you don't need to explain. I saw her, remember?" He said nothing. I looked up into his face, forcing him to meet my gaze. He did so somberly. "I mean, it's where you want to be, right? You still want to go?"

He swallowed hard. "Yes, but—"

"Then go." I hated how flat my voice sounded, like nothing lived inside of me. I hated the way I used Regan to push away his words and my pain. I grabbed the gauze circling her neck to lift her to her feet—ignoring the way her skin gave unnaturally beneath my grip—and propped her between us.

"Your death," I muttered to her, "is going to be a relief." For us all.

Regan didn't answer, and I realized it was probably as close to an agreement as we'd ever come. I looked into her deadened gaze one last time, inhaled lightly of the rotted scent, and knew that, Tulpa's touch or not, Regan had been this gone from the first. Dying even while she was being birthed. Wanting to cause destruction because she was destruction, decay, poison . . . and the enemy of love. She was pure Shadow.

"Here's your candle." I handed it to Hunter, though I guess he already knew how this worked, then pushed Regan in front of the small window, though I guess she did as well. She'd already provided him with a third of her soul . . . at least! "And you blow."

I looked at Hunter and he stared back over the top of Regan's ruined head. I still couldn't put it together. Hunter was Jaden Jacks. Jacks was Hunter.

"One more thing," he said, as an uneven scrape sounded below and behind us. Warren was getting closer.

"Please. No." I didn't think I could take another surprise tonight.

"This is important." He put his free hand on my arm. I looked down but he didn't move it, so I looked up and met his gaze. "Don't believe him," he said softly, almost like he really cared. "Warren, I mean. There's absolutely nothing wrong with you. Not even in the darkest corner of that beautiful soul."

I was unsure what to say to that, not that it mattered. I'd never get words past the lump in my throat. Besides, there *was* something wrong with me. Hunter just didn't know about the pieces of myself I'd left in that other world. I might have told him, but Regan was weary of waiting, of standing . . . probably of living.

"Enough with the long good-bye," she said, leaning forward. "Fuck you both."

It was different than when I'd blown the candle out myself. My arms were dragged forward in the sudden, thickening smoke, like the muscles were being pulled out through my fingertips, causing a terrible tickle to work its way back into my body, but I didn't release Regan. And she, in turn, grabbed onto me, the bones of her still-tensile fingers digging into my skin, strong enough to pierce skin and draw blood. I imagined its infection as her rotting body clung to mine. Even while trading an opened-mouth kiss with death she was attempting to drag me along. Then a pained gasp fled her mouth, and the smoke hissed like it was alive. Then nothing. An absence beside me, though nothing could actually move in that choking muck. It was like a metro turnstile, making sure only one person passed and paid at a time, and as Regan's soul wheeled away, yanked from her body to be used as fuel for another world, her scream sounded, like fangs on a chalkboard. Another moment, no more or less, and the smoke cleared. The candle burned anew in the center of the shelf. And Hunter was gone.

I looked down at Regan, limp in my arms.

"You have caused me, and the men I've loved, a lot of trouble," I told her carcass.

It's what I do, I could practically hear her say as I stared down at what was essentially dust held together by blood and bile, and I knew some of her spirit yet lingered.

"Not anymore," I told it. And I let her body fall. The kill spot that would forever lay at the entrance to Midheaven wasn't mine or Hunter's, but Regan's. It's what I'd long wanted. And everyone, I thought, standing alone, should have their greatest desires.

Right?

24

I met Warren fifty yards from Midheaven's candle, just past another concrete cutout, like the one I'd hid in from the Tulpa and Regan. Though I couldn't say why, I wrapped Hunter's whip around that, safely out of sight. Maybe Hunter would return. If so, it was a part of him and would call to him. I cradled my crossbow. At least I had that back.

Warren appeared, another deeper shadow in the dark, and I fired my glyph to let him know where and who I was. He increased his pace, his lopsided gait even more pronounced in the pipeline's frame, and for a moment it was like looking at him through binoculars. I felt far away and as if I didn't know him at all. Then he drew closer.

"Are you okay?" he asked, then sighed, relieved, at my nod. "Where's Hunter?"

"Gone." I said nothing about knowing Hunter's true identity. In fact, I just stared at Warren, the niggling I'd felt in the kitchen and at Midheaven's entry shifting into a full-blown tingle. It would be nice, I finally thought, if he would finally share something, any truth, with me. Instead he pushed past me and went to look for himself. "I said he's gone."

"And Regan?" he asked, leaping to peer over the ledge. His voice echoed back like it was trapped in a drum. "Oh."

After a moment of hesitation—I think he was trying to climb up without touching the Shadow's remains—he disappeared. Curious—though perhaps a better word was wary—I followed. There wasn't a whole lot of room with Regan's body still sprawled on the floor, but I kicked her aside so I could see what he was doing. "What's that?"

"A new lock," he said, securing it over the small latch. He'd been carrying another lock? In his pocket?

I thought of Harlan Tripp, his body set to a slow boil for eighteen years. "Hunter is over there."

I waited, and finally realized he wasn't going to answer. And I knew then what he was doing here, why he followed . . . why he allowed me to follow Regan and Hunter in the first place. He'd already planned to trap Hunter on the other side of that entrance, just as he'd trapped everyone else before. He wasn't here to save me as much as he was tying up loose ends. Namely?

The man I'd started thinking of as my boyfriend.

"You set him up," I said as he turned to me. "You found out Hunter was acting in tandem with Regan, but instead of confronting him about it, you turned around and made her a better deal."

I could practically hear his offer. *Betray Hunter, Regan, and I'll give you a shot at the Kairos.* He'd had an opportunity to remove Regan from this planet, as a threat, and from my life. And he'd chosen to use her as a means to another of his hidden ends instead.

I said, "You were once adamant about none of us going into Midheaven. You said it was twisted, and that it twisted people in turn."

"And now you see that I was right." He motioned for me to follow him.

I didn't move. "Yes, but you refused to even acknowledge that it existed. And then you sent me there. So why did you open it up now?"

Warren tilted his head. "Because I saw what Ben did to you. How sad you were, how screwed up. I don't want you distracted again."

I ignored the sad and screwed-up remarks because they were inarguable. What I did take exception to was his determination that Hunter was a distraction.

He sighed heavily and shook his head, like I was a teenager putting on a good pout. "It's for your own good. Now let's go."

I looked back at the lock. "Take it off. It's agonizing over there."

"No," he said flatly, and dropped back into the pipeline. "And here. You forgot this."

He threw something up at me, and I fumbled as it hit my chest. My mask. I tied it over my eyes where I was so Warren wouldn't see my hands shaking, my face crumpling. I heard his slap-and-slide gait as he moved out of the way, and I dropped down into a low crouch. He kept walking, still expecting me to follow, but I didn't move.

"You know, superheroes never talk."

He kept walking. "What?"

I spoke more loudly as I stood. "In the comics, I mean. You've got panels and pages of villains who get all this great dialogue, but the superheroes have to sit in silence and brood, you know?"

"What are you talking about?"

I took a step forward. "I'm talking about those not-talking superheroes."

Now he sounded annoyed. "And?"

My eyes began to heat beneath my mask. The red glowed prettily off the wet concrete walls. "Let's chat."

He turned slowly, just his head, his body tense beneath his flowing trench. "About?"

"How about Hunter? How you knew all along of his call-boy cover, that he was hunting for a dark-haired woman. For Solange." I flashed back to Warren and Hunter arguing in the panic room, and how the weight of the argument

hung in the air when I'd arrived. If I hadn't been so preoccupied by my inability to heal, I'd have sensed it then. "And
you also knew that Hunter was Jaden Jacks."

His gaze was dead, his shrug an afterthought. We were
both done with pretense. "Of course. I'm the one who gave
him his new identity."

"How did the others not know?"

"Ask Ben," he said with a wry smile, because he knew I
couldn't. Ben's memory had holes in it the size of moon craters. And Warren was intimating that he'd done that to his
entire troop, without their knowledge, as well. He'd made
them all forget about Jaden Jacks, just as I'd suspected. His
smile made me want to puke.

"You keep things from me."

"I tell you what you need to know."

"You use me," I said in a harsh whisper, and my eyes
turned into red flares behind my sockets.

"Calm down, Joanna. You don't want to call the Tulpa
here, do you?" His strained voice told me *he* didn't want
me to. I calmed my breathing and swallowed down the
acidic heat, but it continued to burn in my chest, so my
eyes teared up. My emotions were too close to the surface,
I knew, so I took another moment, let my breath out slowly,
and eventually managed to dampen them.

When I was done and had nodded, he motioned for me
to walk with him. I did, but only because I was dying to
hear his excuse. "Jaden Jacks—or Hunter, if you'd like—
once fell in love with a Shadow. It blinded him, and cost an
innocent child, a changeling, his life. Of course, that's how
I knew Hunter would glom onto you. You're just his type."

A Shadow. Flawed.

Don't believe him . . . there's nothing wrong with you . . .

I shook my head. "Just to be clear, then . . . you sent me
to Midheaven knowing it would hurt me." I didn't tell him
about the power that I'd lost. I didn't dare now. "And that it
would take away pieces of my very soul?"

"Yes."

I nodded, like this was a reasonable conversation to have. "You want me to hurt?"

He turned on me so fast I almost ran into him, and now it was his eyes that were sharp with passion. "I want you to give yourself over entirely to the troop. Like your mother did. Like I have!" He pounded his chest once, then heaved a great breath. "Don't you see? I must strip you down to nothing so I can build you into the Kairos, the strongest being in the history of the Zodiac!"

Horrified, I looked at him. "I'm a person," I whispered.

"You're a weapon," he shot back immediately, but at least he was cognizant of how he sounded. My sudden tears must have shamed him, or maybe they just pissed him off, because he explained the rest. "Regan was stalking you. She would have taken the opportunity to kill you if given the chance, no matter what the Tulpa wanted . . . as evidenced by her appearance at the kitchen tonight. So I got you out of the way for a while. It was for your own good. Besides, you've no room for righteousness. You knew Hunter was up to something too, and you never told me."

More clarity arrived: I'd been following Hunter, but Warren had been following me. "I had no idea he was working with Regan."

But a thought came quick on the heels of that, flitting through my mind like debris caught in a flood. "Not like you."

Warren stood so still he could have been a statue at Caesar's Palace. Then he thrust out his hand. "Give me your conduit."

I laughed so bitterly it barely escaped my throat, but I handed the weapon over. What did it matter? I'd lasted this long without it. Besides, Warren had already proven I was no match for him. He was always one step ahead, plotting and planning and pushing us all about. I followed close when he began walking again. "You're the one who let Regan know we were at the kitchen today, not Hunter."

I remembered the way he'd looked, pretending to be

shocked by Regan's arrival, deflated by her revelations and incensed by Hunter's betrayal. It was a slam-dunk performance. He should just thank the Academy already. "You wanted that showdown so Regan would get Hunter out of the way once and for all."

Warren huffed unapologetically and picked up the pace. "Now you're beginning to think like the Kairos."

"What about the *troop*, Warren? We're weaker without Hunter."

"That's why I put the lock back on. Now we can fill his star sign and the role of the weapons master, since he clearly isn't coming back."

I thought of Hunter in Midheaven, dying of thirst. I had to remind myself he'd been there before, that I had an entire conversation with him as Jacks, and that he went back willingly. For Solange. Guess she really was worth all that.

There's nothing wrong with you.

But this wasn't about me, and wasn't even about Hunter. This was about Warren. Was it really that simple for him? He just dropped agents when he no longer considered them strong, like Kimber, or useful, like me, or loyal enough, like Hunter? He erased his entire troop's collective memory if that served his purposes?

Warren wasn't looking at me, but I know he felt, and probably smelled, my judgment. I was doing nothing to hide it. "Don't you think I would have done things differently if possible?"

I don't know, I wanted to say. Suddenly I didn't have a clue what he'd do. "It hurts, Warren. I was hurt over there, and Hunter will be too."

He laughed then, a bitter cackle that resonated in the pipeline like it was made of copper instead of concrete. "Well, what doesn't kill you makes us *all* stronger, right?"

I stopped, and feeling it, he did as well. He turned, and for the longest time I stared into the face of the man who'd introduced me into this world, who'd risked his life for mine, only to risk mine again, and all for reasons I couldn't

see. He didn't want to make me stronger for my own sake.
I knew that now. He would benefit from any strength I received, so essentially he wanted me for the same reason the
Tulpa did. Power. He held me in the troop like an Uzi or a
grenade launcher or a rocket propeller.

I'm a person.
You're a weapon.

I nodded slowly, not in agreement, but because my neck
felt heavy under the weight of all this new knowledge. Of
the knowledge, I knew, that was still to come.

He turned again without another word, and with the next
curve, we found the exit. The darkness of the sky outside
was as complete as it was in the tunnels, but this close to
open air I could hear and feel the vibration of thunder, like
the sky had a bellyache it couldn't settle. There was no way
that energized webbing would hold much longer.

Even strong things, powerful things, I thought, shaking
my head as I followed him from the pipeline, could only
take so much.

It was the morning of my twenty-sixth birthday, but you'd
never know it by looking at the rumbling, midnight black
sky. I was looking at my feet, so preoccupied with all of
the other things that had kept me in the dark that I didn't
realize how quiet it was until Warren's surprised gasp rose
beside me. The horror in it, which was a prayer and curse
and a realization all at once, made me want to duck for
cover. Instead, I looked up.

And saw my former doppelgänger hanging naked like
a Norse god, draped above as though pinned to the World
Tree. Skamar wasn't just hanging, of course. Certainly not
voluntarily. The physical body she'd attained only a month
ago, the one she'd so aptly and ably used to battle the Tulpa,
had been crucified. It was an old torment for a new being—
torture using one's own flesh.

The blue jet and heat lightning of the failing sky showed
flashes of cramped muscles, knotted into partial paralysis.

Her limbs were overextended, bent at odd angles so that she hung like a broken doll. Wrought-iron nail heads had severed the new bones of her wrists, the arches of her feet folded together and fastened in the same way, though room for movement had been allowed. It was more painful that way; the smallest correction would shoot searing pain through her limbs and spine, all the way up into her brain. But perhaps worst of all, the abuse had caused the capillaries just beneath the skin to burst, and she was now sweating out blood along with her body's water. Obviously weak and clearly in shock—eyes rolled far into her head, breathing strained and sporadic—she was also still alive.

And once all the power, that'd accumulated over weeks of fighting between the two tulpas, was finally released from the bulging bowels of that iron-hot sky, she'd be more than that. She'd be a living conduit. A funnel for that energy via the pointed metal rising from her back into the sky.

And the power, palpable as tin foil clenched between the teeth, would rain down on the only tulpa left alive. He was, I realized, on the verge of gaining all. A city of rubble and Shadows. Skamar's death. Limitless power. That's why he was smiling so broadly as he appeared from behind Skamar's tortured form. My eyes darted to the steep banks of the storm drain, and I felt Warren doing the same, but I didn't see anyone else.

"My dear girl," the Tulpa said, dapper in a black trench and gloves, matching scarf tied around his neck, a jet umbrella blocking the rain from his oiled hair. He reminded me of a Big Band crooner, all slick presentation and dreamy good looks. I swallowed hard and made sure the toggles on my mask were well secured. "Someone is going to have to talk to you about your temper."

Someone once had. I looked back at Skamar, tears welling. She'd been tethered to the makeshift lightning rod for some time—her wrists were tearing, blood clotting—but it was my anger at Warren that had brought her to this location. The Tulpa had felt it, and now she would die at the entrance to the world where she'd been birthed.

My guess was that's why he was alone. He'd flown there with Skamar as soon as he'd felt my anger. But his troop would find him soon, gladly gathering to watch Warren and Skamar and me all burn down to singed husks in this glorified ditch. I swallowed hard, willing my pulse and thoughts to calm as the sky brewed and belched overhead. They should hurry, I thought, swallowing hard. It wouldn't be long now.

The Tulpa shoved a hand in his pocket as he walked toward us, just like a normal man, though his skeleton popped like a black X ray every time the sky above us flashed. Rain peppered his umbrella, but the wind we saw knocking about debris twenty feet above, along the drain's perimeter, didn't touch any of us. The Tulpa was at the core of that stillness too. I felt it, taking up the slack as he drew closer.

The moment elongated like a rubber band stretched to its max, and I knew that when it snapped, the sky overhead would snap with it. The city would lie in ruins, and all that tethered power would funnel into the too-still man before me.

"Regan is dead," he said matter-of-factly.

"Before she was ever birthed," I said coldly.

"Then she made an awful lot of noise for a corpse."

I couldn't argue with that.

"We were a bit rushed the last time I saw you. I didn't get to ask how you are, what you've been doing . . . if you'd prefer a fast death or slow . . . "

"You don't want me dead."

"Not now," he admitted, then smiled again. "But soon."

Because after the sky fell, after the power from the tulpas' accumulated battles entered his body, he'd no longer need to keep me or Jasmine alive. Which meant Jasmine, wherever he'd stashed her, was still alive now.

"In the meantime, we'll pass the time with a little story."

He sauntered forward, straddling the runoff flowing between his wide stance. Red sprite lightning joined the fray to sear the storm clouds overhead, and I shuddered. It was all I could do to keep my eyes from darting to the banks of the ditch. I could run, but I wouldn't get far, so I decided to keep him talking until I figured out something better. My sarcasm was an excellent stall tactic.

"Because you want to appear more human to me? More relatable? Have a real touching father and daughter moment?"

"Because I want the story of my birth recorded," he said in that velvet voice, before smiling. "But don't worry. We'll still have our touching moment."

The sky squealed like rusted wheels above us. It wasn't any sound a sky should make.

"See, the lack of a recorded name, the very thing *this one* sent you on a quest for," he gestured to Skamar but didn't look at her and refrained from saying her name, "has meant much of my story has, over the years, remained in the dark. It has robbed me of additional power . . . until now." He smiled serenely as he glanced up at the cracking sky. "And that just won't do."

I imagined, as he obviously was, what the power a recorded birth would give him. He'd probably tried to get this history recorded before, but the manuals chronicled our dual sides in *action*. Telling the story at the moment Skamar died, or while he killed the Kairos, practically guaranteed its inclusion. Granted, we already knew the generalities of his past and creation, but the more of his story that was brought to life in the Shadow manuals, the more belief and energy he'd receive from the young minds who so eagerly devoured the tales within. He still couldn't be named—only a tulpa's creator, or a descendant, could do that—but coupling the story of his birth with the amassed energy swirling overhead would make his already formidable strength unrivaled. And I couldn't imagine him more powerful than he was now. I didn't want to.

Warren groaned beside me, clearly thinking the same thing. I could feel his desire to flee, his mind winging to the rest of the troop, muscles twitching with the need to get them to safety . . . wherever that might be. A quick death here—and the Tulpa would give him that; the slow one had a "reserved" sign on it for me—would mean leaving their fate unsecured and unknown. I glanced over to find him breathing heavily, the thought unbearable.

The rivulets of water were swiftly turning to inches, assailing the tunnels and pressing coldly against our ankles. Unconcerned, the Tulpa twirled his umbrella. "Did you know that a tulpa's consciousness takes form prior to his body? It's true, though it doesn't happen all at once. No, it's like that sky above, parts lighting up before burning out, awareness flickering, like an old television. There's a gestation process just like for mortals, though the progress isn't physical. You know when you can feel someone watching you?" He didn't wait for a response. "Well, that's what it feels like for another consciousness to take form in your mind. It crowds out the things you'd ordinarily think of, pushing some aside, like moving boxes into storage, and tossing out others altogether."

The drainage from the entire valley was flowing over the Tulpa's ankles by now, though he hadn't altered his stance. We were lucky not to still be inside—the system was filling up far faster than a foot per minute.

"So you'd think that someone creating a person out of layered thought would clue in to the fact that the selfsame being could read *their* every intention. There was nothing my creator could hide. I knew why he was making me, how he planned to use me, when he needed to take a shit. I knew all of it practically before he did. Being unencumbered by a physical body has its advantages . . . right, doppelgänger?"

He still didn't say Skamar's name, even now that it would afford her little strength. She didn't move. The Tulpa smiled again when he saw me watching her, though his face fell as his eyes landed on my troop leader.

"Going somewhere, Warren?" He said it just as Warren's foot moved. We both fell still. The Tulpa took one step forward. "Because I'm not done with my fucking story."

Above us the sky sparked, a tiny sizzle of electrified power singeing the air to escape, finding Skamar. It was only a fissure crack in the dam of clouds, but it arrowed through Skamar and into the Tulpa, the electricity enough to make her scream . . . and him *glow*.

Pulsing with the trace amount of heat lightning, he smiled. "Don't worry. You're not the only man who has thought of abandoning his charge."

I looked at Warren too, but he wouldn't meet my gaze. He'd been about to bolt? Without me?

Because he knows the Tulpa won't kill me.

So he'd just leave me there?

"Yes," the Tulpa continued, in a loud, clear storyteller's tone. "My creator once considered the very same thing. He felt my power growing, and knew too well what thoughts had gone into creating it. Do you want to have a guess at what those elements were?"

"Snakes? Snails? Puppy-dog tails?" I gave him a bitter smile.

"Venom. Vice. And everything nice."

Warren swallowed audibly next to me.

"When Wyatt Neelson tried to destroy me, when he tried to remove the layers of personality he'd given me and dissolve my consciousness back into the world, it felt like hot knives were carving my thoughts into slivers. When I resisted, he then tried imagining me differently. A kinder, gentler tulpa. He mixed up my personality traits, and tried to imagine them anew. But I was already too strong. I did a cross-feint in his mind, and then I wrapped myself around the coils of his gray matter and I *squeezed*. I could have killed him then and there. I could have brought on an aneurysm that would have created a crater in his mind, or sent him into early dementia.

"He begged. He couldn't form words, but his thoughts were desperate." He licked his lips, gaze faraway as he remembered. "He told me that he loved me, and thought of me as the son he never had. He said if I let him live he'd leave the city forever . . . or he'd stay put and act as a sort of gofer, whatever I preferred. That was the exact word he used too. 'Preferred.' "

The Tulpa looked up at the sky. "What I preferred was for him to stop trying to kill me."

Identical eyes found mine, and I knew he said it as a part of the story, to be recorded, but also for me.

"I made him a deal. I let him live, and he, in return, would spend the rest of his days reinforcing me. Chaste as a monk, as focused as Buddha himself, nothing and no one else would ever come between us. We sealed it in blood."

"And then came Zoe."

"Yes. Zoe then," because she'd killed Wyatt Neelson, "and Zoe now." Because she'd created Skamar. "What a bitch."

"That's my mom." Odd, but under the straining sky, and standing before this demonic creation, I don't think I'd ever been more proud.

The Tulpa shook it off. "So the moral of the story is, I have a right to be here. I fought for life the way nations fight for independence. I was birthed of blood."

"If that's your criteria for greatness, then you have no greater claim over it than anyone else."

"True. I just have more power to back it up."

And that's what it came down to. For some people it wasn't enough to simply have power over their own lives. They needed to assert themselves upon the living landscape of other hearts and minds. For some reason, power only mattered to them when it affected others.

The Tulpa twirled his umbrella, one hand shoved in his suit pocket. The water was at his calves now, a tiny river rushing around him, but he didn't even sway. He was rooted to the earth, like an oak that had been planted there. "Don't look so disgusted. Mortals do the same. It's why monarchies work, democracies ultimately fail, and faith becomes a crutch. And that's fine. Most people want to be told what to do, where to go, when to piss."

"If they do, they generally ask first." They ask with their vote, when they join the church. They don't ask for their lives to be sideswiped by imagined beings on—and here I looked at the splitting sky—a literal power trip. There wasn't much further to go on this one. "I find myself curious about something, though."

"Yes, darling daughter?"

"If you're not going to kill me—" I amended the statement when he raised his brows. "—right now, I mean." He nodded for me to continue. "Because you don't want my *chi* to unite again in my changeling, thereby healing the Zodiac, bringing the fourth sign to life, recording Skamar's name and giving her all the power swirling above in that sky—"

"One little death. So many repercussions."

"Exactly," I said, shortly. "So why'd you kidnap Jasmine?"

"Kidnapping is such a harsh word. I'm merely keeping her safe."

He meant away from me, just in case I decided to take my *chi* back by force. "But you can't touch a changeling."

"No, but she's only half. The other half?" He licked moisture from his bottom lip. "Fair game, same as you."

I clenched my teeth. "Where is she?"

He paused, then jerked his head at the tunnels . . . and the pipeline that was flooding more than a foot a minute. Blood drained to my toes. If a thirteen-year-old girl was in there, the rushing water would already surround her. I looked up. "She'll drown." And she'd do it before this sky had completed its tumultuous belch.

"Have faith, dear. I've prepared better than that." He

smiled grimly. "She's high up in an alcove, quite close to Midheaven, actually. Of course, knowing of your little connection, I had to make her go to sleep for a while . . . but she should be coming around just in time . . . "

He smiled, and left the sentence unfinished. *To die.*

And she was tucked high, because if she drowned before the sky fell, my *chi* would be reunited in *my* body. Then the fourth sign of the Zodiac would come to life, Skamar would gain her recorded name . . . the Tulpa would be defeated. If not, it would all go the Tulpa's way.

But either way, Jasmine would die.

I thought of what she must be going through right now, how small and cold and utterly terrified she must be. The Tulpa looked at me, face devoid of guilt. "Now don't look so shocked. You're the one who gave me the idea."

After I'd been found hiding from him in the cutout after my first return from Midheaven.

I turned to Warren. "We have to save her."

He had the nerve to roll his eyes. "Jo. You're the Kairos."

That was it? That was his explanation? "I know," I said through clenched teeth. No one would let me forget.

He stared at me. "Then let me remind you what that means. The prophesy of the Kairos is that it will forever elevate one side of the Zodiac over the other. Good over evil."

"Not necessarily," the Tulpa sang, ever the optimist.

"So I care about you above all else, and yes, that includes Jasmine."

"We can't stand here and do nothing," I said. "She's a baby!"

"And you," he said, putting his hands on my shoulders while water rushed past our knees, "are a wild rosebush that needs to be pruned back and strengthened."

I'm a person.

You're a weapon.

Warren looked into my eyes with the fervor of televangelists and politicians, his fingers digging into my skin. "I will provide the environment and nutrients you need to bloom, but I also hold the shears, and I will not hesitate to cut off all the branches and suckers that threaten to weaken you."

Like Hunter. Like Ben. Like a mortal we were sworn to protect. A *child.*

I looked at him then, and wondered if he'd forever run off everyone I depended upon and loved. For the first time, I also wondered if he was the one keeping me apart from my mother. I wondered if I professed my love for him, if he'd simply go away. Because that one might be worth a shot.

"If you don't help her, you're just as guilty as he is."

"No, I didn't do that. Besides, don't you see, Archer?" He leaned forward slightly. "I'm putting you above all of us. Including myself."

Always put others above yourself.

Frowning, shaking my head a little, I turned the thought over in my mind. Xavier had been the first person to say that to me, and at the time I'd thought him delirious with guilt and fatigue. But, I thought, looking back at the Tulpa, the second person to say it was Solange. Though a Shadow, she'd once been of this world too.

Put her, always, above yourself.

I glanced up at the sky as the downpour began to beat at my skin in earnest, and swayed as the water rose past my knees. It might already be too late, but if I found Jasmine quickly, if she could be revived, if she knew how to swim, if I just acted . . .

No. If I acted like the Kairos.

Warren read my thoughts as clearly as if I'd spoken aloud. "No, Joanna." He used my real name even though it was pounding hard now and hearing was limited. The Tulpa leaned forward in the downpour, straining. "It's already flooding. She's just . . . "

"She's what, Warren?" I said, turning to face him fully,

not caring if the Tulpa heard or not. I wanted to hear him say it. No, I corrected myself, I wanted him to hear how it sounded when he said it. "She's what?"

Warren clenched his teeth, rain rolling down his craggy face like tears that started at his skull. "It's either her, or there will be thousands dead. We need to save ourselves. In light of that . . . what's one person?"

"No. We need to save everyone we can . . . starting with her."

Warren shook his head. "You've got to choose your battles, Archer. Haven't you learned that by now?"

But if this wasn't my battle, what was?

I stepped away from Warren until we were all an equal distance apart. He shifted, but the Tulpa inched toward me, recapturing his attention. I looked at the two leaders of the underworld, one cocooned beneath an umbrella, the other sodden in a battered trench, and in the thunderous roll of ball lightning—just for a moment—I couldn't tell one from the other.

I'm a person.

You're a weapon.

"Hey, Warren."

He was looking at the Tulpa. "What?"

"Warren," I said, more sharply. He jerked his head, eyes fixed on my birth father.

I sighed, and whispered, "Warren."

This time he looked. I smiled. "Boom."

And I bolted.

25

It was impossible to keep my feet beneath me, so I rode the filthy, rushing waves, the raging current easily whisking me into the dark. I was shocked at how loud the water was inside, and by how many other things were swept away with me; tires, wood planks, unlucky animals, discarded clothing, even sheet metal, which banged against my torso and thighs as I was whipped around and, every so often, pulled under. Flash floods were living things, fierce animals given temporary animation, but if I didn't get to Jasmine before the power fueling this storm fell, then the heavens would fall with it, and the Tulpa would win all. There was little I could do for the city at large, but I could begin with the girl who'd started it all.

Put her, always, above yourself.

"Jasmine!" My voice echoed along the widened corridor, slipping along unlikely corners even the most sadistic of city planners wouldn't have dreamed up. I was in the belly of the paranormal pipeline now, and though the rushing water would keep a mortal from hearing my call, I was hoping our shared *chi* would enable Jasmine to hear me, and give her enough strength to answer in return. I listened, but only heard the sky scream outside.

So I kept swimming, floating, and calling out, growing less hopeful the farther into the system I went. At one point I spotted one of the iron ladders drilled into the side of the sloping tunnel and stopped myself so the swollen water rushed past me. The waves were chest deep even in the largest pipes, and the current kept jerking my feet from beneath me as I tried to link them around the rungs. So when the mewling sound came, I barely heard it.

Until it reverberated in my chest.

"Jas!" I called out again, screaming this time, suddenly certain she was trying to reach out to me. Hadn't she said on the rooftop of her house that she'd felt me drawing nearer? So why would it be any different now? The thought gave me an idea, and I inhaled deeply and submerged myself in the icy flood. I held, one-handed, to the ladder, listening . . . and heard it again.

It was coming from deeper in the pipeline, a different entrance, but closer to the core and Midheaven, as the Tulpa had said. I bobbed for air, inhaling a mouthful before giving in to the current and allowing myself to be sucked under again. Jasmine continued calling, the sound growing increasingly stronger. I was becoming used to the tumult of the waters, almost finding a rhythm to its twisting violence, and was so surprised by the sudden slamming of my body into a wall that I actually sucked in a mouthful of the gritty deluge. Flailing as the water continued to press me against the unyielding concrete, I fought to the surface, which proved even higher than I thought. However, once I managed it, I was rewarded.

"Jasmine," I sputtered, and almost managed a smile.

"It hurts," she whispered, squeezing her eyes shut.

At first I thought she was talking about her restraints. The Tulpa had secured her with ropes that stretched the width of the tunnel, fastening on opposite ladder rungs. It didn't look painful, however, and the rising water kept her

body weight from pulling on the ties, so that couldn't be
it. Of course, when she cringed again, eyes squeezed shut,
short dark hair plastered to her skull as she ducked her
head, I realized she was reacting to something I couldn't
hear. Dolphin language, perhaps.

I looked up.

But her proximity to Midheaven was a more likely bet.

I willed my glyph to life, gaining my bearings in the
meager light. I'd hit the rounded wall that marked the vertical entrance, and the ledge to Midheaven above. Perhaps
mortals couldn't stand to be this close to the entrance. I
suspected the only reason Jasmine could manage it now
was because of the power she shared with me.

"Okay, Jas. I'm going to get you out of here," I said,
going to work on one of the restraints. I latched one foot in
a lower rung, as water continued to rage at the wall, rising
swiftly. I had no idea where to take her once I did free her.
To a broken world where the sky had caved in? Back to
a family that might have been crushed under its weight?
Certainly not to Midheaven. The passage alone would kill
her, even if the way wasn't locked.

As if on cue, a piercing wail sounded, almost directly
through the walls.

So the sky was falling, the water rising—neck height
now—Skamar was dying, Jasmine drowning . . . and I
couldn't get this damned knot untied!

So swim away, you idiot! I glanced up. Because I could.
I could decamp to Midheaven again, disappear into another world, saving myself, escaping it all.

Catching my look, Jasmine smiled, bittersweet. "I wondered how long it would take you to think of it."

I shook my head and went back to work. She winced in
response to some sound I couldn't hear, and I felt the shudder slide into me, as if our bodies had melded where they
touched. "Don't worry. I'm not—"

She cut me off. "I would."

Surprised, I jolted and my foot slipped, sending me far

enough underwater that I got another mouthful of the briny stuff. It was metallic and gritty, trace amounts of gasoline making pretty liquid rainbows off the heaving surface. I spit as I regained my feet and tried to lift Jasmine up. There was enough slack to have her half hidden in the hole leading to Midheaven—and *put her always above yourself* might mean literally, right?—but the higher we got, the worse it was for her. She screamed and the water rolling down her face was from tears, not the flood. But if I left her alone, she'd drown. I didn't know which was the lesser of the evils. So I held her to me.

"I would," she repeated against my chest.

"Shh." I stroked her head, as something in the sky lost its riveting. The tunnels shook.

Jasmine gave up, relaxing against my chest. Water lapped at her lips. Her skin was clammy and cold, like she was already dead. Despite my best efforts to hold her up, the water was winning. She lifted her head in the air so she was staring straight up at me.

"You're not going to get me undone in time. It's okay. And . . . and I'm happy for Li. If I die, it'll be better for her." She bobbed, gurgled a bit, and I lifted her higher. Too high. She screamed in pain.

"I'm sorry, I'm sorry, I'm sorry . . . " I clasped her close again and suddenly tears were rolling down my face as well. I didn't know what to do!

Jasmine coughed, spit out more water. "You should . . . go."

"No. I won't leave you."

"Okay." She shut her eyes. "Then stay with me for as long as possible, okay?"

"Yes," I whispered, watching the water climb past her lips.

"It's okay . . . " She bobbed, gurgled. "You said the first time sucked anyway."

The reference to her virginity had me laying my cheek across her forehead. "Jasmine."

She had fought becoming a woman because it meant letting go of the power afforded changelings, but I knew she'd longed for it too. All girls did, at once excited at the prospect and ambivalent at the unknown. That had been a long time ago for me. Before attacks and a metamorphosis, before superheroes and tulpas and tunnels leading to other worlds. I felt tears sliding down my cheeks, almost burning my skin in contrast to the water infiltrating every pore in icy jabs. I lifted Jas a bit higher. Not too high. Not so the proximity to Midheaven would cause her any more pain. She'd had enough of that.

Her head was pointed straight up now. Her ears were submerged.

"Stay with me . . . " she said again. Water again lapped at her lips.

"I'll go under with you," I whispered, because little girls shouldn't have to die alone. Because when I was not much older than her, I'd been left to do just that. I smiled, then bent, and kissed her like I knew her mother would if she were there.

If the feeling that passed between us was visible, it would have been a hot spark, a welder's fire, a burst like a comet shooting from my mouth into hers. Shocked, I pulled back, and she gasped, sucking in a lungful of the floodwaters.

Put her, always, above yourself.

And in the moment, when I really believed it was the last for both Jasmine and me—for Skamar and Las Vegas, and for Warren's beloved troop—I had the strangest thought. I thought of Suzanne and her blabber about goddesses . . . and how she'd told me I wasn't gray, but full of color. The life of the world. *A fucking rainbow.*

I thought of my mother, and how she'd once given her aura over to me, color blooming behind my closed eyes as she fed her soul into mine, her energy bleeding through and then beneath my skin. Of everything in this world, which oscillated with vibrational energy, lives were the most potent. A death, or birth—a sacrifice of one's own soul—was a detonation that could change the world.

Put her always above yourself.

As my mother had done with me. She'd harnessed her personal energy and then drove it relentlessly into me. I smiled at the memory of power flowing from her mouth to mine.

There was a way to fix Jasmine's shattered *chi* without killing her. A single choice that would give Skamar the power she needed to beat the Tulpa, to force the manuals of Light to be written again so that my allies had havens outside the sanctuary once more. To save this world. I laughed because it was suddenly all so clear and simple.

Jasmine's eyes went wide as she realized what I was going to do, and as she opened her mouth—either to accept or protest, I wasn't sure which—mine came down atop hers to mimic the way my mother had once settled upon mine. I shut my eyes and concentrated on transferring all the remaining aura in my body into hers. I gave it all up, and as it reunited in her body, I felt every ounce of power that had made me super, the Kairos, even the energy keeping me standing, fade away. I fed the entirety of my aura into Jasmine's soul, reuniting the severed *chi*. As for my powers . . . well, they went somewhere. The Universe. Ether. I didn't know. But even as I sagged with the loss, my senses dulled, I kept my lips fastened tight . . . and focusing on sending one final pulse of superpower arching from my body into Jasmine's.

I'd been near death enough times to know I was experiencing it now. This time, though, was both the best and worst because I was choosing it, meeting it full on, playing chicken, but with no intention of dodging at the last minute. I simply gave myself over to it, a release like falling backward into a pool, though the feeling that the pool had moved—that it was farther away than I'd judged—was disorienting.

I felt the tunnel shake above and around me, and realized

Jasmine was freeing herself with that final beat of power, ripping her restraints from the wall, her victorious cry sounding like it was coming from my own throat. There was a pounding like walls cracking. I heard the Tulpa screaming in the voice of a monster. It made me want to smile.

I *was* the Kairos—racing through the tunnels beneath my city, choosing my battles, putting a mortal life above—always above—mine, but the word didn't only signify some preordained savior of the Zodiac. The kairotic moment was defined as the critical time to act. The abandonment of hesitation, the appointed time.

Fate, I thought, and I began, peacefully, to sink.

What's one person?

Warren's words, spoken so callously under a bulging sky at the entrance to the pipeline, were the first that I remembered when I woke.

In a ditch.

On the side of the road.

Alone.

And while it appeared I'd been left in the wake of a flood for some mortals to find, I tried not to give in to the feeling that I'd been thrown away, like refuse, for the second time in my life. After all, I thought as I rose to my knees, Warren wouldn't just dump me anywhere. He always had it well planned out.

Squinting beneath a full blazing sun, I tried to stand and figure out where I was. The latter proved the easiest of the two tasks. I was in the Las Vegas Wash, the end point for all the debris and unwanted things that were pushed out of the city. But I was surprised when my knees buckled and I toppled forward in that wash, surprising myself again when I discovered my arms couldn't hold my own weight. It was, I thought, with a sense of detachment, as if my muscles hadn't been used all year.

Of course, the unyielding earth stopped my fall for me,

and I rose again, more slowly this time, with a mouthful of mud, palms cut where they'd landed atop shattered glass. I knelt among choked weeds and stripped tires, slouched there for at least an hour. I stared at my palms the entire time, sunlight glinting off the cut glass in front of me, finally drying the blood that stained it—though I knew someone, somewhere, would still be able to smell it. But I was anosmic. My muscles were atrophied.

And my palms didn't heal.

I reclined on the slope of one bank, head on a boulder, and decided to lay there just a bit longer. Maybe another hour, like I was sunning myself under that beautiful, sweeping blue sky. Just until some curious mortal came along, a homeless person, or maybe some kids looking to see what the storm had washed away. Someone who'd be wondering, as I was, if there was anything in the wash that could be salvaged.

Finally, I closed my eyes, giving the worry up to someone else's keeping.

26

"How do you feel?"

Feel, I thought numbly, how do I feel?

I stared at the scrubs of the traveling nurse, and after a long moment nodded. It was an inappropriate response to the question, but one I could always blame on being the notoriously flighty and spoiled Olivia Archer.

Formerly *the* Archer.

Xavier's former personal physician, now mine, had told me the day before that I'd make a full recovery. He didn't understand why I laughed so bitterly at that, but he was mortal and had no true understanding of what, exactly, a full recovery entailed. Perplexed by my reaction, and perhaps annoyed, he finally gave me a sedative, and we both went away for a few hours.

With a cheerfulness that was a little more forced, the nurse tried again, chattering about how she was brand new to the valley, but that she'd seen the storms and clouds on the television and wasn't it great that things were back to normal? I turned my head to the window, mentally checking out. Beyond the pane lay a tender blue sky and a sharp winter sun. I knew it was bright and clear, but to me it appeared dim, like blinds had been drawn across my vision. I sighed, wondering if I'd ever get used to mere 20/20 vision again.

The flowers sent by well-wishers were now addressed to me instead of Xavier, though I could no longer scent them moldering in their vases. The equipment left by the physical therapists sat nearby, though I'd refused their help and hadn't touched it yet. On my more positive days I told myself I'd learn to move through this world as a mortal again by myself, and that if my mother could do it, so could I. I was still an Archer, I would think, and I'd strive to make her proud.

At other times I wondered why Warren hadn't just let me die.

Because you're mortal. It's his duty to protect you now.

And he probably would. Like an owner would protect a pet, just because it was theirs. At least he'd leave me alone now that I had nothing he could profit from. To think I'd been worried about him finding out about the powers I'd gambled away in Midheaven. Maybe if I'd told him I was broken, I could have deterred him sooner.

So as the fog of injury and shock gradually lifted, I began to put the events leading up to Jasmine's near drowning in order. So much of what transpired in these last weeks had been planned by either the Tulpa or Regan or Warren that I finally came to the conclusion my real weakness as a superhero hadn't been lost powers, or being a target due to my kairotic status, but that it was my ignorance, my innocence. I was the only one who'd ever gone into that tunnel without a secret agenda. I'd actually believed that with a weapon at my hip and a clear sense of right and wrong, I could blast through any problem or person I came upon. Instead, brains had won out over brawn, and I found out belatedly that I had too little of both.

I didn't yet know the details of everything that'd happened after I gave the rest of my *chi* over to Jasmine, but the sky was evidence enough that I'd succeeded in healing the changeling, and a quick Google search unearthed a news piece about a young girl's miraculous recovery.

Plus, the city hadn't collapsed in on itself like a soufflé.

Meanwhile, in lieu of something as interesting as the weather to talk about, the local reporters used the news of my near drowning in a flash flood to reignite a discussion about the Archer dynasty and its future here in the valley. There was a summary of Olivia Archer's notorious party life, complete with glossy images of her at clubs, with different men, always smiling and beautiful and looking like she hadn't a care in the world, which some reporters pointed to as a moral lesson. The insinuation was that carelessness and excess had nearly cost Olivia Archer her life; the subtext was that she deserved it. And if the inexperienced heiress couldn't even avoid a dangerous seasonal flash flood, then how on earth could she be expected to run a multi-million-dollar company? Archer, Inc. stock prices plummeted and John's blood pressure soared.

I sighed as the nurse continued chattering as she made notes on my condition, a buzzing noise I was beginning to find annoying, but she finally paused for breath, looking up from her chart, pencil stilling in the air. "You know, I was there pretty quickly after they brought you in."

I blinked. "Sorry?"

"At the hospital. Your lawyer flew me in from California as soon as he found out about your accident . . . remember, I just said that?"

I squinted. Had she?

"I mean, not to be vain or anything, but I'm the best there is. I took care of the Von Witt family matriarch and the . . . " She trailed off, seeing she was losing my interest. "Well, whatever the Archer family wants . . . right?"

I huffed, and laid my head back.

She cleared her throat. "Anyway, you were pretty out of it, mumbling about the water and how it was stealing your soul and being lost in the middle of heaven. Getting swept into that tunnel system must have been really rough for you, not just physically, but . . . " She shrugged at my raised brows, realizing she was making me recall something I'd rather not. I turned back to the window. "Well, they sedated you then, and you seem fine now, but I know these things don't just go away. So, you know, if you ever want to talk about it or anything . . . "

Slowly I turned my gaze on her. It didn't burn red anymore, but from the way she startled, I was pretty sure the effect was the same. "Let me see your hands."

"Excuse me?"

"Your hands, Ms. . . . ?"

"Scaglia. But you can call me Angie." She frowned as she came forward, and I could tell I'd insulted her. "I wash them religiously. I know my job."

I looked anyway. Fine whorls and liquid lines were laid like artwork upon each fingertip, the prints marking her as mortal. I swallowed hard, and managed an apologetic half smile as I glanced up. "I, um, read palms. Your arrival here is . . . fortuitous."

"Oh. Really?" She brightened at that, and began to speak again, but before she could get too chatty, I dismissed her.

"Thank you, Angie."

"Oh. Sure." She put her chart away and looked around for something else to do, anything else I might need, but there was nothing. Another small smile and she turned to leave, but she paused in the doorway, looking back at her right hand, wondering what I'd seen there. "By the way, your mother stopped by."

"What?" The word barely passed my lips. I felt like I'd been kicked in the gut.

"At the hospital? After you were sedated." She glanced up, noted my surprise, and realized she'd just said something that could get her fired. If she knew her job as she claimed, she would've read up on the Archer family history. Color spread to her cheeks and she began to stutter. "At least s-she said she was your mother."

"What did she look like?"

Angie opened her mouth, her inhalation hanging on the air like a question mark. She searched for the memory for so long that I knew she'd never find it. Whoever it was had either messed with her memory or was well-disguised.

"Honestly?" she finally said, shaking her head. "She looked pissed."

And Angie, a woman who knew nothing of superheroes or Shadow agents or worlds outside this one, crossed herself as she walked out the door. I leaned back in my stacks of supporting blankets and pillows and imagined what Zoe Archer was capable of when she was pissed. Then I closed my eyes to rest.

Later, alone, with the curtains drawn and the house silent, I studied myself in a hand mirror. I looked past all of Micah's impressive handiwork, tried not to get hung up on my sister's beautiful face, or the physical scars I'd accumulated in the past year . . . beyond it all to that which even Micah couldn't hide. Eyes so dark nothing shone in them. Funny, I thought with a sigh, but before my near drowning, I'd actually begun to believe my mental wounds to be healing.

I leaned forward, scanning my body, tentatively feeling along my forearms, my waist, my neck, fingers finally playing over my face. I swallowed hard, meeting my own gaze, trying to see myself as soft and vulnerable as the world saw Olivia, laughing at parties, taking trips on a moment's notice, lunch dates like they were a part of a regular business day. After a moment I lowered my eyes and shook the visual away. Yes, those were Olivia's pastimes. But not mine.

"All the king's horses and all the king's men . . . " I muttered to myself.

Couldn't put Jo together again.

"Then it's up to you alone," I told myself, lifting the mirror. "Again."

That's when I finally saw something I liked. It was very close to the expression my mother must have worn earlier in the week at my bedside.

I cleared it from my face when Helen entered. She flipped on the overhead light without warning, momentarily blinding me. I dropped the mirror, blinked, and covered my face with a pillow.

"You should let me change your bandages."

I cracked an eyelid to look down at my wrapped palms. They were folded carefully so that my printless fingers were hidden—good habits die hard—though the light caught on the smooth tip of my right thumb, making it gleam like a pearl, a beautiful taunt.

"You should go to hell," I muttered, pulling the covers up to my chin.

The room grew uncomfortably still, though if Helen was going to strike, I'd have been six feet under before I even knew she'd moved. As it was, the undercover Shadow agent left in a huff, slamming the door behind her without another word.

I smiled at the small power. She probably had orders to stick close to the remaining Archer, see if I couldn't be as easily bought as my father, turned into a lackey for a secret paranormal organization. The Tulpa had to be growing increasingly desperate, weak, and with fewer resources than ever before. I thought of the way Warren would pounce on that. How Vanessa would be sharpening the blades of her steel fan while Felix joked about the chances of a Shadowless city by spring. I wondered if Gregor still parked his cab behind the Peppermill in wait of dawn and dusk, and if Micah ever wondered about my long-term medical prognosis.

Tekla, I knew, was probably trying to determine the same via her charts and constellations and diagrams, though one never knew with her. She, more than anyone else, operated autonomously of Warren, and according to her own whim. Kimber wouldn't be sorry to see me gone, that was for sure, and I wondered if Chandra had finally been given my Archer sign.

My heart squeezed at the thought, and I turned away from it so fast I ran smack dab into another. *Hunter.*

I turned away again.

Hunter.

Everywhere I turned.

Hunter. Hunter and me. Hunter and Solange.

"You knew me," I whispered into my pillow, feeling the darkness draw in closer. He'd known me, shared my bed and body—even a surprising ability to wield the same weapon for a while—and he'd said there was nothing wrong with me. I wondered if he'd retract that now. How flawless he'd find me without even two superpower chips to rub together.

Of course, the greatest hurt in all this was that Hunter had been looking for Solange long before Skamar's appearance in this world alerted him to the existence of Midheaven. Even with all of Warren's lies and denials, once he found out about Midheaven, he knew that's where she was, and had been plotting his way to her, and using my greatest enemy's soul to do it. Maybe someday I'd be able to look at the manuals detailing how and why, and begin to understand.

"Unlikely," I said to the empty room, because meanwhile he'd made love to me even while knowing he would soon return to Solange. *Sola*, he had called her, I remembered with a sneer. The worst of it was, I'd really believed he'd felt something for me . . . and maybe he had. Lust. Possibly affection. Probably pity.

Whatever it was, it wasn't strong enough to temper those old feelings. That old love. And he'd had the nerve to be angry with me for revisiting Ben.

It's not what you think. There's more. So much more that you don't know . . .

"Hypocrite," I muttered, but there was no heat to the thought. I remembered all too well the division of the heart, and how difficult it was to step into a murky future when you still had the option of returning to a familiar, if dangerous, past. Solange and Hunter—or Jaden, as I needed to start thinking of him—had a history. He was right; I didn't know what "more" had led to his actions, but in light of what I'd put him through, I couldn't blame him for wanting to shield himself under the tapestry of that past. It was my own fault that I was the one stuck in this world, shivering and mortal and alone.

I looked over at the phone. It was dangerous, stupid to even consider with Helen in the house, but emotions won out over thought. I picked the phone up and punched in a long memorized emergency contact number for the rest of the troop. I felt like a jilted woman drunk-dialing her ex, though without the benefit of alcohol. I felt even more stupid once the electronic voice announced the number was disconnected. I didn't bother checking to see if I'd misdialed.

"I am not disposable," I whispered to myself, repeating it until Hunter, the troop, my mother, and the Tulpa were all smothered under my new mantra. No, I was recyclable, I thought with black humor. I lifted my shirt to reveal a belly with the glyph of the sun fading around a healed piercing. Those things that were recyclable could be reinvented in the world, right? I could become someone new. Again.

"Miss Archer?" Angie poked her head in after a short series of knocks. "You have visitors. A woman named Cher—um, no last name—and her mother?"

A soft smile visited my face, like a hesitant sparrow on its first flight. I nodded for her to send them in.

"I am not disposable," I repeated, smoothing out the bedsheets as I waited. I decided to do the same with the edges of my wrinkled life; find some worth in what remained behind. There was value simply in being human, in being alive, I thought, lifting the hand mirror to finger-comb my hair. Right?

My reflection stared back at me, not looking at all sure.

"My gawd, girl." Cher swooped in on a magic carpet of worry, estrogen, and Chanel No. 5. "Next time you decide to go for a swim . . ."

Suzanne followed not far behind, tears in her eyes. "It was the necklace, wasn't it? It weighed you down?"

Cher hopped on the bed, settling close to me without asking. Angie looked a bit taken aback at this invasion, but I nodded that it was okay, and she shut the door softly as she left. I looked up at the two women who remained behind with me.

"Actually," I told Suzanne, my hesitant smile widening, "I think it was what kept me afloat."

27

In addition to the support of two flighty, mortal women who'd never wavered from my side, it helped somewhat that I had achieved my goal. I discovered Thanksgiving week that in my last completed task as a superhero, I'd finally brought the belated fourth sign of the Zodiac to life. This effectively ferried Jasmine on to the next phase in her life, healed Li, strengthened the agents of Light, caused the manuals to be written again, and gave Skamar a recorded name.

By transferring the rest of my soul, and all of my powers, over to Jasmine in the depths of that flooding pipeline, I had reunited an aura within the changeling, making her whole again. Skamar was resurrected . . . and though I'd missed what had proved to be a stunning climax, I'd read later in the first printing of the manuals of Light that she screamed to life under the power of a broken sky, and rocketed from her cross to pin the Tulpa to the ground with only her thumb. He managed to flee, but she followed, trailing sizzling sparks, like stars, behind her.

As for the fourth sign of the Zodiac—what we'd all been wondering for months now—it had proven more obvious than the previous three: *the Kairos will sacrifice herself for a mere mortal.*

Good thing I hadn't known that one beforehand.

The fifth sign, or portent that one side of the Zodiac was gaining dominance over the other, was also brought to light. I had my driver pull into the strip mall parking lot at Master Comics, and waited in the car while he went inside, partly because I didn't want to risk an appearance by Olivia Archer in the shop—not only because I was lacking powers, a conduit, support, or a troop—but mostly because I couldn't bear facing the changelings. Despite saving one of their lives and restoring the balance between the two sides of the Zodiac, I had a feeling they too would turn their backs on me, and I couldn't take that. Not yet.

This intuitive feeling was confirmed when my driver reemerged empty-handed, and thoroughly confused as to why the owner of the shop had refused to sell him a mere comic book.

"Did you tell him who I was?" I asked, sounding a lot more imperious than I felt as he peered in the passenger's window to give me the bad news. He clearly expected to be sent back into the shop.

He'd also not only told Zane who the comics were for, but offered more money for them, and expressed an interest in a number of collectibles as well . . . all to no avail. His frustration and pure wonderment at the situation—and I was sure part of this was due to my interest in a comic book to begin with—was etched across his normally placid face.

I sighed and leaned back in my seat. "Get in the car, Kevin."

"But—"

"It's fine." I shook my head. "It's . . . fine."

But just as we were sliding from the curb, a figure darted in front of the town car. Kevin slammed on the breaks, narrowly avoiding the small child. He cursed her and wiped his brow, but I slid the tinted back window down and took a good long look at the healthy, glowing, beaming girl.

"Hi, Miss Archer," Li said in a high voice that was as strong as I'd ever heard it.

I could only nod.

"Zane has reconsidered your driver's offer. He'll take the money along with your word that these remain . . . collector's items only."

I cleared my throat. "They're for my personal collection."

Kevin looked puzzled as he watched Li hand me the small stack of comics through the open window. Our fingertips touched as she drew her hands away, and I felt a light squeeze on my pinky, so fleeting I might even have imagined it.

"Thank you," I managed in a whisper.

"No. Thank *you*."

Li turned away, and I twisted in my seat to follow her progress around the back of the car, until she leapt back onto the walkway. "Wait!"

I fumbled at the console until Kevin finally lowered the opposite window for me, and Li turned.

"You, um, you look familiar," I was stuttering, and I reminded myself that high emotions could sometimes be scented. "D-Do you have a sibling?"

"An older sister, but . . . "

"But?"

She frowned, pretty face pinching up. "But we don't hang out much anymore. She's . . . moved on."

The air whooshed out of my chest like it'd been kicked. "Oh, well. I'm sure you'll be close again one day. When you grow up."

The faraway look disappeared as her eyes met mine. Her beautiful, unmarked face widened in a perfect smile. "No rush."

Then she skipped back into the comic book shop, bells jangling before the door shut firmly behind her.

"Weird kid," Kevin commented, before catching my hard gaze. "B-But seems sweet."

I looked down at the manuals, randomly flipping one open. Nothing jumped out at me or flashed or sounded from the pages. Just a normal comic book for a normal person. I let it fall shut on my lap and leaned my head back as we slid from the parking lot. "No, you were right the first time. She's about as weird as they come."

I pored over the manuals once I was alone in Olivia's old penthouse. My driver had been reluctant to leave me and John-the-overbearing-lawyer had sent Angie knocking on my door, but I sent her back and used the mechanical wheelchair to ease around Olivia's penthouse. Someone had put up ramps that ran from the kitchen into the sunken living room, and cleared enough space for the chair. If I still had my powerful sense of smell, I could have said exactly who it was, but the olfactory clues had long disappeared under my mortal nose. So I threw my meds down the sink, shook up a stiff cocktail, and started reading.

The Tulpa, as suspected, had gotten to Jasmine. The deed was drawn in black and white in the brand-new manual of Light, though parts of the experience were missing. That was fine; I was more interested in what had happened to Warren when he returned to the troop without me. His confession was spelled out in full—how he'd been trying to get rid of Hunter because he was worried that the weapons master was a distraction to me, just like Ben. My guess was that anything to do with Hunter would now be omitted because to mention him was to mention his alter ego, Jacks, and Midheaven. My troop knew nothing about either of those things. I could only hope that the fate of both would be revealed in time. There was nothing now.

The manuals did show an argument breaking out between the senior troop members and Warren, the former wanting to at least contact me and thank me for my sacrifice, Warren forbidding it. That made me feel marginally

better, though nobody ever disobeyed his orders by coming
to see me. Warren's argument was that after I'd "betrayed"
them by leaving Shapiro's Kitchen to follow Regan and
Hunter, and by making the choice to give Jasmine my *chi*
rather than taking it back, they no longer had an obligation
to share anything with me. Micah brought up the idea of
sharing some of his protectant with me . . . at least for a
little while. Tekla then wondered if they should at least let
me know about the advent of the fifth sign of the Zodiac.

"She's no longer an agent," Warren replied flatly to them
both, his face half shadowed on the colorless panels.

Fine, I thought harshly, throwing that comic onto the
granite countertop. Because the fifth sign of the Zodiac,
the one that had yet to come to pass? *The Shadow will bind
with the Light.*

"Have fun with that one, Warren," I muttered darkly.
"You asshole."

I glanced at the manuals scattered across my lap, thinking I should put them all away for good. I should put
blinders on and live as ignorantly—no, I corrected myself,
as *happily*—as other mortals.

"Third time's the charm," I said, gathering the comics
together to throw them in the trash. Time to start over.
Again.

But when I lifted the lid of the bin in the kitchen, just
as I was about to release the lot of them, I thought of my
conversation with Solange in her planetarium. *Nobody can
walk through this life unchanged.*

These stories were a part of my past now. If I was going
to build on it, I'd have to remember it all, even if I couldn't
speak of it to anyone. Otherwise there'd be holes in my
mind, and I'd be eternally on the edge, ready to totter into
one. Besides, one year ago I'd been stripped of everything
that provided my life with meaning. I'd then built a new
one, as a superhero, and for the last year the job, the duty,
the identity, and the goal—that need to restore balance—
was all there was. I'd accepted that as the Kairos there

were going to be sacrifices demanded of me, and though I had no clue what they'd be, or how they'd come to pass, for a while it was enough to know I had a place in this world.

And now Jasmine had a place in this world, her proper place. Li did too.

And Ashlyn was going to need help finding hers. Not to mention a safe place to hide from the Tulpa now that he knew of her. Skamar might be keeping him busy, but I knew he'd send Shadows to track the girl as soon as he had a chance. At least he didn't know her full name, or if she was even still in Vegas, so she was safe from him for now . . . and from Warren.

I placed the manuals on the counter and returned to the bedroom to look out the window my sister had once fallen through . . . where it all began. I might not be an agent of Light, I thought, staring out over the city I'd saved more than once, or a protector of these people and this valley anymore, but I had experience in protecting my own. Even in a fragile mortal body—one I assumed possessed only a third of a soul, and lacked an aura altogether—I still possessed a spirit that was fiercer than ever.

Embrace your contradictions, Solange had said, looking like a goddess wheeling among the stars.

"Be myself," I murmured, thinking it sounded simple . . . which was probably why it was so hard.

I glanced down to find Luna, white and liquid, pushing against the wheels of my chair, and I scooped her up, burying my face in her fur as I stared out the giant windows to the city below. The floodwaters had receded. Vegas was back to normal. The agents of Light wanted nothing to do with me.

"Maybe I'll leave town for a while," I said, nuzzling Luna's head. She purred like a freight train. The cat had been like glue since my return, as if mortality made me more approachable. "Besides, one little human can't make a difference, right?"

The cat looked at me like I was an idiot.

"I mean, what's one person?"

But then I thought of Hunter, and the painful pang chimed again like a gong in my chest.

I thought of Jasmine and what I'd done for her alone.

I thought of Li, just a mortal girl, nothing more than a blip on the mental radar of someone like the Tulpa, and sighed.

Okay, so I could leave the city now and go on vacation, but I couldn't lie to myself. I knew the worth of one person.

One person was a vote and voice.

One person was the difference between a resurrection or an apocalypse.

One person, I thought, as the neon blurred before me, was an entire world.